DREAM WARRIOR

DREAM WARRIOR

BOBBI SMITH

KENSINGTON BOOKS

KENSINGTON BOOKS are published by

Kensington Publishing Corp.
850 Third Avenue
New York, NY 10022

ISBN 0-8217-5303-7

First Zebra Paperback Printing: November, 1993
First Kensington Hardcover Printing: September, 1995

Printed in the United States of America

This book is dedicated to the memory of my father, James Smith.

I'd also like to offer a special note of thanks to the following people who have helped me so much during the writing of this book:

Evan Marshall, my agent, for his support and understanding.
Ann LaFarge, my editor, for her kindness and for believing in my work.
Rick Gee, my friend, and his mother knows why.
Pam Monck, lawyer and friend, for her help.
Terry Rau, for the inspiration.
And for Gwen Rice at the Wyoming State Library in Cheyenne for all her invaluable help with research.

Prologue

Spring 1859
Dakota Territory

"Easy, boy." Gray Eyes, the eight-year-old, half-breed Cheyenne boy, spoke quietly as he approached the sleek young stallion he sought to tame. "Easy, Wild One."

It was almost dark, but Gray Eyes didn't notice. His concentration fierce and his expression determined, he closed in on the spirited black horse that had been a gift from his grandfather, Tall Shadow, the chief of the tribe. His grandfather had known how smart and independent the horse was and had offered to help train it, but Gray Eyes had turned him down. He was determined to break the stallion by himself.

Wild One was living up to his reputation for having a mind of his own. Gray Eyes had been working with the horse since early that morning, but had met with little success so far. Still, he refused to be discouraged. He wouldn't let the physical pain and exhaustion he felt or the other Cheyenne boys' mocking laughter stop him. He was going to master this horse, and once he did, it would be the finest mount in the tribe.

As Gray Eyes approached the stallion again, the horse rolled his eyes and laid back his ears as he sidled away. Tired though he was, the horse was just as stubborn as the boy and would continue this struggle for domination. He would not yield his freedom easily.

Driven by his burning need to succeed, Gray Eyes concentrated on mounting again. He'd learned early in life that he was different from the other boys and that the white man's blood that ran in his veins from his now-dead father had somehow tainted him. He'd always felt he'd had to earn their respect, and he'd done so with a vengeance, always working to be the best. It had become a way of life for him, and taming this horse would be no different from any of the other challenges he'd faced. Finally, ready to engage the battle once more, he grabbed Wild One's rein and vaulted onto his back, gripping the stallion tightly with his legs.

The stallion fought with all its strength. Desperate to dislodge the boy from its back, he twisted and turned, bucked and writhed. But no matter what the horse tried, the youth matched its efforts with equal fervor.

The battle for supremacy seemed endless to Gray Eyes. Every violent, jarring movement of the horse sent pain shooting through his already battered body, but he would not admit defeat, he would not give up. Hanging on for dear life, he suffered the stallion's severest test and somehow, ultimately won.

When the steed finally stood quivering beneath him, Gray Eyes let out a whoop of victory. The taunts of the other boys were forgotten. He had done it. He had conquered the proud stallion and made him his own! Gray Eyes held his head high as he rode the prancing Wild One. In his triumph, he looked every bit the future warrior.

Everyone heard his cry and came running. All eyes followed him as he guided the magnificent stallion through the village. His control of the animal earned the respect and approval of all, and they loudly praised his ability as he rode by.

Tall Shadow stood with his daughter, Gray Eyes's mother Morning Wind, watching his grandson. His black eyes shone with pride. "For one so young, your son has done a remarkable job. Few others could have tamed that one. Once again he has proven his worth."

"My son has always known his own worth," Morning Wind told him.

"He will be a fine warrior one day."

"I know," she replied, her smile fading a bit as her gaze followed her son.

"This does not please you?" Tall Shadow heard the note of reluctance in her tone and wondered at it.

"It saddens me that my son does not wish to learn more about his father." As much as Gray Eyes tried to be fully Cheyenne, there could be no denying his resemblance to his father, Jack Marshall. At the thought of her husband who'd died when their son was an infant, an intense longing filled Morning Wind. She deeply regretted that father and son had never gotten to know each other.

"There is no reason to worry. Gray Eyes will grow to be a good man. No father could ask more of his son."

Morning Wind fell silent. She knew her father believed what he was saying, but Gray Eyes was no ordinary Cheyenne boy. He was Jack Marshall's son, and she wanted him to be as proud of his white heritage as he was of his Cheyenne background. Jack had been a fair and honest man, respected by all in the tribe. She wanted Gray Eyes to hold his father in the same high esteem. In honor of his memory, she'd insisted her son take lessons from the missionary who came to their village. Gray Eyes resented the lessons, but she'd remained firm. She would not allow him to deny his father's existence.

Tall Shadow glanced at his daughter and saw the sadness in her eyes. "Your love for this man has never faded."

"No, Father, and it never will."

"There are many warriors who would have you for a wife."

"I want no other man to raise my husband's son."

"A boy needs a father."

"He has you. Who else could do a better job of bringing him to manhood?"

At that moment, Gray Eyes encouraged Wild One to rear as he let out a war cry. The horse pawed the air and then raced away with long, powerful strides as his master gave him his head. The other boys ran for their own mounts to give chase. Their shouts of praise for Gray Eyes's accomplishments filled Morning Wind's heart with joy.

Morning Wind couldn't help but smile again as she watched her son disappear over the hill. She knew in that moment that he would indeed grow to be a fine man. She only hoped that one day he would come to appreciate the ways of his father.

1861

Gray Eyes was weary. For five days now, the ten-year-old boy had survived alone in the wilderness as he'd searched and prayed for a vision from the heavens— a message that would show him the path he was to follow for the rest of his life, a message that would give him the power he needed to become a brave and fearless warrior. But the days and nights had passed without the desired revelation, and despair had begun to grow within him. The fear that his father's blood was a curse upon him that would prevent him from fulfilling his vision quest tormented him. Many of his friends had already received their visions, some in as little time as a day. Yet here he was, still praying and still waiting.

Night came and swallowed the earth, and once again Gray Eyes was alone in the darkness. Settling down beneath the warmth of his blanket, he closed his eyes and tried to sleep. His last thought as he drifted off was that maybe the next day would bring the knowledge he so desperately sought.

The snarling sounds of the savage battle echoed through the night as the ravenous wolves battled the sleek, well-fed mountain lion. The lion was the intruder. For months now it had been stalking the wolves' land and preying upon their game. Food had grown scarce now, and winter would soon be upon them. To save themselves, the pack had to drive the powerful invader from their ancestral territory. There was no avoiding the confrontation any longer.

The mountain lion's pale fur shone white in the moonlight as it fended off its desperate assailants. The monster cat had claimed this land by right of might and would not give it up. With deadly accuracy, the lion struck blow after bloody blow. His defense against the pack proved lethal as he inflicted mortal wounds against the all-but-conquered wolves.

Though bloodied and nearing death, the pack did not, could not, retreat. Starvation drove them as they continued to attack the greedy beast that had stolen by brute force all that was theirs. There would be no honor in retreat; there would be only death.

Driven by hunger, the wolf warriors moved in closer. The largest of the pack was crouched low, ready to leap for the lion's throat when a haunting howl echoed in the distance. It was an eerie sound unlike any they'd heard before— a call that expressed without words the agony of their souls.

Wolves and mountain lion paused to scan the jagged cliffs around them, searching for the one whose cry had stopped the fighting. They caught sight of him then and stared in awe at the mighty wolf standing high above them on a narrow, rocky outcropping. His head was thrown back as he howled his haunting song, and his coat glowed like silver fire.

As if aware that the bloodshed had stopped, the silver wolf turned his shining eyes to the scene below. Making his way fearlessly down from the heights, he moved to stand between his kind and their sworn enemy. Time seemed to stand still. The pack felt the peace of his presence and slipped away into the night.

The lion remained, alone with the silver wolf. It eyed him cautiously, then sensing no threat and believing its power now uncontested, it let out a roar of victory before turning its back and bounding away.

The carnage ended, the silver one returned to the ledge, surveying the land below. From on high he could see that peace reigned— for now. There would be no more deaths that night, and in celebration, he threw back his head and gave vent to the thankful song in his heart.

As if drawn by the silver wolf's call, another wolf, a female, appeared in the clearing. Her coat, too, was the color of moonbeams. She saw the silver peacemaker and climbed to him. Coming to his side, she joined in his haunting song, her voice blending with his in the night.

Across the valley in his small, secluded encampment, Gray Eyes watched and listened. He'd been awakened by the sounds of the fight, and excitement had filled him as he'd realized what he was seeing. Though he was only half Cheyenne, his heart was true and his motives were pure. His white blood had not cursed him. He'd been given that which he'd sought. He'd been given his vision.

Gray Eyes faced to the east and began to pray. His prayers of thanksgiving were fervent and lasted throughout the night. When at last sunlight erased all vestiges of darkness and fear from the land he loved, he stood and lifted his arms to the heavens. Calling out in a loud, strong voice, Gray Eyes declared, "I am Silver Wolf!"

As if destiny intended it, a wolf's cry echoed back to him from across the valley.

Silver Wolf gathered his belongings and began the long trek back to his village. When he'd begun his quest, he'd been a boy, with conflicts in his soul that had haunted him. Now, as he returned to the village, he was a man— a man at peace with himself.

One

1865

It was a dark night, and on the McCord Ranch, the Circle M, all was quiet— all except eight-year-old Carinne McCord. The blond-haired, blue-eyed Cari was filled with childish excitement as she lay wide-awake in her bed. It had been raining all day, a miserable, chilling drizzle, but just at dusk, her father had observed that the wind had shifted and was now blowing out of the northwest. He'd said that it might snow, and the prospect had left Cari sleepless. The thought of playing in the snow thrilled her, and she'd lain awake long after her father and mother had fallen asleep, imagining the good times she was going to have if it did.

Tossing and turning, Cari was beginning to believe that the night was never going to end. It seemed she'd been lying there forever. Eager to know if her father's prediction was coming true, the adventurous young girl just couldn't stay in bed any longer. She got up and tiptoed barefoot across the icy, wood-plank floor to the window.

Cari's eyes widened at the sight that greeted her, and she

could hardly contain her joy. Snow blanketed the countryside in a mantle of pure white. Big, fluffy flakes were still falling, and Cari realized that it must have been snowing very hard for it to be so deep already.

Creeping to her bedroom doorway, she glanced toward her parents' room and wondered if she should wake them to tell them of her wonderful discovery. After only a second's consideration, she decided against it, for it was late and she was certain they would send her back to bed until morning. She wanted to play, not sleep. This was the first snowfall of the season!

Determined to have her own way, Cari hurried to don her slippers and then pulled on her coat over her flannel nightgown. She was very careful to move quietly as she rushed to escape the confines of the house, for she didn't want to risk waking her parents.

The wind was biting as she stepped outside on the front porch and closed the door behind her, but she was so excited she didn't feel it. With carefree spirit, she ran, skipping and dancing, across the yard, twirling joyously about, laughing in pure delight.

Barnie, the big, year-old dog the family called both guard and pet, heard the sounds of Cari's laughter, and rose from her safe haven under the porch to investigate. At the sight of the child playing in the snow, she loped over to frolic with her.

"Barnie!" Cari threw her arms about the dog's neck and gave her a hug. The dog was her best friend, and she was glad for her company. "Come on!"

Leading the way, Cari ran in circles with Barnie following her, their tracks drawing designs in the snow. Though the icy fluff found its way into her slippers, she paid it no mind.

Enchanted by the night, the child ventured farther away from the house than she normally would have, exploring with Barnie by her side. She passed the ranch's outbuildings and only stopped when she came to the steep gully some distance away. A small creek ran at the bottom of the hill. During the warm weather it was one of Cari's favorite places to play. Eager to see the creek in the snow, she edged closer to the drop-off. The dog whined as if to warn her away, but Cari was determined to listen for the sounds of the babbling brook below.

"I can hear it, Barnie. I bet it's pretty down there. Let's go see." Cari meant to walk down the hillside as she always did, but the rain that had fallen earlier had turned to ice beneath the snow and footing was treacherous. Once on the slope, she couldn't stop herself from falling. She slid all the way down the hill, landing in the frigid, rushing water of the creek. Her coat had protected her from any real battering during her fall, but she was still stunned by the shock of her descent.

The dog sensed Cari was in trouble and followed her. When she reached the bottom, Barnie scrambled to hover protectively over the child. When Cari didn't get right up, Barnie grabbed her coat sleeve in her powerful jaws and dragged her up the bank, out of the numbing water.

"Barnie . . . I'm so cold!" Cari gasped as she began to shiver. The sodden weight of her clinging coat and gown chilled her to the bone. "We've gotta go home . . ." she whispered through chattering teeth as she stood. Only then did she notice that she'd lost her slippers in the fall and that they were floating on down the stream.

Knowing there was no point in going after them, Cari tried to climb back up the slope. She wanted to go home and get dry and warm. To her horror, though, Cari discovered she couldn't make it up the hill.

"Barnie, go get Papa! Go on! Get help!"

The dog understood the command, but even her four-footed attempts to claw her way up the icy incline proved futile. She returned to Cari's side, panting from the exertion.

Cari looked around in desperation for a way out. There were a few trees growing on the hillside, but they were out of reach. No matter how she tried, she couldn't reach high enough to grab hold of one.

"Mother! Papa!" she cried into the night, but in her heart she knew her parents were sound asleep and wouldn't hear her. Tears coursed down her cheeks as fear filled her heart. She was stranded in the frigid darkness!

Growing frantic, Cari looked around for a solution. She'd never wandered far downstream and wasn't sure where it led, but she decided to follow its winding path and hopefully find a lower spot where she and Barnie could get their footing and climb out to safety. The pain from her bare feet was agonizing as she hurried, limping, downstream.

They'd walked over half a mile along the twisting course of the creek before Cari finally found a place where the trees grew closer to the water's edge. Using the low-hanging branches for leverage, she managed to pull herself part of the way out of the gully before once again losing her footing and sliding back down. Her efforts grew weaker as cold and exhaustion overtook her. Cari tried to get back up and make another attempt, but this time her numb legs would not hold her. She collapsed on the bank of the stream.

"Barnie . . . I want my mother . . ." Cari began to cry.

The big, furry dog lay down with the child, curling around her protectively to shield her from the gusting wind. Cari sought the solace of her pet's nearness and slid her feet beneath Barnie's warm body. She clung to the dog's warmth as she began to pray for someone to find them. In the distance the sound of a wolf's howl rent the night, frightening Cari even more, and she buried her face against the dog's neck.

The minutes seemed like hours. Cari kept calling out to her mother and father for help, but eventually she grew sleepy . . . very sleepy. It seemed strange to her that after a while she didn't feel the cold anymore, but somehow it didn't matter. All that mattered was that she fall asleep . . .

When Barnie suddenly lifted her massive head and gave a low growl, Cari knew the dog might be warning her that the wolf she'd heard earlier was approaching. Even so, she couldn't summon the strength to move or even look up. She only wanted to close her eyes and drift off. She sighed, too weary to care.

Barnie's growl turned to a menacing snarl as Cari heard someone speak.

"Be quiet."

The deep, male voice was firm and commanding, and as if recognizing a friend, the dog immediately fell silent.

Cari finally stirred. She opened her eyes and stared up at the man who'd spoken to Barnie with such authority. She blinked in confusion, not sure if she was really seeing the young, handsome, buckskin-clad Cheyenne brave standing over her.

"Help me . . ." Cari managed a whisper. The Cheyenne were her family's friends, and she knew no fear of them.

Fourteen-year-old Silver Wolf and his friend, Strong Eagle, had been riding for their village when Silver Wolf heard her cry for help. At first, he'd thought it was the wind playing tricks on him, for Strong Eagle had not heard it, but when they'd paused, both had heard the call. They'd immediately ridden in the direction of the cry and had found the child's tracks in the snow on the creekbank. They'd followed the trail to where the near-frozen girl lay with the dog.

When the animal had risen to its feet and snarled at him, Silver Wolf had been glad for the first time in his life that he'd learned English. And when the dog had responded to his command to be quiet, he'd been pleased . . . and relieved.

Knowing the dog would not interfere, Silver Wolf bent to take the fair-haired child in his arms.

"I will not hurt you, little one," he promised in a comforting tone.

"I know," she sighed.

Her calm acceptance of him surprised Silver Wolf, for most whites hated and feared his people. This child, however, offered no protest as he picked her up. She was as light and fragile as a bird, and it was then, as he held her, that he realized she was wet as well as barefoot. He knew he had to get her to warmth and safety quickly. Handing her up to Strong Eagle, Silver Wolf mounted his own horse and then took her back.

"It is foolish to brave the winter snows alone," he told her as he cradled her against his chest to share in his body heat. He wrapped his buffalo robe around her, making sure her icy feet were covered. "On nights like this, even the animals of the forest know to stay in their lairs."

"But you're here . . ." Cari murmured sleepily, feeling protected in his arms.

Silver Wolf ignored her point as he asked, "You are McCord's?"

Cari managed to lift her head to look up at him. As she studied him in the darkness, she thought God must have answered her prayers and sent him to save her. "Yes, but who are you?"

"I am Silver Wolf. I will take you home."

At his friend's words, Strong Eagle spoke. "It's a good thing that your grandfather is a friend of James McCord. It would be dangerous to ride up to any other white man's house in the middle of the night."

"McCord will know us. There will be no trouble," he told his friend. Then to the child, he said, "Put your arms around me and hold on, little one. You will be warm soon."

Cari wrapped her arms around him and gave herself into his keeping.

As she snuggled against him, Silver Wolf felt a surge of tenderness for her. He fought it down as he kept one arm securely around her and put his heels to Wild One's flanks. They raced for the McCord home with the big dog running along with them, barking. When they reined in before the white man's house, Silver Wolf called out to the man who was his grandfather's friend.

Barnie's barking had awakened James McCord. He'd just been getting out of bed to investigate when he heard someone call his name. Fearing trouble, he tugged on his pants and then snatched up his rifle and ran for the door. His wife, Elizabeth, quickly followed him, wrapping her dressing gown around her as she went. They reached the front of the house at almost the same time, neither of them noticing that their daughter was not in her room.

"James! They're Indians!" Eastern-born-and-bred Elizabeth clutched her husband's arm in an effort to hold him back when he would have immediately opened the door and gone out. She'd never become accustomed to the people of the plains, and the sight of two Cheyenne braves on horseback before her home in the middle of the night frightened her. "What if they're here to cause trouble?"

"If they'd meant us any harm, Elizabeth, we'd already be dead," he told her. "Besides, they're from Tall Shadow's tribe. The one boy is his grandson, Silver Wolf; the other is Strong Eagle. They're our friends." He shrugged off her clinging hold, threw the door wide, and went out on the porch to greet his night visitors.

Elizabeth wondered how he could call them *boys* when they looked so fierce . . . so savage. Their hair was long, worn loose past their shoulders with feathers tied in the lengths. Their buckskin clothing and fur robes made them look to her as if they were only one step above the animals whose skins they wore. She was trembling as she followed James outside.

"Silver Wolf, Strong Eagle, it's good as always to see you, but why have you come to my home so late?" James asked.

"We have come to bring you what is yours." Silver Wolf swung down from his horse, making sure to keep the robe tucked around Cari.

McCord frowned, puzzled by his words. "I don't understand."

"James!" Elizabeth had come to stand behind him, and her whisper was nearly frantic as the young brave came toward them. To her, he was a fearsome-looking wild man, and she had no idea what he was carrying wrapped in the filthy animal robe.

"Be quiet, Elizabeth," James ground out under his breath, afraid of what she might blurt out next.

Silver Wolf climbed the porch steps and stopped before them. Until that moment he'd kept his robe tight around Cari to warm her, but as he moved forward, he let it fall open so they could see it was their child he carried.

"Cari!!" Elizabeth was stunned. "What are you doing with my baby?" Cari was supposed to be in her bed sleeping! How had this creature . . . this half-breed Indian gotten her child? She snatched Cari from his arms.

"Cari? What . . . ? How . . . ?" James gave Silver Wolf a confused look.

"Silver Wolf saved me, Mother," Cari said in a small, quavering voice, sorry the warrior was no longer holding her. Even though she'd been wet, cold, and miserable, she'd liked riding with him. Now, however, she was going to have to face her mother's fury.

Elizabeth cast outraged looks at all of them as she held her daughter to her breast. Then, without a word, she turned and disappeared inside.

"You saved Cari?" James asked. "Where was she?"

"We heard her calling for help as we rode for our camp. We found her by the creek with the dog." He gestured toward Barnie. "The dog is a good dog, but the child should be tethered."

James cast a glance over his shoulder and watched his wife strip the buffalo robe and wet clothes off Cari, then wrap her in a warm, dry blanket. His daughter was shivering, but otherwise appeared unhurt. He turned back to Silver Wolf and smiled, offering his hand in the white man's gesture of friendship.

"I thank you for the gift of my daughter's life, Silver Wolf. You're right. The dog is a good dog. She obeys. My only daughter, however, is young and already has the will of a buffalo. It was my good fortune that you found her and saved her from her foolishness."

Their gazes met, and Silver Wolf, seeing the honesty of his words reflected in his eyes, nodded as he took his hand in a firm grip. "It is good that she will live."

"Will you stay with us and have something to eat?" James invited.

"No. We must return to our village."

"I'm sorry you cannot stay, but thank you, Silver Wolf. You, too, Strong Eagle. You are always welcome in my home."

Silver Wolf glanced past James to where the child sat with her mother before the fire. Her back was to him and her waist-length, white-gold hair was tumbling freely about her shoulders. It struck him that her hair was the color of shimmering moonlight. The revelation disturbed him for some reason, and he turned quickly and walked away. He'd just started to mount his horse when he heard her call to him.

Though Cari was still freezing, she wanted to talk to her warrior one more time.

The young brave looked back to find that the little girl had come out to stand at her father's side.

"Thank you . . ." she said as she hugged the blanket around her.

He did not speak, but swung up on his steed in one fluid motion and wheeled his horse around. He raised a hand in silent acknowledgment and then rode off into the snowy night with Strong Eagle.

Cari remained in the doorway with her father, both watching the two men until they'd ridden out of sight.

"Silver Wolf saved me, Papa."

"I know. He's a good man, just like his grandfather Tall Shadow."

"I like him."

James put an arm around his daughter's shoulders as he offered a silent prayer of thanks to the brave who'd brought his child home. They were starting to go back inside when the sound of a whine stopped them. They looked down to see Barnie sitting at the foot of the porch steps, a hopeful look on her face. The warm glow of the fireplace beckoned, and though James didn't usually allow the dog in the house, to-night he would make an exception.

"Come on, Barnie. You've earned a bed by the fire."

With a bark of happiness, the big dog jumped up and ran indoors. She immediately curled up before the hearth. Warm and toasty at last and secure that Cari was safe, she quickly fell asleep.

Keeping her blanket wrapped around her, Cari sat down next to the dog. "If it hadn't been for Barnie and Silver Wolf, I'd be frozen right now!"

"And just what were you doing outside in the middle of the night, young lady?" Elizabeth asked as she came from the kitchen carrying a steaming cup of tea.

"I wanted to play in the snow," Cari answered honestly as she took the hot brew from her mother and sipped from the cup. She made a terrible face.

"Drink it all," her mother ordered, knowing the whiskey she'd put in it would help to warm her.

Though Cari grimaced at the nasty taste, she obeyed without comment.

"I'm sorry, Mother." She gave her mother a pleading look.

Elizabeth stared down into her daughter's beautiful face and innocent blue eyes and knew that she loved her more than life itself. She took the empty cup from Cari and set it aside before taking her in her arms and hugging her tight.

Cari was relieved by her mother's reactions and allowed herself to enjoy the embrace.

"Oh, darling, if anything had happened to you . . . if that terrible half-breed had hurt you . . ."

"Elizabeth . . ." James said her name sternly, angered by her words.

Cari glanced over at her father as her mother released her. "What's a half-breed?" She had never heard the term before.

"A half-breed is a man who's half white and half Indian," James quickly explained. "In Silver Wolf's case, his father was white, but his mother is Cheyenne."

Cari was intrigued. "Isn't it good to be a little of each? Silver Wolf can be anything he wants to be. He could be a rancher or he could be a warrior . . ."

"Cari . . ." Elizabeth began again, ready to launch into a condemnation of any and all Indians.

"Silver Wolf kept me safe, Mother. He brought me home. He wouldn't hurt me. He's nice."

There would be no convincing Elizabeth that Indians were nice. "Yes, I'm sure you're right, but that's enough talk about Indians for now, Cari. Let's get you tucked into bed where you'll *really* be safe. You can sleep with your father and me for the rest of the night."

Cari loved her parents' big, soft feather bed. Her mother helped her put on a heavy flannel nightgown, and soon she was bundled up under the covers between them. She quickly fell asleep, the liquor in the tea having warmed her to drowsy contentment.

James slept, too. Only Elizabeth remained awake, staring into the darkness. She loved her husband and daughter. They meant everything to her. She and Cari had come here two years ago to join James in this godforsaken wilderness from their life back East because it was what he'd wanted, and she'd wanted to please him. Yet, as much as she adored her husband, this land he loved so dearly terrified her.

Elizabeth couldn't help but imagine what would have happened had that horrible Indian not brought Cari back. A part of her told her she should be thankful to him for saving her child, but she refused to give him credit. Her daughter had almost died! If they'd been living in the city this would never have happened. This was a barbaric land, rugged and untamed, and she was beginning to hate it with a passion.

Tears of bitterness and confusion slid down her cheeks. She wondered if James would ever give up his crazy dream of carving an empire out of the wilderness and return to the comfortable life they'd known before. She wondered, too, if she had the strength to stay by his side if he didn't. Her tears lasted until the first light of dawn.

Cari slept late. When she awoke she discovered that the storm had passed and the sun was high in the sky, reflecting brilliantly off the new-fallen snow. She was surprised that she'd slept so long, and she padded barefoot from the bedroom, rubbing her eyes in a sleepy morning ritual. As she entered the main room, she saw her mother holding Silver Wolf's buffalo robe.

"I don't care what you do with it," Elizabeth was saying to James, handling the robe as if it were too vile even to touch. "You can burn it for all I care. I just want it out of my house."

"Mother, wait!" Cari ran to them. "I'll keep it in my room until we see Silver Wolf again. It's his, and I have to give it back to him."

"She's right, Elizabeth. The Cheyenne set great store by their robes."

It annoyed Elizabeth to keep the thing in the house, but she handed it over to Cari without further comment. Her daughter took it and held it as if it were a most cherished object.

For the next three days, the temperatures remained freezing. Cari played in the snow every chance she could, but even as she did, the Cheyenne brave was in her thoughts. At night, Cari curled up in her bed with his buffalo robe. She spent hours studying the beautiful designs painted on it, trying to figure out what they meant. When she fell asleep each night, she dreamed of Silver Wolf, and she knew she would one day see him again.

A week passed before the temperatures finally moderated and the snow melted. Cari followed her father to the stable one afternoon to talk to him in private, away from her mother.

"Papa, I want to go see Silver Wolf now that the weather's better," Cari told him as she helped feed the horses. "I have to give him back his robe."

"I'll make sure he gets it the next time I visit Tall Shadow," James offered. He'd known one day she would ask, and he wanted to discourage her interest, for he knew it would anger Elizabeth.

"No. I have to see him myself. I want to thank him," she persisted, her mind and heart made up.

James smiled ruefully at the familiar look of determination on Cari's face. He knew full well where she'd gotten her hard-headedness, for he and Elizabeth were both as stubborn as the day was long. "All right, sweetheart. We'll go tomorrow."

Actually, James was glad she wanted to go. He'd long feared she'd be affected by her mother's hatred of all things Indian, and it pleased him to discover that she hadn't been. If they were going to build a successful life there in the territory, it was important that she learn all she could about the Cheyenne. This ranch, after all, would be hers one day.

The next morning, Cari sat before her father on his horse as they rode for the Cheyenne village. She'd feared that her mother would convince her father not to make the trip, but he'd ignored her angry protests. He'd promised her mother that they would return by nightfall, and then they'd ridden off without another word.

The sun was bright and warm, the day unusually mild. Cari rode easily with her father, holding Silver Wolf's buffalo robe in her arms as if it were her most precious possession. She could hardly wait to see Silver Wolf again, and her eagerness showed as she bombarded her father with endless questions about the tribe.

"How did you and Chief Tall Shadow get to be friends, Papa?"

"We met when I first came to the territory. We did some trading. Then one day, I spotted a band of Pawnee heading onto Cheyenne land. I knew the Cheyenne and the Pawnee weren't on friendly terms, so I warned Tall Shadow. He was ready for them when they attacked. We've been friends ever since. He respects me just as I respect him and his people."

"Why doesn't Mother like them?"

"Your mother likes the city, Cari."

"And you don't?" Cari had lived in Philadelphia with her mother until she was six and they'd moved west to join him. She'd thought the city nice, but she preferred living on the ranch.

"Once I saw the beauty of this land, I knew I could never

go back." He reined in his mount. Above them, the sky was blue and cloudless. He pointed to the snow-topped mountains on the horizon. "This is God's country, Cari. It's beautiful and open and free. If a man works hard, he can build a good life for himself here, and I intend to do just that. I'm going to make our ranch the finest in the territory." James drew a deep, satisfied breath as he looked around. After a quiet moment, he urged his horse on.

Cari had never been to the Cheyenne village before, and when they reached it late that morning, she stared in awe. There were more than forty tipis in the encampment. Children were running about laughing and playing in the unusually fine weather. The Cheyenne women who were tending the cooking fires stopped their work to watch them ride in.

Word that they were there spread like wildfire, and Tall Shadow came out of his tipi to greet them.

"It is good to see you, my brother," the chief welcomed them in English as James stopped before him. Tall Shadow had learned the white tongue from the missionary and from James during the years of their friendship.

"It's good to see you, too." James dismounted and helped Cari down.

"So you have finally brought your little one to us." His black-eyed gaze was on Cari appraisingly, remembering what Silver Wolf had said about the pale-haired child he and Strong Eagle had rescued from the storm. "I have heard that she likes the snow."

"Yes, she loves the snow, Tall Shadow." James chuckled.

The chief nodded sagely, but his dark eyes glinted with good humor as he thought of the name his grandson had given the child. "Come inside." He beckoned them into his tipi.

When they had settled in before the fire ring at the center of the room, Tall Shadow bid his wife, Little Cloud, to bring them refreshments. She served them herbal tea while the two men recounted all that had happened since their last visit.

Cari sat beside her father, studying her surroundings with interest. The tipi was big, at least ten feet across, and the inside walls were painted with scenes that depicted the chief's bravery and skill as a warrior and hunter. The beds the family slept on were raised mats, and the covers were furs.

"We have come for a special reason today," James began. "Cari wants to thank Silver Wolf for helping her and to return his buffalo robe."

Tall Shadow spoke to his wife in their native tongue, and she hurried off to do his bidding. When she returned, Silver Wolf was with her.

Cari didn't even try to hide her delight as she gazed up at her warrior. He seemed to fill the whole tipi with his presence. He was every bit as handsome as she remembered him to be, in his soft buckskin beaded shirt, fringed leggings, and moccasins. Tall and lean, he wore his black hair loose with a single feather woven into it. His features were angular and strong; his eyes, his most startling feature, were gray. She jumped up and ran to him, carrying the robe.

"Silver Wolf! I'm so glad you're here. I was afraid I wouldn't get to see you. I wanted to thank you for saving me and I wanted to give you back your robe."

Silver Wolf glanced down at the impulsive child. He saw the open eagerness in her lovely face, and he grew uncomfortable. He was glad to see that she had not suffered from her ordeal, but he was a warrior and warriors had more important things to do than spend time with children.

"There is no need to thank me. I would have done as much for anyone; although a Cheyenne girl would never have gone out in a snowstorm alone."

His words hurt Cari, and her blue eyes darkened in confusion and pain. She let her gaze drop away from his, and her little shoulders slumped. She had hoped he would be her friend as her father was Tall Shadow's. She'd even brought him a present, a treasure that meant a lot to her, but now, fearing he might refuse it, she secretly hid it deep in the folds of the robe.

"Here . . ." she said softly, glancing up at him again as she handed over the garment. "Thank you."

Silver Wolf took the bundle from her, and as he did, he saw her hurt look. Though he kept his own expression impassive, her distress troubled him. It annoyed him to find that he cared about her. He forced himself to shrug the feeling off. "Goodbye, Little Snow." With that, he was gone from the tipi.

Cari turned to her father and Tall Shadow, her expression puzzled. "He called me Little Snow . . ."

"Little Snow is his Cheyenne name for you," Tall Shadow explained.

"I have my own Cheyenne name?" She brightened at the thought.

"You will be called Little Snow whenever you visit our village."

Cari's heavy heart lightened, and she quickly looked outside, hoping to see Silver Wolf one more time, but he had already gone from sight.

For the rest of the day, while her father visited with Tall Shadow, she kept watch for her brave, hoping to see him again, but he didn't return. She was disappointed when they rode for home late that afternoon without ever seeing him again.

Silver Wolf spent the day working with Wild One and seeing to his weapons. That night when he returned to his tipi, he started to put the robe away, and when he did, Cari's present fell out. He picked up the small, heart-shaped white stone and held it in the palm of his hand. It gleamed palely against his darker skin. A strange emotion tugged at him as he stared down at the stone. He didn't want to feel this attachment to the child whose life he'd saved, but he did.

Little Snow. . . . An image of her smiling face appeared before him, touching his heart. He said nothing about the gift, but placed the heart stone in his medicine bundle.

Two

1868

Cari finished her final chore, snatched up her book, and dashed from the house. "May I go down to the creek now?" she called out to her mother who was busy in the garden.

Elizabeth glanced up from her work to see her daughter standing, poised for flight, at the bottom of the porch steps. She could tell by Cari's expression that she was awaiting permission to go, and, remembering her own youth, she had to force herself not to smile. "Are your chores done, young lady?"

"Yes, ma'am."

"All right, go on. Just be back before dark."

"I will," Cari called as she hurried off. She'd worked hard to get all her chores done early, and now she had the whole afternoon to herself. It was a beautiful spring day, sunny and warm. There was just one more thing she needed to make the day perfect . . .

Elizabeth's heart was filled with love as she watched Cari. At eleven, her daughter was just beginning to show the first bloom of womanhood. Her hair had lightened to an even finer hue of silvery-blond. Her body had begun to ripen, and she'd grown taller over the past few months. Elizabeth knew that one day soon she would be a beauty beyond compare. For now, though, Cari was still an innocent, completely unaware of her loveliness, which suited Elizabeth just fine.

Elizabeth's contented expression faded as her daughter disappeared out of sight. There was one thing that troubled her deeply, and though she'd ignored it for some time, she knew she was going to have to confront James about it soon. The thought of that conversation filled her with a sense of foreboding, and she decided that the day was just too pretty to ruin with worries. She would face that dilemma when she had to and not before.

Cari reached the creek and followed its course to the spot that had become her favorite place in the whole wide world— the place where she'd first met Silver Wolf. That winter when she'd been lost and freezing, she'd thought it desolate, but the following spring she'd discovered it was a glorious, wonderful place. Colorful, fragrant wildflowers bloomed there in profusion, and tree limbs grew out over the water, shading it and giving it a feeling of privacy. It was her special place . . . hers and Silver Wolf's.

As she sat on the bank with Barnie beside her and laid her book aside, Cari thought of the Cheyenne brave. She hadn't seen Silver Wolf for quite a while now, and she hoped they would meet again.

Cari wasn't sure exactly how their enduring friendship had come about. When she'd left the Indian village that first time, she'd been certain she would never see him again. Then unexpectedly, he had come to the creek one day while she'd been playing. A bond had been forged between them during that visit, and in the three years since, she and Silver Wolf had become good friends.

Cari enjoyed his companionship and eagerly looked forward to what little time they had together. Silver Wolf taught her about the Cheyenne, while she deliberately tried to stir his interest in his white heritage. Once she'd learned he could read and write, she'd begun to share her books with him. Glancing down at the book beside her now, Cari hoped with all her heart that Silver Wolf would come to the creek today so she could give it to him.

The sun was so warm that Cari couldn't resist the urge to play in the water. Stripping off her shoes and stockings, she hiked up her skirts and went wading. The knee-deep water was cold, and she shivered as it swirled about her bare legs.

"Come on, Barnie!" Cari invited as she tried to splash the dog.

Barnie, however, was no fool. She turned tail on Cari and sought higher, drier ground. A patch of sunlight just out of reach of attack by her mischievous mistress beckoned, and the dog lay down there, hoping for an undisturbed nap.

"Don't go to sleep, Barnie! Let's play!" she coaxed.

Faithful friend though she was, Barnie closed her eyes in answer to Cari's call.

Cari glared at her lazy dog and muttered, "I'm going to tell Papa to get me a new puppy. You're no fun anymore. Who will I play with if you don't play with me?"

"How about me, Little Snow?"

The deep voice came to her from the trees just a short distance downstream, and Cari looked up, smiling brightly as she saw Silver Wolf emerge from the woods.

"Silver Wolf! You're back!" She ran toward him in the water, not caring that she was splashing herself. She knew nothing of flirtation and artifice, so all the joy she felt over seeing him showed plainly on her face. Now her day was perfect!

"Your dog is getting old and lazy, Little Snow," Silver Wolf teased. "She wasn't even aware I was here."

"She knew. She just didn't bark because she knows she can trust you."

Cari was breathless as she stopped before him, and she wasn't sure if it was from the run or just because he was there. She gazed up at him, thinking he looked somehow different than he had last fall. His features had taken on a more hawkish, powerful look. His shoulders were broader, his chest

deeper and stronger, his long, buckskin-clad legs tightly mus-
cled. The changes in him left her feeling shy for a moment,
but then he smiled at her, and in that instant, her trepidation
vanished. He was still her Silver Wolf.

"I missed you," she blurted out.

Silver Wolf gazed down at Cari, not willing to admit that he
had missed her, too. "You enjoyed the winter?"

"There was a lot of snow," she told him with a grin.

"And you were happy." Silver Wolf found he couldn't stop
smiling at her. He told himself he was a seventeen-year-old
warrior with many more manly things to do, yet it didn't seem
to matter. He was drawn to Cari in some elemental way he
couldn't explain. Their meetings at the stream had become an
unspoken ritual for them, and it was one he wouldn't break.

"Not really. I've been lonely, but that doesn't matter now,
'cause you're here. Wait until you see what I've got for you."

Cari took his hand and led him back to where she'd left the
book. As they walked the short distance, she became aware for
the first time just how very warm and strong Silver Wolf's
hand was. She drew him down beside her when they reached
the place and handed him the leather-bound volume. "Here.
It's my Christmas present to you, even though it is a little
late."

"Thank you." His eyes met hers as he took the book from
her. He handled it carefully, paging through it with interest.
"I have something for you, too. Wait here."

Silver Wolf retraced his steps and returned a few minutes
later leading his horse. He took a cloth-wrapped package from
the parfleche bag he'd brought with him.

"This is my gift to you." He handed her the package.

"What is it?" she asked excitedly as she quickly untied the
thong that held it bound. To her delight, there was a pair of
beaded moccasins inside. "Oh! They're beautiful! Thank you!"

He only nodded in response to her thanks, but he was glad
she was pleased with his gift.

Cari donned the moccasins, thrilled that they fit perfectly.
She tiptoed around for a few minutes, enjoying their softness.

Without thought, she went to Silver Wolf and kissed his cheek. "They're wonderful. I love them."

Her kiss surprised him and he stiffened.

"Let's see if I can walk as quietly as you do now!" She was completely unaware of his reaction to her affectionate gesture as she hurried off toward the woods.

Caught up in her enthusiasm, Silver Wolf followed her. They explored the forest in comfortable companionship. He pointed out the tracks of several different animals to her as they roamed the area, and he spoke to her of the many different trees and plants. They ventured into the small, secluded cave they'd discovered on one of their previous walks.

The sun was sinking lower in the sky when they finally returned to the creek bank, but Cari was having too much fun to even consider going home yet. She slipped off her new moccasins, hiked up her skirts, and ran for the water to cool off.

Silver Wolf paused on the bank to watch her for a moment. He noticed for the first time how long and shapely her legs had become and how rounded the curve of her bosom was against the now-damp bodice of her dress. He realized then just how much she'd matured during the past few months. By Cari's age, the girls in his village were almost considered to be women. The thought bothered him, so he refused to dwell on it. He enjoyed the simplicity of their relationship and wanted it to stay that way. He joined her in the stream.

This time, warmed by the heat of the late afternoon, Barnie came charging in, too. She barked wildly as she ran through the water with them.

It was near sunset before Cari realized that she had to leave.

"I've got to go home, Silver Wolf. My mother will be worried," she told him, putting on her moccasins again and then gathering up her belongings.

"Come, I'll take you."

He mounted and then lifted her up before him. Cari leaned back comfortably against his chest as they rode for the ranch. It seemed a very natural thing to ride with him that way. By the time they reached the house it was almost dark, but there was still enough light for her to see her parents standing out on the porch.

"I'm home, Mother!"

Elizabeth and James looked up. Cari could tell that her father was relieved to see her but that her mother looked angry.

"I told you to be here by dark!" Elizabeth's tone was sharp, for she was barely able to contain her unhappiness over seeing her daughter with Silver Wolf. She saw, too, that Cari was carrying her shoes and stockings instead of wearing them, and she wondered what she'd been doing that she would be coming home barefoot.

"I'm sorry, Mother. We were having so much fun I forgot," she apologized, hanging on to her belongings as her father helped her down from the horse's back. She smiled up at her friend. "Thank you."

James smiled at the brave, too, hoping to deflect his wife's ire. "It's good to see you, Silver Wolf. How's Tall Shadow?"

"He is well."

They talked a few moments longer, then Silver Wolf, sensing the white woman's mood, bid them good-bye.

Elizabeth observed Cari as she watched the half-breed ride away. She saw how her daughter's gaze followed him and how her face glowed with happiness. It was in that instant that Elizabeth made her decision. It was time. She could no longer avoid the confrontation she'd known was coming. This friendship between Cari and Silver Wolf had to end, and it had to end now. Silver Wolf was no longer just a young brave. He was a man, and she wanted her eleven-year-old daughter far away from him.

Elizabeth knew Cari was still a child, but soon she would be a woman. This was a very delicate time in her daughter's life, and there was no way she could let Cari continue to be exposed to that Indian's savage influence. She would discuss it with James later tonight when they were alone. It was time to get Cari away from here. It was time to do whatever was necessary to ensure her daughter's future.

James was unaware of his wife's thoughts as he put his arm around Cari. As they headed for the house, he asked, "Did you have a good time at the creek?"

"Oh, yes!" Her eyes were alight with happiness. "I was so glad when Silver Wolf came. He's my friend, Papa . . . and look! He gave me a pair of moccasins!" She paused to lift her skirts to show her father the gift he'd given her.

Elizabeth turned back at her words and the sight of Cari wearing moccasins hardened her resolve. She loved James, but her daughter's future was at stake. No matter what her husband's objections, she was going to take her daughter back East as soon as she could arrange it. She was going to enroll her in a school for girls and make certain she learned to be a lady. Then she was going to see her married to the finest gentleman she could find. Her expression was grim as she went inside.

It was some hours later, when she and James lay in bed together in the dark of their bedroom, that she finally broached the subject.

"James . . . there's something we have to talk about."

He'd known she'd been furious since Cari had returned with Silver Wolf, and he'd been preparing himself for what was coming. "If it's about Silver Wolf . . ."

"No, I want to talk about Cari, about her future."

He frowned into the darkness. "Her future?"

"I think we should take her back East for a while."

"Why?"

"James," she said softly as she rolled to her side and raised up on her elbow to look down at her husband. She rested one hand on his chest as she spoke. "She's a young woman now. She has her whole life ahead of her. She should be getting ready to attend parties and dances and wear ballgowns, and yet here she is . . ."

"Is this such a terrible place to be? Have you been so unhappy?"

"I'm thinking of our daughter. There are no social gather-

ings to speak of. How in the world will she ever meet someone
suitable if she stays on the ranch? I want to take her back to
Philadelphia so she can do all the things a girl needs to do
before she marries and settles down."

"No, I can't go." His answer came quickly and emphatically.
"*I* could take her then."

The thought of all those long, lonely days and nights without
his wife and daughter was just too difficult to consider. "I
don't want you to go. I want you here with me."

With great tenderness, she pressed a soft kiss to his cheek.
"Oh, James, I want to be with you, too, but don't you see?
Cari isn't a little girl anymore."

"She's a child, Elizabeth," he persisted.

"Not for long," she replied, remembering her own youth
and how she'd matured so rapidly once she'd turned twelve.
One day she'd been playing dolls and the next, she'd been all
grown up. It had been exciting, but it had also been frightening. "She's almost a woman."

James remained silent. It troubled him to realize that what
his wife was saying was the truth. He sighed as he slipped an
arm around Elizabeth and drew her against him. "You're
right," he finally admitted. "She's growing up so quickly. I
don't suppose there's any way to stop it, is there?"

Elizabeth gave a soft laugh as she lay her head on his shoulder. "No, dear, I'm afraid not."

"I didn't think so."

James kissed her. His love for Elizabeth had always been
passionate, and the thought of being separated from her again
for any length of time ate at him. The moment took on new
and poignant meaning as they came together. His lovemaking
was intense and powerful as he possessed her, taking her to
the sweetness of ecstasy and beyond. They lay together in the
aftermath of their loving, cherishing the intimacy and trying
to avoid saying what needed to be said.

Finally, Elizabeth broke the silence. "I want Cari to have what
we have," she told him gently, her left hand splayed across his

chest, her gold wedding band gleaming in the soft light that shone through the window.

"I do, too," James agreed slowly, lifting her hand to his lips.

"There's so much she doesn't know . . . so much of the world she's never seen. I'll take her back to Philadelphia. We can live with my parents. She can go to school there. It'll be good for her to be with other girls her own age."

"How long, Elizabeth?" The question was strangled from him. "How long will you be gone?"

"You could come with us," she offered, hoping with all her heart that he would, and that once they were there, he would want to stay.

"I can't leave the ranch for any length of time. You know that."

She fought to keep the bitterness she felt out of her tone. "I don't know. Cari will need at least a few years in school."

"Years . . ." He said the words slowly, painfully. "Are you sure this is what she really needs?"

"What can we give her here, James?"

"We can give her love. We can teach her how to take care of herself and be independent. We can teach her the importance of working with her own hands to build something out of nothing. We can . . ."

"I'm talking about her future. She can't live with us forever. She's a beautiful young woman, and she will need to have the opportunity to meet young men. What kind of life will she have if she never gets to see the world? You love the ranch, because you've been other places and seen other things. Cari's never had that chance. We have to give it to her."

James knew Elizabeth was right, but it didn't make it any easier to accept the fact that they would be leaving and he would be alone. "How soon do you want to go?"

Elizabeth's victory was bittersweet. She pressed a tender kiss to her husband's lips. "I'll tell Cari in the morning, and if we start packing right away, we should be ready in a few days. Will you be all right?"

"I'll be fine," he lied, knowing he was going to be very

lonely without their love and laughter surrounding him. "But I don't know about Cari." He knew his daughter would rebel at being forced to leave.

"I'm not going," Cari declared defiantly as she faced her mother across the kitchen table the following morning. She couldn't believe her mother would even suggest that they move back East, and her expression mirrored her disbelief.

"It's already been decided, Cari. You're going."

"I don't believe you! Papa wouldn't send me away like this!"

She turned her back on her mother and ran from the house to find her father.

"Carinne! Come back here!"

Her mother's call was useless, for Cari wasn't about to return until she'd talked to her father.

"Papa!" she cried as she burst into the stable to find him tending the horses.

James had feared that his headstrong offspring would be furious over Elizabeth's plan, and as he watched her come charging toward him, her face flushed with anger, he knew his fears had been justified. "Yes, Cari?"

"You and Mother can't be serious! You don't really want me to go back East to live, do you?" Her blue-eyed gaze was imploring as she looked up at him. She was desperate for a reprieve from the fate that seemed worse than death. She loved ranch life. She didn't want to leave her father and her home to go to Philadelphia. She didn't care about school or parties or ballgowns or boys. She wanted to stay on the ranch and ride and spend time with Silver Wolf.

It took all of James's willpower to answer her sternly. "Your mother and I discussed it last night, and we've decided it's the best thing for you."

"The best thing for me? Papa! How can you say that? You didn't even ask me what I wanted! I want to stay here. I don't want to leave you and the Circle M."

"Sometimes in life, we don't always get what we want." His

reply was firm. "This will be good for you, and it won't be forever. You'll only be gone a year or so."

"A year or so! That's a lifetime!"

James couldn't help but chuckle. He recognized so much of himself in her. He reached out and took her in his arms, giving her a reassuring hug as he held her close to his heart. "It won't be that bad, sweetheart."

"Are you really going to make me go?" she asked, her face pressed to his chest.

"Yes, Cari. You go to Philadelphia with your mother and learn to be a lady like she is. Then when you come back to me, we'll run the ranch together."

Cari nodded, but didn't look up at him.

"Cari?"

She still kept her face buried against him, and so he took her chin in his hand and tilted her face up to his. It startled him to find she was crying.

"Ah, darling, I don't want you to go, but it's for the best . . ." Tears burned in his eyes, but he fought them back. Elizabeth had convinced him that this was what their daughter needed, and he'd never denied her a thing in all the years of their marriage.

"Yes, sir," Cari choked miserably, her eyes downcast. She could fight her mother, but she couldn't fight her father, too.

"That's my girl," he managed, his smile less than enthusiastic. "Now, help me feed this mare, and we'll go back and have breakfast together."

They worked in silence for a few minutes, then Cari asked, "Papa, will you tell Silver Wolf when he comes back?"

"Of course I will. He'll miss you, I'm sure."

"Do you really think so?"

"Yes, I do."

Cari felt a little better then, but not much. She would rather have spoken to Silver Wolf about the matter herself, but with her mother planning to leave the day after next, there would be no time. It saddened her to think that it might be years before she got to see him again. He was her dearest friend.

* * *

The following day passed in a blur for Cari what with all the packing for the trip. It would be a long trek, and Cari dreaded the coming departure. At night she cried silently into her pillow. She'd offered up unceasing prayers to be saved from this fate her mother was intent upon inflicting on her, but her pleas went unanswered.

The morning of their departure dawned bright and clear. The birds were singing. It was a perfect day, and it seemed to Cari, as she faced it with all the bravado she could muster, that it wasn't fair her last morning on the ranch be so beautiful. It would have been easier for her to leave if it had been a rainy, horrible day, a day just as miserable as she was. Instead, her last view of the ranch was going to be a glorious, beautiful one, and it was going to tear her heart out to go.

"Papa . . . are you sure I have to do this? I promise I'll be good. I promise I won't get into any trouble. Papa, please let me stay . . ." she begged one last time as he loaded their trunks onto the wagon. She'd vowed not to cry or beg him again, but watching him put her luggage on the wagon just made it all seem so final.

James turned and swept her into his embrace. "Honey, I promise you you're going to have a good time once you get back East and settle in. You're going to spend time with your grandparents and you'll make a lot of new friends. I'll come to see you just as soon as I can manage to get away."

"Promise?"

"I promise."

"Will you give this to Silver Wolf for me?" She glanced over her shoulder to make sure her mother hadn't come out of the house yet, then handed him the letter she'd written, telling him what her address would be and that he could write to her and how much she was going to miss him.

James started to take it from her, but then for some reason, he looked up and saw the brave sitting on his horse on the rise above the house. "You can give it to him yourself."

"What?" When Cari twisted around and saw Silver Wolf for herself, her heart lurched in her breast.

"Looks like he got my message," James observed.

"You sent word to him that I was leaving?"

"I saw Strong Eagle yesterday," he answered simply.

Cari threw her arms around him and kissed him. "Thank you, Papa."

"Go on, hurry before your mother comes," he said in a gruff voice to hide the depth of the emotions that were filling him.

Lifting her skirts, Cari ran toward Silver Wolf.

Silver Wolf had been surprised by the message from James McCord, and he'd ridden out before dawn to see if it was true. As he watched the scene below and saw the white man loading things in the back of his wagon, he knew his friend had not lied. Little Snow was leaving . . .

When Cari began to run toward him, Silver Wolf put his heels to his horse's sides and raced to her.

"Silver Wolf! I'm so glad you got here in time," Cari told him as he reined in before her.

"I received word that you were leaving. Why?"

"My mother says I need to go back East to school, but I don't want to go. I want to stay here with Papa . . . and with you," she confessed her misery.

His face was stony, revealing nothing of what he was feeling as he asked, "Your father says you must do this?"

"Yes. He agrees with my mother. We're leaving this morning."

Silver Wolf glanced toward the wagon and saw that her mother had come outside and was standing with her father. "They are waiting for you."

"I know, but I had to see you again and give you this." She handed him the letter. "Will you write to me? The address is inside."

He nodded tersely as he took the letter. He did not open it then, but remained on his horse with his gaze fixed on the scene at the ranch house below.

Cari stood beside Silver Wolf gazing up at him, trying to

memorize the way he looked so she could carry that image of him with her while she was away. "I'm going to miss you."

His eyes met hers, and for a second, Cari thought she saw something there . . . a flash of some emotion she couldn't put a name to.

"Cari!"

Then her mother's distant call interrupted them, and the look in his eyes vanished. The privacy of their moment together was destroyed.

"Go. Your mother calls." Without looking at her again, he turned his horse and rode back to the top of the rise, her letter clutched tightly in his hand.

Cari's heart sank as she made her way down to the house. She felt as if something very special was being stolen from her, and she didn't know how to get it back. Fighting the despair that gripped her, she returned to the wagon where her parents waited. She climbed up and sat between them, then donned the sunbonnet her mother insisted she wear.

As her father slapped the reins on the backs of the team and they started on their journey, Cari turned in the seat to try to get one last look at Silver Wolf. Her spirits leaped with excitement when she found he had not ridden away, but had remained on the rise and was watching them. He looked magnificent on his powerful stallion.

Tears streamed down Cari's face as she waved to him, and she gave a small sob when he lifted one arm in return. Despite her mother's admonitions to turn around and sit like a lady, Cari kept her eyes on Silver Wolf and treasured the knowledge that he remained there, keeping watch until they traveled out of sight.

Three

Reverend Walter Louis, a short, heavyset, dark-haired man, was the missionary who'd been visiting Tall Shadow's village for many years. He sat opposite the chief in his tipi now, his expression serious as he tried to explain the fears he harbored in his heart about the future. "My people are coming to your land, Tall Shadow. There is no longer any way to stop them. Already you've seen the railroad cross the plains and now the towns are here and growing. I have just received word that your land is now being called Wyoming Territory, and there is much talk about it becoming a state."

The chief spoke in disgust. "So it is not enough that we have touched the paper with the pen and that we want to be left alone to live in peace."

"You know as well as I do that as long as one man has something another man wants, there can be no peace. Greed is an ugly thing, Tall Shadow. There are many who try to take what they want no matter what the law says or who it belongs to."

The two men regarded each other in silence.

"I have an idea that might help you and your people," Reverend Louis offered, and at Tall Shadow's questioning look, he went on. "You know I've been teaching Silver Wolf for many years now." He waited until the chief nodded, then continued, "Well, I've taught him everything I can. He's smart and quick, and I want him to go East to school. If he learns how to deal with the white men on their terms, he'll be able to help you with those who are sure to come."

"Why do the white men not send their young to us so they can learn our ways?"

"Because most whites have little respect for other people's ways. They think their way is the only way. That's why it's important we convince your grandson to do this. He has a sharp mind, and since his father was a white man, he'll have insight into both sides. It would be good for the tribe if he were to do this."

Tall Shadow regarded the missionary in silence for a moment, knowing he was right. Tall Shadow had watched as the whites crossed the Cheyenne land, first in their wagon trains, then in stagecoaches, and now on trains. He had seen the destruction they wrought on the land. "I will speak with him."

When Reverend Louis had gone, Tall Shadow sent for Silver Wolf. As he waited for him to come, he thought about the reverend's advice. Tall Shadow knew he was a good friend to his people. He agreed with him that Silver Wolf was a quick learner, but he wondered how his grandson would do, completely surrounded by whites. In spite of his mother's urgings, Silver Wolf had never fully embraced his father's heritage, and the chief worried that he would balk at the idea of leaving the only home he'd ever known. At the sound of a horse coming into camp, Tall Shadow looked up to see his grandson riding toward him. He knew he would soon have his answer.

The chief's summons had surprised Silver Wolf, and he'd hurried back to camp quickly. He reined in before him and dismounted quickly. "You wanted me?"

"I have spoken with Reverend Louis. He thinks it would be wise if you learned more of the white man's ways."

Silver Wolf frowned. "Why? I am Cheyenne."

"It would make you stronger to defend our tribe."

"I will defend our tribe with my bow and lance as my grandfather does!"

Tall Shadow lifted his gaze to the east. In the distance, dark clouds stained the horizon. He suddenly felt old, his insight to the future sapping his strength and spirit. "The whites are no longer just crossing our land. They are as many as the stars in the sky, and they are coming to take what is ours."

"Then we will fight them," he stated with the boldness of youth. "We will drive them away."

"They are too many, Silver Wolf." He put a steadying hand on his grandson's arm, understanding his eagerness to fight and wanting to temper it. "We must find a better way. You could do that if you went to the white man's school."

"Why do you say their way is a better way?"

"I do not. I only know that they will not turn back and that we must do what we can to survive. You alone among our people have the power to help."

Silver Wolf frowned. Tall Shadow had always treated him as a true Cheyenne, but now, suddenly, he was appealing to his white side, and it troubled him. He was Cheyenne, not white! Still, he knew his chief and the missionary were wise men, and he valued their counsel. "I will speak with Reverend Louis."

Silver Wolf left his chief to seek out the missionary, his teacher for many years. He found him sitting at the edge of the village, a group of happy, laughing children gathered round him. Standing off to the side for a while, he watched him with the little ones. The reverend was kind and gentle. Silver Wolf thought a great deal of him, but he had his doubts about this new idea of his.

The missionary glanced at him and smiled. "I'm glad you came, Silver Wolf. I was hoping to talk to you." He turned to the children. "All of you can go play now. I'll see you later for your lessons."

Excited over getting out of their schooling, the youngsters ran off laughing.

Reverend Louis had known Silver Wolf long enough to gauge

his mood, and he saw the shadow of uneasiness in his eyes. "Did Tall Shadow tell you what we talked about?"

"Yes."

"It would be a good thing for you to go East to college."

"I see no reason to go. This is my home. I belong here, not with the whites."

"There is much you could learn there that would help you here."

"How can learning from books help the Cheyenne?"

Reverend Louis stood and went to put his hand on the young man's shoulder. His expression was earnest as he tried to explain. "I'm not talking about book learning. I want you to go so you can learn more about the white ways. I want you to come to know their hearts, how they think and how they act. If you do this you could become a bridge between two worlds. You would have insight to both sides and be able to resolve conflicts between them. I know you have the strength and intelligence to succeed. But I wonder if you have the courage."

Silver Wolf looked deep into the missionary's imploring gaze. He saw the goodness there and the hope he harbored for a peaceful future for all men. "I do not lack courage, but I do not want to go," he said slowly. "I do not want to be white."

"I know, and I won't lie and tell you it'll be easy. It won't be. But if you agree to try, I will travel with you to the school in New York and see you settled there."

"You are sure it will help my people?"

"It's important that there be understanding in our dealings together and you could provide that."

Little Snow slipped into Silver Wolf's thoughts then. Just like his mother, she'd constantly encouraged him to learn more about his father's heritage. She had always wanted him to read and study. He knew what she would have said to him. She would have told him to go and do his best.

Thinking of Little Snow also brought her mother to mind, and he found himself wondering if his going to an eastern school would change her opinion of him. At the thought, he grew annoyed with himself. He told himself he didn't care what Little Snow's mother thought of him. All that mattered was that he do the right thing. He frowned in concentration as he considered the decision that had the power to change the rest of his life.

When Silver Wolf didn't respond right away, the reverend feared he was planning to say no. "While you're learning about the whites, they'll have the opportunity to be learning about *you*. Everyone would benefit."

Silver Wolf considered all he was saying, but still, fear of the unknown nagged at him. He had not known this uneasiness for many summers, and it angered him. He could ride, hunt, and fight with the best of the Cheyenne warriors. He had faced many dangerous situations and not been afraid. Yet, a strong part of him was cautioning him not to leave the land he loved. Denying the fear, he chose the more difficult path, the one that would be best for his people. "I will go."

Silver Wolf made his way to his and Little Snow's favorite place at the stream. He had not been back since she'd left, but today he knew he had to go. He sat down on the bank, and after getting out the paper and pencil Reverend Louis had given him, he began to write.

Dear Little Snow,
I have made an important decision today . . .

As he labored over the letter, he heard a rustling in the brush and looked up to see Barnie lumbering toward him, her tail wagging happily as she neared.

Silver Wolf welcomed her warmly, and the dog curled up beside him on the bank and rested her head on his thigh. As he paused in his writing to pet her the loneliness he'd ignored for so long filled him.

"You're missing her, too," he said to Barnie as he stroked her silken fur.

She raised sad eyes to his in understanding and sighed as only a dog can.

Silver Wolf finished the letter and was about to put it in the envelope when he remembered the many lessons in tracking he'd given Little Snow. Coaxing Barnie down to the water's edge so she'd get muddy, he took her paw and made an imprint of it at the bottom of the page. That done, he sealed the note away.

He stayed at the stream with the dog until darkness forced them to go their separate ways. When he returned to the village, he gave the letter to the minister so he could send it for him.

The next six weeks passed in a rush for Silver Wolf as he traveled east with Reverend Louis. The trip was a revelation to him. He experienced the speed of trains and saw steamboats for the first time. He also saw for himself the vast numbers of white people who lived in the big cities in the land toward the morning sun. Tall Shadow had been right: They were as many as the stars.

It was as they settled in the carriage that would take them on the final leg of their journey to Marywood College that Reverend Louis broached the last subject that was troubling him.

"Silver Wolf, there is one more thing we have to discuss."

"What is it?" Silver Wolf asked.

"I know you may not like my suggestion, but I hope you will listen to me with an open mind and heart. This concerns a matter I think will help ease your transition at Marywood."

"I don't understand. What more can you want from me? I am already wearing white man's clothes, and I have cut my hair so no one will think I'm a 'savage heathen.'" He'd overheard a woman making that comment about him on the first part of their journey. "What more must I do?"

The missionary heard the frustration in his voice and smiled a little sadly. "You need a name to use in white society."

"I am Silver Wolf." He stiffened in resentment. They could take many things from him, but he would not allow them to take his name.

"I know, but there might be some who would not appreciate the sacred importance of your name."

"My father's name was Marshall. If I must do this, I will take Marshall as my name to honor him."

Reverend Louis realized how hard this was for him, and sympathized. "You're like Daniel going into the lion's den."

He studied Silver Wolf, seeing the proud way he carried himself and the intelligence shining in his eyes. For a moment, he almost wished he hadn't brought him. In the territory, he'd been accepted as a fine Cheyenne warrior. The reverend wondered if his plan to help the Indians would really serve to divert disaster, or if he was merely ruining this young man's life by forcing him into another culture, a culture not known for its kindness to those who were different.

"I remember the story of Daniel from your teachings," Silver Wolf remarked with a slight smile. "Daniel came out untouched."

The missionary smiled, too, then said with a confidence he wasn't really feeling, "As you will, my friend. You're as strong as Daniel."

"Then I shall take Daniel for my first name while I am here," he told him. He stared out the carriage window. He was a thousand miles from his people; he had cut his hair and changed his manner of dress. Now, they wanted him to give up his name. It was a difficult thing to agree to, but he bent to the wisdom of the missionary. "I will be called Daniel Marshall."

"Good." This time his smile was real. "You will do well."

Silver Wolf hoped he was right. As the carriage turned up the long driveway that led to the three-story, ivy-covered brick building that was Marywood College, he knew the new life that had been set before him was about to begin.

"Again, I welcome you to Marywood, Mr. Marshall, and I repeat how pleased we are to have you with us," Mr. Dalton, the headmaster, said to Silver Wolf as they concluded their initial meeting. "It seems everything Reverend Louis wrote to me about you is true. I'm sure you're going to do fine here at Marywood. Let's go to the dormitory now and see about getting you settled. You'll be sharing a room with Kyle Mason. He's a good athlete and scholar and comes from one of the best families upstate. I'm sure you'll get along well."

The headmaster led the way outside from the office through the halls of the administration building. They crossed the commons with its lush grass and splashing fountain and entered the dormitory that housed the college's two hundred male students. After climbing the stairs to the second floor, he directed them to a room at the end of the hall. Silver Wolf came face-to-face with his roommate when Kyle Mason answered Mr. Dalton's knock on the door.

"Mr. Dalton!" The nineteen-year-old Kyle, a tall, classically handsome young man with blond hair and cold blue eyes, was surprised to see the headmaster, but he quickly masked the emotion.

"Mr. Mason, this is Daniel Marshall, your new roommate. He's come to Marywood on Reverend Louis's recommendation. I trust you'll take him in hand and help him learn what he needs to know."

Though his expression seemed to indicate that he was pleased, Kyle's eyes narrowed slightly as he regarded the newcomer. He was furious at being saddled with a roommate, and especially one that looked to be a half-breed Indian. Kyle's sophisticated manners served him well, though, and he did not show his disgust in the presence of the headmaster and the reverend. "Come in."

"Thank you." Mr. Dalton gestured his new student and the missionary inside the room ahead of him. "They'll be bringing his trunk up shortly. Which bed will be his?"

"He can have the one closest to the door."

"Fine. Daniel, I leave you in Kyle's capable hands. He'll tell you all you need to know, and if there's anything else I can help you with, just contact me at my office."

"Yes, sir."

The one bag Silver Wolf had been carrying with him contained all his most precious possessions. He laid it on the bed that Kyle had indicated was his, then followed the two older men from the room. Mr. Dalton left Silver Wolf and Reverend Louis alone in the lobby downstairs.

"We made it, Daniel." The reverend deliberately used his new name so he would get used to it.

"Thank you for coming with me."

"I couldn't let you go through this alone. I'll be staying with my family in the area for three more weeks before going back. If you need anything, you can contact me there." He'd already given him the address. "I'm going to miss you, but I think one day you'll come to see that this was the best thing for you. I'll write to let you know how Tall Shadow is and what's happening in the village," he promised. Their eyes locked and their gazes met in full understanding of the challenge Silver Wolf was about to undertake. "You're Daniel now. Remember that. Daniel was not defeated."

Silver Wolf nodded, and they shook hands. He stood in the doorway of the dormitory watching the missionary until he'd gone, then returned to his room.

"Well, well, well, what do we have here?" Kyle sneered out loud to himself as he rifled through his new roommate's bag. So far, he'd found only Indian clothing, a pair of moccasins, and a small rawhide bag that had some designs painted on it.

Daniel had sensed Kyle's resentment, but he'd never expected to find him going through his personal things. Fury filled him as he stared at the arrogant white man holding his medicine bag. "Give me that!" He launched himself at him without thought.

Kyle dodged his attack as he taunted, "Whatever's in here must be important . . . I think I'll take a look."

Daniel put his head down and dove for him just as he was about to open the medicine bag. This time Kyle did not escape, but was tackled heavily. They crashed to the floor together, grappling and fighting for the bag. The sound of their struggle brought the rest of the boys on the floor running, and there was soon a crowd standing at the doorway watching them.

While Daniel was the more fit of the two, Kyle proved strong and wily. The match drew blood as they exchanged blows in the quest for supremacy. After one particularly punishing hit, Kyle's grip on the bag loosened and it fell from his hand. Daniel drew back to snatch it up and had just done so when Philip Porter and Jeremy Michaels, two friends of Kyle's, stepped in and grabbed him.

Daniel fought against them, but he was outnumbered and overpowered and finally forced to hold still. Blood dripped from a cut over his eyebrow, making him look every bit the savage as he fixed his glare on his tormentor. "Put it down, Mason."

"Hey, Kyle. What have we got here?" Philip and Jeremy asked in unison, enjoying the ruckus and wondering why the newcomer was so upset.

Kyle smiled venomously as he slowly got to his feet. His mouth was cut, and he angrily wiped the blood away. "This is my new roommate, Daniel Marshall. I guess he got a little upset because I was helping him unpack."

"You mean he didn't want your help?"

"Doesn't look that way, does it?" he sneered as he took a step closer to Daniel. Kyle was emboldened now that he knew the other boy couldn't attack him. "And all I wanted was to see what was in this little pouch . . ." He snatched the medicine bag out of his hand.

"It's private!" Daniel ground out as he fought again to break free from the two boys holding him.

"Let's see what's so private about it," Philip urged, sensing it must be something important to cause this much trouble.

Kyle was about to open it and dump out the contents for all the boys to see when another voice rang out.

"I don't think you want to do that, Mason."

A hush fell over the group, and the young men standing in the doorway parted to let Benjamin Douglas enter the room. Tall, handsome, dark-haired, green-eyed Ben was the son of a very rich and influential senator, and though he easily could have been spoiled and arrogant, he was anything but. Ben didn't like injustice in any form, and he never hesitated to defend those in need. He was looked up to by the students at Marywood for his intelligence and quick wit, not to mention his superior athletic prowess, for he was an excellent boxer and horseman.

"What?" Kyle looked up, surprised that anyone would have dared to interrupt him.

Ben nodded toward Daniel as he stopped in front of Kyle. "Whatever is in that bag is private."

"Who do you think you are, coming in here and telling me what to do? This isn't any of your business, Douglas."

"I'm *making* it my business. I've got a friend standing by the door downstairs just waiting for me to signal him to go for Mr. Dalton. Return this man's property now and all will be forgotten. If you don't. . . . Well, I think you just might have some explaining to do. I know your parents contribute a lot of money to the school, but if the administration suddenly became aware of some of your other, shall we say, less honorable activities . . ." He let the sentence hang knowing he'd cornered him. Ben had long despised Kyle Mason. He knew he was a lowlife troublemaker, and it felt good to be able to back him down.

Kyle went pale at Ben's unspoken threat and thrust the bag at him. "Here. Take it. I was just having a little fun."

"Didn't look like fun to me," Ben remarked. "Let him go."

When Jeremy and Philip released Daniel, Ben went to the window and waved, then turned around to face the group. "What are you looking at? I'm sure if the professors knew you had this much free time they'd be glad to give you extra work."

The boys rushed to disperse, leaving Kyle, Ben, and Daniel alone in the room. Ben looked at Daniel and saw a flicker of wariness in his eyes. Wanting to gain his trust, Ben handed him the cherished medicine bag. "What's your name?"

Daniel knew a deep abiding sense of relief as he took the bag. "I am Daniel Marshall."

"I'm Ben Douglas. It's nice to meet you." He put out his hand and was glad when Daniel took it. "Get your things, Daniel Marshall. You can stay with me. I think you'll find the atmosphere in my room more relaxed."

Daniel needed no more encouragement. He gathered up the items Kyle had strewn around and followed Ben.

"Thanks for your help," Daniel told him as they strode down the hall to a room at the other end. It wasn't easy for him to admit that he'd needed help.

"You're welcome," Ben returned quietly. He opened the door to his room and gestured him inside. "Take your pick of the beds."

"You sure?"

At Ben's nod, Daniel went to the window and looked out. The view was of the countryside, green and lush, stretching as far as the eye could see.

"I'll take this one."

"Make yourself at home," Ben invited as he stretched out on the other bed. He folded his arms behind his head as he lay there studying Daniel. Ben judged him to be about his own age, and he could tell he was proud just from the way he carried himself. He knew, too, that he had to be smart or he wouldn't be at Marywood. He wondered what tribe he was from and what had brought him to the East. "How did you end up here, Daniel?"

"Reverend Louis has been a missionary teaching in our village for many years. He thought it would be good for me to study here."

"I don't mean to sound ignorant, but I don't know a lot about Indians. What tribe are you?"

Daniel could tell that his question was motivated by a desire to know, not to disparage or insult him. "My mother is Cheyenne; my father was white."

"He's dead?"

He nodded. "He died many years ago."

"Do you have any other family?"

"My grandfather is Tall Shadow, chief of our tribe, but I have no sisters or brothers."

"That's too bad," Ben told him with an easy grin. "But I tell you what, I've got more family than I need, so if you want to borrow a sister or brother just let me know. I'm one of seven children."

"I'll remember your offer."

Ben had a feeling that Daniel was less than happy in his present situation, and he asked astutely, "Did you want to come here?"

Daniel paused as images of his home, buffalo hunts, and Wild One raced through his mind. A wave of homesickness struck him, but as he thought of all that he'd seen since leaving the village, he knew his own desires didn't matter. "I need to be here," he answered slowly as he faced him. "I must learn more about your ways."

"You say 'your' ways, but you're white, too."

"I did not choose to be."

Ben was thoughtful, then spoke in a voice tinged with regret. "After Kyle's actions, I understand. You got your first Marywood lesson in dealing with white men and it wasn't a very nice one."

"My second lesson was better." He paused as their eyes met in understanding. "Not all whites are like Kyle."

Their moods lightened.

"What do you say we go downstairs to the dining room and get something to eat? You can tell me all about your home."

Daniel knew his interest was real, and he agreed. They talked over their meal and beyond, then long into the night, and Daniel told him of the village and his way of life. He even spoke of Little Snow and their friendship. During the weeks that followed they became close friends. Ben helped him adjust to life at the college and taught him how to study. With his help, Daniel adapted quickly and, within a short period of time he was among the best in his class. He studied hard, sometimes staying up long after everyone else had retired to master a particularly difficult subject. It did not bother Daniel to do it. He was used to working hard to achieve his goals.

As Kyle watched Daniel's achievements, his dislike of him grew. He took every opportunity he could to deride and insult him, wanting to make his life so miserable that he would leave and return to his own kind. It frustrated him when his efforts met with little reaction and usually only a cold-eyed stare from Daniel.

Daniel was very much aware of Kyle's viciousness, but he knew better than to be drawn into any conflict with him. Whenever he felt discouraged, he thought of Tall Shadow and his mother, and he kept working to make them proud. He was aware there were many who were waiting for him to fail.

As determined as he was to succeed, the long hours confined in the classrooms tested Daniel's patience. He longed to be outdoors. He missed the thrill of the hunt and his old way of life. Some nights when sleep eluded him, he would escape from the dormitory to the nearby countryside. He'd discovered a stream that ran in the woods not too far from the college and would seek out the comfort of its banks to pass the long night there.

In those hours of secret freedom, Little Snow always stole into Daniel's thoughts. In all the time they'd been apart, he'd received only one letter from her, and it had been written before she'd learned of his decision to go to Marywood. In it she told him how much she disliked her school and living in the city. He'd written back to her, but decided that her life in Philadelphia with her mother was changing her when she'd never replied. Still, he continued to write to her occasionally for their friendship meant too much for him to let it die of neglect. After a while, he managed to ignore the emptiness he felt in his life, but a small part of him always hoped that one day a letter from her would arrive.

As time passed, Daniel acquired a veneer of civilization. He'd grown accustomed to wearing white man's clothing, and he discovered that he could handle most social situations without difficulty. Daniel knew it was important that he learn all these things so he could be successful at the college, but sometimes he feared the Cheyenne part of him was being destroyed. There were days when loneliness filled him and he ached to return to his old ways, free to ride, hunt, and live his life the way it was meant to be lived.

It was during his second year at Marywood, when Daniel

was having dinner with Ben in the dining room, that Kyle and his friends entered and sat at a table near them.

"Jeremy, look what I've just read," Kyle said in a voice louder than necessary as he unfolded his newspaper.

"Bad news?" his friend asked, unaware of Kyle's motive.

"No, this is good news," Kyle told him, his gaze deliberately resting on Daniel.

"What happened?"

"It seems a certain Colonel Baker killed more than 170 Indians in a raid out West somewhere. Looks like he's following in Colonel Chivington's footsteps." Kyle was smiling with open pleasure.

Daniel went rigid at Kyle's taunt. Chivington's unprovoked slaughter of the peaceful Cheyenne years before had been a tragedy, and though his tribe had not been involved, he'd still grieved for the loss of innocent lives.

"Were they Cheyenne?"

"No."

"Too bad."

Murderous rage swept through Daniel. The Cheyenne who'd been murdered by Chivington had just met with white soldiers seeking peace. During the attack, the chief had even raised an American flag to show their loyalty and to try to stop the killing, but his efforts had been futile. They'd been brutally slain anyway. Daniel controlled his fury with a fierce effort, clenching his hands into fists on the table before him. He glanced up to find Ben's eyes upon him.

"Are you all right?" Ben asked softly.

Daniel managed a grim nod. He told himself that Kyle was stupid and that he himself was strong enough to handle anything the other man threw at him.

"I wonder if Colonel Baker will get a promotion?" Kyle laughed, verbally prodding him again.

Daniel wanted Tall Shadow to be proud of him, but even the Great Spirit could not have controlled himself in the face of Kyle's heartless comment. Daniel came to his feet in a single violent movement. His chair went crashing to the floor as he

unleashed the rage he'd long harbored against Kyle. Before Ben
could react, Daniel crossed the distance between the tables.

"Defenseless women and children were murdered!" Daniel
snarled as he attacked.

Kyle's bravado faltered, then failed him completely. A battle
ensued, ending only when Daniel had Kyle flat on his back and
his hands tight around his throat. If Daniel had had his knife,
he would have used it. Only the sudden, calming weight of
Ben's hand on his shoulder stopped him from doing Kyle great
harm.

"He's not worth it." Ben's words penetrated the red haze of
fury that was coloring Daniel's thinking.

Daniel stared down at the choking Kyle. "You're right," he
answered, his head clearing. "He's not." Daniel let go of Kyle
abruptly and stood up, looming over him. "Stay away from me."
His words were spoken quietly, but with deadly intent. He
turned and stalked from the dining room with Ben by his side.

Kyle turned to Jeremy in disbelief as he struggled to his feet.
"Did you see that? Did you see what he did? He almost killed
me!" he gasped, his throat aching and bruised. "He's an animal! There's no telling what he'll do next! They shouldn't let
his kind in Marywood."

"Maybe it's time to stop pushing him," Jeremy suggested,
cowed by what he'd just seen. When Daniel had had Kyle by
the throat, he'd borne no resemblance to the Daniel they were
familiar with. The half-breed was not someone to toy with,
and Jeremy believed it was time Kyle realized it.

Kyle, however, was not about to give up. He gave his friend
a black look as he stormed away. His hatred for the Indian
had grown even stronger.

Four

Hilary Moore stood off to the side of the ballroom, watching the crowd before her. Though her expression was one of mild amusement, in truth, Hilary was bored, and Hilary didn't like to be bored. Having been spoiled by too much wealth, doting parents, and a quick mind that could outwit most of those who crossed her path, she continually sought challenges to add excitement to her life. Just the year before, she'd been dismissed from Miss Parkington's Girls' School in a hushed-up scandal that had left her parents infuriated and Miss Parkington staunchly unforgiving. Hilary herself had shrugged off the incident, for other people's opinions were not important to her. She did what she wanted when she wanted to, and she dared anyone to tell her differently.

Stifling a yawn, Hilary let her blue-eyed gaze sweep the room, once more assessing the worthiness of the men in attendance. Those she saw held little interest for her. She was about to pick the best of the bunch and reward him with her company when she cast one last hopeful glance toward the door. It was then that she saw him.

Hilary's breath caught in her throat as she gazed at the tall, dark-haired man who'd just appeared in the entranceway. She judged him to be young, probably in his early twenties, but his handsome features showed a strength of character she rarely found in men his age. There was a totally masculine air about this stranger that set her pulse racing, and she eyed him hungrily. He was not like the others in attendance tonight. From his black hair worn just slightly overlong to the broad width of his shoulders beneath his perfectly tailored suit, this one was pure male. She could actually feel his power from all the way across the room. At last. Here was her challenge!

One of the young men she might have chosen was close by, and she reached out to touch his arm. "Who is he?"

"That's the half-breed from Marywood College."

"Half-breed?"

"He's half Indian. Calls himself Daniel Marshall, but someone told me his real name is Silver Wolf."

Silver Wolf. . . . Yes, she breathed to herself.

Her eyes shone with excitement as she anticipated the chase to come. Here was a man worthy of her. Here was the man she'd been looking for all night. She wondered what it would be like to make love to him and grew aroused at the images her active imagination conjured up. She set her mind on having him.

Daniel was gazing about the room, looking for Ben and the rest of their friends when he caught sight of a fair-haired woman out of the corner of his eye. He glanced her way, as he always did when he saw a blonde, for a part of him held on to the fragile hope that it might be Little Snow. Lovely though this woman proved to be, she wasn't Little Snow. Ignoring each time the sense of disappointment that filled him, he turned his attention to locating Ben again, and finally spotted him near the refreshment table. He headed that way, the unknown blonde dismissed, his thoughts on enjoying the evening to come with his friends.

Hilary was delighted when the handsome stranger looked her way, but when he turned his attention elsewhere and strode across the room to join a group of young men instead of coming to speak to her, her delight changed to irritation. She wasn't used to being ignored by men. Hiding her pique behind a smiling, flirtatious demeanor, she went after him like a predator stalking its prey.

"So you finally got here," Ben greeted Daniel as he joined them.

"I had to finish some work."

"All work and no play . . ." Ben gave a rueful shake of his head.

"Means I'll graduate and get to go home," Daniel finished.

"Well, just for tonight try to relax and enjoy yourself. You want a drink?"

"No, I've got an early class tomorrow."

Ben was about to tell him what he thought about his endless hours of study when he saw Hilary approaching. His smile faltered, then failed completely as he realized that her hungry gaze was fixed on Daniel.

Ben knew Hilary. He knew her much too well, and the last thing he wanted to do was introduce her to Daniel. He wanted to ignore her, but being familiar with how brazen she could be, he was sure there was no way he could avoid speaking.

Daniel noticed the change in Ben's expression just as he felt a touch on his arm and heard a soft, seductive voice saying hello. He turned around to find the lovely blonde he'd originally mistaken for Little Snow. From a distance her resemblance to Little Snow had been faint, but up close, her blue eyes and shimmering, pale hair were *so* like Little Snow's that the effect on him was like lightning striking.

"Hello," he replied, his gaze intent, almost devouring, upon her.

"I don't believe we've met," she said in a sultry tone.

"I'm Daniel Marshall," he told her, unable to take his eyes off her.

"And I'm Hilary Moore." There was a breathless, seductive quality to her voice. Then, out of the corner of her eye she saw Ben looking on, his expression cold and guarded, and she added smoothly, "Good evening, Ben."

"Hello, Hilary." Ben's response was curt.

She turned back to Daniel, giving him her full attention. "Are you new to the area, Daniel?"

"No, I've been at Marywood for several years now."

"I can't believe we never met before."

"I've been too busy studying to go to many dances, but now that I realize what I've been missing, I may change all that. Would you care to dance?" he invited, having picked up the basic dance steps at the few parties he had attended.

"I'd love to." A spark of desire glowed in the depths of her gaze as she smiled up at him.

"It's been a while since I've danced," Daniel told her as he stared down at her, mesmerized.

"Then we'll practice together until we get it right," Hilary purred.

Without another word, he took her in his arms and whirled her out onto the dance floor. The warmth of her soft, lush curves pressed ever so slightly against him stirred something very primitive deep within him, but it was her eyes that held him entranced, for they seemed to be coming from his past.

Ben stood on the sidelines, frowning. He knew Daniel was smart, he just hoped his friend was smart enough to see through Hilary's sweet, innocent act. Refilling his glass, he took a deep drink of the potent bourbon and forced his gaze away from the sight of Daniel dancing with a woman he knew could be deadly.

An hour before on his way to the party, Daniel would never have believed that he would have been sorry to have a dance end, but when the music stopped, he was no more ready to let Hilary go than he was to stop breathing. Wanting to stay with her, he suggested a walk outside, and he was pleased when she quickly agreed.

"Tell me about yourself," Hilary asked as they stepped out onto the veranda. She wanted to learn all she could about him.

Daniel told her a little about his studies as they walked toward the steps that led out into the flower garden. Hilary took his arm, and Daniel was surprised that her simple touch had the power to send desire burning through him. They talked of Marywood as he led her along the path that wound its way through the lush foliage, and they didn't stop until they were some distance from the house.

The moon was bright in the cloudless night sky, and stars spangled the heavens like diamonds on black velvet. Hilary sighed as she gazed up at the evening's glorious display.

"It's a lovely night."

"Not as lovely as you," Daniel said, turning her to face him.

"Thank you," she murmured, the look she gave him promising more than Daniel could ever imagine.

"Your hair looks silver in the moonlight."

"I had no idea you were a poet." She gave a light laugh, then grew more serious. "Maybe we were meant to be together, you and I. You are called Silver Wolf, aren't you?"

Suddenly wary, he tensed. "How did you know that?"

"I asked."

"Oh." He relaxed again, pleased that she'd been interested enough to ask about him and pleased that she hadn't been disgusted by his Indian heritage.

"I find you very intriguing, Daniel . . . and very handsome." She moved closer and raised one gloved hand to lightly touch his cheek. "I feel that fate has brought us together," she murmured.

Daniel was enchanted. Invitation was in her eyes, and her touch was a firebrand. Driven by an elemental need he didn't fully understand, he bent slowly to her, his mouth seeking hers with unerring accuracy.

No novice at seduction, Hilary moved willingly closer, and as his lips touched hers, she was surprised by the power of her response to him. Linking her arms behind his neck, she clung tightly to him. She'd known Daniel was different from the others, but she'd never expected to feel this way about him.

Daniel was lost in the passion of her kiss. Clasping her close, he deepened the exchange, seeking out the honeyed secrets of her mouth. It took all of his considerable willpower not to give in to the need to have more of her. He ended the kiss and raised his head to stare down at her, his eyes glittering with the power of the emotions that filled him.

Daniel made Hilary feel alive. She sensed a primitive, almost savage, element in him. Hilary knew she was going to enjoy exploring that part of him. "It would have been a long, boring evening without you. I'm glad you decided to come tonight."

"If I'd known you were going to be here, I'd have made it a point to arrive earlier."

Hilary rose up and kissed him, a quick, teasing, taunting kiss. Then she drew away. She had him just where she wanted him. "Shall we dance again? I love being in your arms."

Daniel's eyes darkened at Hilary's words. She fascinated him. Eager to hold her again, he took her arm and led her back to the house.

Inside the ballroom, Ben had grown concerned when he'd realized that Daniel and Hilary were outside together. He knew he had no right to butt into Daniel's business. Daniel worked hard at school and had the right to some fun, but not with this woman. Ben knew the ugly truth about Hilary, and he wanted to protect his friend. He'd known the young man who'd committed suicide after she'd cruelly finished with him, and he would never forget the whole sordid business.

Ben was relieved when he saw them come back inside. He wanted to speak to Daniel, but before he had the chance, they started to dance again. When the music finally ended and Daniel left Hilary for a moment to go to the refreshment table, Ben took advantage of the chance to speak to him alone.

"Daniel, we need to talk," he said as he joined him.

"Hilary's waiting for me, Ben. Why don't we talk later?"

"But it's about Hilary."

Hearing the terseness in his tone, Daniel cast him a curious look. "What about her?"

"I want you to be careful."

"Why? What are you talking about?"

"Hilary isn't what she seems," he began. "She's not like any woman you've ever known."

Daniel smiled at that remark. "I know."

"Damn it! Listen to me . . ."

"Calm down, Ben." He chuckled.

"Don't laugh off what I'm trying to tell you! I'm dead serious. This woman is dangerous. She . . ." He never got the chance to finish.

"And just what are you two handsome men talking about?" Hilary purred as she appeared at Daniel's side and linked her arm through his. It was a deceptively innocent move, but, in truth, she had a good idea what Ben was saying to him and she wanted to interrupt.

"I was just telling Ben what a wonderful time we're having," Daniel answered. "Here's the punch I promised you." He handed her a cup of the sweet concoction.

"Thank you." Her eyes were only on him as she lifted the cup to her lips. As her gaze held his, she ran the tip of her tongue sensuously over her lips.

Ben looked on in helpless frustration as Daniel appeared to fall even more deeply under her spell. "If you'll excuse me . . ."

"Of course." Triumph flashed in Hilary's eyes.

The rest of the evening passed quickly for Daniel. He remained by Hilary's side and couldn't remember a time in the recent past when he'd felt so alive. He laughed more in those few hours with Hilary than he had in all his years at Marywood. She was witty, intelligent, and attractive. When the last waltz of the evening was announced, he grew solemn. He didn't want the night to end. He knew he had to see her again. Thoughts of his studies hovered in the back of his mind, but he ignored them. Right now, Hilary was more important.

"What are you thinking about?" Hilary asked, noticing the change in him. With most other men she could easily predict what they were going to say before they said it, but Daniel was proving different. He intrigued her.

"I enjoyed being with you tonight," he told her honestly. "And I want to see you again."

She smiled up at him from beneath lowered lashes. She wanted him more than she'd wanted any man in a very long time. She actually thought about taking him to her home that very night, but she knew it wouldn't do to move too quickly. She would have him, but all in good time. "There's going to be a fox hunt at my parents' estate next weekend. Would you like to come?"

She doubted he knew anything about riding to hounds, so by inviting him, she believed she'd be in control of the situation . . . and him.

"I'd be delighted."

They had no further opportunity to be alone, so as the ball came to an end, Hilary was forced to bid him a polite, public, good night. With the memory of his kiss still burning in her mind, she departed in her own carriage. Her thoughts were flying as she planned the weekend to come with Daniel. He was going to be hers!

Hilary was glad that there was no one at home when she returned, and she didn't even bother to light a lamp as she entered her bedroom. She wanted time alone to think about Daniel. She started to undress.

"Let me do that for you . . ." a deep voice came to her out of the darkness.

Caught unawares, she gasped in shock.

"Come, Hilary. We both know you're no stranger to having a man in your bedroom . . ." There was laughter in the man's voice.

Hilary's shock turned to good-humored dismay. "Kyle. Only you would be so bold as to break into my home. What are you doing here?"

"I didn't break into your home, my dear. I merely entered without anyone knowing, but that's all the better for us, don't you think?" Kyle kissed her. It was a hot, possessive kiss, and when he drew away he asked, "Did you have a good time tonight?"

"You might say that," she told him. They'd known each other for years, and, in fact, were two of a kind. They took what they wanted, and damn the consequences.

"I expected you home long ago."

"I met a very interesting man. You might know him. He goes to Marywood."

"Really?"

"His name is Daniel Marshall, and he's quite the best-looking man I've ever seen."

Kyle's eyes turned cold at the mention of Daniel's name, but he revealed nothing else of his hatred for the man. "I've heard of him."

"What do you know about him?" she asked, hoping for more information she could use to her advantage in her pursuit of him.

"He's a half-breed and little better than an animal from what I understand."

"Personally, I find him very attractive." She gave a throaty chuckle as she moved away from Kyle to light a lamp. "He's handsome and intelligent and . . ."

"And a savage," he finished the sentence for her.

"And I'm going to tame him." She continued to loosen her gown as she spoke, then let it slip from her shoulders. Her eyes narrowed like a cat's as she turned back to Kyle. Daniel was the man she wanted in her bed right now, but she would satisfy herself with Kyle. There would be time for Daniel later.

Kyle responded to Hilary's unspoken invitation, picking her up and carrying her to the bed. He stripped away the rest of her clothes and eagerly shed his own. They came together in a blinding rush of lust that had nothing to do with love or tenderness. Later, when the passionate frenzy had passed, she lay with Kyle, sated but not satisfied.

"I've invited Daniel to the country next weekend for the hunt."

"What for?" he asked, irritated that she would bring up the half-breed while they were in bed together.

"I want to spend the whole weekend with him. By the time the weekend is over, Daniel Marshall is going to be mine."

"Don't count on it. From what I know about Marshall, the only thing he cares about is studying. He has some crazy idea about going back out West after graduation and working with his tribe. For all that he may look like a gentleman, he's going to end up living in a tipi and running around in a breechcloth."

"Daniel in a breechcloth? Sounds wonderful. I even love his Indian name. Silver Wolf. Maybe I'll go west with him."

"I thought you said *you* were going to tame *him,* darling, not the other way around," he sneered. "I'll tell you what. I'll make you a wager."

"A wager? What kind of wager?" She levered herself up on one elbow to look down at Kyle, her eyes glowing with excitement.

"I'll bet you that you can't bring the 'Wolf' to heel."

She laughed at his word play. "Be careful what you bet, Kyle. I'm very good with dogs, and wolves are quite similar to their canine cousins." A confident smile curved her lips. "What do I get when I win?"

"When you win?"

"Absolutely. I have no intention of failing."

He looked thoughtful, then smiled. "A diamond bracelet. You can have your choice."

She nodded, eager to claim her prize. "I'll tame Daniel, you'll see. I'll have him following me around like a lovesick puppy, eating out of my hand within two months." Already she was imagining the diamond-crusted bracelet on her arm.

"Two months it is, Hilary. But tell me, how will I know if he's 'following you around like a lovesick puppy'?"

"We'll arrange it so you can see us together. How's that?"

"Fine. But, tell me, darling, what do I get if you fail?"

"What do you want, Kyle?" Her eyes were sparkling with bold confidence.

"You, in my bed, for an entire week."

"Done!"

As Daniel lay in his bed late that night, he realized he knew nothing about fox hunting. He decided to ask Ben's advice. "Ben? Hilary invited me to her family's estate for a fox hunt next weekend, and I wondered if there's anything special I need to know?"

Ben had been trying to sleep, but at Daniel's words he stirred, frowning into the darkness, wondering at Hilary's game. "You ride like the wind. You won't have any trouble.

I'll show you a few technical things you'll need to learn during the week. Other than that, you'll be fine."

Daniel was completely unaware that Ben was having misgivings. He only knew that each passing day brought him closer to seeing Hilary again.

When Friday arrived, Ben loaned him the clothing he would need for the hunt, and he was greatly appreciative.

"Any time. Just remember— be careful," Ben advised, not saying what was really in his heart— that he wanted Daniel to run as far and as fast as he could away from Hilary Moore.

Daniel arrived at the Moore's country house and was admitted by a servant. Hilary appeared at the top of the staircase.

"Daniel . . . I'm so glad you're finally here!" Hilary moved slowly down to him, her gaze fastened on him.

As Daniel watched her coming down the steps, he was surprised to find that she again reminded him of Little Snow. He wasn't sure if it was the simple way she was wearing her hair down and brushed out in a glorious tumble of curls around her shoulders, or if it was the fashionable, deep-green daygown she wore that clung to her shapely figure. As she reached the bottom step and their eyes met, though, he knew she wasn't his Little Snow. The look in her eyes was anything but innocent, and the slight pout of her lips stirred his blood. He felt heat rising through him.

"I missed you," she said in a throaty voice.

The heady scent of her perfume encircled him, rousing his senses to an even sharper edge. "I missed you, too," he answered, unable to stop himself from reaching for her.

"I thought today would never come."

Without a thought as to who might catch them, she drew him down to her for a fiery kiss. Their mouths met in a torrent of desire, and when they broke apart, they were both breathless.

"It's going to be a wonderful weekend," she said in a tone that promised even more delights. She led him off to meet her family and the other guests.

Daniel was proving more than amenable to Hilary's direction. He charmed her parents and his skill as a horseman left her breathless. Everyone in attendance was thoroughly impressed with him, including many of the other ladies, who, along with Hilary, thought he looked absolutely magnificent in the scarlet coat and highly polished boots.

Daniel spent every moment he could with Hilary, but it seemed they were always surrounded by a crowd of people. Sunday he awakened early. The night before he'd mentioned to Hilary's father that he might go for an early-morning ride. Mr. Moore had given his approval, and so Daniel was up, dressed, and ready to ride long before anyone else even thought about getting out of bed.

A soft knock sounded at his bedroom door as he was about to leave for the stables, surprising him. He opened the portal to find Hilary standing there, also dressed for a ride.

"I heard you talking to my father last night, and I thought I'd go riding with you to keep you company."

She stepped into his bedroom and shut the door behind her. Her gaze fell upon his bed with its tumbled covers, and she wished she'd been lying there with him all night, instead of spending the long, dark hours alone. She wanted Daniel desperately, but her bet with Kyle had kept her in her own room. A quick, heated coupling wouldn't do it. She had to bring Daniel to heel, and she couldn't do that if she gave in to her desire to make love to him too quickly.

Daniel saw the direction of her gaze, and for a fleeting moment he thought of throwing her onto the bed's softness and making love to her. The idea stirred him, but he respected Hilary and didn't want to put her reputation at risk.

"We'd better go," he told her softly.

"In a minute . . ." She stepped nearer to him and rested her hands on his chest as she gazed up at him. "First . . . kiss me, Daniel."

He crushed her to him, his mouth claiming hers. Hilary reveled in the power of his embrace. She allowed him to hold her until she felt the fever building within him, then she moved away. She used all the tricks of a tease to deliberately maneuver Daniel where she wanted him.

They left the house and made their way to the stables. Daniel saddled their horses and helped her to mount, his hands sure and strong at her waist.

Hilary took the lead, guiding Daniel along wooded bridle paths and across open fields. Having led him the merry chase, she finally reined in at a secluded glade. Unable to resist any longer, they lay together on the bed of sweet grass, sharing kiss after ardent kiss. Suddenly, Hilary needed the feel of Daniel's hands upon her bare flesh.

"It's all right, Daniel. No one will find us here . . ." She unbuttoned the top three buttons on her blouse, then took his hands and drew them to her to finish.

"Hilary . . ." Daniel unfastened the last two buttons and parted the fabric of her blouse to reveal the lacy camisole that remained the sole barrier between them.

She shrugged her shoulders just enough to let the straps of the camisole fall, baring all but the very peaks of her breasts. With a groan of pure desire, Daniel pushed the offending garment down.

"You're beautiful," he said huskily as he cupped her breasts and pressed heated kisses upon them.

"Oh, Daniel . . ." she gasped.

His lips explored her sensitive flesh, and she arched to him, offering him more. Her hands moved over him, unbuttoning his shirt to bare his chest to her caress. Pulling him up to kiss her lips again, she pressed her breasts against his hair-roughened chest. A shudder wracked him, and she smiled in feminine triumph, for she knew that he was close to losing control. She slowed her caresses and whispered, "Daniel. We have to stop . . ."

Daniel tensed. He knew she was right, but that didn't make it any easier to stop loving her. With an effort, he moved away. He sat up, his knees bent before him, his forearms resting on them as he fought to bring his raging desire under control.

"It's time we go back, Hilary." He glanced over to where she lay beside him, her breasts still bared to his hungry gaze, and knew he would regret being honorable for a very long time.

Hilary saw the flaming passion in his gaze and smiled to herself. Her plan was working! He wanted her— desperately! With slow, deliberately provocative moves, she covered herself. She was aware of his heated gaze upon her, and she gloried in the sense of power it gave her. The weekend had been a marvelous success.

Several weeks passed, and Hilary made sure that they spent every possible moment together. She arranged strategic times and places where they would be alone just long enough for her to work her wiles on him, rouse him to a fever pitch, and then leave him.

Daniel was unaware of Hilary's devious planning. He was too enraptured with her and the world she was showing him. Each day seemed brighter, each flower more fragrant, each moment happier since she'd come into his life. He thought of love and wondered if this was it.

One afternoon, seven weeks after he'd met Hilary, Daniel returned to his room after classes to find a note from her waiting for him.

"What is it?" Ben asked casually, as he watched a slow smile spread across Daniel's face as he read the note.

"I'm meeting Hilary tonight." His blood began to heat as he anticipated the rendezvous.

"Don't you have a report due in tomorrow?"

"I'll get to it."

"Daniel, I think it's time you and I had a talk."

"Why?"

"You've worked too hard to throw it all away. Think about what you're doing. You've been neglecting your studies."

"I'm still receiving passing grades," he argued.

"Daniel, there's something you need to know . . . something I have to tell you before you ruin your life. It's about Hilary."

"What about her?" Daniel tensed as he turned toward his friend.

"She's no good. She's using you and she's going to hurt you. It's almost as if she takes pleasure in destroying men. You aren't the first one she's played with like this, and you won't be the last."

"I don't know what you're talking about."

"It's time you heard the truth. She's a slut . . ."

Ben didn't get any further, for Daniel hit him with all his might, sending him sprawling backward onto his bed.

"Don't talk about her that way," Daniel ground out, standing over Ben, furious.

"Listen to me . . ." Ben began again as he struggled to his feet, gingerly wiping the blood from his cut mouth with the back of his hand.

"Good-bye, Ben."

"You're going to regret not listening to me . . ."

"I already regret that I listened to what I did."

"Well, you're going to regret it even more!"

Daniel had already slammed out of the room, leaving Ben staring after him, his heart heavy with the fear that he'd lost his friendship forever.

Hilary was waiting for Daniel when he arrived at their meeting place, her friend Janis's house.

"I'm so glad you could come tonight," she said huskily as she led him into the parlor.

"Where's Janis?"

"Gone, and so is her whole family, and I've dismissed the servants. We have the entire house to ourselves."

Their eyes met and passion flared between them.

"But first, champagne . . ." Hilary poured them each a glass of the fine wine and lifted hers to him in salute.

"To us," she breathed.

Daniel rarely drank, but tonight, after his confrontation with Ben, he needed something to lighten his spirits. He didn't respond to her toast, but downed the glass and waited for her to pour him another.

"Are you hungry?"

"No. Food's the last thing on my mind." He wanted to feel her body against him so he could erase the haunting harshness of Ben's words from his memory.

Hilary needed no other encouragement. She took the empty glass from him and set it aside with hers, then took his hand and led him to the bedroom she'd already prepared for them. Candles flickered, casting the room in a golden glow, and the bed was invitingly turned down. She'd been planning this seduction for a long time and wanted everything to be perfect. Closing and locking the door behind them, she turned back to Daniel and began to unbutton his shirt.

"Tonight, no one will interfere. Tonight, it will just be the two of us."

"Yes." His mouth covered hers as he brushed her hands aside and finished unbuttoning his shirt himself. That done, he sought out the buttons at the back of her gown and unfastened them. When the kiss ended, she stepped away from him and slipped out of her gown. She stood before him unclothed, and he was shocked and excited to discover that she'd worn nothing beneath it.

Hilary walked sinuously to the bed and lay down upon it. She lifted her arms to him in welcome. His blood was pounding in his veins as he moved toward her, shedding his clothes as he went. Daniel meant to be tender with her, but she would have none of it. The moment they touched, she became a wildcat. Tonight, she would no longer deny herself. Tonight, she would prove that he was her slave.

Caught up in the firestorm of her need, his usual rigid control eased by the potent champagne, Daniel was caught up in Hilary's wild fervor. She moved restlessly beneath him, caressing him boldly, begging him to take her. When at last he entered her, she moaned his name in ecstasy and raked her nails down his back, branding him with her mark. The pain she inflicted drove him on, and he thrust harder into her hot depths. Their fierce passions roiled in a cauldron of lust until the sound of her crying out to him in her own pleasure took him to his. Panting from the exertion of their violent mating, they collapsed together.

They rested only a short time before Hilary reached for him and aroused him again. She spun her sensual web around him, trapping him with the power of her desire, and he was her willing captive.

The night was a tumultuous one for Daniel. When he returned to the dormitory, he was glad to find Ben asleep. He was in no mood to have another fight with him, and fight him he would have, because he believed he was in love.

Days passed, and with graduation only a short time away, Daniel began to think seriously about his future. He made his decision quickly. The excitement he felt when he was with Hilary convinced him that they were meant to be together. He wanted to spend his future with her, so he went to a jeweler's and purchased a modest ring. He could hardly wait to see her again, to ask her to become his wife and the mother of his children.

A note from Hilary arrived just after he returned to his room with the ring. He was thrilled to discover that she wanted him to meet her in the garden of her house later that evening. Thinking this would be the perfect night to propose, he eagerly awaited the appointed hour.

Kyle was furious as he rode toward Hilary's home, but he knew he only had to hide that fierce emotion for a few more hours. It was almost over, and when it was, he was going to have what he'd always craved— Daniel's complete humiliation.

When he and Hilary had made their wager about Daniel, Kyle knew he would be the winner, whatever the outcome. If Hilary tamed Daniel, Kyle would make certain that he would be humiliated when the truth came out, and if she didn't tame him, he'd still have her in his bed to do with as he pleased.

Either alternative had suited Kyle just fine in the beginning, but it seemed to him now that something had changed with Hilary. He had bedded her several times since the night of the bet, but the last time he'd taken her earlier that week, she'd been less than responsive. It had seemed as if she were holding back from him. He hadn't quite been able to figure out what the difference was, but he knew he was not imagining it. Then, when he'd learned through one of his numerous sources that Daniel had bought a ladies' ring, it had become obvious to him that Hilary was keeping a lot of things from him. It wasn't just a lark to her anymore. Obviously, she'd tamed the breed, but had enjoyed bedding him so much she hadn't wanted it to end.

It was that thought that had left Kyle rigid with anger, and it had been that anger that had driven him to write the note in his best imitation of Hilary's handwriting asking Daniel to meet her in the garden tonight. He was going to teach them both a lesson they wouldn't forget.

It was late as Hilary lay in bed, thinking of Daniel and wondering what to do about Kyle and the bet. She knew the time was almost up, but she wasn't sure that she wanted her relationship with Daniel to end. The thought amazed her, for she'd never met a man she wanted to stay with this long before. But Daniel was different.

A knock at the door interrupted her thoughts, and when the maid announced that Kyle had arrived and wished to see her, she grew troubled. She dismissed the servant for the night, then quickly freshened up and went down to greet him. When he suggested a walk in the garden, she agreed, but she knew he wanted something and she had to be careful what she said to him.

Kyle's timing was perfect as he walked arm-in-arm with Hilary to the fountain. In just a few moments her Indian lover would show up, engagement ring in hand no doubt.

"You know, Hilary, the time for our wager is almost over. I'm looking forward to having you in my bed very soon," he told her, his meaning clear in his tone as he paused with her before the splashing waters of the fountain.

"Ah, but Kyle, you haven't won yet." She was irritated by his smugness.

"Does that mean you've brought the half-breed to heel, my love?" he taunted.

"Of course. Daniel is mad for me. He'll do anything I ask."

"Then why haven't I gotten to hear his pleas of undying devotion?"

"All in good time, Kyle . . ."

He heard the faint sound of footsteps and knew the moment he'd been waiting for had arrived. "You don't seem to want your prize very badly," he remarked. "Perhaps you're stalling because you really haven't tamed the beast."

"Of course I've tamed Daniel," she insisted. "The man hasn't been born who can resist me when I make up my mind to have him."

"Then prove to me that you have him begging for your attentions, and I'll give you this . . ."

Kyle drew the expensive bracelet out of his pocket and held it up for her to see. The diamonds flashed fire in the moonlight, and in spite of her desire for Daniel, she gasped in delight at the sight of the bauble.

"It's beautiful," she breathed, grasping it. She was very fond of diamonds.

"And it will look lovely on your arm. If you win, that is. . . . If you bring Daniel to heel and I get to witness him groveling before you." Kyle took her in his arms and kissed her, his hand boldly seeking the curve of her bodice.

The hard strength of him against her aroused her, and she arched against him, enjoying the contact. Kyle was no challenge to her. She'd already won the bet, all she had to do was figure out how to collect her prize without losing Daniel in the process. It didn't seem too difficult to her. She'd always controlled Kyle in the past and saw no difficulty in doing it again. Clutching the bracelet tightly, she returned his kiss.

Daniel arrived at Hilary's house, but didn't bother to knock.

As was their custom, he went straight to the garden to meet her. His heart was pounding an excited rhythm as he moved down the path toward the center fountain where they had met before. He'd never thought of proposing before, and he was hoping Hilary would say yes. As he neared the fountain, he was surprised to hear voices, and as he moved within view, he saw that she was already there, talking with another man. Daniel stood perfectly still, not wanting to interrupt. He hadn't meant to eavesdrop, but when he recognized the sound of Kyle Mason's voice, he froze in place.

"Kyle, you haven't won yet."

"Does that mean you've brought the half-breed to heel, my love?"

"Of course. Daniel is mad for me. He'll do anything I ask."

"So when do I get to hear his pleas of undying devotion?"

"All in good time, Kyle . . ."

"You don't seem to want your prize very badly. Perhaps you're stalling because you really haven't tamed the beast."

"Of course I've tamed Daniel. The man hasn't been born who can resist me when I make up my mind to have him."

"Then prove to me that you have him begging for your attentions, and I'll give you this . . ."

"It's beautiful."

"And it will look lovely on your arm. If you win that is. . . . If you bring Daniel to heel and I get to witness him groveling before you."

"Hilary, what the hell is going on!" Daniel couldn't stop himself from confronting them. His gray eyes were steely as he stared at them. Violence gripped his soul. He wanted to tear Hilary from Kyle's arms and shake her and force her to tell him that what he'd just heard wasn't true— that their relationship hadn't been just a game to her.

"Daniel!" she gasped, startled to find him there. Her surprise was immediately replaced by a terrible sinking feeling, for it was obvious from his expression that he'd heard most of what had been said. Her heart cried out "No!", but she knew it was too late. She tried to free herself from Kyle's confining embrace, but to her dismay he only tightened his arms, pinning her against him.

"What is he doing here, Hilary?" Daniel demanded.

"Allow me to explain," Kyle cut in sarcastically, his eyes bright with power as he faced his rival. "I'm here because tonight is special. You see, it's been almost two months to the day since Hilary bet me that she could bring you to heel."

"She *what?*" Daniel's condemning gaze hardened even more as it rested on her and her alone.

"Of course she wouldn't tell you about our wager . . ." he explained with smug casualness. "But you see, she bet me that she could train you to do anything she wanted, even sit up and beg, and when I heard that you'd bought a ring, well, I just knew I had to be here for the happy moment. My compliments to you, Hilary dear, you did an outstanding job. You have him right where you promised you would all those weeks ago." He laughed cruelly and ignored the painful stabbing of Hilary's nails in his arms. He refused to let her go just yet.

Daniel felt cold inside, his heart turned to stone as he looked at the woman he thought he'd loved being held in the other man's embrace. "Hilary. . . . Tell me he's not serious. Tell me what we had meant something to you . . ."

Hilary finally freed herself from Kyle's hold and took a reconciling step toward him. "Daniel, it wasn't supposed to happen this way."

"*It* wasn't supposed to happen this way? How was *it* supposed to happen, Hilary?" he demanded.

"Danny boy, don't be so dramatic." Kyle laughed at his outrage, enjoying every minute of his victory. "Hilary makes a lot of men feel special, if you know what I mean, but when she tires of them, she discards them. You were only different because she'd get a prize if she won your heart." He gestured toward what she was holding in her hand. "Show him your prize, Hilary. Hold it up so he can see."

Hilary didn't have to move for Daniel to see the expensive trinket. The diamonds sparkled like ice in the moonlight—cold, frozen, and hard, just like his heart.

"It's a beautiful bracelet, isn't it? Hilary likes beautiful, expensive things, don't you, Hilary? Tell me, Daniel, did you bring your ring?"

In his pocket the ring he'd selected with such great care felt leaden, as he glanced from the bracelet to Hilary's face, seeing for the first time the truth of her nature. "Everything Ben told me about you was true . . ." Disgust flickered in his eyes, then his expression turned stony.

Hilary wanted to cry out in protest, to tell Daniel that she hadn't known she would feel this way about him when she'd first made the bet, that it had been only a game then. But looking at him now, she knew she would never be able to convince a man like him of the sincerity of her plea. Kyle's conniving little plot had sounded the death knell of what they'd shared. It had been special while they'd shared it, but it was over now whether she was ready for it to end or not.

"You should have listened to your good friend Ben. Here, Hilary, let's put on your bracelet."

Daniel had had all the humiliation he could stand. He grabbed the bracelet from Kyle before he could put it on her wrist.

"So this is all you think 'taming' me was worth?" he snarled, the warrior in him alive and proud.

Hilary blinked, staring at him as if seeing him for the first time. He looked wild, almost savage, in moonlight that now seemed harsh and unforgiving. A shiver ran down her spine as she recognized the raw strength and power in him. "Daniel, I . . ."

"No matter what you think, you never 'tamed' me, Hilary," he said, his expression furious. "Did you really enjoy trying, or did you feel you earned the bracelet? Ben said you were a slut, but actually he was wrong . . ." He paused to look down at the bracelet he held. "You're a whore."

"Stop it!" she snapped.

"Stop it?" Daniel repeated with a cruel laugh as he took a step nearer. He took her chin in his hand, lifting her face so she was looking at him squarely, and his fingers bruised her pale skin as he glared down at her. "I thought you were special, Hilary. Did you enjoy playing me for the fool?"

Hilary stared up at him. The revelation that he was not and never had been an animal she could train shocked her. He was a fierce, proud warrior, and he looked very angry and very deadly. "It was only a game. I didn't know I was . . ."

"Shut up, Hilary. You've said enough." His civilized veneer fell back into place then, and his voice turned flat and emotionless. He let his hand drop away from her as if touching her was suddenly a vile thing. He dropped the bracelet at her feet, then walked away.

Hilary watched him go, her heart beating a painful rhythm in her breast.

Kyle saw how tense she'd become and laughed. "Honestly, Hilary, you're much better off without him. He's little better than an animal. Be glad he's gone!"

At his taunt, Daniel stopped, all the rage and pain he'd carried for the last four years surging forth within him. He turned and hit Kyle with all his might. Kyle was caught unawares, and the powerful blow knocked him flat on his back, unconscious.

Daniel stood there for a minute, staring down at him. He had finally defeated Kyle, but the victory felt hollow. He glanced at Hilary, who was watching. A short time before he'd thought himself in love with her, and now . . .

He walked away.

Hilary looked from Kyle's prostrate form to Daniel's back, then slowly bent down to pick up the bracelet. After all, she had won the bet. But even as she fastened it on her arm herself, the ache in her heart didn't ease, and she wondered if it ever would.

Five

1872

Pen in hand, Cari sat at the desk in her room, gazing out the bedroom window, a distant, dreamy look in her eyes.

"Cari? Are you getting dressed yet? It's almost time . . ." Elizabeth called from downstairs.

Her mother's call interrupted her reverie and forced Cari to push all fanciful thoughts of her father, the ranch, Barnie, and Silver Wolf from her mind. Her mother was right, there really wasn't much time left. She dropped her gaze to the letter she'd begun over an hour ago and stared in dismay at her progress:

Dear Silver Wolf,

I'm writing this one last time to let you know I'm finally coming home. It's been so long since I've heard from you that I'm not even sure you care any more, but I wanted to tell you. My father says you've been back in Cheyenne for over a year now, working for the Indian Bureau. I guess I'll get to see you when I get there.

Cari

She'd signed her given name, though she'd been tempted at first to sign *Little Snow.* The impulse seemed foolish now, for their wasn't much of Little Snow left in her. Her mother had made sure of that with her multitudes of lessons and years of endless study. But as of tonight that would all be officially over, and Cari was excited. Tonight was her graduation. At last, she would be free of the classrooms and lectures that had nearly bored her to tears. At last, she could begin her life.

After writing out the envelope and addressing it to Silver Wolf at the address her father had given her on his last visit to Philadelphia, she sealed it, rose from the desk, and called for Prudy, the maid. She told her to see the letter posted and then come back and help her get ready for the ceremony. The maid returned a few minutes later and began to help Cari style her hair and slip into the beautiful pastel gown she'd chosen.

Half an hour later, Cari stood before the full-length mirror in her bedroom. She wanted to look pretty tonight, not just because it was graduation, but because Elliot Lowell was going to be there. Her expression was pleased as she studied her reflection.

"Cari, dear . . ." Elizabeth knocked briefly at her door and then walked in. Her eyes widened as she gazed upon her daughter for the first time that evening. "You are breathtaking," she said.

"Do you really think so?"

"Absolutely. You're going to be the most beautiful girl there." Elizabeth hugged her, then kissed her cheek. "Your father would be so proud. I'm just sorry he couldn't be here tonight."

"I'm sorry, too." Cari's smile faltered. Her father had visited them only a few months before and had stayed for four weeks, but this was the busy time of the year on the ranch, and he couldn't get away for her graduation. She understood, but, love him as she did, she still wanted him there to see her triumph.

"We'd better go now. George and Elliot are waiting for us."

"They're already here?" She'd been so busy getting ready that she hadn't known they'd arrived.

"Yes, and Elliot's eager to see you."

They hurried downstairs to find the two men waiting for them in the parlor, twenty-one-year-old Elliot Lowell and his widowed, forty-three-year-old father, George.

Elliot was a dark-haired, dark-eyed, slim, yet muscular young man who stood a little under six feet tall. Heir apparent to his father's fortunes, he'd already taken over the day-to-day management of the very lucrative Lowell Warehouses. But it was not money that had attracted Cari to Elliot. She enjoyed being with him and found him to be a true gentleman in every sense of the word. She was looking forward to their evening together, though it was probably the last time they would have for a long while. In less than a week, she and her mother would be returning to Wyoming.

Elizabeth was glad the Lowells were there, too. Graying, dark-eyed George was a longtime friend. They'd met years ago, before she'd married James, and he'd renewed their acquaintance when she'd returned from the ranch to live in Philadelphia. They'd been close friends ever since and were happy that their children had taken a liking to each other.

"Good evening, Mr. Lowell, Elliot," Cari greeted them as she entered the room.

Both men turned her way and smiled when they saw her.

"Cari, you look lovely tonight," George complimented her.

"Thank you." She blushed prettily.

"You're stunning," Elliot told her as he went to take her hands.

Elizabeth sensed an intensity in Elliot that she hadn't seen before, and she cast George a questioning look. He merely smiled benignly.

"Shall we go? Our carriage is waiting," George said.

The two men helped the women with their wraps and then assisted them into the vehicle. When they reached the academy, Cari left them to join her classmates.

The ceremony passed quickly, ending with a blessing upon

the graduates and their futures. Cari's spirits were high, and excitement filled her as she waited to join the procession.

"Cari's almost as lovely as you are," George told Elizabeth in a low voice as they watched her move past them up the aisle.

"George, you really shouldn't say such things." Though his compliments made her feel young and attractive, she couldn't allow him to talk to her in such a familiar manner. She was, after all, a married woman.

"Why not? I'm a firm believer in telling the truth," he persisted.

"You flatter me."

"Hardly." George gave her a look that spoke volumes. A widower since Elliot was five, he'd been lonely and miserable until he'd seen Elizabeth again. When he'd discovered that her husband, James, was living out West while she resided here, he couldn't believe it. If Elizabeth had been his wife, he would never have let her out of his sight. "I think you're the most beautiful woman in the world."

His words were so earnest and so sincere that high color stained her cheeks. She was grateful for the darkness of the auditorium.

Thoughts of James besieged her as she sat beside George. Soon she would be returning to the ranch, leaving behind Philadelphia, the life she so loved, and George. She had never allowed him to be more than a good friend to her, for, even as different as she and James were, James was still the one and only man she loved. Finally, knowing she had to say something to George, she simply thanked him for his compliment.

The ceremony over, the four of them celebrated at one of the best restaurants in town. Elizabeth found herself thinking again of her husband. Her eyes burned with unshed tears as she realized that her time in the East was almost over.

As they left the restaurant, Elizabeth took one last look around at the glittering dining room, the expensively gowned women and handsome, sophisticated men, and realized she

was losing this life forever. James had made it clear on his
last visit home that he intended for them to stay in Wyoming.

She sighed as they made their way back home. If only there
was some way to make James understand, to convince him that.
. . . She stopped herself. Night after night, she'd lain awake
trying to think of a way to persuade James to stay in Philadelphia, but she knew nothing would change his mind. Once he
set a goal for himself, he always achieved it. He planned to
make the Circle M the biggest and the best ranch in the territory, so if she wanted to be with him, she would have to go
to him. It was as simple as that.

And want him Elizabeth did. As much as she liked George,
James was the love of her life. She adored him and had missed
him dreadfully.

Her thoughts were still on her future when they reached the
house. She and George settled in the parlor, while Elliot and
Cari went out on the veranda to spend some time alone.

"You've been so quiet since we left the restaurant," George
said as he poured two brandies and sat down beside her on
the sofa, offering her one. "Is something troubling you?"

"I've been thinking about James. I hadn't mentioned this to
you before, but Cari and I will be leaving to join him next
week."

"But, Elizabeth, why?" He stiffened at the thought of losing
her. "Aren't you happy here?" He'd been determined to win
her away from her hardheaded husband. He'd figured any
man foolish enough to let Elizabeth go didn't deserve her.

"Of course I am, but I promised James we'd go back to the
ranch once Cari had finished school, and the time has come."

George thought James a very poor excuse for a father and
husband. The man hadn't even come back for his only daughter's graduation! Still, he didn't say so for fear of alienating
Elizabeth. He didn't want to put her in the position of having
to defend her absent husband. "Since James isn't here, who's
escorting you back?"

"Cari and I will be making the trip together."

"Then allow me to accompany you," he offered gallantly.

She dropped her gaze. "No, George, I can't do that."

He scowled, but he understood her concern for decorum. Quickly he suggested an alternative, "If not me, then how about Elliot? It isn't safe or proper for two ladies to travel such a great distance without an escort."

"Really, George, we'll be fine."

"I insist. I wouldn't be able to rest knowing you might be in danger."

Elizabeth smiled tenderly, finding it rather nice to have someone concerned about her. "That's very thoughtful of you. Are you sure Elliot would want to do it?"

"My dear," he began, his tone suddenly confiding, "after tonight, it's my hope that Elliot and Cari may be spending much more time together."

"Why do you say that?" She sensed a secret behind his curious statement.

"I have it on good confidence that we may soon be related . . . if the young lady is willing, that is."

"You mean Elliot plans to propose to Cari?"

"Yes. He broached the subject to me last night. At the time, we didn't know you were leaving, of course, but I did encourage him to ask her as soon as he could."

Elizabeth was delighted. She'd long believed that Elliot was the perfect match for her daughter, and she said a silent prayer that her daughter would accept his proposal.

They raised their after-dinner brandies in a silent toast to the engagement they both hoped would soon be announced.

As Elizabeth sipped from her snifter, she thought of the letter Prudy had brought her earlier that evening to mail. It had been another letter from Cari to Silver Wolf, and she'd destroyed it the moment the maid had left her. Ever since they'd moved to Philadelphia, she'd been intercepting and destroying their letters to each other, and it amazed her that even after all this time they still tried to communicate. Their persistence troubled her, but she was firmly convinced that if Cari became engaged to Elliot, her worries about the half-breed would be over. There was no way the Indian could compete with Elliot. She silently repeated her prayer that Cari would accept his proposal.

"Oh, Elliot, tonight has been perfect!" Cari told him. The happiness she was feeling radiated from her lovely features as they walked to the rail of the veranda and stood in the moonlight, looking out across the landscaped flower gardens. "Thank you for sharing it with me."

He slipped an arm around her waist and drew her to him. His kiss was a gentle caress, his lips soft upon hers.

"It was my pleasure," he told her when they moved slightly apart.

Elliot loved Cari and knew it was time to make her aware of his feelings. She was finished with school now, and there was no reason they couldn't marry. He wanted nothing more than to kiss her again, but he didn't. Instead, he paused, taking a moment to draw upon his courage before broaching the subject so close to his heart.

"Cari, there's something I've been wanting to talk to you about." He reached into his pocket for the ring box he'd been carrying all night, waiting for just the right moment.

Her expression was open and unguarded as her eyes met his eyes, expectantly.

"Cari, would you marry me?" He opened the small box and handed it to her.

Cari stared at the beautiful diamond ring. She didn't want to hurt Elliot, for she cared for him deeply, but marriage? She wasn't sure what to say.

Elliot's nerves were stretched taut. He'd never proposed to a woman before and her silence unnerved him.

"Should I take your silence as a *no*?" he ventured, unable to endure the agony of the suspense any longer. He tried to smile, to be light-hearted, but he cared too much.

"Oh, Elliot! I'm sorry. It's just that I'm so surprised!"

He brightened a bit at her candor, consoling himself with the thought that at least she hadn't refused. "You are?"

"Yes. I mean, I love being with you, and we always have a good time together, but I hadn't in my wildest dreams ever imagined you'd propose to me."

He pulled her to him once more, and whispered as his lips sought hers, "Start dreaming about it, Cari. I love you, and I want to spend the rest of my life with you."

"Elliot . . ." She returned his kiss eagerly, enjoying his embrace. But even as she did, Silver Wolf slipped unbidden into her thoughts.

Silver Wolf . . . Cari still carried in her heart the memory of her warrior watching her from the rise above the house as she'd left Circle M seven years ago. He'd looked handsome and powerful, and she wondered what he was like now. Certainly, he'd changed, for though she'd written to him regularly since they'd parted, he'd never answered her. His lack of interest had hurt her, but it had not killed her feelings for him. They went too deep to be lost so easily.

Cari glanced up at Elliot; he was no Cheyenne warrior. He was, however, a very intelligent and successful businessman. If she married him, her life would be perfect— by Philadelphia standards. She would have a big house, plenty of servants, and children who looked just like him, and that wasn't such a bad thing, for he was very attractive. Still, before she made any decisions about her future, she knew she had to see the ranch one more time. *And Silver Wolf,* a little voice in the back of her mind whispered.

"Elliot, I care about you very much, but I'm not ready to get married yet." She handed him back the ring.

"I love you, Cari. I know I can make you happy."

"I promised my father that I'd return to the ranch when I got out of school, and I can't break that promise."

"I see." Elliot understood. She'd often talked about her father, and he knew she loved him dearly. "Do you want time to think about it?"

"Would you mind? There are things I have to do before I can give myself completely to anyone or anything." Her expression was pleading. She didn't want to hurt him. She cared

about him, loved him— maybe. She just needed time to find
out for sure.

"Cari, I'd wait forever for you," Elliot told her with a sad
half-smile. "I'll keep the ring, and when you decide, you let
me know."

"Thank you." She smiled up at him, thinking him the most
thoughtful man in the world.

They went back inside to join their parents.

"Elliot . . ." George began as the young couple sat down
with them. "Elizabeth and I were just talking, and it seems
she and Cari have to go back to Wyoming shortly after Cari's
graduation."

"I know, Cari just told me."

"Well, I don't like the idea of them traveling west alone, so
I suggested you accompany them. What do you think?"

His smile broadened. It was perfect! If he went with them,
he would have plenty of time to convince Cari to marry him.
"Will you be able to handle everything here?"

"I'll be fine."

"Then, if you ladies will have me, I would be honored to
escort you."

Cari was pleased. She was glad he'd be going with them so
he could see the ranch. Being with him in the western setting
might help her make up her mind about marrying him, too.
She knew it certainly couldn't hurt.

Later that night as Cari prepared for bed, her mother came
into her bedroom. "Did you have a good time tonight?"

"It was lovely, Mother."

"Good, I'm glad," Elizabeth said. "Soon, such evenings will
be things of the past."

"You mean when we go home?"

"Yes, Wyoming is still very wild compared to Philadelphia.
We'll be miles away from everything and everybody."

"But we'll be with Papa. That's all that matters really. He

misses us, Mother. You know he does. I bet he's counting the days right now, waiting for us to arrive."

"I'm sure he is."

"Do you love Papa? Love him with all your heart and soul?" she asked.

Elizabeth was surprised by her question, but didn't hesitate to answer. What she felt for James came only once in a lifetime. "Yes, darling, I love your father. He's the only man in the whole world for me."

"And did you know it right away, when you first met him? I mean did you just look at him and know?"

"No, honey. I suppose some love is that way, but not ours. Your father and I had known each other for some time before we even began to see each other socially. Of course, once he kissed me, I knew. But that came after we'd been courting for a while."

"I see . . ."

Cari sounded so perplexed that Elizabeth had to ask. "Why do you ask?"

"Well, tonight Elliot proposed to me."

"How wonderful! He's a nice young man, and he has a promising future ahead of him."

"I like Elliot a lot and I enjoy being with him, but I don't know if I love him. How can you know, Mother? How can you tell if a man's the right one for you?"

"When the time is right, you'll know. What did you tell him?"

"Well, I didn't tell him no. I just told him the truth, that I hadn't thought about marriage yet and that I wanted to go home and spend some time with Papa on the ranch first before I make any decisions."

Her mother's heart sank. "I understand, and I think perhaps it's a good thing that Elliot's coming with us. It will give you two more time together to get to know each other."

"I'm glad he's going, too, and who knows, we might get married after all."

Elizabeth tucked her daughter into bed and kissed her forehead. "If Elliot's the right man for you, you'll know it. I won't have to tell you."

"And if he's not?" she asked quietly.

"You'll know that, too. Good night, Cari. Sleep tight."

Cari curled up, alone in the darkness, and let her thoughts run free. As always, when she lay in that dreamy half-awake, half-asleep state, memories of Silver Wolf came to her— Silver Wolf saving her from the snow, Silver Wolf reading with her on the creek bank, Silver Wolf bringing her the moccasins, Silver Wolf watching her leave . . .

Cari sighed sleepily. It had been so long since she'd seen him. She wondered again how he was and what he was doing. On her father's last trip back he'd told her that Silver Wolf had returned to Cheyenne and was working with the Indian Bureau. The hurt that he had never answered her letters stabbed at her again. She'd thought her friendship was important to him; could she have been so wrong? She knew she would have to find out.

Restlessly, Cari rolled over onto her stomach and clutched her pillow to her breast. She was going home, and Elliot was going with her. She cared for Elliot, and she would decide about his marriage proposal once she'd seen Silver Wolf again. Her eyes finally drifted shut, and as she fell asleep, her last thought was of her warrior.

Elizabeth returned to her own bedroom, but did not go to bed. As much as she told herself everything would be fine, there was still a nagging doubt in the back of her mind even after all these years.

Damn that half-breed! she swore silently to herself.

Silver Wolf was the reason she'd brought Cari east in the first place, and now she was going to have to deal with him again. That troubled her deeply . . . especially since she'd destroyed all their letters. Soon, she would be found out.

Elizabeth chose to ignore any guilt in the matter. She was a mother and entitled to protect her child. To her way of thinking, it would have served no purpose for the two of them to stay in touch. They lived in different worlds. What bothered her now was how Cari was going to react when she discovered her interference. Elizabeth told herself that she would face that if and when it happened. Until then, she could only hope for the best.

George stood on the platform at the train station with Elizabeth. Outwardly, he played the role of the concerned friend. Inwardly, he was fighting to keep from revealing how much he wanted her to stay— with him. He'd already bid Cari and Elliot good-bye as they'd boarded the train, and now, for the first time that day, he was alone with the woman he loved. It pained him to send her back to James, but he knew it would never do for him to declare himself, for it was wrong to want another man's wife. Elizabeth had made it clear that she loved her husband, and George cared for her so much that he would do nothing to try to damage that marriage. He would sacrifice his own love for her happiness.

"When will you be back?" he asked.

"I don't know, George, maybe next year for a visit . . ." She let her voice trail off as she regarded him, her gaze searching his face. She saw kindness and gentleness there, along with an inner strength that marked him as a good man. She loved him as a friend. Perhaps in another time and place, there could have been more between them, but James would always hold her heart.

"Will you write?"

"Every chance I get. You're my friend, George. I want to keep in touch."

"I will always treasure your friendship, Elizabeth. If you ever need anything, anything at all, you have only to let me know and I'll be there."

She took his hand and held it in hers. "Thank you. You'll never know how much that means to me."

Their gazes locked, and for an instant she could see the flame of hopeless passion glowing in his eyes.

"I have to go . . ." she said quickly, frightened by the intensity she'd seen in his gaze. She dropped his hand and started to move away.

"Elizabeth . . . wait . . ."

She had taken two steps, but stopped and turned back to him.

"Take care of yourself . . ."

"You, too." There was a catch of betraying emotion in her voice as she gave him one last fleeting smile, then she boarded the train that would take her into exile in the land she hated, but it would also take her into the arms of the man she loved above all others. She did not look back.

George stayed on the platform until the train pulled away. He watched until it disappeared down the track. His heart was crying out to Elizabeth to stay with him, but his mind told him there was no hope. She belonged to another man and always would.

He was glad he had work to keep him busy. Work had saved his sanity after his wife died, and it would save him now after the loss of his beloved Elizabeth. He turned back to his solitary life, the days stretching bleakly and endlessly before him.

Six

1874

Sam Larson was the spokesman for the group of outraged ranchers who'd come to Fort D.A. Russell to complain to Captain Greene about the rustling that was taking place on their land. He stood before the officer's desk glaring at the captain who sat so calmly before him. "I'm telling you, Captain Greene, we know it's the damned Indians who are doing it, and we want help from you! How many more head of cattle must we lose before the Army does something? Run the damned Cheyenne out of the territory now!"

Joshua Greene's blue-eyed gaze was cool and steady as he regarded the angry rancher. He'd seen Larson's kind before, the shoot-first-and-ask-questions-later type, and it worried him that the man was the leader of this group. Greene's job was to keep peace in the area, not start a war, and he didn't like the sound or mood of these men. "How many head of cattle have you lost, Mr. Larson?"

"I've lost six so far." He motioned to his companions.

"McKeon, there, has lost four, Johnson at least six, and Bryant, nine that we can be sure of."

"What proof do you have that it was the Cheyenne?"

"Who else would it be?" Sam demanded. "Over twenty-five head are missing. You want more proof than that?"

"Look, Captain Greene." McKeon spoke up in a more conciliatory tone. "You've got to put a stop to this stealing. We own big ranches and we can't be everywhere at once."

"I can appreciate your problems." He let his gaze sweep over the group. "And you have my word that I'll look into this right away. I'll consult with Daniel Marshall, the agent from the Indian Bureau, and take whatever action is necessary."

"Marshall . . . that filthy half-breed . . ." Sam spat the name. He hated the arrogant, college-educated breed almost as much as he hated the Cheyenne. "What good will it do to talk to him? He's only going to defend his people and claim they didn't do it!"

"Your complaint has been taken under advisement, Mr. Larson." Greene pinned him with an icy look as he rose and stood behind his desk, a move that signaled the interview was over.

Feeling dismissed, Sam was even more enraged.

"What are you going to do about it, Captain Greene?" Sam's twenty-two-year-old son Mark asked. "Just talk? Talking isn't going to stop them from stealing. A gun is the only thing those Indians understand."

"Marshall and I will decide on an appropriate plan of action. You'll be notified."

"You trust that Marshall? Hell, he ain't no better than the savages who're stealing my stock! He's probably involved in this!" Sam was practically shouting.

Captain Greene managed to control his temper, but it took an effort. Blind ignorance like Larson's was hard to deal with. "Good day, Mr. Larson," he said coldly.

"To hell with your 'appropriate plan of action'!" Sam refused to give up. "I want those damned heathens out of the territory! It isn't safe there for decent folks. You know damn good and well we gotta get rid of them!"

"Thank you for your comments, sir." Greene turned a frigid gaze on the men as he circled his desk to open the office door for them.

"You ain't heard the last of this, Greene," Mark Larson told him as he led the way outside.

The others filed out after him, and they had just reached the parade ground when they saw Daniel Marshall coming toward them.

"There's the half-breed now." Mark pointed him out.

"Marshall, we were looking for you," Sam called as he and the others walked toward him. His expression was belligerent, his movements aggressive.

Daniel had been back for two years now, and during that time, he'd learned that there were more men like Kyle in the world than there were men like Ben. Though he would never understand them, he'd finally managed to learn how to deal with their blatant prejudice and hatred. He met Sam's gaze levelly with no show of emotion as the rancher and his group stopped before him.

"Hello, Mr. Larson, Mark." He nodded to the others, who he knew by sight but not by name. "What can I do for you?"

"You can keep your thieving friends and relatives off our land!" Sam snarled. "The damned Cheyenne have been stealing our stock, and we're going to see that something's done about it!"

"Have you spoken with Captain Greene?"

"He ain't no help," Mark put in, eyeing the man who represented both the Indians and the government. He didn't like him. He acted as if he were as smart as whites, and that didn't sit well with Mark.

"You mark my words, Marshall. If the rustling doesn't stop, we're going to take matters into our own hands."

"Are you certain it's the Cheyenne who are doing this?" Daniel pressed.

"We know it, Marshall, and if another steer turns up missing, there'll be hell to pay," one of the others threatened.

Daniel said nothing for he knew it was pointless to argue. He watched the men as they stormed away.

"Marshall, come in here a minute."

The captain's words cut into his thoughts, and he looked up to see Joshua Greene standing in the doorway of his office.

Josh waited until they were inside and the door was closed before he spoke. "Larson's trying to stir up trouble. I want you to make sure none of your people are involved. It's going to get ugly if they decide to start shooting off more than their mouths."

"I know. I'll ride up to Tall Shadow's camp just as soon as I finish my business here."

"Good. Tall Shadow seems to be an honorable man."

"He is."

"Make sure his people know that there could be trouble if this stealing continues."

Daniel's expression hardened at his insinuation. "I can guarantee that Tall Shadow's people are not a part of this."

"If they're not, then find out who is. I want them caught! I'm trying to avert trouble here."

"I'll see what I can do."

Daniel's mood was black as he left the office. He wondered if the whites' hatred of the Indians would ever end. Certainly, it hadn't improved since he'd graduated from Marywood and gone to work for the Indian Bureau. He'd spent a month at home after he'd gotten out of school, then taken a job with the Indian Bureau in Washington, D.C. He'd worked there for over a year, trying to make changes that would help his people. It had been a slow, tedious, frustrating game, played with politicians who said one thing and did another. When the opportunity finally came to work back in the territory, he'd taken it.

Ben had been intrigued with life out West, and after visiting Daniel in Cheyenne, he'd decided to join him there. They'd bought a building in town. Ben had set up a law practice in offices downstairs while they kept rooms for themselves upstairs. They'd been there ever since, each trying, in his own way, to bring justice to the territory.

Daniel wondered, though, if justice could ever prevail for his people. He held on to the hope the Reverend Louis had instilled in him that it could and would triumph, somewhere, some time.

Daniel hurried on to finish his business at the fort. It was urgent he alert his grandfather's people of the possible danger and warn them to stay far away from the land the ranchers considered to be their own.

"I think that takes care of it, James," Ben said as he made the final correction on the legal document that lay before him on his desk in his law office in Cheyenne.

"It looks that way. I appreciate your advice, Ben. Making up this will was something I'd been meaning to do for a long time, and I'm glad I finally got around to it."

"You're satisfied with the way everything reads?" Ben glanced at James.

"Yes, thanks."

"I'll see you get a final copy soon, and I'll keep one on record here."

"That'll be fine." James stood, eager to be on his way. While putting the final touches on his will had been important, he had a far more exciting reason for being in town today. Today, Elizabeth and Cari were coming home.

Ben rose and extended his hand to his client. "I understand your wife and daughter should be arriving soon?"

"On the noon train," James told him with a smile, checking his pocket watch one more time as he started for the door.

"Have a wonderful reunion, and if I can do anything more for you, just let me know."

"I certainly will."

Ben accompanied James to the door and watched as he headed for the train station.

James was excited. There had been many times during the last seven years when he'd thought this day would never come, but it was here at last, and his joy knew no bounds.

It had been months since he'd journeyed back to Philadel-phia, and the trip this time had been a revelation for him. Though he loved his wife and child to distraction, the visit had left him frustrated and miserable. He'd grown up back East, but had discovered that he was no longer an easterner. The crowded cities and bustling traffic left his soul screaming for the peace and quiet of the ranch. Even the sophisticated social life that had once been such a source of pleasure for him had left him cold.

What had troubled him the most, though, was the change in Cari. He'd always known Elizabeth loved living in the city. She came alive in the constant, frantic swirl of activities. He'd thought his daughter was different. Early on, when she'd first gone to live in Philadelphia, Cari had written to him telling him how much she'd hated living there. He'd always believed she would remain that little girl who'd left him so reluctantly all those years ago. When he'd seen her on this last visit, though, he'd been shocked to find that she'd changed completely. No longer did she seem to miss the ranch and their old way of life. Now, she was the belle of the ball, the center of attention, and she'd been enjoying every minute of it. The crying, sorrowful little girl who'd left him, was gone.

James knew he should have been thrilled that Cari had grown into such a lovely, sophisticated young woman, but all he felt was regret. Cari had been an open, innocent child who'd delighted in their way of life on the ranch, and he was afraid he'd lost her forever. He supposed today would be his day of reckoning. Today, he would find out how she really felt.

"How you doing, James?" Ken Madison, the stationmaster, stopped to say hello.

"I'm fine, Ken."

"Big day for you, isn't it? Aren't your ladies due in on the noon train?"

"They sure are." He was beaming.

"Think they're going to like the changes you made out at the ranch?" He and James had been friends since he'd arrived there with the first trains back in the late sixties. They visited whenever James came to town for supplies, and he knew how hard his friend had been working to make his ranch the best in the territory, how he had bought that prize Hereford bull to improve his herd.

"I hope so. The house is certainly a darn sight better than it was when they left." James hoped with all his heart that the improvements he'd made would please them. He wanted them to be happy.

"They will," Ken assured him, thinking of the two-story, white frame structure James had built to replace the original small log cabin. It was one of the finest ranch houses around. The hundred-thousand-acre Circle M was becoming quite a showplace. It had excellent water rights, good grazing, and James running it, so Ken had no doubts that it would prosper for years to come.

James smiled at his encouraging words, but the smile hid the worries that were haunting him. He could not forget how much Elizabeth disliked living on the Circle M.

"There it comes now!" Ken told him as he caught sight of the train down on the track. He clapped James on the shoulder as he hurried back to work.

"Nothing's changed," Elizabeth muttered to herself as she studied the passing landscape from the train window. She'd been gone for years, and yet everything looked exactly the same. She'd heard people back East calling the territory the Great American Desert, and looking at it now, she definitely thought they were right. Where were the cities? Where were the people? Where was life?

"Did you say something, Mrs. McCord?" Elliot asked, looking up from where he sat next to Cari, opposite her.

"Nothing seems to have changed since Cari and I left." She voiced her disillusionment.

"Well, we're not at Cheyenne yet," Cari put in cheerfully. "Let's wait and see. Papa said Cheyenne was quite a town now compared to what it was."

"Your father's idea of a town and my idea of a town are two different things," Elizabeth pointed out.

"I know, but there's always hope," Cari told her with a laugh.

Elizabeth gave Cari a loving look. When they'd left the territory, her daughter had been a lonely child; now, she was returning a beautiful, confident woman. Glancing at Elliot, Elizabeth thought they made an exceptionally handsome couple. It was her fondest dream that Cari would realize he would make the perfect husband and accept his proposal. Her only regret was that she hadn't already accepted him. If she had, Elizabeth knew her worries would be eased about her daughter seeing the half-breed again.

"Look, that must be Cheyenne!" Cari was staring avidly out the window.

Elizabeth and Elliot both joined her, watching as the town came into view.

"It actually looks almost civilized . . ." Cari remarked in surprise. When they'd left, Cheyenne had been a booming railroad town, crowded with people, but little else. The only buildings had been tents and hastily erected shacks. It had definitely improved.

"There's Papa!" Cari exclaimed as she saw her father waiting on the station platform. Her eyes were filled with tears of joy as she turned to her mother. "We're home!"

"Yes, dear, we are," Elizabeth managed to sound pleased, but her heart was heavy with dread. True, Cheyenne did look much improved and she did love James, but she wondered if she would be able to stand the isolation and loneliness that went with living here again. Refusing to ruin their reunion by dwelling on her fears, Elizabeth stood as soon as the train came to a stop and hurriedly made her way toward the exit with Cari and Elliot following right behind. James was there. Her James . . .

"James!"

"Papa!"

The two women flew off the train and into his arms, while Elliot decided to remain discreetly off to the side. James's heart nearly burst with the love he was feeling as he hugged Elizabeth and Cari to him. They were home at last! They'd come back to him! He closed his eyes, fighting back tears as he gave silent thanks to God for their safe return. He was a happy man, a contented man. His years of loneliness were over.

"Oh, Papa, it's so good to see you!" Cari told him, kissing his cheek.

"Cari, love, I've missed you," he responded gruffly, his voice choked with emotion. "And Elizabeth . . ."

James smiled tenderly at his wife as Cari discreetly moved away to join Elliot. James thought Elizabeth was as gorgeous as ever, and his gaze devoured the sight of her, like a starving man at a feast. "Welcome home, darling."

"Oh, James." She realized with a pang just how much she had missed him. She buried her face against his shoulder, savoring the feel of his arms around her. He was her heaven. She'd forgotten how wonderful it was to be with him.

Her voice was a soft caress upon his love-starved senses, and he couldn't resist kissing her. Gently, yet passionately, his mouth sought hers, and for a moment, nothing existed in the world but the two of them, reunited at last.

When they finally moved apart, James glanced over at Elliot and smiled as he extended his hand in welcome. They'd met before on his last visit to Philadelphia. "Good to see you again, Elliot."

"You, too, sir," he returned, shaking his hand.

"Elliot traveled with us to make sure we got home to you safely, Papa," Cari explained. "He's going to stay and visit for a while."

"Good. Glad to have you."

"Thank you, sir."

They shared a silent moment of happiness, and then James said, "Let's go home."

He saw Ken standing off to the side and motioned him over. "Ken, come say hello to Elizabeth, my daughter, Cari, and her friend, Elliot Lowell."

"Glad to have you back, ladies. Nice to meet you, Mr. Lowell." Ken hadn't seen two such fine-looking ladies since he'd traveled to St. Louis a couple of years before. James's wife was as lovely as he remembered, and his daughter had grown into a gorgeous young woman. If he hadn't been happily married, he'd definitely have given that Lowell boy a run for his money with the beautiful Cari McCord.

Cari and Elizabeth extended their gloved hands to him, and Ken nervously wiped his hands on his pants before taking theirs, then Elliot's.

"Hope you ladies like what James has done out at the Circle M. He's been working like a madman to make that place shine for you."

"I'm sure he's done a wonderful job." Elizabeth cast an adoring glance at her husband.

"I did it all for you, sweetheart. Now, let me get your trunks on the buckboard, and we'll head home."

"I'll help you," Elliot offered.

The two men moved off to begin picking up the many pieces of luggage they'd brought with them. James was eager to get on the way. He wanted to give them a quick tour of the town and then head out to the Circle M to show them all he'd accomplished in their absence.

"I'll help you there, too." Ken quickly went to their aid. When everything had been loaded, he bid them good-bye. "Be careful on your ride out to the ranch, and remember, there's that big dance at the social hall a week from Saturday night. We'll be looking forward to seeing you."

"I'll remember. Thanks for your help." James handed Elizabeth and Cari up onto the seat, waited for Elliot to climb up, and then joined them there. It was a tight fit, but they managed. "See you later."

"Take care. Welcome back to the territory, ladies."

James slapped the reins on the horses' backs, and they moved off, heading home. He gave them a quick tour of Cheyenne, showing them the fine churches, public and private schools, the theater and the stores.

Elizabeth murmured her approval. The rugged western town was better than she'd expected, but it was still raw and wild-looking compared to Philadelphia. As she stared about herself, she wondered dazedly what she was doing there. Then she glanced at her husband. His eyes were upon her, warm and loving, and their gazes met. When James reached out and took her hand, she reveled in that unspoken expression of intimacy and knew in that moment the answer to why she'd returned.

As they rode for the ranch, Elliot asked many pertinent questions about the territory, and both James and Cari were quick to answer.

The ride was long, but Cari didn't notice. While she maintained the outward demeanor of a lady, a part of her was thrilling to the sight of her home— the distant mountains and the beautiful open land. The depth of her feelings about her homecoming surprised her. It was as if she felt a kinship with the land, as if her soul belonged there.

"I didn't tell you when I visited you in Philadelphia because I wanted to surprise you, but now that you're home, it's time." They were about to top the low rise that gave them a full, unobstructed view of the ranch in the valley below.

"You have a surprise for us?" Elizabeth gave him a pleased look.

"Yes, sweetheart. I built you a new house." He reined in as he spoke. Turning to her, he lifted a hand to caress her cheek. Her skin felt like satin to him, and the anticipation of the night to come filled him with a low, burning heat. "I want you to be happy here."

She leaned into his touch, her eyes never leaving his. "Oh, James." Her words were a sigh.

"Look!"

Elizabeth and Cari both looked down at the same time, and they stared in awestruck wonder at the thriving ranch below. The white, two-story house was impressive, yet it also had a welcoming air. Green shutters framed the windows, and a wide veranda surrounded it on three sides.

Elliot was impressed. It looked to him like an oasis of civilization in the midst of the wilds.

When the women didn't say anything right away, James began

to worry that they didn't like it. "Our old house is the bunk-house for the hands now. We've got six men working for us."

"James, it's wonderful," Elizabeth told him at last as she leaned closer and kissed him.

Relief swept through him. "I'm glad you like it." He urged the team onward. "Wait until you see the inside."

As they neared the house, Elizabeth saw a flower box on the porch near the front steps, and she turned an amazed gaze to him. "You planted flowers?"

"Just a few wildflowers," he said, embarrassed. "I wanted today to be special, and I know how much you like them."

Tenderness shone in her eyes. "Thank you."

Cari watched her parents. Though her mother had never said much about it, Cari knew she'd been happier in Philadel-phia. The closer they'd come to Cheyenne on the trip back, the more tense her mother had become. That mood had dis-appeared now, and Cari was glad.

James stopped the buckboard before the house. He helped Elizabeth descend, while Elliot made it a point to aid Cari. Two cowhands appeared then, and James quickly introduced them as Hank and Fred. The men carried the trunks, while James led the way inside.

Just as Cari was about to close the door behind her, she heard a distant bark and looked out. She gave a laugh of pure exuberance as she spotted Barnie running toward them.

"Barnie!!" she cried. Forgetting the manners and decorum she'd learned in school, she ran to meet her long-lost pet.

Cari hadn't been sure Barnie would remember her, but she did. They came together in a rush, Cari dropping to her knees beside her. She threw her arms around the old dog's neck and hugged her fiercely.

"I'm so glad to see you! How've you been?"

Barnie gave her a big wet kiss, and Cari laughed even harder.

"Cari?"

At the sound of Elliot's call, she realized how silly she must look to him. "I'll be right there!"

Getting up, she dusted off her skirts and, after giving Barnie one last pet on the head, hurried to the house. The dog followed on her heels and sat down on the porch to await her return.

"Barnie remembered me," she told her parents and Elliot as she joined them.

"She missed you," James said simply. "But not as much as I did."

"Well, we're home now." Cari was smiling brightly.

"Home . . . I like that. It didn't seem like home without you." James was still having trouble believing that Elizabeth and Cari were really there. His smile matched his daughter's. "Now it will."

"The house is lovely, James." Elizabeth was looking around, impressed. The hallway divided the house, running front to back, and it was wide and cool. The staircase to the second floor rose before them.

"The parlor, dining room, and kitchen are downstairs," he explained. "There are four bedrooms upstairs."

The parlor and dining room were on opposite sides of the hall and both were large. The kitchen ran the complete width of the house across the back. While it lacked the warmth of a woman's touch, the house was clean, neat and spacious.

When they went upstairs, James showed Cari to a large, airy bedroom at the back of the house that he'd thought she would want for her own, and then showed Elliot to the largest extra room. Leaving them to unpack, he then took Elizabeth to the master bedroom.

"You did a wonderful job, James. It's all beautiful," Elizabeth told him.

"I did it all for you," he said earnestly as they faced each other. He pushed the door shut behind them, then took her in his arms. "Life has been hell without you, Elizabeth. I don't ever want us to be apart again. I want you here with me always."

He kissed her deeply, and she responded without reserve. It was heavenly to be in his embrace again. She was savoring the intimacy, when abruptly he drew away from her, frowning.

"What is it?"

"Someone's coming . . ." He scowled, unable to believe anyone could have such terrible timing. He moved to the window to look down the drive.

Elizabeth heard the horses approaching, too, and she followed James to see who it was.

"Damn!" he swore under his breath as he recognized their visitors. "It's Sam Larson and his son Mark . . ."

James sounded angry, and Elizabeth wondered why. "He's one of the neighbors you told me about, isn't he? The one who owns the land to the west of us?"

"Yes."

"Maybe he's just come over to say hello," she offered naively.

"This isn't Philadelphia. Sam Larson doesn't make social calls. A visit from either one of them usually means trouble."

"Why?"

"Sam hates Indians, and he doesn't hold a high opinion of anyone who disagrees with him." He cast her a glance, remembering all the fights they'd had about his friendship with Tall Shadow's tribe. "I'd better go see what he wants." James headed for the bedroom door.

Elizabeth remained at the window, studying the two men who'd already reined in and dismounted. The older man was heavily built, almost to the point of being hulking, and his expression was stern as he walked toward the house. His son was on the slighter side. They looked nice enough, she supposed, but then she knew looks could be deceiving.

"I'll get Cari and Elliot and come downstairs with you. The Larsons are our nearest neighbors, so I think it's important we meet them," she called to James as she followed him from the room.

James found his unwanted guests waiting on the front porch.

" 'Afternoon, Sam . . . Mark. Good to see you," he greeted them as he stepped outside. "Would you like to come in?"

"Nope. We're here to talk serious, and the porch is as good a place as any," Sam answered tersely.

"What's wrong?"

"We were just wondering if any of your cattle are missing."

"No, why?"

Sam and Mark exchanged a look, then Sam spoke. "There's been a lot of rustling going on. We're missing head. So are McKeon, Johnson, and Bryant. Looks like your damned Cheyenne are at it again."

James had figured the Larsons meant trouble, and he'd been right. It wasn't the first time they'd come there to complain about the Indians, and he knew it wouldn't be the last. "The Cheyenne are not 'my damned' anything. And just because some steers are missing doesn't mean they did it— "

"Who else, if not the thieving redskins?" Mark interrupted.

"Have you got any proof?"

"We're losing stock, and you're not. That's enough proof for me!" Sam snarled.

"It's not for me."

"Look, James, you've got more to lose than we do. If anything happens to that bull of yours, what will you do?"

Everyone in the area knew the fortune James had invested in the animal to improve his breeding lines. "Nothing's going to happen to the bull," he insisted.

"How can you be sure, unless you know the thieves are from Tall Shadow's tribe and they've promised to leave you alone?" Sam countered with malice. James was known as an Indian-lover, who had the best ranch, a prize bull, and the respect of most everyone in town— and that infuriated Sam. Sam hated James with a passion and wanted to see him and all his Indian friends gone from the territory. If that happened, there would be no stopping his own plans for the future.

James stared at his neighbor with cold eyes. "I can assure you, that's not the case."

"Look, we could use your help. We've already talked to Captain Greene and warned him that if any more stock disappears, we're going to start shooting. You really ought to think about joining up with us before it's too late."

"Captain Greene's trying to keep the peace here. If you start shooting, he's not going to like it."

"He hasn't offered to do anything to help us— other than

talk—and we've got the right to protect what's ours," Mark told him, his hand moving to rest on his sidearm.

"Protect what's yours, yes, but to start killing people without reason is insane. No one will win if the killing starts."

"The hell we won't!" Sam gave vent to his hatred. "I'm going to tell everyone in town what's been going on, and if we get enough guns, we can . . ."

"James? Do we have guests?" Elizabeth recognized that the men's tempers were rising and had deliberately stepped outside to join them. Cari and Elliot were with her.

"Yes, dear, meet our neighbors, Sam Larson, and his son, Mark. Sam, Mark, this is my wife, Elizabeth, my daughter, Cari, and our friend from Philadelphia, Elliot Lowell."

"Hello, gentlemen, it's nice to meet you."

"Ladies," Sam responded, then nodded toward Elliot. "Lowell."

"Hello." Mark's brown eyes lingered on Cari with open interest. He'd heard James talk about his family before, but he'd never imagined his daughter would be this pretty. Cari McCord was a real looker. "It's nice to meet you."

"Would you like to come inside for some refreshments?" Elizabeth invited graciously.

"No thank you, ma'am. I said my piece to your husband, and now we'll be going," Sam addressed her before turning to James. "You'd better tell the bas—, er, uh, Cheyenne that we're not going to stand for anymore! You got that, James?"

James didn't respond.

"Ladies . . ." Sam started from the porch.

Mark flashed Cari a quick smile. "We got a dance coming up in town. Hope to see you there, Cari."

Cari returned his smile as she politely replied, "I'll be looking forward to it."

When the Larsons had ridden away, the McCords went back inside. James was worried. He didn't like either the father or the son. He knew they were troublemakers, always trying to stir up a fight with the Indians. Sam seemed bound and determined to force the Indians from the territory, and he took every opportunity to increase the hatred and mistrust between the whites and the Cheyenne. Trouble was, Sam wasn't alone. There were a lot of people who hated the Indians and wanted them gone.

"Elizabeth?"

She looked up at him expectantly.

"Lord knows I don't want to leave you so soon, but I'm going to have to ride out to Tall Shadow's village first thing in the morning."

"Why?"

"I've got to warn him to keep his young braves away from Larson. That man's looking for an excuse to start a war. He knows if the cavalry comes into it, the Indians will be driven from the territory, and that's exactly what he wants. He's a greedy, hate-filled man, and that makes him especially dangerous."

"Will you be gone long?"

"Just the day. You're welcome to ride along with me, if you'd like," he invited.

"No. I'll stay here. I've had quite enough traveling for a while."

"What about you, Cari? Elliot? Would you like to ride out to the Cheyenne village with me?"

"I'd like that very much." Elliot was excited at the prospect.

"I'll go, too, Papa. If it's all right with you, Mother?" Cari answered, smiling at the thought that she might see Silver Wolf.

Elizabeth was dismayed, but could only agree. She knew she had to get used to it. Despite all the years away, James's feelings about the Cheyenne had not changed.

"Of course, dear, go with your father and Elliot."

James, Cari, and Elliot began to discuss the trip, but Elizabeth paid little attention. Her thoughts were elsewhere as she worried that Cari might run into Silver Wolf. She told herself that it was inevitable that they meet again one day. It was just that she had wanted their reunion to take place only after Cari had become engaged to Elliot— or even better yet, after she was married.

Elizabeth tried to convince herself that her fears were unfounded; yet, she couldn't forget all the letters she'd burned over the years. The next day was going to be a very long one for her.

Seven

Elizabeth and Cari cooked a simple dinner. After eating, everyone went on the porch to sit and relax. Barnie joined them, curling up devotedly at Cari's feet. It was the first quiet moment they'd had, and they took the time to tell James all that had happened in Philadelphia since his visit. As the sun sank in the western sky, the conversation turned to the ranch and James's plans for the future.

"The Circle M is going to be the best ranch in the territory."

"Isn't it now?" Elliot asked. He'd been impressed by all he'd seen that day.

"We're close," James said. "But I know I can make it better. Beef is the future. The demand for it is growing. That's why I invested so much in the Hereford bull. There's no reason why within five or ten years, with our water supply, range, and access to the railroads, the Circle M can't be delivering the finest beef west of the Mississippi."

"Do you really think Lord Anthony will make that much difference?" Cari asked. She remembered her father talking about the prize bull when he'd been in Philadelphia, and she was curious about it.

"Lord Anthony?" Elliot repeated, confused.

"That's our bull's name. Sounds rather elegant, doesn't he?" Cari laughed.

"Your father's probably right; if he's royalty, he certainly will add to the line." He grinned.

"The bull's the key to our success. Without him, we're just another ranch, but with him, we can boast of the best beef and mean it," James said.

"When do we get to see him?"

"I've got him out on the north range. I'll take you out to see him, day after tomorrow. He's quite a sight."

"What about the Indian trouble we hear so much about back East? Is it as bad as they say?"

"It depends on whose side you're on," James answered cautiously, unsure of Elliot's thoughts on the issue.

"Basically they tell us that the Indians are 'murderers, killing defenseless white settlers in their beds.' " He quoted one particularly inflammatory article he'd read.

James gave a harsh laugh. "The truth is far from that. We've come onto this land uninvited and stolen what has been theirs for centuries. We sign treaties with them that we do not honor. We try to put them on reservations, box them in on land that's dry and lifeless. They're a nomadic people, and when they refuse to go where we tell them to go, we choose a different more insidious way to force them to comply. We kill the buffalo and try to starve them into submission, or to death— whichever comes first."

"So, ugly things have happened on both sides," Elliot interpreted. "What about the rustling the Larsons were talking about?"

"It's not the Cheyenne. I know Tall Shadow and his people. They do not steal."

"Then who could it be?"

"Hard to say. Could be poor whites or some renegades. . . . The trouble is, the Cheyenne get blamed, and the hatred just seems to escalate. One of these days, I'm afraid there's going to be a terrible confrontation."

"What can be done to help?" Elliot asked.

"Silver Wolf, Chief Tall Shadow's grandson, is a half-breed who went away to college and is back now working for the Indian Bureau. I hope he can make a difference around here, but sometimes I wonder when I talk to men like the Larsons."

At the mention of Silver Wolf, Cari's heartbeat quickened. "Will Silver Wolf be at the village tomorrow?" She managed to sound casual.

"It's hard to say, sweetheart. I saw him a week or so ago, but he travels around a lot. Sometimes he's out at Fort Russell, other times he's in Cheyenne. By the way, I don't know if I told you this or not, but when he's dealing with the whites, he goes by the name of Daniel Marshall. He took his father's last name when he went off to school."

"So his father was white?" Elliot questioned.

"Yes." James explained Silver Wolf's parentage. "We've been friends for many years, ever since he rescued Cari."

"This Silver Wolf rescued you?" Elliot gave her a curious look.

Cari told him the story of her snowy escapade. "We became close friends after that. He taught me a lot about the Cheyenne, and I tried to get him interested in our ways."

"You obviously did a good job if he went away to school."

"I doubt it was my influence. Father said it was the missionary who worked in the village who convinced him to go."

"Then you haven't seen him since you left for Philadelphia?"

"No. The last time we saw each other, I was eleven and he was seventeen. I'm sure we've both changed a lot since then." There was a touch of sadness in her voice as she thought of all her unanswered letters, but no one noticed except her mother.

Dusk had given way to nightfall, and the soft breeze cooled the land. James had been longing to get Elizabeth alone ever since the kiss in their bedroom earlier that afternoon. Determined to finish what he'd wanted to start then, he stood up.

"We'll leave you young folks alone now. It's been a long day," he announced.

"Yes, it has," Elizabeth agreed, trying not to look too eager to be with her husband as she rose with him. "Good night, Cari, Elliot. We'll see you in the morning." She gave Cari a soft kiss on the cheek and then went back to James.

"Don't forget that we'll be leaving at first light," James told them as he put a hand at Elizabeth's waist and guided her indoors.

Elliot had enjoyed Cari's parents' company, but he was glad to finally have a few minutes alone with her. He wanted desperately to kiss her; in fact, he'd been thinking about little else all day. He'd managed to control his desire— until now. Rising, he took her hands and pulled her up to him, then led her over to the porch railing so they could gaze up at the night sky. It was a black velvet, starry canopy, and on the horizon the moon rose, full and silver.

"I'm glad I made the trip with you. I understand now why you love this land so much and why you wanted to come back."

She was pleased by his understanding and thought all the more of him for it.

"I'm fascinated by all this. I've read everything I could about the 'wild' west, but nothing could equal the real thing. It's impressive."

"It's my home," she answered simply.

Elliot wanted to tell her that he could be happy there, that his home would be any place she was, but he refrained from speaking. She had yet to mention his proposal again, and he wouldn't push her. Deciding to take advantage of their time alone, he turned to her and kissed her with utmost tenderness.

Cari enjoyed Elliot's kiss. He made her feel fragile and cherished.

When they moved apart, the love Elliot felt for Cari was plain to see in his serious, dark-eyed gaze. It took a lot of control for him not to take her back in his arms and show her just how much he really wanted her.

"We'd better go in now if we're going to be up and ready at dawn," she said.

The easy grin he gave her belied the strength of his desire, and he was forced to remind himself once again of his resolve to give her time to make her decision. He held the door for her and saw her to her bedroom.

Cari got ready for bed and lay down to sleep, but it did not come quickly. Though her body was tired, her mind churned, conjuring up memory after memory of Silver Wolf and their time together. Finding no rest in her bed, she wandered to her bedroom window.

Gazing out across the night-shrouded land, she sighed. No matter how she tried, she couldn't put Silver Wolf out of her mind. Her homecoming was incomplete without him. She wanted . . . no, she *needed* to see him again.

Staring up at the star-studded heavens, Cari wondered if her warrior ever thought of her. She wondered, too, where he was and what he was doing tonight. Finally, her weariness drove her back to the comfort of her bed, but it was still a long time later before she fell asleep.

Silver Wolf completed his business at the fort late that evening, but rather than spend the night within its confines, he chose to ride out alone and sleep under the stars. The ranchers had left him restless and worried. He didn't trust Larson, and he didn't doubt for a minute that the vicious cattleman might cause serious trouble in the very near future. It was imperative that he ride for his grandfather's village as soon as possible, so he could warn them.

The air was cool and the sky was clear as Silver Wolf bedded down for the night. As he lay staring up at the myriad of twinkling stars, Little Snow crept into his thoughts. Ben had told him a few weeks ago that she had been due to return home today. He wondered if she really had come back. It had been so long that he'd almost convinced himself she would never return.

Silver Wolf was certain that she'd changed. The Little Snow he'd known had begged him to write to her; the woman she'd become had never bothered to answer his letters. He tried to conjure up a mental image of her as a woman full grown, but he could only see her childish face with her sparkling eyes and bright smile.

In spite of himself, Silver Wolf smiled into the night. He had missed his Little Snow, and he knew he would have to see her, if for no other reason than to find out why she'd never written. Gazing up at the heavens, he wondered where she was and what she was like now.

James came awake slowly. The bedroom was still dark, but the chorus of birds told him it would soon be light. He sighed. For the first time in years, he was content. The night he'd just passed in his wife's loving embrace had been ecstasy for him, and he knew the future held the same promise of love.

Cautiously, he shifted positions and raised up on an elbow so he could gaze down at Elizabeth. A tender smile curved his mouth as he watched her sleep. She really was there, at his side. It hadn't been just another dream. She had come home to him. He needed nothing more to be happy.

James let his gaze trace the delicate outline of her features and then drift lower to the soft curve of her throat, and then on to her breasts. They'd spent the better part of the night making love. It was wonderful to be so intimate with her again.

As if sensing his attentions, Elizabeth stirred and came awake. When she opened her eyes and saw James already awake and watching her, she smiled.

"Good morning, my love," she purred, stretching in a sensual motion.

"Is it?" he asked in a husky voice as his desire for her flared to life again.

"You tell me," she countered, drawing him down to her and moving against him in an unspoken offering.

She lifted her hands to frame his face, and he turned to press a devoted kiss to her palm. The rasp of his beard against her hands was arousing, and she sought his lips with her own as she nestled her hips against the hardness of his. She wanted to *show* him just how much she loved him, not *tell* him.

James's passions soared anew. "You'll never know how many mornings I woke up and wished you were here with me like this."

"Yes, I can. I felt the same way." Elizabeth's eyes were glowing as she kissed him again.

Filled with a sudden urgent need to be one with her, James moved, bringing her beneath him. They melded perfectly, his strength filling her softness. They blended together in shared rapture.

This morning their need for each other was so fresh and new that they felt like newlyweds. They celebrated their love. The memory of all the months apart fueling the power of their desire. It had been so long . . .

James slowed his pace, forcing himself to take his time, wanting to enjoy every moment of their mating. As dawn proclaimed the new day, ecstasy claimed them. They exulted in their shared pleasure and lay in each other's arms, sated.

"You will be back by tonight, won't you?" she asked softly.

For just those few blissful moments he'd forgotten all about his need to see Tall Shadow, and now regret filled him as he thought of having to leave her so soon after their loving. He grinned wryly to himself.

"You're smiling. . . . Why?"

"What I really want to do today is lock the door and spend every waking minute right here with you. I don't want to leave this room until we're so weak from hunger we have to, and the way I'm feeling now, that might take a week or so." His hand caressed the fullness of her breast as he seriously considered the possibility.

"What would Cari and Elliot think?" she asked, a hint of humor in her tone.

"That we love each other?" He raised an eyebrow as he smiled wickedly down at her.

"I hope they already know that."

"I'm sure they do."

The sun's rays brightened the room, and James knew he could put off getting up no longer.

"I'll be back tonight," he promised.

"I'll be waiting," she breathed softly.

Riding sidesaddle and wearing a fashionable riding habit and matching hat, Cari looked quite the woman of the world as she accompanied her father and Elliot to the Cheyenne village. For all that her outward appearance bespoke of sophistication, though, she felt more like an excited child. The possibility that she might get to see Silver Wolf today filled her with anticipation.

Cari couldn't help but wonder at his reaction upon seeing her again. As close as they'd once been, she hoped he'd be glad, and she knew it would hurt to discover that he hadn't missed her at all. The only thing that she was certain about was that Silver Wolf was no longer the young Cheyenne warrior of her childhood dreams. He was a twenty-four-year-old man now. That he was also known as Daniel Marshall, pleased her. It indicated to her that he had come to terms with his white heritage, and she wondered, now that he'd been away to school, which name he preferred. In her heart, though, she knew it didn't matter. To her, he would always be Silver Wolf.

As they crested a hilltop the village came into view spread out across the valley floor below. They reined in to enjoy the scene.

"There is the village," James told them.

Elliot studied the setting with great interest. The tales of Indians and their warring ways and bloodthirsty viciousness bore no resemblance to the quiet scene before him. Peace seemed to reign amid the tipis that were painted with colorful designs depicting the achievements of the owner.

"They look almost civilized," Elliot remarked with some amazement.

James's smile was rueful as he glanced at the young

easterner who still had a lot to learn. "Sometimes, I think they're a lot more civilized than we are."

James urged his horse forward and they rode into camp.

As always, news traveled quickly through the village, and Tall Shadow was waiting for them when they arrived. Their greeting was warm and open.

"This is Elliot Lowell. He's a friend who accompanied my wife and Cari on their trip home," James explained. "He'll be staying on with us for a while, and, of course, you remember Cari."

Tall Shadow's expression never changed, but his black-eyed gaze rested on Cari with great intensity as if he were trying to find the little girl he'd known in the woman she'd become. "Little Snow has changed in her time away from us."

"Yes, Tall Shadow, I'm grown up now," she replied with a smile, enjoying hearing Silver Wolf's pet name for her. It had been so long . . .

"Little Snow?" Elliot gave her a puzzled look.

"It's the name Silver Wolf gave me when I was small." She glanced around, hardly able to contain her excitement any longer. "Is he here today, Tall Shadow? I was hoping to see him."

"No. My grandson rode to the fort several days ago to meet with the soldiers. I do not know when he will be back."

Cari was forced to hide her disappointment. "Will you tell him I was here?"

"I will tell him."

"Tall Shadow, I need to talk with you alone for a moment," James said.

"There is trouble?" He saw the concern in his friend's expression.

"There might be."

The chief nodded. He called out to one of the Cheyenne women working nearby to bring refreshments for Cari and Elliot, while he and James went inside his tipi to talk.

"The Larsons came to see me last night. They're accusing

your braves of stealing their cattle, and they're threatening to start trouble."

Tall Shadow knew of the Larsons; it wasn't the first time that the greedy rancher had tried to cause disruption for his people. "We have not stolen from him."

"I know that, but he's hell-bent on blaming you. Keep your braves far away from him and the other ranchers to the south of him. This man's crazy enough to start something for no reason . . ."

"When Silver Wolf gets back I will tell him of Larson's lies."

"Good. Maybe he can help us avoid trouble. In the meantime, I'll see if I can find out who's been doing the stealing."

While the two men talked, Cari and Elliot remained outside, eating the fresh berries the Cheyenne woman had given them. When they finished, Cari showed him around the village, pointing out things she remembered from long ago.

"How did you learn so much?" he finally asked her.

"From Silver Wolf," she answered, searching each brave's face in hopes that it was him and thinking how empty the village seemed without him.

They stayed long enough to share a meal with Tall Shadow, then headed home. Cari's mood was less than jovial as they rode back. She wondered if Silver Wolf would seek her out when his grandfather told him of her return. She hoped so, but judging from his lack of interest over the past seven years, she had her doubts.

"Daniel! I'm glad you're back. How did it go?" Ben asked, looking up from his work as his friend entered the office the next morning.

Silver Wolf gave him a disgusted look as he dropped into the chair before the desk. "Sometimes I wonder if I'm doing any good at all. Captain Greene is a reasonable man, but there are others . . ."

"Trouble?" Ben probed.

"I have a feeling that there are white men out there just

looking for an excuse, any excuse, to either drive my people out of the territory or massacre us all and put a permanent end to the 'Indian problem,' as they call it. God knows, they're trying their best to starve us to death with the way they've been slaughtering the buffalo.''

Ben and Silver Wolf had been outraged when they'd discovered that the white hunters were killing buffalo for sport, sometimes hundreds at a time, and then just leaving the carcasses to rot.

''We can file complaints again, but I doubt they will do any good. According to law, the hunters' actions are legal.''

''I know, but that doesn't make it any easier to accept.''

''Who says we have to accept it? We'll keep trying, just like we always do.'' Ben tried to sound optimistic.

''One day there'll be justice.''

''I hope so.''

They shared a tired smile. In the years they'd been friends, they'd faced many battles together. Silver Wolf had always believed that things would improve, but now he wasn't so sure anymore. Still, they had no intention of giving up. If anything, they would try harder.

''James McCord was in town yesterday to pick up his wife and daughter.''

At this, Silver Wolf quickly looked up. ''So they really did come back. Did you get to meet them?''

''No. James stopped by before they arrived. Why? Are you curious to find out what your Little Snow looks like now that she's grown up?'' Ben missed very little and he'd noticed how Daniel had reacted to the news that she was back in town.

Little Snow . . . Silver Wolf still remembered the day she'd ridden away with her parents and how she'd watched him from the seat of the wagon until they'd traveled out of sight. He still found it hard to believe that the young girl who'd seemed to care so much had never answered his letters.

''Seven years is a long time. How old is she now?'' Ben asked.

''Eighteen,'' he answered.

"Why don't you ride out to the ranch and pay them a visit? I'm sure James would be glad to see you."

"I would, but I've got to go to my grandfather's village."

"Well, there's a dance coming up next Saturday night. Why don't you come with me? Maybe she'll be there."

"If I don't get the chance to see her at the Circle M, I just might do that." He rose and headed from the office to go upstairs to his rooms to pack for his trip to the village. "I'll see you when I get back."

It was late when Silver Wolf reached the village.

"Silver Wolf! I am glad you've come. There is much we have to talk about." Tall Shadow welcomed his grandson home.

They shared a meal with his mother and grandmother, and then when the women left them, Tall Shadow told Silver Wolf of McCord's visit.

"James says that Larson believes we are stealing his stock, and he fears there might be trouble. I have told our people of his warning."

"Good. That's the reason I'm here. I met the Larsons and their friends at the fort," Silver Wolf told him. "Those men are full of hate. You're wise to tell your braves to stay away from them."

"We do not want to fight with the whites. We only want to be left alone."

"That's all well and good, if Larson will leave you alone, but the man is first cousin to a snake. Watch out for him."

"We will take care," Tall Shadow assured him. "Did you know that Little Snow is back? She came to the village with James and another man named Elliot Lowell. She wanted to see you and was sorry you weren't here."

"Did she say how long she was staying?"

"It is my understanding that she and her mother have come home to live."

"And this other man. Who is he?"

"James said he was only a friend, but he looks at Little Snow with the eyes of one who cares."

"Perhaps I will go to the ranch and see her tomorrow."

"That would be good."

Feeling the need to get outside, Silver Wolf left the tipi. He strode away from the campsite to the bank of the stream that ran nearby. As he listened to the sound of the brook, it reminded him of the place where he and Little Snow always met. He turned his gaze in the direction of the McCord ranch and knew tomorrow would be the day he'd see her again. He smiled in the darkness.

Eight

It was late morning when Cari, Elliot, and James started back to the house from their visit to see Lord Anthony.

"I can see why you invested so much in him. He's one fine animal." Elliot was impressed with the huge, white-faced bull.

"With Lord Anthony's cooperation, I should have the best herd in the territory in a few years," James told him with pride. "And just as soon as he's finished servicing the females, we'll move him back closer to the house."

"Are you worried about the rustling, Papa?" Cari asked. The memory of the Larsons' visit had been hovering in her thoughts all morning.

"There's no sense in tempting fate, sweetheart. Lord Anthony's the Circle M's future, so we'll take all precautions to keep him safe."

When they reached the ranch at noon, they found that Elizabeth had a hot meal waiting for them. After they had finished, James rode out with Elliot again to show him more of the ranch operations, while Cari stayed behind with her mother.

Cari and Elizabeth planned the evening meal, and then Cari began helping her mother with the housework. After an hour or so, Cari grew restless. Several times she paused to look out the window, longing to be outside, longing to go down to the creek. Silver Wolf hovered in her thoughts, and she wondered if he was there waiting for her. Finally, unable to stand being cooped up in the house anymore, she sought out her mother.

"I'm going for a walk, Mother. I'll be back."

Elizabeth had noticed Cari's look of longing as she'd gazed out the window, and she'd known the direction of her daughter's thoughts. As Elizabeth watched Cari cross the yard heading for the creek, she grew angry and frustrated. She feared the reprieve she'd been given when Silver Wolf hadn't been in the village the day before was about to come to an end, and she was helpless to prevent it.

"Be careful," Elizabeth called from the doorway where she stood watching until Cari had disappeared from sight with the dog trailing faithfully behind her.

Tension filled Elizabeth as she went back inside to her work. Her thoughts were on her daughter and the half-breed, though, and her anxiety grew with each passing minute.

Cari reached the top of the incline and stared down at the sparkling stream below. The faint gurgle of the rushing waters drew her like a siren's song, and she hurried down to her favorite childhood place, hoping that maybe, just maybe, Silver Wolf would be there waiting for her.

"Come on, Barnie!" she called to her dog. "Let's go see what's changed."

Barnie gave a bark, and they started down the hillside together. Cari was wearing a simple white blouse, leather riding skirt, and boots, and she was glad for the freedom the comfortable clothing gave her as she hurried down the incline with all the eagerness of a little girl.

The stream was crystal clear and rushed by with an enchanted gurgle. The trees had grown in her absence, reaching higher and filling out so that their lushness spread over the creek in a translucent, emerald cover. When she reached the bottom of the hill, Cari paused, feeling as if she were entering a fantasy world.

Cari knew Tall Shadow had said Silver Wolf was at the fort and might not be back for days, but somehow she held on to a thread of hope that he'd returned early. Her hope faded and died, though, as she reached their spot and found it deserted.

Sighing her disappointment, she sat down on the grassy bank and took off her boots and socks. The rippling brook was calling to her, and, unable to resist, she laughed in delight as she waded out into its cold current. She played there for a while, reliving all the joyous moments of her childhood. If there was a paradise on earth, she was certain this was it. Wildflowers were blooming everywhere, and Cari thought of them as a welcome-home bouquet. The idea soothed her soul. Finally wearying of her solitary fun, she returned to her place on the bank amidst the blossoms.

The low drone of the insects and the sweet songs of the birds had a quieting effect on her, and after a while, Cari relaxed and lay back upon the bed of sweet grass. She folded her arms behind her head and stared up at the sky through the arch of the leafy limbs. Barnie came to lie beside her, and Cari lazily scratched her ears. There was no reason to worry about hurrying back, for her father and Elliot wouldn't be returning for hours. She was in heaven.

Closing her eyes, she let herself drift away, and as she slipped off to sleep, she whispered softly, "Silver Wolf . . . where are you?"

Silver Wolf rose with the sun and, shedding his white man's clothes, he dressed as one of his people. He became a different man when he donned his breechcloth, leggings, and moccasins. The Cheyenne clothing freed him from the restraints of the whites and left him once more feeling at one with the land. He passed the morning in the village, visiting with his mother and with the Reverend Louis, who was still there working with the children. The minister's vision for a future with a peace among all peoples was as strong as ever, and Silver Wolf came away from their talk reaffirmed in his belief that he was doing the right thing and that harmony was truly possible between the whites and the ranchers.

By the time Silver Wolf rode for the creek, it was afternoon. He told himself he was going only because he was curious about Little Snow, but as the miles passed, the eagerness within him grew. The power of it surprised him. Since Hilary, he'd spared little time for women, devoting himself almost exclusively to his work. But now, with the news that Little Snow was back, an afternoon at the stream with her held great appeal. He'd learned his lesson well from Hilary, though, and would never allow himself to trust or care too deeply for a woman again, but this was his Little Snow, not some sophisticated eastern flirt.

Silver Wolf put his heels to Wild One's side, urging the stallion to go even faster. He didn't slow their breakneck pace until they neared the woods. He reined in and directed the stallion with care through the trees. Dismounting as he reached the bank of the stream, he left Wild One there and continued on foot.

Silver Wolf's tread was silent. He moved with the sleek, powerful grace of a man who was one with the forest as he made his way toward their rendezvous place. Though he'd learned the white ways and used them to his benefit when he dealt with them, his heart and soul remained Cheyenne.

At the edge of the trees near the small clearing, Silver Wolf paused. It was then that he saw her, lying on a bed of colorful wildflowers on the stream's bank with Barnie by her side. For a moment, the years disappeared, and he remembered the first time he'd come upon Little Snow, curled up with her dog in almost the exact same location. The memory was both warming and chilling, for he recalled how close to death she'd been that night. At the thought, his expression darkened, and he suddenly worried that something was wrong—that she'd been injured or hurt in some way. He left the safety of the trees and moved toward her.

Barnie sensed his movement and lifted her head to look in his direction. She gave a welcoming thump of her tail when she saw him, and rose to greet him.

Silver Wolf paused only long enough to pat the dog distractedly on the head. He never glanced away from Little Snow, for the worry that gripped him was almost painful in its intensity. He reached her and dropped to one knee beside her. Only then did he realize by the easy, steady rhythm of her breathing that she was asleep. Reassured, some of the tension eased from him.

Silver Wolf remained kneeling next to her and took the opportunity to study her as she slept. She was his Little Snow, and yet the pretty child he'd known was gone, and in her place was a stunning young woman, a Greek goddess slumbering amidst the wildflowers. She had grown into a beauty.

Silver Wolf was enthralled, and his gaze was hungry as it traveled over Cari. Her features were delicate, her cheekbones high, her nose straight and feminine. Her complexion was creamy, and a light flush colored her cheeks as she slept. Her figure was sweetly curved, her breasts high and round against the soft white material of her blouse. Her waist could be spanned by his hands and her hips were slender. Her legs were long and shapely. She was as beautiful as he'd always known she would be, but it wasn't the kind of worldly beauty that had been Hilary's. Little Snow's beauty was innocent and pure. She was everything Hilary hadn't been, and the knowledge touched him deeply, stirring feelings within him he'd never known before.

He lifted his gaze to her hair. It was the same silver-gold color he remembered, and though she was wearing it confined in a knot, a few tendrils had escaped the restraint. A curl lay enticingly against her cheek, and he reached out to touch that silken tress. As he did, his knuckle caressed the sweet curve of her cheek, and a jolt of unbidden desire surged through him, settling hot and heavy in his loins.

Silver Wolf went still, electrified by his reaction to that single touch. Suddenly, it was just the two of them, alone in their own private world. The delicate, heady scent of her perfume urged him closer, and an instinct older than time filled him. He wanted her . . . wanted to take her in his arms and hold her close. Never before had a kiss seemed so important, so urgent, so necessary. He bent nearer, his lips almost brushing hers . . .

"Cari!"

His lips were but a breath away from Little Snow's, but at the sound of a man's distant call, Silver Wolf hesitated. He paused, listening. At the sound of approaching footsteps, he drew quickly away and stood up, his gaze sweeping the area for some sight of the intruder. The man calling her name was not James. Silver Wolf reasoned that he was the one his grandfather had told him was visiting the McCords from back East.

Silver Wolf knew it was only a matter of minutes before the man reached them. Angered by the intrusion, Silver Wolf scowled blackly as he stared down at Little Snow. He'd wanted their first visit to be special, a time when they renewed their friendship free from outside interference.

"Cari?"

The second call was much closer now, and Silver Wolf knew the stranger was almost upon them. Disappointment filled him as he faded into the foliage, disappearing as surely as if he'd never been there.

Little Snow was dreaming of Silver Wolf. In her dream, her warrior was on his stallion atop the hill that overlooked the ranch, watching her ride away with her parents. A terrible longing welled up inside her as she slept. *Silver Wolf was her dream warrior, and she had missed him so. . . .* Until she'd returned to the stream, she hadn't realized just how much the years had dulled her true feelings for him. But being there without him brought back all the pain of missing him again. She wanted to be with him, and suddenly it seemed as if she could actually feel his presence again, as if he were so close she could just reach out and touch him . . .

Elliot had been following the stream in the direction James had told him to go to find Cari. Dinner was almost ready, and Elizabeth had suggested he find her and bring her back.

All day he'd been thinking of the kiss he and Cari had shared on the porch, and he'd been longing for the chance to be alone with her again. He'd been more than happy to go after her, for he'd believed they'd have a few minutes to themselves before having to return to the house.

Elliot had just begun to worry about Cari, when he caught sight of her sleeping on the bank of the creek just ahead of him. Taking care to move as quietly as he could, he made his way to her. Barnie was nearby, and she gave a slow wag of her tail when she saw him.

Thrilled to be alone with Cari, Elliot dropped quietly down beside her and took advantage of the moment to watch her sleep. She was lovely, everything he'd ever wanted in a woman, and the desire to wake her with a kiss was overpowering. Bracing his arms on either side of her, Elliot leaned down to her and gave her a soft, gentle kiss.

Cari's entire being was focused on her dream warrior, and at the touch of lips upon hers, she believed it was Silver Wolf and she lifted her arms to embrace him.

Elliot was surprised by her eager response, and he deepened the kiss, parting her lips and claiming the sweetness of her mouth for his own as he lowered himself to her.

At such bold contact, reality jarred Cari fully awake. Dragged from her dreamy reverie of Silver Wolf, her eyes flew open to find that Elliot was the man holding her and kissing her. Startled, she stiffened as she broke off the kiss.

"Were you having sweet dreams?" Elliot asked in a husky voice as he remained where he was, holding her.

"Elliot . . ." She blinked, her confusion real.

"You looked so beautiful sleeping that I couldn't resist the opportunity to wake you with a kiss."

"Why are you here?"

"It was getting close to dinnertime, and your parents told me to look here for you. Your father said this was your favorite place, and now I know why. It's very beautiful here . . . so secluded and peaceful."

"I've been coming here since I was a little girl," she told him as she shifted positions. She was glad when he moved away so that she could sit up. "It was always my favorite place to play."

"It looks like you've been playing, too," he told her, smiling at the sight of her bare feet.

"I hadn't gone wading in so long . . ."

As she remembered the last time she'd frolicked in the creek, memories of Silver Wolf came flooding back. Elliot's company was not the same as being there with her warrior.

"I missed you this afternoon," he said earnestly, his eyes glowing with the devotion he felt for her.

"Did you have a good time with my father?"

"He was trying to teach me about ranching, but I was having trouble concentrating."

"Why?" She couldn't imagine what could have been distracting him.

"I couldn't get you out of my mind, Cari," he told her in a soft voice as he leaned toward her, slipping an arm about her shoulders and drawing her to him. "Marry me now . . ." His lips sought hers once more in a cherishing kiss.

Cari accepted his kiss. It was sweet and nice, and she wondered anew if this warm, comfortable feeling she had when she was with him was love. When they ended the embrace, she gave him a tremulous smile.

"I care about you, Elliot, I really do, but I'm just not ready to get married yet." She lifted a hand to caress his cheek.

His disappointment was real, but he hid it behind a bright smile. "When you finally do decide you're ready, I'll be waiting."

"I know."

Standing up, Elliot offered her a hand and drew her to her feet. The ground was a little uneven, and when she swayed for a moment trying to get her balance, he steadied her, taking her in his arms and stealing one last kiss.

Cari relaxed against him. She knew Elliot would never pressure her to do anything she didn't want to do.

"I guess we'd better go back," he finally said with a sigh.

Realizing that her time at the stream was over, she lifted her gaze to look around. A fleeting sadness crossed her expression, for there was no sign of Silver Wolf. He hadn't come. . . . Taking Elliot's offered hand, she allowed him to draw her away from her secluded retreat.

Silver Wolf remained in the shadows of the trees watching Little Snow walk away with the white man. His expression was grim. He'd been ready to protect her with his life if need be, but had realized the folly of his gallantry when she'd kissed the other man so willingly and seemingly without restraint. He'd stood in silent rage, watching as they'd kissed and embraced again.

Silver Wolf had known he should go, but somehow he'd found himself rooted there. Memories of Hilary had seared him. Suddenly it seemed as if the innocence he'd seen in Little Snow's sleeping features had only been an illusion. Little Snow had been gazing up at the stranger the same way Hilary had gazed up at him, her expression no doubt leading the other man to believe that he was the only man in the world she cared about. Silver Wolf wondered angrily if Little Snow's years in the East had changed her into a woman like Hilary. The thought filled him with bitterness.

He stayed beneath the shelter of the trees until she had walked away with the other man. Only when they had gone from sight did he step forward into the sunlight.

Barnie ran gleefully to him as soon as she saw him.

Silver Wolf petted her with great affection, feeling she was the only link left to what he and Cari had all those years ago. "Barnie!"

The dog wavered anxiously, trying to decide whether to stay with Silver Wolf or follow her mistress. When Little Snow called again, Barnie had no choice. After one last lick of Silver Wolf's hand, she bounded faithfully away.

It was late in the day and Ben was tired, but he refused to quit working just yet. The contracts spread out before him on his desk had to be finished, and he wasn't going to stop until they were done. Leaning back in his chair, he stretched the stiff muscles of his neck and shoulders, then raked a hand through his thick dark hair. It had been a long day, and it looked like it was going to be an even longer night.

Ben was about to get back to work when he heard the door in the outer office open and someone come in. His clerk had already gone for the day, so he rose to investigate.

"Ben?" Melanie Wells knew she was being a little brazen by coming to Ben Douglas's office this way, but she didn't care. She wanted to see him, and she was tired of waiting for him to come to her. Her daddy had always told her that if she wanted something, she should go after it. She wanted Ben Douglas. So she was taking his advice.

Ben was surprised to find Melanie there. "Melanie. . . . This is a pleasant surprise."

"I was hoping you'd think so." She gave him a bright smile as she let herself through the small half-gate that separated the waiting area from the clerk's desk. He was so incredibly handsome with his broad shoulders, dark hair, and those incredible green eyes that she couldn't wait to get closer to him.

"What brings you here this afternoon? Is there some legal matter I can help you with?"

"This is a purely social call." Melanie narrowed the distance between them, her gaze warm upon him. She hadn't seen him since the social two weeks before. They'd had a nice time that day and she'd expected to hear from him afterward. He hadn't come calling, though, and her frustration had mounted. Today, she decided to take matters into her own hands. She wanted him, and she meant to have him.

"I just wanted to make sure I'd see you at the dance Saturday night," she said as she came to stand before him. She lifted her dark-eyed, sparkling gaze to meet his as she rested a hand upon his arm. The feel of his hard muscles beneath her fingers sent a tingle of excitement through her.

"I'll be there." Ben suddenly felt trapped, but he managed a smile. He'd met Melanie about six months before when he'd asked her to dance at a party. While he thought her pretty and enjoyed her company, he had no intention of seriously courting her. They'd shared a simple kiss or two, but she had the look of a woman who wanted a husband, and he knew beyond a shadow of a doubt that he wasn't going to be that man. He had yet to meet the woman who could make him want to settle down.

"Good. I'll be looking forward to it," she said in a husky tone. "Are you busy right now?"

"My clerk's already gone for the night, but I've still got some contracts I have to finish up."

Hearing that there was no one else in the office, she felt suddenly reckless. She was determined to do whatever was necessary to win this man.

"I was hoping," she began coyly as she slid her hand up his arm to his shoulder, "that I might be able to convince you to walk me home."

She rose up on tiptoe, leaning close enough so her breasts brushed against his chest as she pressed her mouth to his.

Her move surprised Ben, and he accepted her kiss passively. Realizing that walking her home might be the quickest way to get back to the task he'd set for himself for the night, he put his hands at Melanie's waist and held her slightly away from him.

"I'd be honored to walk you home," he offered, and he was rewarded with a beaming look.

Melanie wanted to kiss him again, but she had to avoid appearing too aggressive. She knew it was bad enough that she had gone to the office. "Oh, good."

She stared up at him adoringly as she linked her arm through his, and they left the office. Ben paused only long enough to lock the door behind them before they started on their way toward her home.

They were making small talk about the dance to come, when the sound of angry voices down the street in front of one of the saloons drew their attention. Though Melanie would have kept going, Ben stopped to see what was going on and saw a big, ugly man menacing a Cheyenne maiden.

"Don't walk away from me, you squaw!" the man bellowed as she tried to evade him. "I'm talkin' to you!" He grabbed her by the upper arm in a bruising grip.

"Don't . . ." The girl tried to get away from her assailant, but his hold kept her captive.

"Don't what, little sweetheart? I ain't doin' nothin'. I jes' wanted a little company for a while, and you looked mighty entertaining." Harky Tavers leered down at the ripe young woman, his gaze dwelling first on her wide, frightened eyes, and then dropping lower to her bosom. He felt his desire rise. He liked women to be scared of him. If they were scared, they fought more when he took them and made it more lively.

"Let me go!"

"What's your name, darlin'? Tell ole Harky, and he'll treat you right. I'll be real nice to ya. Not like those wild braves you got out at your camp."

"The men in my village never have to force a woman." Star Blossom faced the evil stranger as bravely as she could. She was afraid, but she refused to cower before this man. She'd already learned just how terrible white men could be, and she knew he would take pleasure in degrading her.

"I ain't forcin' you," he said as he yanked her closer. "You'll be begging for it in a minute . . ."

He started to reach for her breast, and she jerked away from him with all her might. He was too strong for her, though, and she could not break free. She kicked out at him, managing to make contact with his shin, but her moccasined foot did little damage except make him angrier.

"You little bitch! Think you're too good for me, do you?" Harky snarled, dragging her against him and grabbing and pinching her breast. "I got me a yearning for a taste of some red meat, and I mean to have it . . ."

Ben had watched the interplay with growing fury, and the minute the man laid a hand on the girl, he started to go to her aid.

"Ben? What are you doing?" Melanie asked, puzzled.

"I'm going to put a stop to this," he told her.

"But it's none of your business."

"She's a woman," he argued.

"She's just an Indian, for heaven's sake. They do this kind of thing all the time. They're just heathens . . ."

Melanie was shocked and hurt when Ben turned his back on her and walked toward the drunken cowboy and the Indian slut. She couldn't believe that he would just leave her that way, but he had. Melanie was tempted to stalk off in a huff, but she wanted to be with Ben and so she decided to wait for him.

Though rage consumed Ben at seeing the other man's hands upon the girl, his expression was deceptively mild as he stopped before Harkey.

"Let the young lady go," Ben ordered in a slow, deliberate voice.

"Lady? This ain't no lady. This is a squaw. Now, you go on about your business and leave me to mine." Harky glanced at Ben. Though Ben was a big man, Harkey saw how he was dressed and dismissed him as an interfering dandy. Harky was wanting a woman. He'd found this one, and he meant to have her. No town fella was gonna stop him now. She was his.

"I said, take your hands off her, friend," Ben ground out. His jaw was clenched as he struggled to stay in control. He wanted to avoid violence if he could, because he didn't want to chance that the girl might be hurt.

"I ain't your friend," Harky growled.

"I know."

"She wants me. She tol' me so. We was just on our way to the hotel so we could enjoy ourselves for a while. Have a few drinks . . ." He tightened his hold, daring her to contradict him.

Ben glanced at the girl for the first time then and was so taken by her clear brown eyes and delicate beauty that he could only stare at her for a moment. She was by far the loveliest woman he'd ever seen. Her beauty was pure and natural and owed nothing to artifice. She barely topped five feet tall. Her complexion was flawless, her features lovely; her raven hair was parted in the middle and worn in two long braids. Her dress was of fringed buckskin and it clung to her figure, emphasizing just how petite she really was. Ben had been angry before when he'd seen the other man assaulting her, but now, seeing how small she was, he was filled with an even greater surge of protectiveness.

"She doesn't look too willing to me." Ben spoke with slow deliberation. "If she's so eager to go with you, why are you holding her like a prisoner?"

"She wants me."

"What do you say we leave it up to the girl to decide?" Ben met the girl's brown-eyed gaze. Though she was trying her best to hide it, he could see the panic and fear in her eyes. "Do you want to stay with him?"

"No! I do not know this man . . ." she protested.

Ben's green eyes hardened to icy emerald brilliance. He took a step closer. "You heard her. Now, let her go."

It was a command, not a request, and for the first time, Harky began to have some doubts.

"What's she to you?"

"She's a woman."

"She's a damned squaw!"

Harky never realized what hit him. One minute, the girl was in his grasp; the next, he was flat on his back on the ground with the other man looming over him. Shocked by the suddenness of his attack, Harkey stared up at Ben in furious disbelief. He would never have guessed the gent could have packed such a punch.

"She's a woman, and, as such, she deserves your respect," Ben said threateningly.

Harky knew he didn't have a chance and shot him a dirty look. "All right."

"I'm glad you're finally seeing things my way. Now, get out of here."

Ben was aware of the girl standing nearby, but he waited until Harky had scrambled to his feet and disappeared back into the saloon before turning to her. He took a step toward her, but she froze him with a look of hatred so burning and real that he stopped. "Are you all right?"

Star Blossom stared at him, all the bad feelings she harbored toward whites showing clearly in her expression. Save her though he had, this man was still a white man, and that condemned him beyond any hope of redemption in her eyes. "I am fine. I must go now."

She started to leave without another word, but Ben found he couldn't just let her walk out of his life. He wanted to talk to her, to find out her name, to make sure she got home safely. There was something vaguely familiar about her, and he wanted to know if he had seen her before somewhere.

"Wait . . ." He reached out to stop her, but the moment he touched her arm, she stiffened just as she had when Harky touched her. He dropped his hand away.

She turned on him, the anger still evident in her regard. "Are you no better than the other man? Would you stop me from returning to my people?"

"I meant no harm." He stared down at her, thinking her breathtaking.

She nodded tightly then turned with great dignity and walked away.

Ben watched her go, noting the straightness of her back, the way she held her head up with pride and the gentle, very feminine sway of her hips as she walked. He was filled with a great sense of disappointment when she moved out of sight.

"Ben? Is it over now?" Melanie appeared at his side, finally believing it was safe to come forward now that the filthy Indian was gone. Her face was pale, her expression strained.

"Yes. It's over." He glanced at her, finding her presence intrusive and obnoxious and almost wishing he could go after the Cheyenne girl. There was something about her that had touched him deeply, and he knew he wouldn't forget her soon.

"Thank heaven," Melanie babbled. "I was worried about you. Why in the world did you put yourself at risk over that squaw? Don't you realize those women like that kind of treatment? She probably asked for it . . ."

At her words, Ben grew furious.

"She was Cheyenne, Melanie, and Cheyenne women are known for their virtue," he told her tightly. "They wear chastity belts until they marry, and any man who dares touch the belt before the wedding night is at risk not only from the girl but from her whole family. The Cheyenne women are very well guarded and very chaste."

Melanie thought he was being deliberately insulting, since she'd kissed him so brazenly in the office. "If she's so virtuous, why was she wandering around town all by herself? Where are the rest of her people? You know, personally, I don't think they should let them come into town anymore."

"Perhaps you're right," Ben replied, letting her think she was right, but really believing the Cheyenne would be safer far away from the whites. With men around like Harky and women like Melanie who hated without reason, the Indians had little hope for a continuation of their centuries-long peaceful nomadic lifestyle. He thought about trying to convince Melanie that she was wrong about the Indians, but gave up the idea as hopeless. "Let's get you home, shall we?"

"Yes, please." She smiled up at him as she took his arm again. She began chattering about the dance once more.

Ben only half listened to her. His thoughts were on the maiden, and he wondered if he'd ever see her again.

Nine

Silver Wolf was mentally arguing with himself as he shrugged into the jacket of his best suit. He adjusted his cuffs, then paused before the mirror to check his appearance. A quick glance at his reflection told him he looked every bit the gentleman his years in the East had forced him to become. His dark suit was tailored just for him, fitting his broad shoulders to perfection. His shirt and tie were without flaw; his boots were polished to a high gleam. Despite his civilized appearance, though, there was nothing "gentlemanly" about Silver Wolf's mood. If anything, the word "savage" best described it.

Since seeing Little Snow kiss the other man by the creek, Silver Wolf had tried to convince himself that he didn't care, that what they'd shared had ended years before and that she meant nothing to him now. But the strength of the emotions that seared him whenever he thought of that afternoon belied his very logical contention.

Silver Wolf had been determined to put Little Snow from his mind and turn his full energies to his work, but the memory of her loveliness had haunted him, day and night, ruining his ability to concentrate. At the most inopportune times, a vision of her sleeping among the blossoms would float through his thoughts and with that vision had come the memory of how soft her skin had felt when he'd caressed her cheek. He remembered, too, the intoxicating scent of her perfume and how close he'd come to waking her with a kiss . . .

As always, though, when Silver Wolf remembered how tempting her lips had been, he also remembered the other man kissing her and her response to him. It was that memory that brought a scowl to his darkly handsome features now, and he wondered not for the first time why he felt compelled to go to the dance tonight.

Silver Wolf hated dances and all the pretense that went with them. Though he was always invited, he knew that he was not really wanted at these social occasions. Usually, he did not attend, only going when a valuable contact might be made to help with his work, but tonight was different. Tonight had nothing to do with work. Tonight was personal, and that was what was bothering him.

A knock sounded at the door.

"You ready?" Ben asked as he walked casually inside Daniel's room without waiting to be invited.

Not wanting to reveal the uneasiness he was feeling, he quickly, almost tersely, replied, "Let's go."

"I was afraid you were going to say that," Ben groaned, drawing a surprised look from his friend.

"I thought you always looked forward to these things."

"I do . . . or at least, I did, until Melanie Wells set her cap for me."

"You don't think you can handle her anymore?" Silver Wolf was smiling as he thought of the outspoken, spoiled young woman who'd been aggressively pursuing Ben.

"The point is, I don't *want* to handle her. While you were gone, she paid me an unexpected, after-hours office visit," he explained. This was the first opportunity they'd had to talk, since Daniel had only returned from his trip to his grandfather's village that afternoon.

"There are a lot of men in town who would love to have Melanie chasing them."

"Good, they can have her," Ben said in exasperation.

"Having trouble discouraging her, are you?"

"Trouble isn't the word. I don't think she'll take no for an answer."

"You think she's going to propose?" Silver Wolf laughed.

"I wouldn't put it past her," he remarked as they started from the room. "What about you? Did you ever get out to the McCord ranch and speak to Cari?"

"No," Silver Wolf answered, taking care not to lie. He had *not* spoken to her.

"Well, she's in town with her parents. I hear they're staying at the hotel for the night, so they could be at the dance. It should be an interesting evening for you. I'm looking forward to meeting her myself."

They headed across town toward the hall and could hear the sound of the music as they approached. Ben and Silver Wolf entered the crowded hall and made their way around the room, greeting friends and acquaintances. When the adoring mamas of the marriageable daughters caught sight of Ben, their expressions brightened. He was one of the richest, best-looking, available men in town, and more than one woman wanted him for their son-in-law.

At the same time they noticed Ben, however, they also saw Daniel, and, attractive and eligible though he might be, their reaction to his presence was altogether different. Though their adventurous daughters might find him exciting and desirable because of his Indian blood, for the very same reason they found him unacceptable. Concern marred their features, and as they spoke to their husbands in hushed whispers, the men turned cold, unwelcome gazes on him. Educated though he might be, Daniel Marshall was still a half-breed.

The young ladies, however, were unconcerned with their parents' opinions. The moment they saw Daniel, a titter of excitement raced through them. Melanie Wells had already set the group of flighty females straight about Ben, claiming him as her own personal property, so the excited group turned all their attention to Daniel, watching his every move with breathless wonder. He seldom came to these parties, and their hearts beat faster as they waited breathlessly to see if he would ask one of them for a dance.

Ben and Silver Wolf were oblivious to the hungry-eyed stares of the young women. They got drinks from the refreshment table and settled in along the sidelines to watch the dancers glide by. Ben was scanning the room trying to see if he could locate the McCords, when he noticed Daniel grow tense. He let his gaze follow in the direction of his friend's and saw a beautiful, fair-haired young woman dance by with Mark Larson.

"Is that Cari McCord with Larson?" Ben asked.

"That's her." Silver Wolf's gray-eyed gaze had turned to silver fire at the sight of her dancing with Mark, and he downed the rest of his punch in one swallow, wishing it were something much more potent.

"She's very pretty," Ben told him with undisguised appreciation.

"Yes, she is," he answered tightly, unable to look away from her. The turquoise gown she wore was stylish and displayed her figure enticingly, hugging the swell of her bosom and nipping in at her slender waist before flaring out over her gently rounded hips. Her hair was done up in a glorious tumble of curls and held by a single ribbon, the same color as her gown. He remembered how soft the single curl had been against her cheek, and he longed to untie the ribbon, free the tawny mane, and sink his hands into its satiny length. His gaze drifted lower, studying her face as she turned toward him in the dance. Her eyes were sparkling, her cheeks flushed, and she was smiling as if she were having a wonderful time. Silver Wolf couldn't hear what Larson was saying, but when she gave an enchanting laugh, his mood grew even darker.

"Has she seen you yet?" Ben asked.

"No."

"Are you going to ask her to dance?"

Silver Wolf was saved from having to tell his friend to mind his own business by Melanie's timely arrival.

"Ben, darling, it's so good to see you," Melanie cooed, taking his arm and rubbing subtly against him. "You were so late getting here that I was afraid you weren't going to come."

"We just arrived, Melanie," he answered, annoyed by her clinginess and trying to free himself from her grip.

"Well, good. I wouldn't want to have missed a minute of your company." She gazed up at him with wide, adoring eyes. "The more I thought about the other night, the more I worried about you. You weren't hurt, were you? I realize now that it was a very brave thing you did, defending that little squaw, but I was still concerned that you might have been injured."

At the mention of a squaw, Silver Wolf glanced questioningly at Ben. "What happened?"

"A drunk was bothering a Cheyenne girl, so I broke it up."

"He was wonderful," Melanie bragged. She'd realized her previous attitude hadn't worked with him and so was trying a new strategy. "Of course, if the Indians would just stay where they belong away from the whites, it wouldn't have happened in the first place, but that doesn't matter as long as Ben's all right."

Silver Wolf wanted to ask her where the Cheyenne belonged if not on the land that had been theirs for hundreds of years, but he said nothing. He gave Ben a grateful look.

"Let's dance," Melanie declared enthusiastically, allowing Ben no chance to escape. After he'd handed Daniel his glass, she practically hauled him from the side of the dance floor out among the other couples.

Trapped for the moment, Ben could do nothing but capitulate. In his mind, though, he was already planning his escape. As he whirled Melanie about the dance floor, his thoughts were on the Indian maiden again. He couldn't forget the look of utter disdain she'd given him when he'd tried to find out more about her. He was a man used to attracting women, not repulsing them, and it had been a shock when she'd reacted to his touch with such contempt. He wondered what had happened to her to make her feel that way toward whites, and he wondered, too, if she was safe right then.

"You're the loveliest woman in this room," Mark complimented Cari as he held her in his arms.

"Why, thank you, Mark. That's kind of you to say," she replied, taking care to keep the look on her face sweetly insipid. She remembered how angry her father had been over the Larsons' accusations against Tall Shadow's people, and she wasn't about to let Mark become too familiar with her. She would be nice to him— smile and laugh at the appropriate times, and do all the things a lady was supposed to do— but that didn't mean she had to like doing it.

Of course, that was exactly the reason why good manners had been invented— to give one the polish necessary to convince someone you liked them even when you couldn't stand the sight of them, and Cari was drawing heavily on her years of etiquette training right then. She seriously doubted Mark would be quite so enamored with her if he knew what she was really thinking.

Mark was pleased with himself. He'd managed to get a dance with Cari, and she seemed quite taken with him. He thought her even better-looking tonight than he had on the day they'd met, and he wondered what his father would think if he decided to court her. Marriage would be an easy way to get the Circle M with all its good water and grazing land, but the Widow Green certainly knew how to please a man, as did several other women in town who shared their beds with him, and he wasn't ready to give them up yet.

The music ended, and he was sorry to let her go. "I look forward to dancing with you again, Cari."

"So do I, Mark. Thank you." She smiled benignly at him as she turned away to find Elliot there, waiting for her. He took her arm and led her to the side of the room to join her parents.

Ben finished the dance with Melanie, and seeing the McCords all together, he excused himself. He was eager for an introduction to Elizabeth and Cari, for he'd heard so much from James about them. He glanced around for Daniel, wondering when his friend was going to speak to the girl, but he didn't see him anywhere. He approached the McCords, and greeted them.

"Ben, good to see you," James responded. "I want you to meet my wife, Elizabeth, and my daughter, Cari. This is Ben Douglas, my attorney here in town."

"It's a pleasure, ladies," he told them warmly, thinking them both beautiful.

"Ben went to college with Silver Wolf. In fact, it's because of him that Ben's out here working now," James explained.

"Is Silver Wolf here tonight?" Cari's eagerness was obvious.

"He's around somewhere," Ben replied, and he was rewarded with a bright smile.

Elizabeth saw her daughter's happiness and had to fight to keep her disapproval from showing. She'd known this moment of reckoning would come, but she'd never dreamed the half-breed would come to a social occasion in town.

The next song, a waltz, began, and Elliot claimed Cari for the dance.

"Enjoying yourself?" Elliot asked as he held her as close as propriety would allow, his action definitely possessive. It had sorely tested his patience to stand by and watch Cari dance with Larson. Now, however, he had her all to himself again, and he meant to savor every second.

"Yes, are you?" she answered, but she couldn't help but wonder where Silver Wolf was.

His grin was rueful. "I would be, if it was just the two of us. You're the belle of the ball tonight."

"Only because I'm new in town, and the proportion of men to women is six to one," she laughed. "Once I've been here for a while, all the attention will fade."

"Is that what you want, Cari? To stay here?" It was the question he'd been wanting to ask her for days. He had to find out what she was thinking and feeling so he could know what his chances were with her.

A niggling of guilt washed through Cari, for she knew she was keeping Elliot dangling. She hadn't really meant to. She liked him, liked him a lot, but she still wasn't sure that she wanted to marry him. "I care about you, Elliot. You mean a lot to me . . ."

Elliot was about to urge her to be totally honest with him and give him an answer, when a powerful hand clamped down on his shoulder and a deep, hard voice interrupted them.

"I believe this dance is mine."

Silver Wolf had gone to refill his drink while Little Snow had finished her dance with Larson. Intent on seeing her, he'd set the glass aside and started across the crowded room to where she stood with her parents, Ben, and the stranger who'd kissed her at the creek. He was only halfway there, when another melody began and the stranger took her in his arms. At the sight of him holding Little Snow again, the low-burning fury Silver Wolf had kept banked within him ignited to a raging inferno.

Silver Wolf had been aware that people were watching him as he crossed the dance floor, but he didn't care. He was going to dance with Little Snow, and nothing and no one was going to stop him. He'd suffered through her dance with Larson. There was no way he was going to stand by and watch her dance with this man.

As he reached them, he heard Little Snow say, *"Elliot. You mean a lot to me . . ."*

A violent emotion shook him, and he had to restrain himself from doing more than just putting his hand on this Elliot's shoulder to cut in.

"I'm sorry, but . . ." Elliot began, stopping in the midst of the waltz to face the man who would take Cari from him.

"Silver Wolf?" At the sound of that familiar voice, his name escaped her in an excited gasp. He'd come to her at last!

"Hello, Little Snow." He said her name softly.

An expression of pure radiance lit her lovely features as she pivoted to see him, coming face-to-face with her dream warrior for the first time in seven years. Cari could only stare at him with a mixture of joy and surprise. She'd known that he must have changed in the time they'd been apart, but she'd had no idea he would look like this. Her blue-eyed gaze swept over him, taking in every detail of his appearance. Her warrior was gone, and in his place was a man who appeared as civilized and sophisticated as Elliot. Cari wasn't sure whether to be disappointed or happy. Silver Wolf's shoulder-length black hair had been cut, the style he wore now only a little longer than that of the other men in the room. His suit was expensive, his manner totally proper. She almost felt like she was meeting a stranger for the first time, until she looked into his eyes. They were the silver-gray she remembered so well, and right now they were warm and welcoming upon her. "It's you. . . . It's really you."

"Yes, Little Snow. Will you finish this waltz with me?" he asked, totally ignoring Elliot who was standing in silent confusion beside them.

"Cari?" Elliot bristled at being so coolly dismissed. He glanced at Cari and felt a flare of primitive jealousy, for her expression was rapt, and in all their time together she'd never looked at him that way. "Do you want to dance with him?"

Elliot remembered James saying that Silver Wolf had gone to the East to college and was now working for the Indian Bureau, but he'd never expected him to look like this person. He'd expected him to look like the braves they'd seen at Tall Shadow's village, not a debonair, sophisticated gentleman.

"Yes, Elliot, please. This is Silver Wolf, the friend I told you about."

Silver Wolf turned his guarded gaze to the white man as he waited for his response.

Unable to do anything else without making a scene, Elliot reluctantly handed Cari over. "It's nice to meet you."

The two men's eyes met as Silver Wolf took Cari's hand. The look they exchanged was fleeting yet powerful and spoke of possession and dominance, and Elliot knew he had a more than worthy rival in this man.

Silver Wolf drew Little Snow to him, his hand settling possessively at her waist as he whirled her expertly out onto the dance floor. They paid no attention to the gossips who were watching them with only barely concealed outrage. The rest of the world with its prejudices and hatreds faded away. It was only the two of them, wrapped up in themselves and the beauty of this much longed-for moment.

Cari had never known a waltz could be so exciting. She was in heaven as she followed Silver Wolf's smooth lead. His arm around her was strong and sure, and the heat of his hand at her waist sent tingles of awareness through her. He danced as well as he seemed to do everything in life, and they moved in perfect unison, as one to the music.

"I'm so glad you came tonight. I've been home for over a week, and I was beginning to think I'd never see you again," Cari told him, the happiness she felt at being reunited with him shining in her eyes. She was thrilled to be with him, and she didn't care who knew it.

"I was busy at the fort, but I'm back in town now."

"I missed you while I was gone," she confessed in all honesty, completely forgetting all the things she'd learned about how to flirt and attract men. This was her Silver Wolf, and none of that mattered.

"You were away a long time," he replied. As genuinely happy as she seemed to be to seeing him, he still could not forget the scene at the stream. He wondered if she'd become a sophisticate like Hilary, a woman learned in the art of seduction, a woman who looked at every man the same way she was looking at him right then— as if there was not another man alive in the world but him, as if he were a king among men in her eyes. He wanted to believe she hadn't, but . . .

"I was away too long," she admitted freely. "School was nice, I guess, but I'm glad to be home." Cari met his eyes then, and the intensity of his silver regard took her breath away. It was almost as if he were trying to look into the very depths of her soul.

"What did you learn while you were away?" His question was double-edged.

"I took the usual subjects at school, but Mother insisted I take dance lessons, too, and though I hated it at the time, right now I'm glad for them. I never knew a waltz could be so wonderful. You're a very good dancer."

Unwelcome thoughts of Hilary intruded again. He tried to push them away, reminding himself that this was his Little Snow.

"My father told me that you went to school in New York. Why didn't you write to me? We were just in Philadelphia, and I might have been able to visit you." A little of the hurt she'd felt over his not answering her letters was reflected in her voice.

Her words surprised him, but before he could reply, the tempo of the music changed and he knew the waltz was about to end. Unwilling to relinquish his claim to her, he maneuvered them toward a side door.

"Let's go outside so we can talk."

Cari didn't even consider refusing his suggestion, though she knew her mother would be scandalized if she found out. Being with Silver Wolf was much more important than anything else.

Silver Wolf took Little Snow's hand and they slipped from the hall, escaping into the black velvet night. He knew others would come looking for them soon, but at least they'd have some time alone together before they did.

"You didn't answer my question, Silver Wolf," Cari said as they moved away from the lights and noise of the hall. "Why didn't you write to me? Why didn't you answer my letters?"

He stopped and looked down at her, studying her face in the softness of the moonlight, searching for some sign of deception, but he found none. "Little Snow, the only letter I ever received was the one you wrote right after you left. There were never any other letters."

"But I wrote every week . . ."

"And I wrote to you, too, several times a month at first."

"There's no need to lie about it," she began, not wanting to argue about the issues. She supposed now that they were back together again, it really didn't matter anyway. She was startled when, the words having barely left her lips, he gripped her by the upper arms, his expression hardening.

"There's one thing you've apparently forgotten about me, Little Snow. I never lie," he told her brusquely as he released her.

Confusion marred her lovely features for a moment, and then understanding dawned on her. If Silver Wolf had written to her, there was only one person who could have kept his letters from her.

"My mother . . ." she said slowly, the ugly truth hurting her. She put her hand on Silver Wolf's arm and could feel the tension in him. "It had to have been my mother. I wrote to you every week, telling you how much I missed you and begging you to write back and tell me how you were. But I never received an answer. She must have destroyed them all." Her gaze lifted to his as they came to grips with the injustice done them. "I'm sorry . . ."

At last Silver Wolf understood. Her mother had hated him for as long as he could remember. It didn't make the lonely years apart any easier to accept, but the knowledge that Little Snow hadn't abandoned him did ease the tension in him. All that really mattered was that she had written to him. He touched her cheek with a gentle caress. "So am I."

"I should have realized . . . should have known she would try to keep us apart," she agonized, humiliated. "I should have believed and trusted in you."

"It's over now."

"But we missed so much. Can we start again?"

"There's no need to start again. We're here, together. Nothing's changed."

His hand dropped away from her cheek and they walked on

to a secluded place behind the hall where they could talk without fear of interruption.

"It really is a beautiful night," Cari sighed as she gazed up at the moon and stars above them. She was home and she was with Silver Wolf.

"Not as beautiful as you are," he said softly, coming to stand close beside her.

She laughed lightly as she turned to him, her mood happy once again. "You said nothing's changed, but *you* have. My Silver Wolf would never have said anything so . . ."

"Do I have to keep reminding you? Your Silver Wolf always spoke the truth."

She looked at him through the eyes of a woman now, and not those of a child. Her voice was soft, almost a whisper, as she asked, "Do you really think I'm pretty now?" Somehow, suddenly, it was very important to her to hear him say it again.

"You were a pretty child. Now, you're a beautiful woman."

The stars, pale moonlight, and the distant strains of the music from the dance all came together, swirling around them with intoxicating intensity. Silver Wolf gazed down at her, seeing in her all the simple truth and beauty that had been missing from his life for so long. His Little Snow had grown into the most lovely woman he'd ever seen, and he could no more have stopped himself from kissing her right then than he could have stopped breathing. The tension and the wanting had become too powerful. He had to kiss her. With infinite care, Silver Wolf bent to her, his lips seeking and finding hers.

It was a tentative exchange at first, their lips meeting in a gentle test, a gentle exploration. Cari had kissed Elliot many times, and it had always been a pleasant experience. But this one simple kiss from Silver Wolf shattered all her notions about how kisses were supposed to be. As his lips touched hers, drew away, then sought hers again, she sensed he was holding back, and she was filled with a longing to know more.

A small sound escaped Cari, a whimper almost, and it was all the encouragement Silver Wolf needed. Wrapping his arms around her, he drew her fully against him as his mouth covered hers, hot and demanding. His lips parted hers, and when his tongue sought the dark, honeyed depths of her mouth, Cari swayed weakly against him. She clutched at his shoulders, glad for his strong arms around her. As she clung to him, she knew a vague and distant thought that this was what she'd always wanted . . . that this was what she'd always needed—to be in Silver Wolf's arms.

Silver Wolf felt the eagerness in her response and tightened his arms around her. The fullness of her breasts crushed against his chest excited him, and he had to force himself to remember where they were. He ended the kiss to save his sanity, yet unable to bring himself to release her, he remained holding her to his heart.

"The last time I held you like this, you were almost frozen to death, and I had to keep you warm while I took you home," he told her in a husky voice as he fought to quell his raging desire for her with memories of her as a child.

"I don't have to be home just yet," she whispered, remembering that night, too, how he'd saved her and how wonderful and safe she'd felt in his arms. She'd only been a little girl, but somehow, instinctively, she'd known even then . . . "Silver Wolf . . ."

His name on her lips fired the flame of his desire for her to white-hot pitch, and he cast his intention to stop aside. His mouth slanted over hers, searing her with the power of his need, and she returned his passion full measure. They strained together, caught up once more in the vortex of emotion that swept them along beyond the realm of reality to a place where only they existed.

Ten

"Are you having a good time?" James asked Elizabeth as he squired her about the dance floor.

"Of course, I always have a wonderful time with you." She'd been looking forward to tonight for she loved dancing with her handsome husband.

James's hand tightened at her waist, letting her know he felt the same way. "I know this isn't Philadelphia, but I was hoping you'd enjoy yourself."

At the mention of the city she loved best, a flash of longing shone in her eyes. "I won't lie to you and say that I don't miss it. I do. I'm just sorry you couldn't get away to be there with us for the season so you could have seen Cari. She was so popular, you would have been proud of her."

James heard the disappointment in his wife's voice, and pain stabbed at his heart. It seemed no matter how hard he tried to make the Circle M home for Elizabeth, she would never think of it that way. It saddened him, even as it frustrated him. "Young Elliot seems to have won her favor."

"I hope so. He's a fine young man. The perfect choice for her actually. I hope she doesn't take too long deciding to accept his proposal. He's proud, and while I do believe he loves her, I don't think his patience will last forever."

"Does she love him?"

"I wish I knew," Elizabeth said slowly, her gaze seeking out her lovely daughter as she danced with Elliot. Cari looked as if she were having a good time.

The dance ended, and Elizabeth and James moved to the side of the room. He left her alone for a moment while he went to get them drinks, and while he was gone, Elizabeth took the time to look around the hall. Festooned though it was, the hall was still terribly rustic compared to the fancy ballrooms in Philadelphia. A pang of discontent stung her. She loved the life she'd left behind, and no matter how she tried, she would never feel the same way about life here in the territory. James returned to her side with a cup of punch and, after taking a sip, she turned to him.

"James, do you suppose we'll ever live in Philadelphia again?"

Elizabeth's question caught him off-guard, and he was hard pressed to mask the hurt. He'd done everything he could to please her— everything except give up his dream for the ranch, and that was the one thing he wouldn't do. He was building up the Circle M for her and Cari, and Cari's children. Why couldn't Elizabeth understand he was building a dynasty for the future generations of McCords?

"No, Elizabeth," he finally responded. "We'll visit there, but the Circle M is home."

"All right," she agreed in subdued tones. Resigned to spending the rest of her life there, she tried to lift her spirits by searching the dance floor for Cari. "Have you seen Cari?"

"Not for a while." He glanced around the room. "There's Elliot, but Cari's not with him."

"I wonder where she is . . ."

Before she could say anymore, several of James's friends from town gathered around. After introducing Elizabeth, James was drawn into conversation with them.

"I'll go see if I can find Cari." She smiled as she left him to his ranching talk and went to speak with Elliot.

Elliot's mood had not been good when Silver Wolf cut in, and it deteriorated to positively surly when Cari disappeared with the man at the end of the waltz. Elliot knew the Indian was her friend and that they probably had a lot to say to each other, but enough was enough. He'd give her a few more minutes and then he was going after her.

Glancing up, Elliot found Elizabeth making her way to his side. He smiled at her. "Are you enjoying the evening?"

"Oh, yes. James and I are having a wonderful time. He's with some friends now, talking about the ranch, so I thought I'd come see what you and Cari were doing. She *is* here with you, isn't she?"

"*No,*" he answered curtly.

"Where did she go?"

"Her friend Silver Wolf showed up and she went off with him."

Elizabeth gasped, growing pale.

Elliot wondered why she seemed so distressed. "He cut in on our last dance, and when it ended, I looked for her, but I didn't see her."

Elizabeth went cold. Cari had gone off with that filthy Indian! Didn't she know what that would do to her reputation? Didn't she realize that people would talk? "We have to find her . . ."

Together they began to make their way around the room in search of Cari.

As Cari had begun to dance with Silver Wolf, horrified whispers had swept the hall, and when Nettie Jones, a sharp-eyed, gossipy matron, had seen them disappear out the side door, she'd quickly relayed the news to others. It was bad enough that the half-breed had asked a white girl to dance, but to take her outside was unthinkable. Of course, Nettie realized that Cari McCord was probably just being her father's daughter, for everyone knew how James McCord felt about the Indians. For that reason she hadn't spoken directly to James and Elizabeth about it, but when Elizabeth asked her if she'd seen Cari, Nettie took the opportunity to tell her every juicy detail she knew.

"Yes, my dear, I'm afraid I do know where your daughter's gone."

"Excuse me?"

"She's outside with that . . . that half-breed Daniel Marshall. They've been gone quite a while, too," Nettie informed her with glee. "You know, it really wasn't proper for her to dance with him, let alone go outside unchaperoned. Of course, knowing how savage 'they' are, he might have forced her to go, though I certainly didn't think she looked as if he were making her do it against her will."

Elizabeth's regard turned icy as she stared at the gossip. "Thank you for your concern, Mrs. Jones."

"Of course. A reputation is such a fragile thing and so hard to reclaim once it's been ruined."

Elizabeth walked rigidly away with Elliot, her manner stiff, her nerves frayed, her temper about to explode. "I should have realized something like this would happen. Cari never gave a thought to her reputation. She just went with him . . ."

"Shall I go look for her?"

She paused and put a hand on his arm, the appreciation she felt showing in her eyes. "Please."

Elizabeth went to speak to James, while Elliot went out the front doors in search of Cari. Elizabeth was relieved when she found her husband by himself, and she drew him even farther away from the others to speak to him.

"Do you realize what your daughter's done?" she demanded.

"Cari? What's happened, Elizabeth? Is something wrong?"

"I'll say something's wrong!" She was seething. "It was bad enough that he showed up here in the first place . . ."

"What are you talking about?"

"The half-breed! Silver Wolf! He cut in on Elliot and Cari.

Then, if that wasn't bad enough— he took her outside alone! Nettie Jones told me.''

"Elizabeth, Nettie Jones is a busybody and a troublemaker, and the whole town would be better off without her." James stared at his wife. He saw the anger blazing in her eyes and was saddened by it. Elizabeth saw no honor in Silver Wolf's accomplishments and achievements. In her eyes, because of his Cheyenne blood, he would never be good enough.

"James, you have to do something."

"Why? You know how much Cari missed Silver Wolf. I'm sure they just went to talk for a few minutes. They haven't seen each other for years."

"I want her back inside now," Elizabeth demanded, refusing to give in. "I already sent Elliot to look for her."

"I'll look, too." James gave a weary sigh as he agreed, simply to keep peace.

Cari was lost in the bliss of Silver Wolf's embrace. It seemed as if she belonged in his arms, as if they'd been made for each other. His lips upon hers evoked feelings within her she'd never known existed, and she gave herself over to the wonder of it, blending together with him in a haze of passion.

"Cari!"

The distant call echoed through the night. Cari wanted to ignore it. She wanted the whole world to go away so she could stay in Silver Wolf's embrace. When the call was repeated, and this time closer and much louder, she tensed. There was no mistaking Elliot's voice now, and the realization that the man who'd escorted her to the dance was looking for her, possibly with her mother in tow, frightened her. She forced herself to draw reluctantly away.

"Someone's coming," Cari said nervously, fighting to regain her composure. Her lips felt hot and swollen from his kisses, and she wondered how she looked— if the excitement she was feeling showed too clearly on her face.

"So?"

"He might see us."

Silver Wolf recognized Elliot's call, too, and was cursing silently under his breath. He felt the change in her, how she stiffened when she heard her boyfriend's voice and it infuriated him. "Does it matter if he sees us?"

"Of course it matters," she insisted, though she wasn't sure quite why, for all she really wanted to do was throw herself back in his arms and stay there.

"Why?" He pressed her for an answer; he could remember when nothing could have driven her from him.

"Because I shouldn't be out here alone."

He grinned wickedly. "You're not alone. You're with me."

She smiled back at him. "That's the point. Propriety dictates that I should have a chaperone. I'm grown up now, you know. I'm not a little girl any longer."

"I've noticed." His glittering gaze raked over her.

The effect of his silver eyes upon Cari was as powerful as any physical caress, and she stood unmoving, breathlessly waiting as he closed the distance she'd put between them and leaned down to her. He paused, his lips hovering over hers.

"Would you really rather be inside dancing?" he asked her in a soft, seductive voice, knowing the easterner would soon be upon them.

"Well, I . . ." Mesmerized, she met him in the kiss, and it was more exciting than anything that had gone before. She was shocked by her eager response to it. Worries about her mother disappeared as she surrendered to the forbidden desire to kiss Silver Wolf just once more while there was still time . . .

Elliot was about to call Cari's name again when he rounded the corner of the building and stopped. For a moment, he could only stand in silence, for there before him stood Cari and Silver Wolf kissing. Jealousy exploded within him, and he was jarred to action.

"Cari . . ." Elliot said her name in a tight voice as he strode forth with every intention of breaking up the cozy little scene. "I think it's time to return to the dance."

"Elliot . . ." she gasped, tearing herself from the dreamy pleasure of Silver Wolf's embrace.

"Your mother's looking for you. She sent me to find you and bring you back inside." His gaze went from Cari to the man standing so close beside her. He'd meant to step forward and take her arm, but even in the darkness he could see the look of pure male power in the other man's face, and he hesitated. To Elliot's annoyance, Silver Wolf seemed to sense his hesitation, and a look of something akin to amusement shone in his eyes.

Cari was unaware of the silent challenge issued between the men. She glanced up at Silver Wolf and gave him a tremulous half-smile, hoping he knew just how much she didn't want this moment to end. "I have to go."

"I'll escort you," Elliot offered, stung by Silver Wolf's unspoken mockery.

But Silver Wolf would have none of it. He took her arm. "Little Snow left with me, and she'll return with me." He said the words quietly, but the meaning was clear.

Elliot could only watch as they walked away.

"I'll see you inside, Elliot," Cari called over her shoulder as Silver Wolf drew her toward the hall. She felt guilty over leaving him that way, but every fiber of her being wanted to be with her warrior.

"What is he to you?" Silver Wolf asked as they neared the door.

Cari stopped walking and forced him to pause, too. She turned to him and rested a hand on his arm. "Elliot is a friend, and nothing more."

"He acts as though he has some claim on you."

"I have no control over his feelings, only my own. He has proposed to me, but— " she answered.

"You'll never marry him," he interrupted harshly before she could finish.

Cari gave a stubborn lift of her chin. "I never said I intended to, but I haven't refused him yet," she countered. But she knew she would and soon. She could no longer encourage Elliot. She knew she could never settle for less than Silver Wolf.

They entered the building, but didn't have the chance to say another word before Elizabeth descended on them.

"Thank God you're back! We've been looking everywhere!"

"I'm fine, Mother. I was with Silver Wolf." She wanted to soothe her as quickly as possible.

"Why do you suppose I worried?" she demanded, turning to look at Silver Wolf for the first time. He'd matured into an extraordinarily handsome man, who looked more cultured and civilized than many of the men in the room, and the realization only upset her more. Addressing him, she asked tersely, "Do you realize what you've done?"

"I don't think a few minutes alone with me has ruined Cari's life." He smiled derisively.

Elizabeth's temper was frayed. "I hardly think you're in any position to make that decision. James told me that you'd been educated, but obviously you didn't learn the one lesson you needed to learn most."

"And what was that?" Silver Wolf regarded her levelly, betraying no emotion. Though he knew she'd always despised him, she was Cari's mother and James's wife, and, as such, still deserving of his respect.

"Your place!"

A murmur swelled through those within earshot, but Elizabeth was too distraught to notice. Her worst fears were coming true.

"If you weren't so concerned about appearances, you might be more accepting of others," he countered.

"Cari . . ." Elizabeth said her name in a command. "Come with me."

"Mrs. McCord, maybe you should stop trying to control Cari and trust her to make the right decisions."

His words pushed Elizabeth over the edge, and, livid, she slapped him.

Cari had been miserable as she'd listened to the exchange. Discovering her mother's interference in their correspondence had devastated her, and hearing her say these things to Silver Wolf upset her even more. But when her mother actually slapped him, she was so horrified she could only stare at her in total disbelief. She hadn't thought her mother capable of such an act. She was stunned and rendered speechless.

Silver Wolf's face was schooled into a stony mask, but his eyes flared with intensity as he stood rigidly before Elizabeth. He'd been insulted before, but this time, in front of the townspeople, it was particularly humiliating. He glanced at Cari, waiting for her to say or do something— anything— but she stood in silence, looking at her mother with an expression he couldn't read. A deadly coldness filled him as no word was said in his defense. A terrible sense of betrayal overwhelmed him, and he knew he was alone.

Silver Wolf turned and walked from the hall. He passed Elliot on the way out. Elliot had witnessed the scene and, seeing the look in his eyes, quickly got out of his way.

Going out the side door, Silver Wolf skirted the building, heading toward the street. As he passed beneath one of the open windows, he overheard two matrons talking in scandalized tones.

"Did you see what happened? The McCord girl was outside with that half-breed for the longest time, and I guess her mother took exception to it! Thank goodness the girl's back inside now and talking to that nice man from back East. But heavens, did you see the way Elizabeth McCord slapped Daniel Marshall? I would never have had the nerve!"

"Why, she's lucky he didn't pull a knife on her and slit her throat right there!"

Silver Wolf kept on going. His thoughts were on Cari. He had gone to the dance tonight only to see her, and now that he had, he would leave town. For a few moments, he'd allowed himself to believe that they shared something special, but the pain of her betrayal had destroyed that foolish notion. According to the two women he'd heard gossiping, she was already back with Elliot again. Obviously his encounter with her mother had just been a temporary embarrassment for her and nothing that could disrupt the good time she'd been having.

Emerging on the street in front of the hall, Silver Wolf changed his mind about going straight back to his rooms to pack. He didn't drink very often, but tonight was the exception. He stalked off toward the nearest saloon.

As soon as Silver Wolf left the hall, Cari finally spoke up.

"Mother, how could you?" she demanded through gritted teeth.

"How could I?" Elizabeth turned to her, white-faced and still furious. "How could *you?* You know how I feel about him."

"And I also know how *I* feel about him!" she countered angrily. "Silver Wolf and I talked, and we know the truth now. We know how you intercepted and destroyed our letters to each other."

"I did it for your own good," she defended herself. She was very aware that Nettie was watching them with great interest, and she was trying not to draw any more attention to them.

"My own good? How can breaking my heart be good for me? Silver Wolf means . . ."

Before she could say anything more, Elliot reached them, interrupting what she'd been about to say. "Cari, are you all right?" he asked.

She paused, and, realizing this was no place to argue with her mother, she chose her words carefully. "I'm afraid I'm suddenly not feeling very well, Elliot. Please take me back to the hotel."

"Of course."

"Cari, you can't leave. It's early yet." Elizabeth stopped her. Now that the half-breed was gone, the rest of the evening promised to be more entertaining.

"Good night, Mother." Her words were cold and final.

Elizabeth barely controlled her temper. "We'll talk about this when your father and I return to the hotel."

Cari didn't even bother to answer as she walked away with

Elliot. They were about to exit when she caught sight of Ben Douglas.

She asked Elliot to wait for her. "There's someone I need to speak to before we go," she explained.

Cari knew she was being more than a little bold by approaching Ben, but she was worried about Silver Wolf.

"Ben? Could I talk to you for a moment?"

Ben was surprised to find Cari McCord by his side. She looked troubled about something, so he quickly excused himself from Melanie and her mother, who'd been holding him hostage in conversation.

"I need your help," Cari told him when they'd reached a place where no one else could hear their conversation.

"Why? What happened?"

"You haven't heard the gossip?"

"Heard what gossip?"

Cari drew a deep breath. "My mother had words with Silver Wolf and she slapped him. He walked out before I could say anything."

Ben was stunned.

"She's never liked him, and when she found out we were outside by ourselves, she got upset."

"Where did he go?"

"I don't know. I wanted to talk to him, but he disappeared out the side door. Find him for me, Ben. Please . . ."

Ben's green eyes darkened with concern. "I'll find him. Don't worry."

Cari returned to the waiting Elliot, and they started back toward the hotel in silence.

"Feeling any better?" he finally asked.

"A little," she answered distractedly. Her every thought was on Silver Wolf. She kept looking for him as they made their way through town, but she saw no sign of him and hoped Ben was having better luck. Her heart ached for Silver Wolf and she wanted to tell him she was sorry. She wanted to kiss him and hold him and never let him go. But he was gone, and she wondered desperately when she'd see him again.

"Do you want to talk about what happened?"

"No. There's really nothing to say."

They entered the hotel and he escorted her to her room. She gave him the key and he unlocked the door for her. As she started to go inside, he put a hand on her arm.

"Cari," Elliot said softly. "You know I'm your friend. If you ever need me, I'm here for you."

She smiled tenderly at him. "You are truly a kind man, Elliot." She reached up and kissed him gently on the cheek. "Thank you. Your words mean more to me than you'll ever know."

With that she went inside and shut the door, leaving Elliot alone in the hall.

In his quest to find Cari, James got caught up in conversation with some old friends. When he finally heard rumblings about what had happened, he sought out his wife.

"I just heard that there was some trouble with Silver Wolf," he said quietly. "What happened?"

"I told him what I thought about him taking Cari outside unchaperoned, and when I did, he was very rude to me."

"Is it true that you slapped him right here in front of everyone?"

Elizabeth heard the accusation in his tone and knew he was going to defend the half-breed. Her anger returned. "He deserved it! How dare he put Cari's reputation at risk!"

James grew furious as he regarded his wife. He loved her, but he wanted to shake her now. "How dare you humiliate him. Did it ever occur to you that Cari wanted to be with him?"

"That's what she said before she left with Elliot, but I don't care. What will people think if she cheapens herself?"

"Why do you care what people think? It's what Cari thinks that matters. Not anyone else," he ground out.

"She's too young to know her own mind," Elizabeth defended her own actions.

"You said she left. Where did she go?" His anger was clearly showing in his face now.

"Elliot took her back to the hotel."

"And Silver Wolf? Where is he?"

"I have no idea, nor do I care."

For the first time in his life, James wanted to throttle his wife. He knew it would do no good, though. All he could do was find Silver Wolf and apologize. "Wait here for me. I'll be back."

"Where are you going?"

"To try to repair some of the damage you've caused." James left the hall, his outrage obvious in his expression and his stride.

Nettie was watching as he spoke to Elizabeth. It was easy to tell he was angry, but she believed his fury was directed at the half-breed. It never occurred to her that he was furious with his wife for insulting a close friend. She spread the word that James was going after Daniel Marshall for the liberties he'd taken with his daughter.

Eleven

It was a sordid scene in the half-lit, sparsely furnished room above the bar in the Sundown Saloon. The man was hulking in size and far too big to be mounting such a small woman, but he didn't seem to care about anything but his own pleasure. As soon as the dark-haired girl had shed her clothes, he practically threw her on the bed atop the already soiled linens and thrust within her. His eyes were closed in concentrated ecstasy as he selfishly sought his own release. She was a whore to him, a receptacle for his needs and nothing more. His hands pawed at her small breasts as he quickened his demanding pace.

Beneath him, the woman moved uneasily as he tormented her with deliberately painful caresses. She turned her face away from the vile heat of his panting breath, her brightly painted lips twisting into a grimace of disgust. Squeezing her eyes shut, she fought against the tears that threatened, but to no avail. One lone tear escaped and traced a path down her heavily rouged cheek. When finally the man shuddered, gave a guttural groan, and collapsed beside her, relief flooded through her.

Jenny Moore lay still, waiting nervously to see what Dex was going to do next. When he didn't move right away, she held her breath in fearful anticipation and inched carefully from his side. The stench of his unwashed body and too much whiskey was nearly overpowering, and her stomach was roiling in protest. For not the first time that evening, she cursed the Saturday nights that brought all the cowboys to town looking for a good time.

Dex stirred and mumbled something. She froze, biting down on her bottom lip to keep from crying out her fear that he might come fully awake and want to take her again. Already her flesh was starting to bruise from his harsh treatment, and she couldn't wait to be free of him. When he promptly fell back asleep, she breathed a sigh of relief and scooted the rest of the way out of the bed.

Escape. . . . The word echoed through Jenny's mind. She wanted to get away from him as fast as she could, but she felt so dirty that she had to wash first. With silent urgency, she scrubbed herself clean at the washstand, erasing all vestiges of his touch from her skin. She trembled as she thought of his hurtful gropings and silently prayed that he wouldn't wake up. When she was done, she threw on her clothes, and as she adjusted the low-cut neckline of the red-and-black satin gown, she hoped the marks he'd made on her body didn't show.

Dressed at last, Jenny cast a glance at her reflection in the small mirror over the washstand. She needed to make certain that she looked all right, for it wouldn't do for Ed the bartender to discover she'd been crying. She was glad to find that her makeup was still intact. She added another touch of red to her lips, then pasted on a bright smile to convince Ed that she was enjoying her job. It never ceased to amaze her how old she looked with rouge and lip color on. She doubted anyone would guess she'd just turned sixteen.

Jenny's thoughts drifted for a moment to what her life had been like the year before when she'd fled her home after her mother had died and her father had remarried. It had been hell living with the hateful, domineering woman. She'd thought things would be better if she left, but now sometimes she wondered . . .

Jenny looked worriedly back to the bed where the drunken cowboy thankfully still slept, then fled the room. As she closed the door and rushed down the hall, she wondered why she was hurrying. There were only more drunken cowboys waiting for her below, along with Ed, who watched and criticized her every move. She'd just started down the steps when the door to her room was thrown open.

"Hey! Jenny! Where d'ya think you're going?" Dex hollered as he staggered naked out into the hall after her.

Jenny stopped where she was, paling a little under her heavy makeup. She had to fight down the panic that welled up inside her.

In the room below, all the bar's patrons looked up. Laughter echoed through the crowd at the sight of the naked cowboy lurching toward the girl.

"Why, Dex, I'm going down to the bar and have a drink. Where do you think *you're* going?" she asked archly.

"Well, come on back up here, little darling!" he demanded. "I ain't done with you yet!"

"You sure could have fooled me. I could've sworn you were more than done," she replied with a laugh. "You were sleeping like a baby."

At her clever words, the patrons roared again with laughter. Dex flushed bright red and disappeared back into the room, slamming the door.

Thrilled to have gotten away from him, Jenny continued on down the stairs and went to speak to Ed at the bar. She could tell he wasn't pleased with her, but she refused to be sorry that she'd outwitted the rough cowboy and saved herself from further mistreatment.

Silver Wolf had entered the crowded Sundown Saloon with the purpose of getting drunk. He'd elbowed his way to the bar, paid for a bottle of the best whiskey and a glass, and settled in at an empty table in a corner at the back of the room. He sat with his back to the wall as he poured a healthy amount of the potent liquor into the tumbler.

Lifting the glass to his lips, Silver Wolf took a deep swallow. The liquor burned going down, but he didn't care. He refilled the glass and took another drink. Studying the bottle soberly, he wondered how long it would be before it began to work and he would feel the blessed numbness he so desperately sought. He drank steadily as he tried to erase the memory of Little Snow's betrayal from his mind. He wasn't sure how much time had passed when he heard a commotion on the stairs that led to the rooms on the balcony above where the saloon girls plied their trade.

He watched in mild amusement as the naked man tried to chase down one of the girls at the bar. The encounter ended quickly, though, so he turned his attention back to his bottle, refilling his glass and downing another deep drink.

"Need anything else tonight, handsome?"

Silver Wolf lifted his gaze to find the same girl he'd watched outwit the naked man standing before him. He'd thought her moderately attractive as he'd watched her from a distance but up close, he found she was actually quite young and very pretty beneath all the harsh makeup she wore. He wondered why she thought she needed such artifice. Her hair was dark; her eyes were a warm brown, and, though not buxom, she had a good figure. Another man, in another mood might have desired her, but Silver Wolf was haunted by the memory of Cari's golden beauty and her slender, enticing curves pressed against him.

"No," he finally answered flatly.

"You could have fooled me. A good-looking man like you shouldn't be alone on Saturday night. My name's Jenny." She edged closer, knowing Ed was keeping an eye on her. "You see the rest of these fellas?" She gestured toward the loud, drunken men lined up at the bar. "Well, they just aren't gentlemen like yourself."

He took another big swig as he thought of Elizabeth McCord's opinion of him. He met Jenny's gaze. "You obviously don't know who I am."

"Oh, yes I do. You're Daniel Marshall. I've seen you around town."

At her use of his white name, Silver Wolf frowned. She thought of him as Daniel Marshall, but who was he really? Right now, he wasn't sure. "Why don't you sit down, Jenny?" At least she thought he was a gentleman, and he meant to prove her right.

"I'd love to." Jenny flashed him a wide smile as she slid into the chair next to him. "How about a drink?"

"Help yourself," he offered, thinking she would get a glass and then pour herself one from the bottle.

She surprised him, though, when she picked up his glass, and, in a way the other girls had taught her, she turned it to drink from the exact same spot he had. Her eyes met his. "You've got good taste in whiskey."

He shrugged, unmoved by her arousing display. "After the first swallow, it all tastes the same."

"Don't let the barkeep hear you say that," she advised. "If he thinks you don't know the difference, when you ask for more he'll switch some of the cheap stuff for what you got here."

"I'll remember your advice." He doubted he'd need another bottle tonight, though.

"Now, Daniel," she purred, scooting her chair even closer to his. He wore a clean-smelling cologne, and she found the scent exciting. If she had to be with another man that night, she wanted it to be him. She boldly put a hand on his knee. "What do you feel like doing tonight?"

Silver Wolf chuckled, but it wasn't a happy laugh. "What I feel like doing and what I'm going to do are two different things."

"Ooh, sounds intriguing. What is it you *feel* like doing?"

"Don't ask me that."

Jenny heard the coldness in his tone and knew he was deadly serious. "All right, then, what are we going to do?"

"I'd like to sit here, and just drink and talk."

"Talk?" she repeated as she cast a nervous glance back toward the bartender. She knew Ed wouldn't be pleased.

"Talk," he repeated. "Why don't you get yourself a glass and join me?"

"All right. I'll be right back," Jenny promised.

She hurried to the bar and earned a disapproving look from the bartender. "I need a glass, Ed."

"I ain't paying you to sit and drink."

"I'm just going to have one with him and then I'll get him up to my room."

He snared her wrist in a viselike grip. "You'd better. I just had to give Dex a free drink to shut him up. You'd better deliver on this one."

"I will!" Her eyes widened in fear.

"Don't think I ain't watchin' you." He gave her wrist a painful twist.

"Ow . . . I know!" Jenny tried to pull free. "Don't worry!"

"That's right. Don't worry," Silver Wolf said in a low voice as he came up behind her. "Let her go."

Though he hadn't been able to hear what was being said, Silver Wolf could tell that the bartender was giving Jenny trouble. When the man grabbed her wrist, Silver Wolf had had enough. His temper had been frayed when he'd come into the saloon, but seeing the man abusing the girl pushed him to the limit of his control.

"Jenny's with me, and she will be for the night," he told him tersely, tossing enough money on the counter to pay for her services. He watched in disgust as Ed quickly released Jenny and pocketed the cash.

"Have a fine time," Ed said magnanimously, handing her the glass she'd wanted.

"Let's go up to your room," Silver Wolf suggested, wanting to get as far away from the greedy bartender as he could.

"I'd like that," Jenny agreed, gazing up at him. She was surprised by his defense of her. It was very seldom that anyone stuck up for her.

They retrieved his bottle and glass from the table and went

upstairs. The lamp was still burning low, revealing the bed and its tousled covers. Jenny closed the door behind them, then set the bottle and glasses on the small nightstand. She turned up the lamp, then faced him.

"I always did like a good conversation. Since we aren't going to be using the bed for anything else, we might as well sit on it." She plumped up both pillows and braced them against the headboard. "Take your pick."

Silver Wolf sat down on the side of the bed closest to the table, poured another drink, then settled back against the headboard, stretching his long legs out before him. "So, tell me about yourself, Jenny."

"I'd rather talk about you," she countered as she sat on the other side of the bed, cross-legged, facing him. She studied him with open interest. She recognized his Indian heritage in his strong features, but felt no fear or loathing because of it. He'd already proven himself to be more of a man than any of those others downstairs, and he was just about the handsomest man she'd ever seen. "I'm sure you're much more interesting than I am."

Silver Wolf saw the earnestness in her expression. There was an open, appealing quality about her. "I asked you first. Why are you here at the Sundown?"

Jenny could see in his eyes that he really did want to know, so she decided to be honest. "I never wanted to do this. But my mother died, and then my father remarried. It was hard enough without my mother, but then when Caroline came into our house and took over. . . . My little sisters managed all right. But for some reason she hated me."

Jenny paused, remembering all the cruel things the other woman had done to her. Caroline had constantly belittled her and criticized her to her father. The worst of it all had been when her father had started believing Caroline's lies. The final straw had come the day he had taken his wife's side against her. When she'd stood up to him and tried to argue her point of view, he'd slapped her. She'd started to flee the room in tears and had turned around to find Caroline standing behind her, smiling.

Silver Wolf could see the pain in the depths of her dark-eyed gaze. "I'm sorry."

"So am I," she managed. "I loved my father and my sisters, but I couldn't stand it anymore."

"Do you ever think of going back?"

"Once in a while. But I'm sure they're fine without me. Besides, there's no point now. I'm sure my father would be outraged by what I've done." She shrugged as she dropped her eyes from his.

Silver Wolf reached out and gently lifted her chin so she was looking at him. "Jenny . . . what you did, is survive. There's no shame in that." He waited, letting his words sink in. "You're very pretty, you know. You don't need all this paint on your face."

His touch was gentle and his words were so precious to her that her heartbeat quickened. No man had ever told her she was pretty before. For the first time in her life, she felt a genuine response deep within the womanly heart of her.

When his hand dropped away, Jenny couldn't stop herself from leaning toward him and kissing him. It was a delicate, emotion-filled kiss, and the warmth within her grew. She drew back, awed by this strange new feeling. Her gaze met his, and she bent toward him again. This time she put everything she had into her kiss, wanting him to know what she was feeling for him.

Jenny was accustomed to men who wanted her physically. It surprised her when Daniel didn't readily respond. Without ending the embrace, she began to caress him, sliding her hands over his chest and down to his belt. She managed to unfasten it and was reaching for his pants when he caught her hands and stilled them. Neither of them noticed when his medicine bag slipped from his belt and fell among the covers.

"Jenny, wait. I didn't come up here for this," Silver Wolf said softly. Her embrace was pleasant, her kiss was sweet, but sex wasn't what he wanted.

"I want to be good to you, Daniel. You're the only man who's ever been nice to me."

Silver Wolf saw her confusion and felt sorry for her. "Just stay with me, Jenny. Like I told you downstairs, all I want to do is talk, and it would be nice if I were talking to a friend."

She drew away from him, disappointed that he didn't desire her, yet strangely happy that he wanted her company. "I'd like that. I'd like to be your friend."

As he refastened his belt, she settled on the bed next to him again. Neither of them noticed that the medicine bag was lost in the jumble of bedclothes.

An hour later, Silver Wolf, with a little help from Jenny, had more than done justice to the contents of the bottle. The tension within him had eased somewhat. Jenny had kept him entertained with undemanding conversation. He hadn't noticed right away how witty she was, and was chuckling over something amusing she'd said and was just reaching for his glass when she put her hand over his.

"Don't you think you've had plenty to drink?" She'd kept hoping he would change his mind about bedding her, but his main interest during the past hour seemed to be drowning whatever problem was bothering him in liquor.

"Why? Aren't you enjoying yourself?" he asked, his words slurring just a little as he fought to focus on her.

"Of course I'm enjoying myself, Daniel. I was just hoping you might have changed your mind about . . ." she said invitingly.

Silver Wolf suddenly noticed the hungry look in her eyes. She was ready and willing, but there was only one woman he wanted to make love to right now, and she was probably dancing with Elliot. At the thought of Little Snow, he shook off Jenny's restraining hand, picked up his glass, and took another drink.

"No, I won't be changing my mind. Why don't we go back downstairs for a while?" Silver Wolf suggested as images of Little Snow haunted his thoughts. He stood up and grabbed the bottle, swaying unsteadily.

"Whatever you want."

Whatever he wanted. . . . Her words repeated in his mind, and he gave a low growl of irritation as he started from the room.

What he really wanted, he realized, was to forget Little Snow, but the memory of her betrayal was burned into his consciousness.

What a fool he'd been. He'd believed after they'd talked at the dance and he'd found out the truth about the letters that she was the same as she had been when they were younger. He'd believed that her years back East hadn't changed her. But now, thinking about the way she'd acted, first, when she'd heard Elliot coming and then when they'd gone back inside, he had to wonder. He took another big drink of the potent whiskey. He noticed that it no longer burned. When they got downstairs, he settled back in at the same table with Jenny sitting right next to him.

Since he'd left Elizabeth at the dance, James had been searching everywhere for Daniel. He was relieved to finally locate him, even if it was in one of the worst saloons in town and with one of the girls from the bar practically sitting on his lap.

"Daniel?" James said his name as he neared the table.

When Silver Wolf looked up, he was surprised to find his vision blurry, and he had to blink twice to clear it. When he realized the man standing before the table was James, his expression hardened. "What do you want?"

"I need to talk to you," James told him.

"I'm busy." His words were slurred.

James realized just how drunk he was and he was shocked. He'd known Silver Wolf a long time and had never seen him drunk before. Had Elizabeth been there, he might have strangled her.

"This won't take long," he promised, giving the girl named Jenny a distracted smile as he pulled up a chair. He sat down opposite Silver Wolf in spite of his friend's objection. "I heard what happened at the dance, and I came to apologize."

"Why? You didn't do anything."

"I'm apologizing for Elizabeth."

"We both know she meant every word she said, so it's better if you leave it alone."

Jenny heard the iciness in his voice and realized that something very serious must have happened and that was why he'd been drinking so heavily. She wondered who Elizabeth was as she glanced from Daniel to the man who'd just joined them. The tension was heavy between the two, so she remained quiet not wanting to interfere. She was, after all, his friend.

"But, Daniel, it's important to me that you know how sorry I am."

For a moment, they regarded each other across the table. The older man's gaze was open and revealing, but Silver Wolf's expression was shuttered, revealing nothing. Before either could say more, Ben strode up to the table.

"Good evening, James . . . Daniel," Ben said. He, too, had looked all over town for Daniel, and in total frustration had finally begun checking the saloons. Judging from Daniel's condition and the near-empty bottle on the table, he was sorry he hadn't started there. "Is this a private party, or can I join you?"

"You might as well sit down, too," Silver Wolf answered, grabbing the bottle.

"I've never known him to drink before," James whispered to Ben.

"Normally he doesn't, and tomorrow morning he's going to remember why."

The two men exchanged knowing looks.

"Is he going to be all right?" James asked quietly.

"I'll take care of him. You can go on if you want."

James wanted to say more to Silver Wolf, to tell him how deeply he regretted his wife's words and actions, but he knew that this wasn't the time or place. Reluctantly, he stood. "I'll see you out at the ranch soon."

Silver Wolf only nodded in response and watched James walk away. Only then did he smile at Ben. He was glad his friend was there to distract him. "Why are you here, Ben? Did you come to meet Jenny? Jenny, this is my friend, Ben."

"Hello, Jenny," he said smoothly, then went on. "I'm here because I've been looking for you."

"Why?"

"I was worried about you."

"You didn't have to worry about me. I can take care of myself."

"I can tell. Looks like you've been doing a great job of it tonight."

"Jenny's been keeping me company."

"That was very nice of her, but what do you say we get you out of here while you can still walk?"

"Sit down and join us, Ben. Have a drink." He picked up the bottle and held it out to him.

"I'll pass for now," he declined.

Daniel shrugged off his refusal and took another swig, straight from the bottle this time. "You don't know what you're missing."

"Oh, yes I do, and *you're* going to find out in the morning. I think it's time we head home."

"Home . . ." His home was with his people in the village under the stars, not in the cramped, stuffy rooms over the law office. "It's a long ride to my home, Ben, and I don't think I'm quite up to makin' it tonight."

"All the more reason to come with me now. Tell Jenny good-bye."

Daniel slowly pushed away from the table.

"You're leaving?" Jenny asked, disappointed.

" 'Fraid so." He picked up the bottle, then got to his feet. He touched her cheek. "Bye, Jenny. Take care of yourself."

"You, too."

"Why don't you leave the whiskey here?" Ben suggested, seeing how glazed his eyes were.

"Nope, I mean to finish it." He took another swallow as they left the saloon and stepped out into the night.

Ben gave him a look of despairing amusement. "You're going to be sorry."

Daniel only shrugged again. He was unsteady on his feet, so

Ben kept a close eye on him as they made their way toward their rooms. They'd walked a block or so before Ben finally spoke up.

"You want to talk about what happened tonight?" He thought that might help Daniel. He was shocked when his friend stopped dead still and turned on him. Moments before, his expression had been slack, almost easygoing; now it was hard and cold.

"If you're my friend, you won't mention tonight again." He started to walk on.

Ben remained where he was, stunned, trying to grasp the sudden change in him. He realized that what had happened between Daniel and Mrs. McCord had been serious. He caught up with his friend and walked the rest of the way without speaking.

"Are you going to be all right?" Ben asked when they reached their rooms.

"Sure," he answered as he fumbled with his door, trying to juggle the bottle as he got out his key.

"See you in the morning." Ben watched Daniel until he'd gone in, then sought the quiet of his own room.

Silver Wolf entered his tiny, airless bedroom and shut the door behind him. He stood in the dark, trying to make up his mind whether or not to light the lamp. Deciding it wasn't worth the effort, he moved to his dresser and set the bottle down. Shrugging out of his jacket and taking off his tie, he tossed them both in the general direction of a chair.

The room was stifling, and he was badly in need of a breath of fresh air. He headed for the window to open it, then took a deep breath of the sweet night breeze, before going to the bed. He lay down and folded his arms beneath his head. He sought peace and quiet and forgetfulness, but every time he closed his eyes, the room seemed to go in motion.

Suddenly, everything seemed to be closing in on him, and he knew he had to get out. He practically threw himself from the bed, and quickly changed clothes. Once he was dressed to ride, he capped the whiskey bottle and stuffed it and the few other things he needed into his saddlebags. He scribbled a short note to Ben telling him he'd be back in a few days and slipped it under his friend's bedroom door on his way out to the stable.

Silver Wolf didn't breathe any easier until he'd left the lights of the town behind and had disappeared into the night. He welcomed the darkness and the solitude. He needed time alone. He needed time to think.

Since he'd been paid in advance for Jenny's services for the night, Ed offered no protest when she went upstairs after Daniel had gone.

Jenny stepped inside her room and closed the door, glad to be free of Ed and the others. She stared at the bed and thought of Daniel and the time they'd spent together. Just being with him had meant a lot to her, and though nothing physical had happened between them, she'd never felt closer to any man. He'd touched her deeply, in ways she didn't understand.

Jenny crossed to the bed and sat down on the side where Daniel had been and picked up the pillow. The scent of him was on it, and she held it to her breast, closing her eyes as she thought of him. She kept remembering what Daniel had said about her being pretty and not needing makeup, and, after a moment, she got up and went to the washstand. Wondering if he was right, she poured fresh water in the bowl and washed her face. Jenny stared at her own reflection, pink-cheeked now from cleanliness, not paint. Tears burned in her eyes as she saw not the woman she'd become in her mirror image, but the girl she'd left behind.

Pain and loneliness stabbed at her, and she returned to the bed, clutching the pillow to her as she lay down. She was reaching for the covers when she felt something strange among them. Brushing the blankets aside, she was startled to find a small leather pouch. She realized it must have fallen off Daniel's belt when she'd unfastened it.

Jenny picked up the medicine bag and thought about returning it to him right away, but decided it would be wiser to wait until the next morning. She sat up and moved closer to the light so she could see what was in it. Shaking out the contents into her hand, she stared at the strange collection, puzzled. There was no money in the pouch, only a strange-looking animal tooth, a chunk of mineral that looked to be silver, a pocketwatch without a chain, and a small white rock that was shaped like a heart.

Curious about the watch, Jenny opened it to find an inscription on the inside: *To my son, Jack, on his twentieth birthday. From your father, George Marshall.* She put it back, along with the tooth and silver, but kept the heart-shaped stone out to study a little longer. It felt warm against her palm, and she wondered where it had come from. She was sitting with the pouch in hand when the door opened without warning.

"Jenny! What are you doing up here already?" Mark Larson demanded as he brazenly walked right in on her.

"Mark . . ." She managed a smile as she quickly stood up. He was one of her regulars, and while he was no Daniel, he had never hurt her in any way.

"Evenin', girl," he said warmly. He'd had all the good manners and polite talk at the dance he could stand for the night. He was ready for some real fun now, and Jenny, he knew, was just the girl for that. She certainly knew how to please a man.

As he crossed the room toward her, he noticed that she was wearing no makeup. "What did you do to yourself? I don't like you this way," he complained.

His words hurt, but she didn't let him know. "I was about to go to bed."

"Well, good. We can go there together." He noticed that she was holding something in her hand. "What have you got there?"

It was then that he recognized the pouch and snatched it out of her hand. "Where did you get this?" He glared at her. "Was that half-breed with you tonight?"

"Yes, Daniel was here, but . . ."

"What in hell were you doing with that damned Indian?" Mark's temper exploded.

He backhanded Jenny viciously, sending her sprawling to the floor. As she fell, the stone slipped from her grip and slid beneath the bed. She had no time to think of the stone as Mark closed in on her.

"Mark . . . don't . . ." she cried. She couldn't believe this was happening. She didn't know what she'd done to deserve it.

Mark hated the half-breed with a passion, and he gave Jenny no chance to escape as he hit her again. He grabbed her up by the arm and gave her a vicious shake. "You're filth, you little whore! You'll give yourself to anybody for the right price, won't you? Pack your bags and get out of Cheyenne! There isn't a white man in town who'll want you now that you've been with an Indian!"

Jenny was sobbing. Blood trickled from her mouth and her eye was already swelling shut. "But nothing . . ."

Mark didn't care about anything she had to say. He slapped her again with all the force he could muster and then practically threw her down, as if touching her was contaminating him.

"If I ever hear that you were talking about anything that happened tonight, I'll find you and see that you pay even more!"

He turned his back on her, his temper appeased as he stared down at the medicine bag. He opened the pouch, picked up the watch, quickly reading the inscription. He smiled, reassured that he did indeed have a treasure of great worth. They'd been hoping for an opportunity to bring the arrogant half-breed down, and now, between his fight with the McCords at the dance and this, they had him. Mark gave Jenny one last disgusted look as she lay, nearly unconscious on the floor, and then he rushed off to find his father and show him the prize.

Jenny was dazed by the force of Mark's blows, and she lay still, tears streaming down her face. Nothing had happened with Daniel, but Mark had never given her the chance to explain.

Daniel . . . Jenny thought of his kindness and his gentle ways and knew he was ten times the man that Mark was. With a pained sob, she crawled toward the bed. Groping beneath it, her hand finally closed around what she sought: the heart-shaped stone. She held it tightly as she collapsed back on the floor. She knew she had to do what Mark said or face more of the same, and yet she clung to the memory that at least Daniel had been kind to her.

Twelve

For the third night in a row since they'd returned to the ranch from town, Cari lay in bed, wide-awake and waiting. It was after eleven, and she was beginning to wonder if her parents would ever go to sleep. When at last the house grew quiet, she got up, shed her nightgown, and dressed. This time, instead of donning her normal shoes, though, she slipped on the moccasins Silver Wolf had given her so long ago. She was glad they still fit, for she needed to walk silently tonight.

Opening her bedroom door, she peeked out into the hall to make sure everyone really was in bed. Once she was sure it was safe, she crept from her room and out of the house. Barnie was sleeping on the porch and she looked up when Cari stepped outside. Cari hastened to pet her so that she wouldn't bark and rouse her parents, then silently moved away from the house.

The moon was bright as Cari headed for the stream in the hope of seeing Silver Wolf. She was desperate to talk to him again. The memory of his kiss had haunted her every waking moment, and her dreams, too. She wanted to be with him again, to tell him how much he meant to her and how sorry she was for what had happened between him and her mother.

Since the night her mother had slapped Silver Wolf at the dance, Cari had barely managed to be civil to her. She'd expected the woman to admire him for what he'd achieved, and she couldn't believe she still held his Indian blood against him. As much as Silver Wolf meant to Cari, she couldn't let her mother go on thinking such terrible things about him. She wasn't sure how she was going to change her mother's attitude, but she definitely intended to try.

A soft breeze sighed through the trees, and the sweet song of a night bird lilted across the land as Cari moved down the hill and along the bank. It was a beautiful night, and she was hoping and praying that he would be there waiting for her.

Silver Wolf savored the solitude of the wilderness as he sorted through everything that had happened. That first morning alone there had reminded him of why he never drank. Not only had he had a pounding headache that had made it difficult for him to think, but he'd discovered that he'd somehow lost his medicine bag the night before. He remembered having it when he'd arrived at the saloon, but everything after that was confused. He hoped when he returned to town that he'd find it in his room. The bag contained his special "medicine," and he'd never been without it since he'd reached his manhood. He'd been tempted to return to town just to get it, but he'd found himself riding for the Circle M instead.

Silver Wolf had told himself he was being foolish returning to his and Little Snow's meeting place. He'd told himself he should go back to town and forget her, but he couldn't. He'd tried to strike her from his thoughts, but instead of fading, the memory of holding her in his arms and kissing her had just become all the more vivid. She'd been an innocent temptress, a fire in his embrace, and the thought that she might accept Elliot's proposal tormented him. In spite of her betrayal, he knew he had to see her again. That was why he'd come here this night.

Reaching the stream at dusk, he'd made camp and settled in for the night. Little Snow had never visited him after dark, so when sleep didn't quickly come to him, he decided to take advantage of the small pool nearby to bathe. Stripping down, he dove into the cool waters.

Silver Wolf was standing in the waist-deep water when he heard someone coming. He froze where he was to watch, not knowing who it might be. It was then that he saw her emerge from the sheltering cover of the trees.

Little Snow was a vision of beauty to him as she moved slowly forward, drawn toward the small campfire he'd built. He could tell that she was looking for him, but he remained where he was, taking the time to enjoy watching her. She was wearing her hair down, loose about her shoulders, and he remembered how silken it had been to his touch when he'd seen her here before, sleeping among the flowers. The dress she wore was simply styled, but the soft material hugged her body in a sweet caress. Enchanted, he could only stare.

Cari didn't know why she felt compelled to return to the clearing every night. Silver Wolf had never met her there after dark. Still, she'd had to come, the hope that he *might* be there driving her on. As she neared the clearing and saw the soft glow from a campfire, her heart leapt within her breast. She hurried forward, forgetting everything he'd taught her about moving quietly.

Reaching the edge of the clearing, Cari stared about the small glade, looking for Silver Wolf, but she could find no sign of him. Only the low-burning fire let her know that he was there. Cari heard something then, and she lifted her gaze to look farther downstream. Her breath caught in her throat as she saw him, standing motionlessly in the waist-deep pool of water. Silver Wolf. Her dream warrior! Moonlight shone down upon him, turning the glistening water on his bare chest and shoulders to a silver sheen. He looked like a magnificent creature of the wild, and she was mesmerized by the sight of him.

She said his name in a voice just above a whisper. "You're here . . . I was hoping you'd come."

At the sound of her voice, heat surged through him and

settled heavily in his loins. He knew a driving urge to take her in his arms, but he remained stoically where he was, allowing the cool waters not only temper his desire, but also shield his state of undress from her.

"Why were you hoping to see me, Little Snow?"

Across the darkly shadowed distance, their eyes met, and she saw reflected in his gaze the caution that held him in its grip. She started toward him, wanting him to trust her again. She stopped before him at the water's edge. "I've been coming here every night since we got back, because I had to tell you that I'm sorry for what happened between you and my mother. She was wrong, Silver Wolf, very wrong."

"Are you so sure?" His pride held him immobile, though he really wanted to hold her and kiss her and never let her go.

"I'm sure. I know you, Silver Wolf. I've known you all my life. No matter what my mother or the gossips think, you would never do anything to hurt me."

Cari knew she had to prove to him again just how important he was to her. She bent and slipped her precious moccasins from her feet. Lifting her skirts, she ignored the chill of the water and waded out toward him.

The water was cold and swirled chillingly about her slender legs, but she hardly noticed. Her need to touch him again was foremost in her mind. She moved forward, knowing that she was getting her dress wet and not caring. She came to stand before him, and her gaze was open and honest as she looked up at him in the moonlight.

"I love you, Silver Wolf." She lifted one hand to tenderly caress the cheek her mother had slapped.

Her words erased all the pain and all the doubts he'd been feeling. Giving in to his need to hold her, he swept her up in his arms and crushed her to his chest.

"What about Elliot?" His eyes were a dark, stormy gray as they challenged hers.

"He's a friend," she told him as she wrapped her arms about his neck.

"Little Snow . . ." At her response, he could bear it no

longer, and he said her name in a groan of passion as his mouth descended to claim hers.

Cari clung to him. She realized that this was what she'd been longing for ever since they'd parted so painfully at the dance.

Silver Wolf held her close, savoring the moment. When the kiss ended, he strode toward the bank with her in his arms, taking care to keep her dress from getting wetter. Carrying her up on the bank, he laid her down upon the soft grass and then stretched out beside her.

Cari was thrilled that they were finally together, alone, and she smiled up at him in the moonlit darkness. "I was afraid I wouldn't see you again," she told him, her heart shining in her eyes. "Even though we were only apart three days, it seemed like eternity to me."

"I missed you, too," he said softly as he bent to kiss her.

She looped her arms about his neck and drew him down to her as she returned his kiss. He was the living, breathing standard to which she'd compared all other men, and by which all others had failed.

Cari met Silver Wolf in kiss after desperate kiss, unable to deny the power of her love for him. She ran her hands over his bare chest and shoulders, sculpting the hard-muscled planes. They'd embraced before, but there had never been this awareness between them— this knowledge of man and woman and desire. His kiss was her heaven. They had waited so long, and now . . . now it just seemed right.

When Silver Wolf began to caress her, his hands skimming over her in a light but arousing touch, she shivered in anticipation, and when he freed the buttons at the bodice of her dress and bared her breasts to his hungry gaze, she was panting with excitement. No man had ever touched her this way before, but it didn't matter. This was Silver Wolf. She knew now that she'd been saving herself for just this moment.

"Please, Silver Wolf . . . teach me . . ." Cari urged him.

"Are you sure, Little Snow?" Silver Wolf drew slightly away, giving her the chance to think about what she was saying. He'd known she would be warm and loving and responsive to him, and he desired her as he'd never desired another, but he wanted her to be certain.

"Oh, yes. I love you. I always have and I always will . . ."

He gazed down at her and saw the joy in her eyes. He knew then that there would be no stopping. With utmost care, his lips moved over hers in a deep, hungry exchange, and then he moved lower to trail hot kisses down her throat. Excitement pulsed through Cari, and she began to move restlessly beneath him as he sought to lave her breasts with kisses.

"You're lovely, Little Snow." Silver Wolf lifted his head to look down at her, his eyes glittering with desire as he gazed upon her tender flesh.

She was embarrassed by his words and shifted to try to cover herself. He smiled gently at her.

"Don't be shy, love. I've always known you would be this beautiful."

The feelings he was creating within her were as exciting as they were strange, and though she wasn't sure what was going to happen next, she trusted him completely. She framed his face with her hands. "I think I've waited all my life for this moment . . . for you . . ."

Silver Wolf kissed her again. His lips were soft and persuasive upon hers, and then he moved to the sweetness of her throat once again. He explored the hollow there and the fluttering, rapid beat of her pulse, before seeking out the fullness of her breasts. Cari began to tremble beneath him as he caressed her.

Cari gasped in pleasure at his intimate touches. When she was almost to the point of being mindless with wanting him, he stopped, and she looked up at him with wide, questioning eyes.

"I need to see you. All of you," he explained hoarsely.

He shifted a little away from her to help her shed her dress, and she gasped at her first sight of his naked body. He reminded her of one of the statues she'd seen in a museum back in Philadelphia. His body was perfect, from the strong width of his chest and shoulders roped with powerful muscle to the narrow leanness of his waist and hips. Silver Wolf was no cold marble sculpture, though. He was a flesh and blood man who wanted her, and she rejoiced in the knowledge.

Silver Wolf gazed down at Little Snow, his heart filled with more emotions than he could ever possibly express. She'd always been the woman he'd adored above all others. She had held his heart since that very first winter night. Few others ever knew the kind of closeness they shared, and now he wanted— no *needed*— to be one with her. He moved over her, fitting himself to her, feeling how perfect they were for each other, yet being careful and gentle, for he knew this was new to her.

The heat of him against her seared Cari, and she trembled.

"Are you all right?" he asked, tensing suddenly for fear that he'd hurt her.

Cari smiled as she wrapped her arms around him and hugged him close. She'd never known emotions so intense before. "I'm fine," she answered, smiling up at him. She'd loved him since that first icy night when he'd appeared out of the darkness to save her, and she gazed up at him now with the same heartfelt trust she'd felt then.

He looked down at her, enraptured. With reverence, he pressed a soft kiss to her forehead, then met her lips in a cherishing kiss. When at last her trembling subsided and he felt she was ready, he freed the passion chained within him. He was thrilled when Little Snow responded without reserve.

Cari wanted to show him how much he meant to her. She wanted to please him as he was pleasing her, and she caressed him with an eagerness that took his breath away.

No longer able to deny himself the glory of union with her, Silver Wolf rose up over her. With great care, he positioned himself and pressed forward. The tight heat of her as he slowly sheathed himself within her left him breathless. She stiffened instinctively against him.

"Easy, my love," he whispered against her lips, and at his words she forced herself to relax.

Silver Wolf kissed her deeply then as he thrust forward, piercing her innocent body with the proof of his love and claiming her for his own. A whimper escaped Cari as he began to move, but he stilled her pain with loving kisses and caresses. His hands traced paths of fire over her silken flesh, and soon she forgot the initial discomfort and was reveling in the wonder of the moment.

Around them the night was Elysian. The moon high above them shone softly down on them as they tasted for the first time the pure ecstasy of their love. Their each caress built upon the last until suddenly the breathtaking heights of love's exquisite reward claimed them. Spellbound, they clung together, soaring to the heavenly peak as one.

The night birds' serenade blended with the stream's musical passage to create a symphony. Enchantment was theirs. They lay together, glorying in the beauty of what had just passed between them.

Silver Wolf cradled her in his arms, marveling at the power of the love he felt for her. For the first time in his life, he felt truly alive.

A sense of peace and contentment stole over them, and, as in the distance a wolf's song echoed through the night, they slept.

Elizabeth could not sleep. She and Cari had barely spoken since the night of the dance, and her heart was heavy with unhappiness over the distance between them. She loved her daughter more than life itself, and she only wanted what was best for her.

Afraid that she'd disturb James with her tossing and turning, Elizabeth rose from bed and, after pulling on her robe, went to Cari's bedroom. She didn't know if her daughter was asleep or not, but she wanted to check. If Cari *was* awake, Elizabeth thought this would be a good time for the two of them to talk, uninterrupted.

Taking care not to wake either James or Elliot, she reached Cari's door and gave a very soft knock. When there was no answer, she turned the knob, and finding it unlocked, she opened it to peek inside.

Cari looked to be sound asleep under the covers. A rush of love filled Elizabeth, and wanting to make peace with her daughter, she tiptoed inside to give her a good night kiss just as she'd done when Cari was a baby. To Elizabeth's horror, though, when she reached the side of the bed, she discovered that Cari was not there. The bed was empty, camouflaged to make it look like she was sleeping.

Elizabeth went cold inside as she looked around and noticed Cari's nightgown tossed negligently across a chair. Her one desperate hope was that Cari was with Elliot. As Elizabeth stood in the darkness considering that a terrible feeling overcame her. Cari and Elliot had been cordial since the dance, but hardly acting like lovers. No. As much as she would have liked to deny it to herself, she knew exactly where her daughter had gone.

Fury filled Elizabeth. She gave no thought to the time when she was young and madly in love with James. All she could think of was her precious daughter lying with that terrible half-breed. Ready to fight the fiercest battle of her life, she was determined to put a stop to this nonsense once and for all. Snatching up a lamp from the hall, she lit it and then headed straight for the stream.

Cari hadn't meant to fall asleep, and she awoke to find Silver Wolf still beside her. He was awake and had braced himself up on one elbow to watch her. She smiled dreamily up at him.

"Hello."

His kiss was his greeting, and she sighed in contentment. She lay quietly for another moment, treasuring the wonder of being with him, wanting it to never end. Reality soon crept in.

"Silver Wolf, I have to get back," she murmured apologetically even as she made no move to leave his side.

"I know," he answered, the regret he was feeling over parting from her sounding in his voice.

"When will I see you again?"

"If I had my way, I would never leave you." He bent to her

and kissed her, telling her with his passionate embrace just how much she meant to him.

"I want to stay with you, too." A sigh from the depths of her soul escaped her. She had never wanted to leave him— not when her mother had dragged her off to school and not now.

"Marry me, Little Snow . . ."

At his words, she gazed up at him, her eyes glowing with excitement. "Oh, Silver Wolf. . . . There's nothing I want more than to be with you."

They kissed again, unwilling to move apart. It was with great regret that Silver Wolf finally put her from him. He knew if he didn't let her go now, he might *never* do it. He stood and, taking her hands, he drew her to her feet and along with him down to the pool.

"The water's going to be cold . . ." Little Snow argued.

"Hasn't it always been my job to keep you warm?" he said with a smile as he picked her up and strode into the water.

She thought about trying to escape him, but her trust in him won out and she hung on to his neck for dear life, expecting at any minute to be freezing to death in the icy water. To her surprise, though, the water in the quiet pool felt warm, and she immediately relaxed. His hands were gentle as he set her on her feet and, with cherishing caresses, bathed her.

Little Snow stood still under his arousing ministrations, learning things about her own body. His hands sought out her most intimate places, building a throbbing need within her, and she gripped his shoulders tightly for fear that her knees might buckle for the ecstasy of it. Silver Wolf caressed her, enjoying giving her pleasure. When they'd made love, they'd both been satisfied, but now he wanted just to please her. He knew her virgin's body would not be able to stand another joining with him, and she was so responsive that he couldn't resist loving her this way. At the touch of his lips upon her breasts the need within her exploded to breathtaking heights that left her senses reeling.

"Silver Wolf . . ." She gasped his name as she held tightly to him.

They stood, embracing in the waters, each having found in the other the meaning of true bliss. He had never known giving pleasure without seeking his own reward could be so fulfilling. He held her in the circle of his arms until the splendor of the moment had passed, and only then did he carry her from the stream.

He donned his breechcloth and leggings and then helped her to dress. He resented the clothing that covered her sweet curves, hiding them from his view, but he knew she had to get back to the house.

Silver Wolf drew her into his arms for one last embrace. It was a passionate, blazing exchange that neither of them wanted to end . . .

The condemning voice when it came out of the night slashed at the young lovers and drove them apart.

"I knew I'd find you here with him!" Elizabeth's words were as cold and icy as her heart as she stared at the two of them embracing.

"Mother!" Cari couldn't believe that her mother had come after her and she tore herself from Silver Wolf's arms.

Silver Wolf could sense Little Snow's upset, and would not let her face her mother's anger alone. He put his arm around her waist and kept her close to his side as he greeted the woman.

"I should have known you'd sneak around behind my back like the savage you are. Cari! I want you to go back to the house right now!" Elizabeth ordered in a tone that brooked no argument.

"It's not what you think . . ." she began, but her mother would have none of it.

"I know exactly what went on here, my dear. I want you to go back to the house and stay in your room until I've had time to talk to your father."

At the dance, Cari had been caught unawares by her mother's hostility, but now she would not remain silent. "No, Mother. I won't go."

Elizabeth seethed in the face of her defiance.

"Cari's not a little girl anymore, and she's made her decision, Mrs. McCord."

"You kept us apart by stealing our letters for all those years, Mother, but you can't keep us apart any longer."

"I was trying to protect you, to make sure you had a better life!"

"A better life than what?" Cari challenged.

"Than sneaking around with a man who isn't worthy of you!"

"Worthy of me?"

"Do you realize what kind of life you'd have with him?" Elizabeth sneered. "People would talk about you and belittle you. Your children would be outcasts. Do you want that kind of life?" She turned on Silver Wolf then, daring him to refute her words. "Do you want her to have that kind of life?"

"What other people think or say doesn't matter to us, Mrs. McCord."

Elizabeth bristled.

"I love Silver Wolf, Mother, and I want to be with him."

"We'll see about that! Just look at you!" Elizabeth's gaze went over Silver Wolf. Tonight, dressed in his Indian garb, he looked the heathen again. "Stay away from my daughter!"

Cari would have none of her interference. "Mother, your hatred has blinded you. Please, listen to me. Silver Wolf has asked me to marry him, and—"

"You'll *never* marry him! Your father and I have already talked about this, and he's in complete agreement with me! There will be no marriage between you!" Elizabeth exploded. "Now, let's go!"

Cari looked up at Silver Wolf, her heart in her eyes. "I'd better go with her."

"I'm coming along," he declared staunchly.

She put a gentle yet restraining hand on his shoulder. "No, please. Not tonight. I'll deal with it myself. Trust me. No one will separate us ever again."

"Little Snow, I . . ." He glanced up at Elizabeth, not trusting her and fearing that something would happen to destroy the beauty of what he and Little Snow had shared tonight.

"Cari, I'm waiting for you," Elizabeth called out in a terse tone as she fixed them with an icy glare.

"We plan to be together, Mrs. McCord," Silver Wolf declared as he met the woman's condemning look.

Cari rose up on her tiptoes to give him a quick kiss. "Give me a few days to convince her."

"All right, if that's what you want."

"It is."

"I'll be back," he promised.

Elizabeth watched her daughter kiss Silver Wolf, and she began to shake with the power of her fury. She stormed back to the house with Cari following her.

James awoke when he heard noise, and thinking that it meant trouble from intruders, went downstairs to see what had happened. He frowned as he found his wife and daughter in the kitchen, their expressions angry, their manner strained.

"What's going on?" he demanded.

"Take a good look at your daughter, James. I just caught her with that Indian down by the creek!" Elizabeth told him.

He looked from his wife to his daughter in confusion. "Why did you sneak off in the middle of the night?" he demanded of Cari.

"You and Mother don't approve of him, and so Silver Wolf thought he wasn't welcome here, Papa."

"And he *isn't* welcome here!" Elizabeth declared.

"Silver Wolf is *always* welcome in this house," James said adamantly, drawing a desperate look from his wife.

"James! I don't want Cari anywhere near him!" she protested, afraid that her worst fears were coming to pass.

James heaved a sigh of agitation. "Let's all go to sleep and talk about it in the morning."

"I want to talk about it now! How can you expect me to sleep knowing what went on tonight!" She'd been patient; she'd been tolerant; she'd suffered through years of living in the middle of nowhere just to please her husband, but she refused to see her daughter suffer the same fate. She wanted better things for Cari. She wanted her to enjoy life. Elliot was the perfect man for her, not the half-breed.

"Elizabeth, Cari is the one who must choose who she wants to marry. It's not our decision."

"How can you say such a thing? Just look at her!"

James smiled a crooked smile. "I'm not so old that I don't remember when you looked that way when I took you home. Let's go to bed, Elizabeth. Good night, Cari."

He started upstairs, his heart heavy. He fully understood Cari's passion, but he also wanted to keep peace with his wife. She had finally come back to the ranch to live, and he wanted her to stay with him.

"What are you going to do, James?" Elizabeth asked when they were alone in their room.

"I don't know yet," he answered.

"You have to do *something!* What if they run off together?"

"Would that be so terrible?"

"Do you want your only daughter married to an Indian?"

James took her by the shoulders as his gaze bore down into hers. "Elizabeth, the day is coming when you're going to have to change your way of thinking. I don't know why you hate Silver Wolf and his tribe so much. Lord knows I've tried everything to help you understand that they're good people."

She trembled beneath his hands. "They're little better than animals . . ."

His grip tightened on her shoulders as if he could somehow force her to understand. "Silver Wolf has more education than I do. Ben Douglas is his best friend, and he's a senator's son. Silver Wolf has worked in Washington, and he deals with the Army on a regular basis. He's more civilized than most of the whites around here, Elizabeth. You'd be wise to remember that."

She wasn't ready to concede anything in Silver Wolf's behalf, and she stood silent and unchastened before him.

Disgusted, he released her. "Let's go to bed. Dawn's going to come soon."

Thirteen

At his wife's words, James lifted his head to stare at her across the kitchen table. He couldn't believe the demand she'd just made of him, and his dark eyes were cold, mirroring his displeasure with her request. "No, Elizabeth. You're not taking Cari back East again."

Elizabeth had plotted all night, but now as she confronted James with her plan to keep Cari and Silver Wolf apart, her hopes sank. "It's the only way to make her see reason! Don't you realize—"

"I realize plenty," he cut her off brusquely, "and though I've always gone along with your wishes concerning Cari, this time is different. She's staying here."

"She can't!" Elizabeth panicked.

"And why not?" he railed. Then after getting control of himself, he continued in a gentler, more conciliatory tone. "Elizabeth, listen to me. Cari's happy here on the ranch. She doesn't want to leave."

"You don't understand. She should have the best life has to offer!"

James's pain grew, and he said quietly, "I thought I was giving you both the best life has to offer."

"You gave us what you thought was the best." She was unable to stop the words of bitterness as they spilled forth. "You never asked us what we wanted. You just did whatever suited your fancy. You always thought about pleasing yourself. You never gave one thought to me or my needs. If you wanted to go west, you went. If you wanted to buy a ranch, you bought it. You've never cared about me and Cari. All you've ever really cared about is this damned ranch!"

Tears streaming down her face, Elizabeth was mortified that she'd blurted out all the pain and anger she'd kept hidden within her for so long. She loved James, but his devotion to the Circle M had hurt her. Many times his quest to build the ranch had taken precedence over his family. Even as recently as Cari's graduation, the ranch had come first! Tears burned her eyes as she remembered how she'd longed to have him with her on that graduation night, and how they'd ended up celebrating the evening with Elliot and George.

James's face was set like granite as he finally accepted that nothing had ever really changed between them. She didn't share his dream of a dynasty in the territory, and he knew now that she never would. In fact, other than their marriage bed, it occurred to him that they shared precious little. Her weeping stabbed at his heart, and it seemed obvious to him that she thought him a failure as both a husband and a father. He stood up slowly and picked up his hat.

"I'm leaving." His words were gruff and final.

"Where are you going?"

"Who knows? Anywhere but here would be inviting."

"I don't want my daughter married to that Indian," she repeated.

"You've made yourself quite clear on the subject."

"And?"

"And what?"

"What do you plan to do about it?"

His expression saddened. "You have a very different dream

for our daughter's future than she has for herself, and you've made it very clear to me that I must give up my dream for making the Circle M a success if I want you to be happy. Are you only happy when things go the way you want them to? Must you take everyone's dreams from them?"

"James!" She gasped at the harshness of his observations. "That's not fair! You know how the Indians live . . . how uncivilized they are. I just want Cari to be happy, and she won't be happy with him."

James shot her a black look as he jammed his hat on his head. "That's your opinion, not hers. Now, I've got a ranch to run and stock to tend."

He stalked out of the house, heading toward the stables where his saddled mount was waiting for him. His heart was heavy as he mounted up, his mood solemn and pensive. He glanced back at the house he'd so lovingly built for his wife, but there was no sign of her. It looked deserted and lifeless. He rode away and didn't look back again.

James rode at a steady, ground-eating pace and didn't stop until he was far from the house. He needed some time alone, and he sought out the rocky outcropping with the expansive view that had become one of his favorite places on the ranch. After turning his horse loose to graze, he sat down to gaze out across the land he loved, the land that was his world.

The hours passed, and still James found no peace. It was a dilemma that tore at the very fabric of his soul. He admired Silver Wolf, and loved him almost as a son. If Cari wanted to be with him, he had no objection. Silver Wolf was a fine, intelligent man. As much as he wanted to completely ignore Elizabeth's arguments against them being together, however, she did have one important point. As prejudiced as some of their neighbors were, it wouldn't be an easy life for Cari being married to Silver Wolf. Still, James believed if they loved each other enough, none of the other things would bother them.

James thought about giving up his dream to please his wife, but something deep within him balked at the idea. He wondered if what Elizabeth had said was true. *Was* he being selfish?

He loved the ranch, that much was true, but he'd been doing all the work for his family.

Only when the sun began to sink low in the western sky did James even think about heading back. He believed Cari was old enough to make her own decisions, and he believed she should be allowed to do that. For himself, it looked like it all came down to a single choice. He could have the Circle M or he could have Elizabeth. From the way she'd been acting when he'd left, he doubted seriously that he could have both. Reluctantly, he started toward the house. He rode slowly.

It was dark by the time James reached the pasture where Lord Anthony was being kept. Charlie Houser, one of his men, was camped in the area to keep an eye on the expensive animal, and James was watching for some sign of his campfire. He spotted the soft glow of a fire in the distance and was riding toward it, when he heard what sounded like a bellow of distress from the bull. Reining in abruptly, he waited in silence, listening closely as he tried to figure out from which direction the sound had come. It came again, distant and troubled from near the fire, and he quickly went to investigate.

James didn't want to think that the Larsons were right, that there might be rustlers. He hoped this wasn't trouble, but he was glad he had his rifle with him, anyway. He topped a low rise, and from that vantage point could see more clearly the small campfire in the distance. He could make out Lord Anthony tied up there and three men moving around the fire.

James knew something was wrong when he didn't recognize any of the trespassers. There was no sign of Charlie. The only good sign was that the men were definitely white and not Cheyenne. So, while the Larsons might be right about rustlers working the area, at least they weren't Indians.

Determined to put a stop to their activities, James pulled his rifle from its sheath. He knew he was outnumbered, so he thought it important that he have the element of surprise on his side. He rode quietly toward the campfire, his rifle at the ready.

"Well, boys, is there a good reason why you're on Circle M land tonight?" His voice was deep and powerful as he reined to a stop just outside the campfire's circle of light. He kept the barrel of his rifle pointed at them so they would have no doubts about the seriousness of his intent.

The three cowboys in the camp looked up in surprise to see James McCord sitting on his stallion, his rifle aimed straight at their chests. He looked as mean and fearsome as they'd heard tell he was, and the rustlers grew nervous.

"It's McCord . . ." one of them gulped in surprise.

"You're damned right, it's McCord!" James thundered. "Who the hell else did you think it would be? This is my land, and that's my prize bull you've got tied up over there. There a reason why you're here on my property?"

"We're just passing through and made camp here for the night." One rustler tried to smooth-talk his way out of trouble.

"And I suppose my bull was going to just pass on through with you, right? Where's Charlie?"

"We don't know . . ."

James didn't believe a word of what they were saying. "Well, if you all are just passing through, then you won't mind stepping over by the fire in the light so I can see your faces real clear. I want to see who I'm dealing with here."

They did as they were told, and James studied their faces closely. "You certainly aren't Cheyenne, are you? In fact, at first I didn't think I knew any of you, but now that I can see you in the light . . ."

James didn't get to finish the sentence as a blinding pain slammed into his chest. The impact of the bullet threw him from his horse, and his rifle went flying from his grip as he hit the ground.

Distantly, he heard someone say "Nice shot!" as he lay unmoving, his life's blood draining into the dirt. He stared up at the sky, seeing the pinpoints of light that were stars and the sliver of a moon that did not give off enough light to brighten his way. He wanted to get up and continue the fight, he wanted to save the Hereford bull, but he couldn't move. Weakness overcame him, and his limbs felt leaden.

James was vaguely aware of someone giving a menacing

laugh as he moved closer in the darkness, but his ability to think clearly was deserting him. He struggled to get a look at the man who'd shot him, but his assailant stayed out of sight and he never learned his identity.

Elizabeth slipped into his thoughts, and the realization that he was dying and would never see her again was more painful to him than his mortal wound. He fought with all his might to live. He loved Elizabeth! He would give up the ranch and everything he owned if only he had the chance to tell her once more that he loved her! They had parted in anger, and now . . .

"Elizabeth . . ." Her name was a choked whisper that died on his lips and was lost on the night wind.

Death. . . . There would be no tomorrow for James so he could ease the pain of their parting. There would be no second chance for him to set things right with the woman he adored. There was only silence and coldness and a terrible emptiness in the night.

"Wasn't there some way to avoid this?" Sam demanded of his son as he came to kneel beside McCord's body.

"Do you think I wanted to kill him? He rode in with his rifle ready and caught the men with the bull," Mark defended his act. "We'd already had to kill his hired hand to get the damned Hereford, and then he came riding in out of nowhere . . ."

"Did you have to shoot him?"

"What else was I going to do?" Mark exploded. "Challenge him to a duel? There was no time, Pa. I had to get rid of him. He'd already seen the men, and he'd have gotten a look at me next. It came down to him or me."

Sam finally nodded, his expression sober as he planned their next move. "You still got the half-breed's medicine bag?"

"In my saddlebag."

"Get it."

Mark brought it to his father, and Sam took it and pressed it into James's lifeless hand.

"I knew it would come in handy. Somebody will come looking for James in a day or two, and when they do, they'll find
him, and the medicine bag, too." Sam Larson stared around
the campsite. "When it's found, it'll be the hangman's noose
for Marshall. . . . If he lives long enough to make it to a hanging, that is."

The thought of a lynching brought a sharkish smile to Sam's
face. With James murdered and Marshall blamed for it, it
would be a simple thing to stir up the ranchers and the Army
against the Indians. He might just get his wish after all.

"What about the bull?" he asked.

"The boys will take him to the box canyon and keep him
there until things settle down."

"I have a feeling that may be a while."

"That's all right. The Hereford's worth waiting for. Make
sure our tracks are covered as we leave. There's too much at
risk here for us to be careless. One stupid mistake could ruin
it all."

Mark erased all evidence that they'd ever been there. The
men took one last look at James McCord, then rode away.

After James left, Elizabeth agonized over their argument.
The more she thought about what he'd said, the more she
realized he'd been right about a lot of the things. She'd accused him of selfishness, but her own self-centeredness was
inexcusable. She loved James, and she wanted to make him
happy.

Suddenly, Elizabeth knew it was important that she prove to
him just how much he meant to her. She'd seen a beautiful
piece of material at a drygoods store in Cheyenne, and she
decided to buy it so she could make a new dress and look
pretty for James when he returned. Shopping had always made
her feel better when she'd lived in Philadelphia, and she hoped
it would help now, too.

When Elliot joined her for breakfast and she suggested they
make the trip to town, he readily agreed. Cari came down a

few minutes later, her expression and manner guarded, and Elizabeth was glad Elliot was with her, for his presence kept them from dredging up what had happened the night before.

"I need to pick up a few things in town, and Elliot's agreed to accompany me. Would you like to come with us?" Elizabeth hoped that if she pretended nothing had happened, then they might actually have a pleasant outing together.

"Where's Papa?" Cari ventured cautiously.

"He's gone out to see to the herd, and he didn't say when he'd be back, so I thought it would be a good time to make the trip into town."

"All right, I'll go," Cari agreed, surprised that her mother was acting as if absolutely nothing unusual had occurred.

"Good, we'll have a nice time."

Cari wasn't so sure, but she smiled in agreement anyway, glad for the momentary reprieve from another confrontation with her about Silver Wolf. She'd passed a miserable night, lying awake for hours, trying to figure out a way to convince her that her love for Silver Wolf was real, but she could think of no new argument to sway her. Her mother seemed determined to hate him, and she was at a loss how to change her. She hoped this short trip together would help ease things between them. Elliot's presence would prevent them from discussing the previous night in any great detail, and Cari thought that was just as well. Until she spoke with her father and found out what had been said that morning, she was better off keeping busy.

"We're getting such a late start that we'll probably have to spend the night, so pack a few things," Elizabeth told her. "I'll leave a note for your father so he doesn't worry, and we'll be back first thing tomorrow."

In a very short time, they were on their way. Cari managed to keep up the small talk on the trek into town, but even as she spoke of inconsequential things, her heart and thoughts were centered on Silver Wolf. She wondered where he was, what he was doing, and how soon he'd return to the ranch to see her. He'd said he'd be back, and she hoped it wouldn't be

very long before he returned, for she longed to be in his arms
again.

They reached town later that afternoon and took two rooms
at the hotel for the night. After settling in, they went off to
the store to see about the material Elizabeth wanted to buy.

Cari felt a little awkward with Elliot. She knew it was time
she told him the truth, but she wanted to do it privately when
it was just the two of them. The opportunity came sooner than
she expected, for her mother, hoping Cari and Elliot's being
together in town would rekindle their feelings for each other,
decided to retire to her room for a rest after their shopping
trip. Alone together, they went into the hotel dining room for
a drink. When the waitress brought them their glasses of lem-
onade, Cari bravely broached the subject so close to her heart.

"We need to talk, Elliot," she said as she took a sip of her
cooling beverage.

The expression in his eyes saddened as he looked at her
across the small table. "About Silver Wolf?"

"You know?"

"It wasn't difficult to figure out, Cari," he told her. "I was
awake last night and heard part of the discussion between your
parents."

Color stained her cheeks.

Elliot didn't want her to be embarrassed; he just wanted to
know the truth. "I think I've known how you felt about him
since I saw the way you looked at him at the dance . . . but
tell me the truth, Cari. Do you love him?"

"Oh, yes," she answered, her eyes glowing with happiness
as she met his probing gaze. "I've loved him ever since I was
a little girl."

Cari's smile faltered as she realized how badly she'd just hurt
him. She reached across the table to touch his hand. "I like
you, Elliot. I really do. I'm sorry I couldn't love you."

He took her hand in his. "So am I." He paused briefly before continuing sadly. "I could tell your mother's not happy about it. Do you think she'll come around?"

"I don't know. She's never liked Silver Wolf. I think he's the reason she took me back East in the first place, and then when she destroyed all our letters . . ." Cari explained the lengths her mother had gone to to keep them apart.

"I hope things work out for you." Elliot let his gaze go over her lovely features, committing them to memory. He'd loved her for a long time now, and it wasn't going to be easy to let her go.

"Thank you."

"Since I'm in town, I think I'll walk on down to the train station and check the schedule."

"I'll go with you," she offered.

A flash of pain shone in his eyes. "No. I'd rather do this by myself," he answered abruptly.

"You don't have to leave yet, you know. You can stay as long as you like."

Elliot could only manage a lopsided grin. "I appreciate your hospitality, but I think it's time I go."

"I'll miss you." Cari felt him drawing away from her.

"Oh, no you won't." He laughed dryly as he rose from the table. "Silver Wolf will see to that."

They shared a bittersweet smile, knowing they would never be lovers but that they would always be friends.

After he left her, Cari felt lonely and at loose ends. Talking about Silver Wolf had left her missing him even more. She thought about going up to the room, but knew her mother would ask her where Elliot had gone, and she didn't want to brave that conversation right then. Deciding to go for a walk around town, she made her way from the hotel alone.

When Cari returned a little later, she found that Elliot was back and visiting with her mother. He'd made arrangements to leave on the train the following week, and Cari could tell that her mother was distressed by the news. There was little conversation during dinner, and they retired early, for they wanted to get an early start on the ride back to the ranch in the morning.

* * *

Elizabeth was anxious to see James, and she was watching the house as they rode up, eagerly anticipating that he would come out to greet them. When he didn't, she thought he might still be angry with her and she hurried inside to find him and apologize. She was startled to find her note right where she'd left it and no sign that he'd been home at all.

"Papa isn't back yet?" Cari asked as she followed her inside.

"I don't know. It looks like he didn't come home last night," she answered worriedly. They'd had fights before, but they'd never spent a night apart in anger.

"I'll go out and check with the hands. Maybe he's with them or maybe they've heard from him," Elliot offered.

Elliot had no news when he returned, but the hands had told him not to worry, that sometimes James ran into a problem out on the range and stayed out an extra day or two to take care of it.

This news didn't make Elizabeth feel better. She was sorry for the fight and wanted to make it up to him. She'd finally come to realize in this time apart, that though she'd always professed to love him, she'd always tried to change him, to make him cater to her wishes and desires. If she truly loved him, she asked herself, shouldn't his happiness be more important to her than her own?

Elizabeth grew contrite as she finally realized that James had been right, that it had been her own selfishness that was ruining what they had together. Tears came to her eyes as she thought of the flowers he'd planted for her homecoming. She thought of her irrational fear of the Cheyenne and of how cruel she'd been to Silver Wolf even though he'd saved Cari's life.

She suddenly understood that she'd failed James miserably. As she wiped away her tears, she vowed to change. She would give up her childish desire to go back East and she would become a true rancher's wife, a wife James could be proud of. She would work by his side and help him build the Circle M into the best ranch in the territory. She would forget about

Philadelphia and her wish for Cari to marry Elliot. She loved James, and she was going to prove it to him . . . if he only would hurry home so she could!

Curling up on her cold, solitary bed late that night, Elizabeth lay awake, listening anxiously for the sounds of his horse's hoofbeats. The minute she heard him returning she planned to meet him at the door. It was long past two in the morning when she finally fell into a troubled sleep.

When Elizabeth awoke the following morning, she was devastated to discover that James still hadn't returned. She made her way downstairs to find Cari fixing breakfast.

"I owe you an apology, Cari."

Her mother's change of heart was so unexpected that Cari glanced up at her in surprise. "What?"

"I was trying to force you to live *my* dream instead of *yours*. I'm sorry. I thought I knew what was best for you, but I realize now that I didn't even know what was best for me."

"Oh, Mother . . ." Cari forgot all about cooking and went to hug her.

"I'm sorry, dear and I only hope your father gets back soon so I can apologize to him, too."

"I love Silver Wolf, Mother."

"I know." She met her daughter's gaze, and for the first time, understanding existed between them.

Elliot came downstairs a short time later, and they all breakfasted together. As the hours passed, Elizabeth's concern about James grew. She tried not to let it show, but every time she heard a noise, she rushed to a window to see if he was returning. She managed to keep herself busy with housework and cooking, but when darkness fell and their third night apart began, she couldn't ignore her fears anymore. Something was wrong, very wrong. She called several of the hands to the house and told Hank and Fred to start searching for James at first light.

Elizabeth didn't sleep the rest of that night. The hours passed in miserable torment for her. At first light, the men

rode out as she'd directed, and it was late the following afternoon when she heard Cari call her. Elizabeth thought her
daughter sounded excited, and she dropped what she was doing and ran from the house, smiling because she thought
James had finally come home. What she saw when she
emerged from the house to join her daughter and Elliot on
the front porch sent shock waves through her. Hank and Fred
were riding up to the house leading two horses, and the horses
looked to be ladened with bodies.

Elizabeth stared at them, her heart in her throat, unable to
breathe, unable to speak. When she realized that Cari was already running toward them, she started to follow, but Elliot
grabbed her arm to stop her.

"Wait!" he cautioned.

But she would have none of it. A terrible feeling was welling
up inside her, and she was desperate to know the truth. She
broke free and ran after her daughter.

"What is it? What happened?" Cari asked frantically.

"It's your father, Miss Cari," Fred told her miserably.

"What?"

"We found him . . ."

"You found him where?" Elizabeth demanded as she
reached them.

Fred saw the desperate looks on their faces and knew he had
to speak the truth, no matter how painful. He glanced at Elliot,
who'd come with Elizabeth, and gave him a man-to-man look
as he told them, "James is dead, Mrs. McCord. He was shot.
We found his body with Charlie's up where they were keeping
the Hereford."

A scream tore from the depths of Elizabeth's soul, but she
wasn't even aware that she'd made the sound. A wild look shone
in her eyes. Elliot tried again to prevent her from going to
James, but she was too quick for him. She tore at the ropes that
held the covering over his body and went pale when it fell away.
Her eyes widened in horror at the sight of her dead husband.

"James! Dear God . . . no!!" she cried. She swayed as black-
ness closed in around her, and she slumped to the ground.

Cari rushed to her mother's side and dropped to her knees beside her. "Mother . . ."

Elliot knelt beside her, too, and started to take Elizabeth in his arms. "I'll take her into the house."

"Miss Cari . . . ?"

She glanced up, and through her tears, she could see the two hands standing over her. "Fred, help Elliot with my mother . . ."

Fred hurried to do as she'd ordered.

"You want me to ride for the sheriff?" Hank asked.

"Yes, Hank. Please . . ."

The ranch hand rode for town immediately.

Cari got up and moved slowly to her father. She touched him with trembling hands and knew the terrible finality of death. When last she'd seen him, he'd been hurt, disappointed, and angry, and now . . . now she would never be able to make it up to him. She would never be able to tell him how much she loved him.

"Oh, Papa . . ." Her voice was a ragged whisper that echoed her devastation. Her shoulders slumped, and sobs wracked her as she gazed at his lifeless body.

Fred had returned and was standing nearby, wanting to help her in some way, yet not knowing how. "Miss Cari?"

"How did it happen?" she asked miserably.

"We found him near Charlie's camp."

"But why?" she asked, desperate to make some sense of the horror. "Everyone liked Papa. He had no enemies. Why would anybody want to kill him?"

Elliot hurried back to Cari after he'd seen to Elizabeth.

"How is my mother?" she asked as he came to her.

"She's awake, but in shock. Someone should probably be with her, but I didn't want to leave you out here alone."

"I'll go in to her in a minute . . ." she said distractedly.

Drawing Fred aside, Elliot quietly questioned him. "What happened up there? Were there any tracks, any clues?" He wanted to know everything.

"Had to be rustlers, the bull's missing. It was probably the Indians, just like the Larsons' been saying all along."

Indians . . . When Cari heard this, she looked up at them, her expression even more stricken. "How can you say that?"

"Your father was clutching some kind of bag that belonged to one of them. Hank's got it with him. He's gonna show it to the sheriff."

Cari couldn't believe any of this. Tall Shadow's people would never have hurt her father, and yet . . . Fred said there was proof . . .

Her gaze rested upon her father again, and she gave a deep, heart-rending cry. She wished Silver Wolf was with her. He would have known the truth. He would have helped her.

"Cari, you don't need to be out here," Elliot said gently, slipping an arm around her and turning her toward the house, away from the sight of her father.

"I'll take care of your pa for you, Miss Cari," Fred promised.

Cari leaned heavily on Elliot as he led her back to the house. When they reached the steps, her father's horse gave a forlorn whinny. It was a sad, haunting sound, and it reinforced to Cari the nightmare her life had suddenly become.

"James McCord was murdered, so was Charlie Houser, and that fancy bull of McCord's is missing," Hank told Sheriff Dixon as he raced into his office in Cheyenne.

"James is dead?" It was after midnight and the sheriff had been awakened from a sound sleep by the frantic hand from the Circle M.

"Fred and I found him this afternoon," he quickly explained, "and he had this in his hand." Hank gave the lawman the medicine bag.

Dixon opened it and checked the contents, then looked up at the cowboy, dumbfounded.

"I don't believe this. It belongs to Daniel Marshall. There must be some mistake." The sheriff ran a weary hand over his face, trying to come to grips with the terrible news.

"I hope you're right, Sheriff, but Fred was there, too. He'll back me up if you don't believe me."

Dixon buckled on his gunbelt. "I'm going to see if Marshall's in town."

"I want to go with you," Hank offered. "I liked James McCord, and I want to see the bastard who shot him hang."

"Now, Hank, this medicine bag is not firm proof that Marshall did the killing. You can come with me, though, just in case I might need your help."

Dixon and Hank left the jail and headed for Marshall's room over the Douglas law office. They had their guns drawn when Dixon pounded on the half-breed's door. Both men jumped when Ben opened the door to his room behind them.

"Sheriff? What's the matter?" Ben asked sleepily, having been awakened by their knocking.

"Where's your friend?" Dixon demanded.

"I don't know where Daniel is right now. I haven't seen him since he left town Saturday night. Why? What's wrong?"

The sheriff holstered his gun as he faced Ben. "Hank just rode in from the Circle M to tell me that James McCord's been murdered and his bull's been stolen."

"What?" Ben stared at the two of them.

"It looks like Marshall was involved," Hank spoke up.

"That's ridiculous. They're good friends."

"Well, we'll just see about that when I bring him in for questioning. If you see him before I do, you'd better tell him to turn himself in. It'll go easier for him if he does."

Ben watched the two men leave, then he went inside and began to dress. He wasn't sure where Daniel had gone, but he intended to find him before the sheriff did. Within minutes, he was on his horse heading for Tall Shadow's village. The going would be slow in the dark, but he didn't care. He had to find Daniel as fast as he could.

Fourteen

Ben was not afraid to ride into Tall Shadow's village. He'd been there several times with Daniel and had made friends among the Cheyenne, and they greeted him now as he made his way toward Tall Shadow's tipi. Ben let his gaze sweep the village hoping for some sign of Daniel, but his friend was nowhere to be seen.

Tall Shadow came out to welcome Ben when he reined in before his home. "It is always good to see you, Ben Douglas. What brings you to our village today?"

"Hello, Chief Tall Shadow. I've come looking for Daniel. Is he here?" he asked hopefully as he dismounted and approached the older man.

"No. I have not seen my grandson in many days," the chief replied. He saw how Ben's expression grew troubled at this news. "Is something wrong?"

"Very wrong," he admitted as he came to stand before the chief. Their eyes met as he told him, "James McCord has been murdered."

Pain knifed through the chief's heart. "How is this possible?"

"I don't know all the details," Ben replied. "All I know is that James was shot and his prize bull was stolen."

Anguish was etched on Tall Shadow's face. "James was a friend to all. Why would anyone kill him?"

Ben's expression grew even graver as he went on. "There's more. For some reason, the sheriff thinks Daniel was involved."

"Silver Wolf? Why would they think my grandson would do this?"

"I don't know. All I know is that Sheriff Dixon said he was the main suspect. That's why I came here looking for him. I was hoping he was with you. I wanted to find him before the law does, so I could try to help him."

Tall Shadow's gaze was tormented as he gestured toward his tipi. "Come inside, we will talk more."

Ben started to follow him then for some reason, he paused and glanced back around the camp. It was then that he saw her, and his heart lurched in his chest. The maiden he'd saved in town was standing by a cookfire, looking just as beautiful as he remembered. He let his gaze sweep hungrily over her, taking in the loveliness of her features and the gentle curves of her slender body beneath her soft buckskin dress.

Ben wanted to go to her. He longed to hear the melodic sound of her voice again, but he remembered all too well how she'd acted in town that day and he remained where he was. When he realized that she was watching him just as he was watching her, Ben nodded slightly in her direction. It took an effort on his part, but he managed to turn away and follow Tall Shadow inside.

Star Blossom had been on her way back from the stream with buckets of water, when she'd noticed a white man talking to the chief. She'd recognized him immediately as the man who'd rescued her in town, and her pulse had quickened. She'd stopped where she was, wondering if he'd come there looking for her. Panic surged through her and she considered fleeing. After a moment, the comforting sounds of the village, the children laughing, and the women talking, eased her fear, and she realized she was safe. There was no need to be afraid. Drawing a deep steadying breath, she continued on to the cookfire where the women awaited the water.

"It is unusual for Ben to come here without Silver Wolf," Morning Wind was saying to her friend Laughing Crow as Star Blossom joined them. "I wonder why my son did not ride with him."

Star Blossom was surprised at Morning Wind's words. "You know the white man who talks with Chief Tall Shadow?"

Silver Wolf's mother looked at her expectantly. "He is Ben Douglas, my son's friend."

The two older women knew of Star Blossom's tragic past— of how white hunters had murdered her mother and sister and how she'd hated whites with a passion ever since, and they were puzzled by her interest in Ben.

"Why do you want to know?" Morning Wind ventured.

"When I went to the town with my father, this man saved me from one who was drunk and would have hurt me."

Morning Wind nodded. "There are not many whites who would help us that way. You were fortunate that he was there that day. Ben Douglas is a good man."

"There are no good white men!" Star Blossom countered quickly, not wanting to hear anything good about him, even though his behavior that day had already proven it. It troubled her to hear that he was different from the rest of the whites she'd known. Hate was a much easier emotion to deal with than this confusing feeling she had every time she thought of this man.

Star Blossom could still remember how helpless she'd been that day in the face of the drunk's brutality. She remembered, too, how this white man had treated her with respect and how he had let her go when she'd demanded he do so. She had never been able to banish the memory of the look in this man's emerald green eyes when he'd gazed down at her. His expression had been open and honest and had struck a chord deep within her. She'd responded to his kindness instinctively, and that had unnerved her. Her hatred of whites ran deep, and she'd countered his kindness and caring in the only way she'd known how—with anger. All the loathing she'd felt for her attacker, she'd turned on him. Now, though, as she listened to Morning Wind and watched him talk with Chief Tall Shadow, she wondered . . .

Star Blossom glanced Ben's way again, and she was startled when he looked up and captured her gaze with his own. He made no move toward her nor did he do anything else other than just smile slightly as he nodded in her direction. That simple recognition sent an unwelcome surge of tingling excitement racing through her, and her confusion deepened, nearly overwhelming her. Once he'd disappeared inside the tipi, she hurried away.

Tall Shadow's mood was grim as he faced Ben across the width of the tipi. "James warned me that the ranchers thought we were stealing cattle from them."

"And now James is dead and his bull is missing. Something terrible is going on here. I have to find Daniel right away before the men from town do."

"I will send my braves to look for my grandson. We will search for the guilty ones, too."

"If you find Daniel before I do, tell him to be careful. Some of those ranchers are just looking to start trouble, and they'd just as soon shoot him as talk to him right now."

The chief nodded in understanding. "Will you stay with us and share a meal?"

"I'd like to," Ben answered sincerely, "but I can't. It's important I get to the McCord ranch and see if I can do anything for Elizabeth and Cari."

Tall Shadow would have liked to have gone to Little Snow himself, but he knew how her mother felt about him and his people, and thought it best to stay away. "Tell Little Snow and her mother that James was my friend and that I hold a great sorrow in my heart."

Ben heard the strain in his voice, and promised to give them his message.

They rose to leave, and as Ben went outside, he immediately looked over to where the maiden had been standing. He was disappointed to find she was gone.

"Chief Tall Shadow? Who was the girl with Silver Wolf's mother earlier?"

Tall Shadow missed very little. He'd seen how Ben had stared at her, and he smiled slightly. "Her name is Star Blossom."

"She's very beautiful."

He heard the admiration in his tone, but knew he had to caution him. "Yes, she is, but for one so young, she has known much sorrow."

"What happened to her?" he asked quickly, needing to know.

The chief explained about the murders of her mother and sister.

"Were the men punished?"

"Several warriors and I hunted them down. They will never hurt anyone again."

"That's good."

Tall Shadow heard more than just a passing interest in Ben's tone. "Why do you ask about the girl?"

"Star Blossom was in town a while ago, and a drunk was bothering her. I ran him off, but when I tried to talk to her after he'd gone she wouldn't even tell me her name. Now I understand why."

"When a maiden goes for water, a warrior will often wait by the path to speak to her as she returns. Sometimes, a warrior sits outside her tipi at night and sings of his love for her. It is up to the woman and her family to decide whether she will talk to him or not."

Ben gave Tall Shadow an uncertain look. He wasn't thinking about marrying this girl. He just wanted to talk to her. Ben almost laughed out loud at the idea of singing outside her tipi. He knew it was a good thing he wasn't a Cheyenne warrior, for if his state of wedlock depended on singing ability, he'd probably be a bachelor to the end of his days.

Tall Shadow called out to one of the women nearby to ask where Star Blossom had gone. When the woman told him that she'd returned to the creek, he showed Ben which path would lead him to her.

Ben moved slowly down the path. He wanted to talk to Star Blossom, but he was unsure how she would react to seeing him again. Certainly, when he'd smiled at her earlier, she hadn't seemed overly receptive. He stopped halfway to his destination to debate with himself. He argued that the smart thing to do would be to forget the whole thing. Finally, though, he decided to brave it out. The worst thing that could happen, he reasoned, would be that she'd refuse to speak to him, and she'd already done that once.

Ben moved down the narrow trek that would lead him to her. A pretty flower blooming along the side of the walkway caught his eye. He picked it and hurried on. As he neared the water, the sound of feminine voices came to him. Moving closer, he saw her, standing with several other young women. Suddenly, he felt a little foolish holding the flower, and he hid it behind his back.

"Star Blossom . . ." He called her name.

Star Blossom was startled by this unexpected intrusion. The girls who were with her giggled nervously as they saw the white man, and they quickly disappeared, leaving the two of them alone.

Star Blossom watched Ben coming toward her and wondered why she hadn't noticed before just how very handsome he was. His shoulders were broad and strong, his waist was trim, his legs long and hard-muscled. It was his eyes that mesmerized her, though, for in their emerald depths she saw a gentleness that soothed her tortured soul. "What do you want, Ben Douglas?"

At the sound of his name on her lips, he grinned, feeling pleased that she knew who he was. "You know my name."

"The women at the cookfire were speaking of you."

"And what were they saying?" he urged.

She tried to reply indifferently. "Only that you were Silver Wolf's friend, and they wondered why you had come to the village without him."

"I came looking for him, but he's not here. The trip wasn't a total waste of time, though, for I found you."

"I was not lost," she said with a haughty lift of her chin.

"You were lost to me. I'd been hoping to see you again ever since that day in town," he said softly as he slowly closed the distance between them.

As he drew near, a part of her wanted to bolt and run, yet another stronger part of her said to stay. She remained, but she watched him warily.

Ben saw the edge of fear in her eyes, and he wanted to do something that would put her at ease. "I've brought you a present," he said, and in a most gallant move, he presented her with the wildflower. "I hope you like flowers."

She looked from the flower to Ben and then back again. "I am named for a flower," she answered, and then she smiled in spite of herself as she reached out to take it from him.

"It must have been a very beautiful blossom," he told her in a low voice.

Their hands touched as she took his gift, and it almost seemed as if a current passed between them. She lifted her startled gaze to his as she cupped the delicate flower in her hands. The expression in her dark eyes took his breath away. It was a look of longing and desire, tinged with fearful apprehension. Suddenly, he wanted to take her in his arms, hold her close, and promise her that no one would ever hurt her again.

Ben had never known such a strong, urgent need to protect anyone before, and the power of it surprised him. He ached to hold her, but a last thread of sanity warned him to stop and think before he acted. Such a move on his part would frighten her, and that was the last thing he wanted to do.

Ben remained where he was, his common sense holding him at bay, while he let his gaze feast upon her. She was so beautiful . . . so delicate . . . He felt awkward and more than a little

silly as he wondered what to do next. He certainly didn't want
to leave her so soon, and yet there wasn't a lot he could say
without blurting out the truth of what he was feeling. Confusion filled him.

"Why did you follow me here to the creek?" she asked, trying to understand why her heart was pounding so wildly. She
told herself it was fear making her feel this way, but a little,
taunting voice in the back of her mind teased her with the
knowledge that it was excitement and not fear that was causing
her heart to beat in this frantic rhythm. She glanced away from
him, afraid of her own feelings.

"I needed to speak with you again," Ben replied honestly.

"There is nothing more to be said between us," she told
him, reminding herself firmly that he was a white man and
she knew what they were like— mean, vicious killers. But then
as she lifted her gaze and looked into Ben's eyes again, all
the firmly held beliefs she had about white men suddenly
seemed wrong. She saw no ugliness in him. She saw only
warmth and kindness, and she knew a great urge to reach out
to him, to touch him . . .

"I think there is. I've been worried about you, and I wanted
to be sure that you'd made it back to the village without any
more trouble," he explained. He knew he couldn't tell her that
he'd wanted to see her again because he couldn't get her out
of his mind. True though it was, he doubted she'd believe him.

"It is because of you that I am safely here now," she admitted, lifting the flower to her nose to smell of its delicate scent.

"I'm glad." His eyes were warm upon her, and he smiled
crookedly as he had a sudden mental image of sitting outside
her tipi tonight, singing to her. *Sit outside her tipi and sing?*
The thought was ridiculous. Ben gave himself a furious mental
shake, wondering at his own sanity to even think such a thing.

Ben suddenly realized that his crazy musings had distracted
him from his real reason for coming there in the first place.
He had to find Daniel. The memory of James's death and his
friend's peril intruded, and with great regret he knew he had
to leave. Ben was disappointed that Star Blossom still seemed

indifferent to him, but he had no time to stay and court her. He glanced back up the path.

"Now that you have seen that I am safe, you will go?" she asked, sensing his sudden uneasiness.

Ben wasn't sure if she was trying to get rid of him or if she understood the urgency of his mission. "I have to find Daniel. It's very important." Unable to stop himself, he lifted one hand to tenderly caress her cheek.

"I hope you find him soon." Star Blossom knew he was going to touch her and yet she did not try to avoid it. She held herself rigidly as his hand gently caressed her cheek, then dropped away.

Ben was disappointed by her stiff carriage, but he didn't let it show. Knowing now what he did about her, he understood her fear and her reluctance to trust him. It would take time, but he fully intended to prove to her that not all white men were as evil as the ones from her past.

"I'll miss you while I'm gone, Star Blossom. Will you think of me, even a little?" His question was daring, but he thought he had nothing to lose.

Her gaze dropped to the flower she held as she said in a soft voice, "Good-bye, Ben Douglas."

"This is not good-bye." His eyes were warm upon her, preserving in his memory the sight of her holding his gift. "You will see me again."

His gently voiced declaration sent a thrill through her, but she was still too unsure to say anything. She watched him walk away, tall and handsome, confident and proud. She warned herself again that he was white and that she shouldn't have these feelings for him, but even as she cursed her attraction to him, she looked down at the flower she still held and smiled. She whispered, "I will think of you, Ben Douglas."

Elizabeth's expression was haunted as she sat, dry-eyed, staring out her bedroom window. "I drove him away from me, Cari."

"I'm sure you didn't mean to, Mother," Cari reassured her. It was late morning, and she was exhausted. She'd been up all night, trying to comfort her distraught mother, but it seemed a hopeless task.

"At the time, maybe I did, but after I'd thought about it, I realized your father was right. I shouldn't have been so selfish. I should have believed in him more." She lifted her troubled, burning gaze to her daughter. "I should have apologized."

"You would have, Mother. It's not your fault that this happened."

Tears welled up in Elizabeth's eyes. The nightmare memories of her last, harsh words to James echoed through her soul, and she would forever bear the guilt of knowing that she'd hurt him that morning. "If only I could believe that. But I know what I said to him . . . and I'm so sorry."

Cari went to her and held her close. "I'm sure Papa knows."

"Oh, God, I hope so, Cari."

After a moment, Cari suggested that she lie down for a while and try to get some sleep. "We still have a few hours before the minister comes," she pointed out.

"All right," she agreed meekly, too tired to argue.

Cari stayed by her side until she'd finally fallen into a fitful sleep, then went to her own room to lie down.

Cari had intended to nap, but the blessed respite of sleep would not come. Memories of her father kept slipping into her thoughts, and a tremendous ache built up within her. She longed to be with him again, to feel his arms around her, and to hear him tell her that he loved her. They'd been apart for so long, and now at last she was home, and . . . and now he was dead. Gone. Lost to her forever.

The dam she'd erected around her own emotions to help control herself while she was with her mother broke, and she began to cry. Once she started, she couldn't stop. She had never known such painful, intense emotion. It seemed as if the ache in her breast would never ease. A flood of grief poured forth from her soul. Moans of agony mixed with her sobs, and she buried her face against her pillow to muffle the sounds.

After a time, her weeping eased. Drawing a shaky breath, she sat up to stare around herself with sightless eyes. She felt hollow and empty, as if all her crying had somehow drained her body of all life and soul. Distractedly, Cari thought maybe that was good, for at least the pain had been dulled for the moment.

Cari felt so very alone. She longed with all her heart for Silver Wolf to come to her. She needed him desperately. She needed the comfort of his arms about her. Elliot had been wonderful and helpful, but Silver Wolf was the man she needed. Cari prayed he'd return to her soon.

At the sound of horses approaching, Cari got up and rushed to the window. She was hoping it was Silver Wolf, but her hopes were dashed when she saw Sheriff Dixon and a group of men riding toward the house. A chill frissoned down her spine as she realized the sheriff might have news about her father's murderer. Anxious to speak with him, she ran from the room. Elliot was already outside with the lawman when she emerged from the house.

"We're looking for him now," Dixon was telling Elliot as they stood together out front. The rest of his men had remained in the saddle, but the sheriff had dismounted to speak with him.

"I just can't believe it . . ." Elliot was obviously stunned.

"We've got proof. It's just a matter of finding him."

"Finding who?" Cari asked as she reached them.

"Why, hello, Miss McCord." The sheriff adroitly avoided her question as he took off his hat and offered his sympathies. "I'm sorry about your pa. He was a good man."

"Thank you."

"How's your mother doing?"

"She's finally resting. It's been a long night."

"Please give her my condolences."

"I'll do that." Still wondering what he and Elliot had been talking about, she deliberately asked, "I only heard a part of what you were saying to Elliot about 'having the proof and finding him.' Does that mean you know who killed my father?"

"We know," he responded tersely.

Cari was filled with a burning need to know. "Who did it? Who killed him?"

"Cari . . ." Elliot said her name gently, trying to discourage her from pursuing it, but she would have none of it.

The hair on the back of Cari's neck rose as she sensed she was close to finding out the truth. She turned back to the sheriff. "This is my father's murderer we're talking about! My father! I have a right to know!"

The sheriff could see no way to avoid telling her, and so he answered her bluntly. "The medicine bag that was found with your father was identified as belonging to Daniel Marshall. It looks like he's the one who killed your pa."

"No . . ." Cari was shocked to the depths of her soul. She turned frantically to Elliot. "That's ridiculous. He and my father were friends. Good friends."

Dixon snorted derisively at her words. "It's time you learned that you can't be friends with Indians, Miss McCord. They're nothing but bloodthirsty, thieving savages. We've been trying to tell your pa that for years, but he wouldn't listen. And now . . ."

"It looks like the Larsons were right, Cari," Elliot added. "And Lord Anthony is missing."

The sheriff continued. "Near as I can figure it, your pa must have caught Marshall stealing the Hereford, and Marshall killed him. Of course, there may have been more to it than that."

"What do you mean?" Cari had no idea what he was talking about.

"Well, Nettie Jones came into the office and reported that the night of the dance she saw your mother and Marshall have a fight right out in public. She said your pa got real mad and went storming out of the hall looking for him right afterward. Nobody knows what happened after that, but now that James was found dead holding Marshall's medicine bag, it doesn't look good for the breed."

"This can't be true . . ."

"Well, Miss McCord, it's a known fact that Cheyenne warriors keep their medicine bags with them all the time. They're supposed to bring them good luck or something." The sheriff gave a dry laugh. "It looks like Marshall's luck just ran out."

Cari realized how damning everything seemed. Her first response had been that there was no connection between any of it, and then she remembered the ugliness of her mother's words to Silver Wolf at the stream. Cari's thoughts were in turmoil as she tried to come to grips with everything the sheriff had told her. The horrible possibility occurred to her that her father had met with Silver Wolf and that they'd had a terrible argument.

With all her heart, Cari wanted to believe Silver Wolf was innocent. She wanted to believe that he was the same man she knew to be honest and forthright.

"What do you intend to do, Sheriff?" Elliot asked.

"We're looking for him now. I stopped here so I could let you folks know what was going on. I figured you'd be worried."

"Thanks for keeping us informed."

"You can rest easy. We won't be back until we get him. We'll see that he pays for what he's done."

Cari heard the fierce determination in the lawman's voice and went pale. The Silver Wolf he described was a cold-blooded killer. The Silver Wolf she thought she knew was honest and kind. He'd held her in his arms and made love to her. Which man was he? Would she ever learn the truth? Though she didn't speak, her torment was mirrored on her ashen features.

Elliot saw her distress and slipped a supportive arm about her waist.

"We'll be waiting to hear from you," he told Dixon.

He and Cari watched as the sheriff and his posse rode away.

"None of this is true," Cari said in an agonized tone as she turned to face Elliot. She was clinging desperately to her faith in her warrior. "Silver Wolf would never have hurt my father."

Elliot didn't want to be the one to force her to face reality, but he knew someone had to. "Cari, they found his medicine bag in your father's hand. If he didn't do it, how did his bag get there?"

She lifted her agonized gaze to his. "I don't know, Elliot. I don't know."

"What are you going to tell your mother?" Elliot asked as they started back indoors.

Cari was about to answer when Elizabeth spoke.

"She won't have to tell me anything," Elizabeth said in a flat voice. "I heard everything Sheriff Dixon said."

"Mother, I . . ."

"Do you see now, Cari? I was right about Silver Wolf," she said slowly, the weight of her torment evident in her tone. "Your father convinced me the other morning that I was wrong, and I believed him. But now the truth is out. I was right . . ." She gave a choking laugh. "I was right about him the whole time! How I wish to God I hadn't been . . ." Elizabeth didn't say another word, but disappeared inside.

Cari wanted to cry out, "No! You're wrong!" But the words wouldn't come. On Elliot's arm, she followed her mother inside.

Four hours later, Cari stood next to her mother, listening as the minister intoned the final prayer and blessing over her father's grave. Since the sheriff's visit, Cari had fallen to the depths of despair. She didn't want to believe a word of what he'd told them, and yet she knew what he'd said was true— Silver Wolf never went anywhere without his medicine bag. The evidence was damning, but even as she faced the facts, her heart railed against them.

"Amen," the minister pronounced.

Cari, Elizabeth, Elliot, and the neighbors who'd heard of

James's death and come for the funeral responded together, "Amen."

The preacher closed his Bible and sought out Elizabeth and Cari.

"Mrs. McCord, I'm so sorry about your loss. It's such a sense-less tragedy. If you need anything, anything at all, just let me know," he told her sympathetically.

Elizabeth tore her gaze away from her husband's grave and looked up at the clergyman. Her pain was evident in her ex-pression. She wanted to tell him that there was something she needed . . . she needed her husband back, but she knew it would do no good. For all his heartfelt kindness and prayers, the minister couldn't bring James back to life . . . no one could. Instead, she simply thanked him. There was no point in saying any more.

Everyone began to move toward the house, every-one except Cari. She remained behind, wanting to spend a few minutes alone with her father.

When the others had gone, Cari stood over the fresh grave, listening to the sounds of silence. She closed her eyes and remembered the big hug he'd given her at the train station when she'd returned from school. She let her thoughts drift back through the years then, recalling his laughter and all the joy he'd taken in her accomplishments— large and small. She remembered all too clearly the day she and her mother had left to go back to Philadelphia, and how he'd contacted Silver Wolf for her so they could see each other one more time before she had to leave.

At the thought of Silver Wolf, the memory of the sheriff's accusations returned, and Cari's pain grew almost unbearable. She'd lost her father. But had she lost Silver Wolf, too?

"Oh, Papa. . . . What happened that night?" Her question was caught up and lost on the wind.

Silence was her only answer. She turned away from the grave, feeling completely desolate. As she started back to the house, she whispered to herself, "Silver Wolf . . . where are you?"

An hour later, Cari sat on the sofa in the parlor, listening to, without really hearing, the conversations going on around her. She supposed she'd been saying all the right things at all the right times, but she couldn't be sure, for she felt as if she were encased in ice. She was numb with misery. It seemed she was living a terrible nightmare in which the truth was a lie and lies were the truth. She wondered if it would ever end.

"Cari, I am so sorry about your father . . ."

She looked up to see Mark Larson standing over her. "Thank you, Mark."

"You look like you could use a breath of fresh air. Do you want to go outside for a few minutes?"

Though she didn't relish being in his company, she desperately needed a reprieve.

She stood, and Mark took her arm to escort her.

"I'll be out on the porch if my mother needs me," she told Elliot.

Elliot wished he was the one spending a quiet moment with Cari, but he knew it was important he stay near Mrs. McCord. She'd been holding up reasonably well, all things considered, but he knew her fortitude wouldn't last forever.

Cari and Mark went outside and stood at the porch railing. The sun was dropping lower in the sky, and it would soon be dark.

"It was good of you and your father to come."

"When we heard the news, we couldn't stay away. That's what neighbors are for." His answer was honest as far as it went. They certainly hadn't wanted to stay away, for they had both been anxious to hear what was being said about James's murder.

So far, it looked like their plan had worked. From what they'd heard inside, the medicine bag coupled with Nettie Jones's rumors all added up to a hanging party for the half-breed once the sheriff found him, and that was just fine with them. They had Lord Anthony safely hidden away, James was dead, and soon the Indians would be run out of the territory. Life looked good.

"Everyone's been very kind."

"Have you given any thought to what you're going to do?" Mark ventured.

"What do you mean?"

"I mean, it's not safe for you and your mother to live out here alone. If something like this could happen to your father . . ." He let the sentence hang.

"It's all been so sudden. We really haven't had time to talk about it yet." Cari was surprised by the pang of loss she felt at the thought of leaving the ranch.

"Of course you haven't, and I'm sorry. I was just concerned about you." He paused for effect.

"There's no need for you to worry."

"Ah, but there is. Like we told your father, we know the Indians are doing the stealing and now we know they're killing, too. There's no safe place in the territory anymore, and there won't be until all the savages are driven out and put on reservations."

"I'm sure there are many who agree with you."

"Now that your father's been murdered, it's just a matter of time until it happens," he told her confidently.

Cari had had all she could stand of Mark. "I think I'd better go back in now."

Ever solicitous, he started to take her arm when they heard a horse coming. Looking up, they caught sight of Ben Douglas riding in, and Cari waited there to greet him.

Ben reined in before the house and dismounted. He gave Mark a curt nod of recognition as he came up on the porch, but his entire focus was on Cari. He took her hands and pressed a tender kiss on her cheek.

"Cari, I came as soon as I could. I'm so sorry," Ben told her earnestly.

"Thank you, Ben."

"How's your mother?"

"As well as can be expected, I guess. Elliot's with her right now. Please, come in. I'm sure she'll be glad to see you. We both know how fond Papa was of you."

They found all the visitors preparing to leave. An emotionally numb Elizabeth was accepting their expressions of sympathy and thanking them in return for their thoughtfulness. Sam Larson kissed her cheek and then motioned for Mark to join him.

"We'll be going now, Elizabeth, but if you should ever need us, just send one of the hands out to the ranch."

"You've been so kind, Sam. We appreciate everything."

When the last person had gone, Elizabeth finally turned to Ben. James had told her how close Ben and Silver Wolf were, and she faced him now with uncertainty. The look of heartfelt sympathy in his eyes immediately erased her concern about him.

"Elizabeth . . . I'm so sorry." He kissed her cheek as he had Cari's.

"So am I," she said wearily, the exhaustion she'd held at bay finally claiming her. "I thought James and I would spend the rest of our lives together. I never dreamed it could all end so soon." Words failed her, and her expression, so carefully schooled for the others, faltered. "I don't know what I'll do without him . . ."

Elliot put an arm about her shoulders, and she leaned gratefully against him, appreciating his strength.

"Do you want to go upstairs, Mother?" Cari asked.

"I think I'd better."

"Ben, will you stay the night?" Cari invited, knowing they had much to discuss and this was not the time.

"If you want me to, I'll stay."

"Please. We'll speak with you in the morning."

Cari and Elliot took Elizabeth upstairs, and while Cari helped her mother prepare for bed, Elliot went back down to keep Ben company.

"Would you like a drink?" Elliot offered. James kept his liquor in the cabinet, and after the day that had just passed, he knew it was time for a whiskey.

"Thanks. I could use one," Ben answered as he sat down on the sofa. He accepted the glass and took a deep swallow.

It had been a long two days, and the ordeal was far from over. In fact, it was only just beginning.

"Did you know the sheriff's looking for Silver Wolf?" Elliot asked as he sat down with him.

"He came by Daniel's rooms last night, searching for him," he answered, his disgust evident in his voice.

"They're convinced of his guilt."

"There's been no trial yet," he answered harshly.

"According to Sheriff Dixon they have proof."

"I know. That's why I was so late getting here today. I rode out to Tall Shadow's village trying to find Daniel before anybody else did, but he wasn't there."

"Do you think he ran?"

Ben bristled at Elliot's insinuation. "I've known Daniel for seven years. He doesn't run from anything." His words were terse. "Daniel is no murderer."

"Everyone else seems to think he is, and judging from what I heard here tonight, they're up in arms about it."

"Anyone who knew Daniel and James would realize the whole idea of Daniel killing him is ludicrous. They cared about each other. James had a special place in his heart for Daniel ever since the night he rescued Cari. Over the years, they've grown close. They were almost like father and son sometimes. There's no way Daniel had anything to do with this."

"He's going to have a hard time proving it."

The two men regarded each other in silence for a minute. Ben was firmly convinced of Daniel's innocence; Elliot leaned toward believing the evidence and the sheriff.

"Then we'll just have to prove them wrong." Ben spoke quietly, but with deadly intent.

Fifteen

Silver Wolf lay by his campfire trying to rest. He knew he should be sleeping, but thoughts of Little Snow were keeping him awake. It had been four days since he'd seen her, four long, lonely days since he'd held her in his arms and made love to her. Memories of the passion they'd shared flooded through him as he lay alone in the darkness. He remembered the softness of her, the sweetness of her scent, the taste and feel of her . . .

Against his will, the heat of his need for her rose within him, then settled low in his body. He stifled a groan as he gritted his teeth against it. He eased the glorious agony by telling himself it would only be one more day until they were together again. Just one more day . . .

When Silver Wolf had left Little Snow, he'd ridden to the place where he'd received his vision quest. He'd camped there for several nights, clearing his mind of things that were unimportant and concentrating on what he felt for Little Snow and what their future together might be. He knew her mother had been right when she'd claimed that some whites wouldn't understand their being together. But he believed that their love was strong enough to survive any hardships, as long as they faced them together.

It had occurred to Silver Wolf on his second day out alone that he hadn't told Little Snow that he loved her that night. He deeply regretted not saying the words to her, though he'd felt them in his heart, and he intended to make up for it as soon as they were together again. He hadn't been ready to admit it before, but he acknowledged now that Little Snow had held his heart in her keeping ever since that first night when he'd found her in the snow. He'd loved her then, and he loved her now, and he wanted to spend the rest of his life with her. Satisfied with that knowledge, he'd headed back for the Circle M. He would reach the ranch tomorrow. He couldn't wait to see her and tell her of his feelings for her.

Only one more day, he told himself, and they would be together. He hoped she'd worked things out with her parents, and remembering the kiss she'd given him as they'd parted, he felt confident that she had.

At the memory of her kiss, Silver Wolf's hunger for her grew. With an effort, he denied it, but he was forced to shift positions again to seek his comfort once more. One more day, he repeated to himself. Just one more day. . . . Sleep was a long time coming, but it finally claimed him. His fire burned down low, and the night grew quiet.

Wild One's low warning whicker and the sound of a twig snapping in the underbrush nearby brought Silver Wolf instantly awake. He wasn't sure how long he'd been asleep, and he lay still, listening, trying to orient himself. Wild One's restless movements convinced him that someone was near, and a sense of foreboding settled over him. As quietly as possible he moved, reaching for the handgun he kept close beside him.

"Don't do it, Marshall!" A man's voice rang out in the night. "We just might have to shoot you if you go for your gun, and we'd hate to do that."

Silver Wolf stopped and called, "Who are you and what do you want?"

"This is Sheriff Dixon."

"Sheriff?" He recognized Dixon's voice and frowned. "What's going on? Why didn't you just ride in?"

Sitting up slowly, Silver Wolf peered into the darkness. The glow from the dying fire provided little light and made it difficult to see, but he thought he could make out the sheriff standing just beyond the edge of the low-burning flames' glow.

"We've been looking for you for a couple of days now."

"Why? Is something wrong? Has there been trouble?" Silver Wolf demanded, suddenly worried about Tall Shadow and his people in the village.

"You're damned right there's been trouble!" Dixon thundered. "You're under arrest."

Silver Wolf wondered if he was dreaming, but then he saw the glint of the gun barrels that were pointed at him and knew everything was far too real to be imagined. This was no dream. "For what?"

"The murder of James McCord."

The news hit him like a physical blow and jarred him to the depths of his soul. "James is dead?"

One of the deputies gave a harsh laugh. "As if you didn't know, half-breed. Now get up real slow. We're taking you in."

Silver Wolf knew he had no choice. He stood up, taking care to keep his hands where the sheriff could see them. "Sheriff Dixon, I have no idea what this is all about. I didn't know James was dead. I haven't seen him or spoken with him since late Saturday night."

"Yeah, we know all about Saturday night, half-breed," another man called out to him in a taunting tone. "We saw you with McCord's daughter, and we know how mad he got—"

"Shut up, Morgan. Go help Collins tie him up," the sheriff cut him off.

"There's no need for that. I didn't kill James, and I'll go into town with you willingly," Silver Wolf offered.

"You think we're stupid?" Morgan scoffed. "We don't trust you. Now turn around!"

The two men moved toward him. They hated all Indians and considered half-breeds no better. Just because this man had had a college education and spoke and acted like a white man didn't make him their equal. It would have pleased them greatly to kill him right there and save the town the trouble of a trial, but the sheriff was with them.

"Sheriff Dixon, James McCord was my friend. I didn't kill him," Silver Wolf insisted.

"Save it for the trial, Marshall," Dixon replied without emotion.

"But I didn't do it!"

"Well, the proof we got says that you *did* do it!" Morgan snarled at him.

"What proof?"

"He had your medicine bag on him when he was found," Dixon explained.

"My medicine bag?" Silver Wolf was startled by the revelation. He started to tell them that he'd lost it some time Saturday night, but Morgan and Collins grabbed him and he didn't get the chance. Collins dragged his arms behind him to tie them, while Morgan held a gun on him.

The posse had been excited when they'd stumbled onto Marshall's camp. They'd tied their horses a short distance away so they could move in quietly and have the element of surprise on their side when they arrested him. Now, leaving Morgan and Collins in charge of their captive, the sheriff and the others went to retrieve the horses.

The two men were thrilled to have a few minutes with the half-breed out from under the sheriff's watchful eyes.

"So you like white girls, do you?" Morgan asked as he pressed his gun against Silver Wolf's chest. He remembered how outraged he'd been when he'd seen him dancing with Cari McCord, and he slowly dragged the barrel of the gun down his body until it was aimed below his waist. "You ain't got no right touching white women, Indian."

"Yeah. . . . Maybe, it's time you learned that lesson," Collins chuckled as he pulled the rope that bound Silver Wolf's wrists extra tight.

Fury and frustration filled Silver Wolf, but he fought to keep his expression carefully blank. He knew what kind of men these were and knew this wasn't the time or the place for a confrontation. He stood still and kept his gaze focused straight ahead.

"It would be a real shame if this gun accidentally went off, wouldn't it, Collins?" Morgan smiled as he toyed with the hammer, watching Silver Wolf's face as he did. "It would be real easy to put a bullet in you . . ." Morgan was getting annoyed because the half-breed wasn't showing any fear. He would have taken great pleasure in shooting him right then.

"You better not," Collins cautioned, still holding Silver Wolf immobile. "He's going to be hung within the week anyway, so why make it easy for him? It'll be good to watch him suffer."

Morgan paused as if in thought. "It would be hard to explain to the sheriff why I shot you there. So maybe . . ."

In a lightning move, he brought the gun up and pistol-whipped Silver Wolf. The force of the blow staggered him, cutting him over the eye and leaving him bleeding. Silver Wolf tried to jerk free of Collins's hold, but his captor only tightened his grip.

"You trying to escape, breed?" Morgan demanded, hitting him in the stomach with all his might. The power of his blow drove him to his knees.

When he dropped down, Collins let go of him, and Silver Wolf took advantage of this moment of freedom. Lunging forward, he rammed his head and shoulder into Morgan's stomach, knocking him on his back and sending the gun flying from his hand.

"You son-of-a-bitch!" Collins swore as he tackled Silver Wolf from behind.

Beneath the weight of his assault, Silver Wolf fell heavily. He managed to roll to one side and throw off his attacker. He was struggling to his feet when another deputy who'd already returned with his horse came charging into the fray. The deputy grabbed him as the other two came at him.

"Gag him. We still got a minute before the sheriff gets back," Morgan ordered angrily.

Once they'd gagged Silver Wolf, Morgan hit him, and he enjoyed his grunt of pain. Collins joined in, and they didn't let up their abuse until the sheriff rode back into the campsite.

"What the hell are you doing?" Dixon demanded as he saw the slumped and nearly unconscious Marshall, supported by two of his deputies.

"He was trying to escape," Morgan lied coolly, sorry that the sheriff had returned so soon. He had just begun to enjoy himself.

"Yeah, he was giving us trouble, so we thought we'd teach him a lesson," Collins added.

"He was giving you trouble with his hands tied behind him?" the sheriff challenged.

"He's an Indian, Sheriff! You know what animals they are!"

"Get him on his horse," he ordered in disgust. "I want a trial, not a funeral!"

The three deputies dragged Silver Wolf's limp form to his horse and practically threw him on Wild One's back.

Silver Wolf was barely aware of what was going on, but he instinctively gripped his horse with his legs. Blood flowed from the cuts over his eye and in his mouth, and his side felt as if it were on fire.

"Think the white girls would like him now?" Morgan asked Collins as he picked up Wild One's reins and swung up onto his own saddle.

"I don't think so. He ain't so pretty anymore."

"He sure ain't. It doesn't matter, though. The McCord girl knows he's guilty, and she ain't never gonna want anything to do with him again. Did you see the look on her face when the sheriff told her that he killed her daddy?"

"Yeah, the wife, too. They're going to enjoy watching him hang."

The two men laughed in vicious triumph.

In spite of his pain, when Silver Wolf heard them talking about Little Snow, he tried to focus on what they were saying. It tortured him to discover they'd told Cari he'd killed James. He wondered if what they were saying was true. Had she really believed them? The possibility filled him with even greater pain than his physical agony.

Morgan holstered his handgun, but pulled his rifle out of its sheath. He leaned toward Silver Wolf and prodded him in the ribs with it. "I'm going to be right behind you. I'm going to be watching your every move. You do anything, anything at all, and you're a dead man. Hear me?"

Their gazes met, and Silver Wolf saw pure hatred in the white man's cold blue eyes. He nodded and wondered if he was going to live long enough to make it into town.

The following morning, Elizabeth and Cari joined Ben in the parlor.

"I know this isn't a happy time, but it is appropriate that we read James's will now," Ben said solemnly as they all sat down.

Elliot was standing in the doorway, and Ben cast a questioning glance in his direction.

"I'll wait in the other room," Elliot offered.

Elizabeth hurried to invite him to remain. "No. Please stay, Elliot. You've been through so much with us already. There's no reason for you to be excluded now. Please."

He nodded solemnly and went to sit with them as they waited for Ben to begin.

Ben opened the sealed envelope and took out the document he'd drawn up for James. He paused a moment, thinking of the day when they'd gone over the changes, of how happy James had been because Elizabeth and Cari were coming home, and of how much he'd been looking forward to the future. A great sadness weighed upon him as he turned his attention to the will. When James had drawn it up, he could never have known that these would have been the circumstances

under which it would be revealed. Ben was filled with a terrible sense of dread as he began to read.

" 'I, James McCord, being of sound mind and body, do hereby
leave one-half of my ranch to my wife, Elizabeth McCord. I also
leave my wife all of my other worldly goods. The other one-half
of the Circle M is left to Daniel Marshall . . .' " He got no
further.

"What?" Cari gasped in astonishment.

All the color drained from Elizabeth's face as she stared at
Ben. "Read that again," she commanded tersely.

"The other half of the Circle M is left to Daniel Marshall. He
is a close and trusted friend, and this share of the ranch is a
small recompense for saving my daughter's life many years ago."

"I don't believe this!" Elizabeth whispered tightly.

Ben's tone was serious. "There's more, if you'd like me to
go on."

She gave a curt nod.

" 'If, in the event of my death, my wife chooses not to remain
on the Circle M, her half shall pass to my daughter, Cari, who,
I hope, will stay on the ranch and run it with Daniel.' "

"Ben, you can't be serious," Elliot remarked, stunned by this
disclosure.

Ben handed him James's copy of the will. Elliot perused it,
noting the initials and signature at the bottom. He showed it
to Elizabeth and to Cari before handing it back to Ben.

"James was very serious about this arrangement. As I told
you last night, Elliot, they were very close. He always felt as if
he owed Daniel a great debt for rescuing Cari and I guess this
was his way to repay it. He also felt that Elizabeth and Cari
would need a man to help run the Circle M and Daniel was
the one he trusted the most."

Elizabeth started to laugh hysterically, and Cari, Ben, and
Elliot all looked at her, surprised. Laughter was the last thing
they'd expected from her— rage, heartbreak, disappointment,
maybe, but never laughter.

"Mother . . ." Cari addressed cautiously, not knowing how
to deal with her strange mood.

"Don't you see how terribly ironic this is?" she asked as she gave another high-pitched laugh. "Silver Wolf's a fool! He's a complete and utter fool!"

"What are you talking about?" Cari asked, not following her reasoning.

"He could have had everything but he got greedy. Now, James is dead and he's lost it all."

"Daniel did not kill James," Ben told them adamantly.

"That's not what the sheriff says!" Elizabeth pinned him with a condemning glare.

"He's not guilty. I don't know who did it, but I know it wasn't Daniel."

"Are you trying to convince us or yourself, Ben?" Elizabeth charged. Then, her calm somewhat restored, she stood and started from the room. She was in no mood to talk to anyone. "If you'll excuse me?"

When she'd gone, Elliot left, too. Cari sat with Ben.

"Your mother is convinced Daniel's guilty. What about you, Cari? What do you think?" Ben knew how Daniel felt about Cari. She was the love of his life, but Saturday night something terrible had happened between them.

"Four days ago, I would never have believed any of this, but . . . there's so much proof that he did it, and now this will . . ." She paused. "When the people in town hear that my father left half of the ranch to Silver Wolf, it's going to give them one more reason to suspect him."

"You didn't answer my question, Cari." Ben captured her eyes with his, trying to read the secrets she held within her.

Cari wanted to think Silver Wolf was innocent, but she knew how important his medicine bag was to him. "I don't know," she finally answered hesitantly.

"If you love him, you'll believe in him. He didn't know about this inheritance. Your father made certain the provision in the will was kept secret."

Her expression was tortured. "But he never went anywhere without his medicine bag, and they found it with my father!

How can I forget that? He had to have been there, and if he was . . ."

"I don't know how the pouch ended up there. All I do know is that . . ." Ben was about to say more when they heard one of the ranch hands yelling outside.

Cari jumped to her feet and ran out on the porch. She saw the sheriff and his posse riding toward the house. Ben, Elliot, and Elizabeth came out, too, to see what the excitement was all about.

"Looks like they found him, Miss Cari!" Hank was shouting jubilantly.

The sheriff said something to his men and left them a short distance away from the house as he rode up to speak to the family.

"Afternoon," Sheriff Dixon greeted them with a tip of his hat as he reined in before them. "Mrs. McCord, I just wanted to let you know that we found Marshall." He motioned back toward the posse. "We're taking him in now."

"Thank you," Elizabeth said, relieved. "Is there anything you need us to do?"

"No, ma'am. I'll be in touch."

"I'd like to speak with Daniel, Sheriff Dixon," Ben said with terse authority.

"I don't think he's in much of a mood to talk right now," the sheriff answered, wanting to discourage him.

Ben frowned and started toward the posse.

Cari had tried to stay back with her mother and Elliot, but when Ben went to Silver Wolf, she knew she had to go to him, too.

"Cari! Stay here!" Elizabeth ordered. "He's a killer! He murdered your father! Keep away from him!"

She knew all the evidence agreed with her mother, but logic wasn't governing her actions. She ignored her command, and hurried after Ben.

Ben reached the posse and forced his way through the crowd of riders to reach his friend. When he saw Daniel sitting on his horse, his shoulders slumped, his face battered, he stopped. For a moment, he could only stare at him.

"Daniel . . ." He said his friend's name in a pained voice, knowing just by looking at him what he'd suffered at the posse's hands.

Cari reached the posse just as Ben did, and when she saw Silver Wolf for the first time, she froze in place.

"Silver Wolf . . ." She gasped his name out loud, unable to stop herself. Her heart thudded painfully in her breast at the sight of him sitting on Wild One surrounded by the band of armed and leering men. His face was bruised and bloodied, almost to the point of being beyond recognition. He was gagged, and his hands were bound tightly behind his back. The condition of his bloodstained clothes testified to the struggle he'd put up resisting the men who'd come after him. One of the deputies was holding Wild One's reins, so Silver Wolf could not possibly escape, while another pointed a rifle at him. He was their prisoner, totally and completely in their control, and, as such, he was at their mercy.

A part of her wanted to run to him and throw her arms around him and gently tend his wounds, but terrible, doubting questions pounded at her. Why had they beaten him? Was it because he'd tried to run from them because he was guilty? Had he been so desperate to flee that they'd been forced to beat him into submission?

The sound of her voice penetrated the pain-drugged numbness that had settled over Silver Wolf as he'd suffered the ride back toward town. *Cari.. . .* He raised his head for the first time and looked for her in the blur of faces surrounding him. His heart was dying to see her, he needed to know she was there and that she was all right. He needed to see her face and know that she didn't believe any of the lies they'd told her. He needed her . . .

Across the distance that separated them, their eyes met. For just an instant, his gaze, stormy gray now and pain-filled, searched hers, looking for, aching for, some indication that the love they'd shared had been real, that she believed and trusted in him. What he saw in her expression, the look of horror and doubt, filled him with a different, terrible kind of agony. He looked away, unable to bear what he thought was her lack of faith in him.

"Daniel!" Ben jarred himself to action, striding forward to grab Wild One's bridle as he turned on the two deputies. "What in hell is the meaning of this? What did you do to him?"

"He was trying to escape. When we caught him, he resisted arrest, so we subdued him. He's just lucky we didn't shoot him," Morgan told Ben with smug superiority.

"Untie his gag. I want to talk to him."

"Can't do that unless the sheriff says so," the deputy refused.

Sheriff Dixon rejoined the posse. "You have a problem, Douglas?"

"I want to talk to Daniel. Ungag him."

"Sorry, but he's nice and quiet right now, and I want him to stay that way until I get him back to town and in a nice safe jail cell."

"You've made a bad mistake, Sheriff. This man is innocent."

"That's up to the court to decide. Now, I'd appreciate it if you'd move away from our prisoner. We're taking him in to stand trial for the murder of James McCord."

Elizabeth had come out to the posse with Elliot, and, at the sheriff's words, she began to cry. Cari heard her distress and went to her. When she glanced up again, she was shocked to find Silver Wolf's eyes upon her. His expression this time was emotionless, and his eyes were a flat, shining silver that appeared cold and lifeless. For that one moment, Cari could almost believe he was a killer. She shivered as she looked away from him.

Elliot saw how upset she was, and he put his arm around her and drew her to his side protectively. Silver Wolf saw his move, but his expression didn't change.

"I'm riding to town with you, Sheriff Dixon. I want to make sure my client is protected on the trip," Ben declared.

"Marshall's very well protected," Morgan jeered.

"And I intend to make sure he stays that way!" Ben snarled,

more than ready to even the score with the cruel deputy if he could get the chance.

"We'll give you five minutes to get ready, Douglas, and that's all. The whole town is screaming for justice, and I intend to see it done just as fast as I can."

"I don't think I need to remind you, Sheriff, that a man is innocent until proven guilty."

"If he's so damned innocent, why did he run?" Collins taunted.

"I'm not so sure he did run," Ben replied, turning an accusing gaze on him.

Ben was livid as he bid Elizabeth, Cari, and Elliot a hurried good-bye. Within minutes, his horse was saddled and he was ready to ride.

Cari watched them leave. As they disappeared in the distance, her heart cried out in anguish. Though she was with her mother and Elliot, she suddenly felt very alone.

When the posse reached town, they rode straight for the jail. Ben dismounted, intending to help Daniel inside, but the deputies refused to let him near his friend.

"We'll handle this," Morgan told him, and with Collins they dragged Silver Wolf from his horse's back.

Ben stood aside and watched in helpless frustration as the sheriff's deputies roughly pushed Silver Wolf ahead of them into the sheriff's office, then shoved him into a cell. Only then did Sheriff Dixon remove the gag and untie his hands. The lawman turned to Ben.

"You can have ten minutes with him and that's all."

"Thank you." Ben entered the cell and waited until the sheriff had closed and locked the door and left the area before he spoke to Daniel.

"Should I get the doctor?"

"I'll be all right," he managed through his swollen lips. His mouth was raw and sore, and he tasted blood.

"What happened? Where have you been? I've been out look-ing for you ever since I heard about James."

"I was camped out by myself for a few nights."

Ben muttered a curse under his breath. "Did you see any-body? Talk to anybody?"

"No."

"What about your medicine bag? How did that end up with James?"

"I don't know. I must have lost it when I got drunk after the dance, but I have no idea where or when."

"Did you have it when you were at the saloon with Jenny?"

"I had it when I went in, but I don't remember if I had it when we left. I might have lost it in my room or when I rode out the next morning."

"Damn . . ." Ben fell silent as he tried to figure out what to do next.

"Does it look that bad?" Silver Wolf asked, reading his friend's worried expression accurately.

"It doesn't look good. You can't prove where you were when James was murdered, and your medicine bag was found with the body." He paused, lost deep in thought as he tried to piece together everything he knew. "I know you didn't kill him, but I want you to tell me who hated you enough to frame you for his murder." His gaze was piercing.

Silver Wolf gave a hoarse, pained laugh. "Every white man in this town hates me. There isn't a one of them who wouldn't like to see me dead."

"Not *every* white man," Ben corrected him in a low voice as he moved to put a hand upon his shoulder. "What about James? How many enemies did James have? Who wanted him dead? And why?"

"I don't know . . ."

"Think, Daniel!" he commanded. "Your life's at stake! Who hated James so much that they'd kill him? Who had the most to gain?"

"The Larsons, I guess. With James out of the way and Elizabeth inheriting the ranch, there would be no one left to stand up to them and fight their hatred of the Cheyenne."

Ben met Daniel's gaze as he prepared to give him the news he'd yet to hear. "Elizabeth only inherited half of the Circle M."

"Then Little Snow got the other half," he finished for him.

"No."

"No?" Silver Wolf looked at him puzzled. "Who got the other half?"

"You did. James left it to you."

He stared at Ben. "I don't believe it."

"It's true. He wanted to thank you for saving Cari's life, and he thought that would be the best way."

Silver Wolf stood up and turned his back on Ben for a minute as he tried to deal with his turbulent emotions. "I didn't know," he said in a choked voice.

"He wanted it that way."

"He was a good man. I wish he were alive right now."

"So do I," Ben said heavily. "We can't bring him back, but we can sure as hell find the ones who killed him."

"Start with the Larsons . . ." he told him, suddenly intent on making the ones really responsible for his friend's murder pay. "They hated the fact that James was my grandfather's friend. They were the ones stirring up the trouble over the rustling, too. Maybe there's something there."

"I'll do it. Did you know the bull was stolen?"

"No."

"They think James must have caught the rustlers stealing him, and it cost him his life."

"If they haven't found the bull, he may still be alive. Get word to my grandfather. If the animal's still in the territory, my people can find him."

"I've already been out to the village. I went there looking for you as soon as I heard about James. Tall Shadow said they'd search."

"Thanks, Ben."

"There's no need to thank me."

"Yes, there is." He looked him straight in the eye. "You believe in me."

The fear and uncertainty both men were feeling went unspoken as they regarded each other solemnly before the sheriff broke their gaze.

"Your time's up!" Sheriff Dixon announced.

Ben gave Daniel one last hopefully reassuring look before he started from the cell.

Determined to prove his friend's innocence, Ben went straight to the Sundown Saloon to speak to Jenny. He didn't know if she'd be any help in finding out what happened to the medicine bag, but at least it was a starting point. To his surprise, the bartender told him Jenny was gone and that he didn't know when or if she'd be back. Ben asked several of the other girls if they had any idea of where he could find her, but none of them did. He'd been worried on his way over to the saloon, and he was even more troubled when he left.

Sixteen

A few hours later Cari sat on the bank of the stream watching the water rush by. Everything seemed so simple for the stream. It had a beginning and an end, and while sometimes its course didn't flow in a straight line, at least it knew which direction it was going.

Cari looked up at the sky, wishing her life was as simple as the stream's. It seemed her very existence was in ruins, as if a vast and devastating flood had swept through her life and had scoured away all vestiges of happiness. Nothing was left, and there was no escape from the torment. *Her father was dead. They believed Silver Wolf killed him . . .*

Tears traced down her pale cheeks, but she didn't bother to wipe them away. Since the moment she'd seen Silver Wolf, beaten and bound in the posse's custody, her heart and mind had been waging a terrible battle. Bewildered, turmoil churning in her soul, she struggled to understand the war within. The law said there was proof that Silver Wolf had murdered her father. Her heart argued that he could never have hurt her father and that it was all some terrible mistake.

Though she was deep in despair, Cari glanced around when

she heard the soft, lilting melody of a bird's song. She found herself gazing out across the pool where she'd first seen Silver Wolf on that wonderful, magical night. It seemed impossible that it had been less than a week ago when they'd made love there. So much had taken place since then that it almost seemed as if it had happened to someone else in another lifetime.

Since the moment she was told that Silver Wolf had murdered her father, Cari had refused to think about their night together by the stream. But now, as she let her mind touch upon those hidden memories, exquisite images of Silver Wolf came surging back and would not be denied. His passionate kisses and arousing caresses had shown her an ecstasy she'd never known existed. She thought of his tenderness when he'd loved her and of the fierce devotion he'd shown later in the face of her mother's vicious attack. She remembered, too, the terrible look in his eyes when their gazes had met just before he'd been forced to ride away with the posse, and her doubts of his guilt grew even more overwhelming.

Cari knew what she had to do. She had to go into town and talk to Silver Wolf. She had to look him straight in the eye and ask him for the truth. Until she did, she would know no peace.

Coming to her decision left her feeling better. She stood and hurried back toward the house, eager to ride to town. When she reached the top of the hill, she was startled to find Elliot coming her way.

"I've been looking for you," he told her.

"I had some thinking to do, and I needed to be alone."

"I was doing some serious thinking myself."

She glanced at him curiously.

"I was thinking about you and your mother, Cari. You know I've already made my plans to go home, but if you want me to stay, I'd be glad to, at least until the ordeal over your father's death is over. I don't want to leave you and your mother here to face the trial and whatever happens by yourselves." It hadn't been a difficult decision for Elliot to make. He knew Cari didn't love him, but that didn't change his feelings for her.

Love her as he did, he wanted to protect her and help her in any way he could.

Cari was touched by his offer, and she put a hand on his arm as their eyes met. She saw the depth of his caring mirrored in his gaze, and she reached up on tiptoes to press a kiss to his cheek. "Thank you."

Elliot savored her nearness but did not fool himself into thinking it was anything more than friendship. They walked back to the house in companionable silence. When they told Elizabeth of Elliot's plan to stay with them a while longer, she was pleased and thanked him for his thoughtfulness. She secretly hoped that Cari would change her feelings for Elliot now that she knew what kind of man the half-breed was.

Cari's thoughts were far different from her mother's, though, as she pleaded exhaustion and retired to her room shortly before dinner. Cari had decided not to tell her mother of her intentions beforehand to avoid the argument that would surely follow. She went to her room and waited until she could slip away from the ranch unnoticed. Cari knew there was an element of danger in making the trip alone, but she was so desperate to find out the truth, she took the chance. She had to see Silver Wolf again. She had to learn the truth from him. Until she did, nothing else mattered.

Sarah Jane had worked for Ed at the Sundown for many years. She was statuesque by nature and flame-haired by plan; her hair color had become her trademark over time. She was immensely popular with the men. They loved trying to match wits with her, for she always had a quick comeback for them, but they knew better than to make her angry. Her temper was legendary, and as fiery as her hair.

When little Jenny had been beaten by the younger Larson, Sarah Jane was angered. She'd told Ed what she thought of him for not protecting the girl, but he'd only shrugged; the Larsons were influential in town, not to mention good customers, and she knew he didn't want to offend them. Since the girl had had no place to go, Sarah Jane had taken her in, and she was staying with her in the little run-down house she'd saved enough money to buy. Jenny had been close-mouthed about what had made Larson so angry, but if he was prone to violence, it was best that he not know where Jenny was. Sarah Jane had told no one that the younger girl was recuperating at her house. She would do what she could to keep her safe, since Ed obviously wasn't going to help.

Sarah Jane left the Sundown a little after five to go home for a few hours. Business would pick up later that night, and she would be back by then, but right now, she just wanted to rest for a while.

"Things got pretty exciting at the saloon today," Sarah Jane told Jenny as she entered the house.

"What happened?" Jenny asked her, glancing up from where she was sitting at the kitchen table.

The older woman still was not used to the sight of Jenny's battered face. She grimaced inwardly as she saw once again her bruised and swollen features. Larson had sorely abused her, and she knew it would be at least another couple of weeks before the girl would feel comfortable going out in public again. "Remember I told you the rancher, James McCord, was found murdered?" At the girl's nod, she went on. "Well, the sheriff brought in Daniel Marshall this afternoon. They arrested him for it."

"Daniel? But they were friends . . ." Shock shone on Jenny's face.

"I don't know that much about it. I'm sure we ain't heard the last of it. You should have heard all the talk down at the saloon."

"What kind of talk?"

"Some of the men are all riled up over an Indian killing a white man. There's even wild talk about getting a lynching party together."

"But they don't know for sure he's guilty!" Jenny stared at her. Though she'd only met Daniel for those few hours on that one night, in her heart, she was certain of his innocence.

His Indian blood had nothing to do with it. She knew he wasn't a murderer.

Sarah Jane gave a harsh laugh as she thought of the hate-driven men in town. "He's half Indian, and to their way of thinking, that's enough to convict him."

Jenny was sickened by the realization that she was right. "The sheriff won't let them take him, will he?"

"Who knows? If there's enough of them, how's he going to stop them?" Sarah Jane moved off into her bedroom to lie down and rest for a while. She closed the door behind her, leaving Jenny alone.

Though Jenny hadn't left the house since coming there, the thought of Daniel being lynched spurred her to action. There was no way she could stand by and let him be hung for something he hadn't done. She had to help him.

It was starting to get dark outside, and Jenny was glad, for she didn't want anyone to see her in her present condition. She remembered that Daniel had told her she was pretty without her makeup, and she wondered if he'd still think so now, disfigured as she was by Mark's cruelty.

Jenny was desperate to help Daniel, but she knew Sarah Jane kept no weapons in the house. Frantically, Jenny searched the kitchen until she found a knife that looked threatening enough so he could use it to save himself if he had to. She wrapped it in a piece of cloth, then donned a dark cloak and crept from the house. She didn't want Sarah Jane to know she was gone. Keeping to the back alleys, she finally reached the rear of the jail.

Silver Wolf was lying on the cot, his arms folded behind his head. He was staring up at the ceiling, trying not to think. When the first pebble rattled against the bars of his cell window, he paid no attention, but when there was a second, he sat up, suddenly alert. After glancing out toward the office to make sure the sheriff was occupied with his own business, he stood on the bed to try to get a look outside.

"Daniel?" Jenny called his name in a hushed whisper.

"Yes," he answered just as quietly. He had to strain to hear the voice and didn't recognize it at all.

"There's talk of a lynch mob. Take this and be careful."

The small parcel was tossed up to him, and he was relieved when he managed to catch it on the first try. "Who are you?" he called back softly.

"A friend . . ."

"But . . ."

Footsteps were all that came to him. Puzzled, he quickly climbed down and sat on the cot. Thinking of the warning he'd just been given, he unwrapped the parcel and stared down at the knife with a mixture of relief and surprise. *A knife. Who would have brought him a knife?* Daniel knew it hadn't been Ben. Ben respected the law too much to even think of arming him. Then who? *A friend . . .*

Silver Wolf frowned as he hid the knife in his waistband, then stuffed the cloth out of sight under the thin mattress on the cot. He lay back down to wait. He hoped there would be no lynch party storming the jail tonight, but if there was, at least he wouldn't be completely defenseless.

Jenny rushed through the alleys back to Sarah Jane's house. No one saw her, and she was thrilled to find that the other woman had slept the whole time she was gone. Her breathing was ragged and her hands were shaking as she settled in, trying to look as if nothing had happened, as if she hadn't left at all. She silently prayed that no harm would come to Daniel.

After sneaking away undetected from the ranch, Cari rode like the wind to town. She was desperate to talk to Silver Wolf. She needed to get to him as fast as she could. Once she reached the sheriff's office and tied her horse outside, she'd had to force herself to walk like a lady into the jail.

"Miss McCord? Why are you here? Did something happen out at the ranch?"

"No. I'm here because I need to talk to Daniel." She could tell that Sheriff Dixon wasn't pleased by her request.

"But this is— "

She interrupted him. "It's important."

The look on Dixon's face was one of misgiving, but he slowly stood up. "All right."

He picked up the keys and led the way back toward the cell area.

"Marshall!"

His secret visitor had warned him of impending trouble over an hour before, and since then, Silver Wolf had lain tensely on the cot. At the sound of the sheriff's call, he sat up quickly, expecting trouble.

"You got a visitor!"

Relief swept through him. He expected it to be Ben. He glanced toward the door to the office, and the sight of Little Snow coming toward him brought him automatically to his feet.

Hard emotions pummeled him as Silver Wolf stared at her, drinking in the sweet sight of her. Joy surged within him. For just one fleeting moment, it reflected in his eyes, and then his sanity returned and he quickly masked it. He didn't know why she'd come, but he told himself that she wasn't there because she cared about him. He would never forget the way she'd looked at him at the ranch.

"Miss McCord wants to talk to you, Marshall. Stay away from the door while I open it," Dixon told him.

Silver Wolf fought to keep his expression carefully blank as he remained where he was, unmoving as the lawman unlocked his cell to let her in.

"You can go on in now," he said as he held the barred door for her. "Are you sure you want to?"

"It's important that I speak with him, Sheriff. I'll call if I need you," Cari assured him.

"Ten minutes is all you get. I'll be right outside, Miss McCord."

"Thank you, Sheriff," she answered politely.

Dixon shot his captive a threatening look as he started to lock the door behind her.

Silver Wolf didn't know why Little Snow had come, but certainly, her timing was perfect. The sheriff was alone in the office now, and there would never be a better opportunity to escape. He reacted on instinct. Moving with blinding speed, he grabbed Little Snow at the same time he knocked the door out of his jailer's grip. Hauling her back against him, he brought the knife to her throat in one smooth savage move.

"What the . . . !!" Dixon started for his gun.

"Don't do it, Sheriff. I'll use this on her if I have to!" he threatened, pressing the blade against her tender flesh.

A look of panic crossed the lawman's face as his hand froze over his sidearm, and Silver Wolf was glad. It meant he was in control.

Cari was stunned by Silver Wolf's move, and she held herself rigid against him. She had come here to see him because she'd thought him innocent of her father's murder. Why was he doing this? Was she wrong? Had he really shot her father?

"Don't say a word or try anything, Cari," he ordered sharply. "Sheriff, get in here and sit on the cot. Then shove your gun across the floor toward me! Don't make any fast moves. I'd hate for anybody to get hurt."

The sheriff stared at Cari's ashen face and knew, as much as it infuriated him, that he had to do what he was told. "All right. Just let the girl go, and everything will . . ."

"Nobody's going to get hurt as long as you do exactly what I say!"

The sheriff never took his eyes from Silver Wolf as he inched over to the cot and sat down. His movements were slow and deliberate as he drew his gun and then carefully slid it across the floor to him. Silver Wolf kicked the gun out of the cell and then backed out, too, dragging Cari along with him.

"If you don't want to see him die, go get a rope and something I can use to gag him," Silver Wolf told her as he let her go.

Cari jerked away and turned on him. Her gaze was wild as she frantically searched his stony expression for some sign of the man she loved. But there was no warmth of any kind in his hardened features.

Torn by his coldness, yet knowing she had no choice but to

obey, Cari rushed to get what he needed. In the outer office, she stopped and stared at the door that beckoned to her to safety. It was unlocked, and she knew there was no one to stop her if she wanted to go for help.

In that moment when freedom was hers for the taking, she made her choice. There was no logic in her decision, for logic told her that he wasn't the man she'd believed him to be and that she should run from him while she could. Her choice was based on a deep, gut-wrenching terror that any help she sought would end up in bloodshed and possibly death. Silver Wolf's

. . .

Cari knew how the townspeople felt about him, and if they found out that he was trying to escape, there would be no second thoughts on shooting first and asking questions later. She turned her back on the door and went back to her warrior's side with the rope and gag.

Silver Wolf had armed himself with the sheriff's revolver while he'd awaited her return. When she came back to him with the rope and gag, he gestured her back into the cell.

"Get in there, and tie his hands behind him and bind his ankles. Then gag him tight. I don't want anybody to find him right away. We need time to get away."

"We?" she repeated, staring at him in shock.

"You're coming with me," he stated flatly.

"That's insane!" Cari argued.

"Tie him up." It was an order.

"Marshall, you already killed her father! What do you want with the girl? Leave her here!" Dixon shouted at him, wanting to protect Cari if he could.

"She goes with me," he repeated, his resolve strengthened by the sheriff's certainty that he'd murdered James.

"Silver Wolf, don't you realize what will happen if you force me to go with you?" Cari pleaded with him as she finished tying the sheriff's hands and feet. "I'll just slow you down. If you go alone, you have a better chance to get away."

"I'll take the chance," he answered curtly.

"You're making a big mistake, Marshall!" Dixon shouted at

him, wild-eyed, as Cari prepared to gag him. "They'll hunt you down like the mad dog you are!"

"They already did that once." Silver Wolf's smile was savage as he glared at him. "Only that time, I didn't know they were after me. This time, I'll be ready."

"They'll shoot you on the spot for this!" he promised heatedly. "Leave the girl here!"

"Gag him," Silver Wolf repeated.

Cari stuffed the gag in his mouth.

"Good, now get out of there," he dictated harshly.

Dixon feared for Cari's life, and he twisted and fought his bonds, trying to break free. She had tied him too well, though. Frustrated, he could only watch as his prisoner made his escape.

Silver Wolf locked the cell door once Cari had come out. "We'll go out the back door."

Cari stopped and faced him, looking up at him with an imploring gaze. She was afraid— desperately so— and terribly confused. She knew what was going to happen to him if he ran and the posse caught him again. There would be no quarter given this time. They would be out for blood . . . his blood, and they wouldn't care how they got it. "Don't do this, Silver Wolf. It's like the sheriff said. They'll come after you. They'll hunt you down . . ."

"They won't do anything as long as I have you with me." His gaze met hers.

Cari shivered, for she could read no emotion in the hard silver of his eyes.

"Go by yourself! You can travel faster alone. You don't need me with you."

"You're my insurance," he said, taking her by the arm as he started for the back door. "Just keep quiet and nothing will happen to you."

Cari could see how implacable his expression was and realized there would be no changing his mind. She went with him.

Seventeen

Silver Wolf and Cari went out into the alley behind the jail. It was deserted, and he was grateful that at least *that* was going his way. Drawing Cari along with him, they made their way to the street and stood in the shadows unnoticed by passersby. He could see her horse tied up in front of the sheriff's office.

"Get your horse." His tone brooked no argument. "But don't get any ideas about trying to get away. Remember, I'm watching you and I've got the gun."

His threat chilled Cari as she moved away from him and headed to her waiting mount. She managed to appear calm as she walked down the street. Her hands were unsteady, though, as she untied her horse. She mounted and rode quietly away from the jail. No one could tell she was involved in a jailbreak and being held hostage at gunpoint.

When Cari reined in before Silver Wolf, he swung up behind her and reached around to take the reins. Dressed as he was in his warrior clothing, Silver Wolf knew his appearance would draw attention if anyone saw them, so he kept to the dark backways, avoiding any and all light as he took the shortest, quickest route from town.

Cari's heart was pounding as Silver Wolf made their way out of town. She was terrified that someone would find the sheriff before they had enough time to escape. Every fiber of her being was tense with the expectation of being discovered too soon, and she held herself rigidly before Silver Wolf, struggling to stay in control.

When at last they reached the edge of town and disappeared into the darkness of the countryside, Silver Wolf put his heels to the horse's sides and urged it to a quicker pace. Cari was relieved when they made it out of town without being discovered, and it was that very sense of relief that puzzled her and added to her emotional turmoil.

Cari had come to town to talk to Silver Wolf and get the answers she so desperately needed about what had happened to her father, but all she'd gotten were more questions. Confusion filled her— confusion about his motives, and about her own. As she rode before him as his captive, the thought that tormented her the most was that there was no reason for him to run if he was innocent. The thought repeated itself relentlessly in her mind as they traveled on in silence through the night.

As the miles passed, Cari's fear that they would be caught at any moment lessened. As the tension drained from her, she found she couldn't hold herself so stiffly anymore, and she slumped a little. The minute she did, she regretted it, for she found her back pressed solidly against the hard, muscular width of Silver Wolf's chest. Shock waves radiated through her at that contact, and she immediately tried to draw away from him again. As she straightened, however, his arm encircled her waist and held her pinioned against him.

"Relax. We've got a long ride ahead of us."

She acquiesced, but she couldn't really relax. There was something too intimate about the contact. "Where are you taking me?"

"Someplace where we won't be found."

"But why? Why are you doing this? If you're innocent, why did you break out and run?" At her words, she felt him go rigid.

"If, Little Snow?" he responded bitterly. "Your faith in me is easily shaken."

Silver Wolf had been hoping that she'd come to the jail to see him because she believed in him. Now, though, he realized his hopes had been foolish. He didn't know why she'd come, but it hadn't been to tell him that she thought he was innocent.

"My faith in you?" she returned angrily. "How can I believe in your innocence when they found your medicine bag in my father's hand? I know how important it is to you— you always wear it! You never go anywhere without it! If you weren't there, how did it end up with my father that night?"

"I don't know. I lost it the night of the dance."

"You lost it?"

"After I left you, I went to a saloon and started drinking. The following morning when I woke up, it was gone."

"You got drunk that night? But you don't drink . . ."

"I did that night."

Guilt stabbed at Cari as she heard the flatness in his voice, and she could form no reply. A heavy silence descended on them as they continued their night-shrouded flight.

Cari remembered the press of his knife against her throat when he'd taken her hostage at the jail, and she wasn't sure who to trust anymore. Did she trust in the law and the proof that pointed to Silver Wolf as her father's killer or did she put her trust in Silver Wolf, the man she believed she loved? The conflicting thoughts left Cari reeling. Her heart ached as she struggled to come to grips with her feelings.

Cari said nothing more as they rode on through the night. Caught up in her fierce inner turmoil, she was aware only of the solid feel of his arms around her and his body pressed against her as he guided their steed expertly across the deserted land.

As soon as word reached the Larsons that Daniel Marshall had been caught and would stand trial for the murder of James

McCord, the father and son rode for town. They headed for the Sundown Saloon to find out what was going on.

Sam was in a good mood. He drank heavily in celebration of the way things had turned out. Outwardly, Mark seemed as happy as his father, but, in truth, there was one loose end that was troubling him. As he downed his whiskey straight, he kept thinking of Jenny and wondering where she'd gone. He had to make sure she didn't show up at the sheriff's office and tell him the truth about the medicine bag. The odds were that Jenny was long gone, but until he knew her whereabouts for sure or Marshall was convicted and hung, he wouldn't be able to fully relax.

"To hell with a trial! I say we go get him tonight!" one man was shouting, red in the face and drunk beyond reason.

"Yeah! To hell with a trial!" Howard, another drunk, joined in. "What d'ya say, Tom?"

"He's guilty. We all know that," the man named Tom agreed.

"The sheriff's got all the proof we need! We know Marshall gunned James down in cold blood!" Howard declared.

"He's a damned half-breed. Who knows how many others he's killed the same way!"

"He's gotta pay for what he's done!"

"Then let's do it! Let's string him up tonight!"

Sam cast his son a satisfied look. "Sounds like we might not have to wait for justice to be done."

Mark raised his glass in salute. "That sounds good to me."

"Damned Indians!" Howard was raging. "We oughta run 'em all out of the territory!"

"We can't let him get away with murder!"

Their frenzied hatred pleased Sam. As riled up as the men in the bar were, he figured it wouldn't take much to get them to attack the Indian village, too, once they'd finished with Marshall. His plan to rid the territory of Indians was succeeding far beyond his wildest imaginings.

"Why're we just jawin' about it? Let's go hang the red devil and be done with it!!" Tom urged.

A roar of approval greeted his words, and the drunken men

surged en masse toward the swinging doors that led out onto the street. Sam and Mark weren't about to miss out on any of it, and they joined in the bloodthirsty crowd. The rumble of the mob's discontent echoed through the streets of Cheyenne, and their numbers grew as word of their purpose spread. The drunks stormed the few blocks to the sheriff's office with vengeance on their minds.

"Dixon! Sheriff Dixon! We want to talk with you!" Howard called out.

When no answer came right away, the crowd grew angrier and even more restless.

"Sheriff! We want Marshall and we want him now! Send him out or there's going to be trouble!" Tom shouted.

Again silence answered the hostile demand, and one of the drunken men threw a rock at the office window. The glass shattered, and the sound crashed through the night in a terrible echo. Still there was no response from the lawman.

"Maybe he's not there!" someone suggested.

"Maybe he heard us coming and got Marshall out."

"I'll go see," Howard announced.

Drawing his gun, he approached the jail. He tried the door and, to his amazement, found it unlocked. Once inside, he could hear something that sounded like grunting coming from the back room, and he rushed back to find the sheriff gagged and bound, locked in one of the cells. He tried to open the cell door, but found it was locked and there were no keys.

"What in hell happened to you?" he demanded as he reached through the bars to untie the gag.

"The bastard Marshall had a knife! I don't know how I missed it on him when I searched him, but I did!" Dixon told him, cursing vilely under his breath as he turned his back to Tom so he could free his hands.

"Where are the keys so I can get you out of there?"

"Marshall took them with him. You'll have to get the blacksmith to break the door open, and tell him to hurry! We can't let him get too big of a headstart on us. He's got the McCord girl. He took her hostage!"

"He *what?*" Howard had started from the cell area to go tell the others what had happened, when he stopped dead-still at this news.

"He kidnapped Cari McCord at knife point and forced her to go along with him."

"How long has it been since he broke out?"

"A couple of hours at least, damn it! I kept hoping someone would come in, but no one did." He was humiliated over the state of things.

Howard ran out front to deliver the news.

"The half-breed's broken out and taken the McCord girl hostage!"

"We knew he was guilty and this proves it! Let's find the son-of-a-bitch and hang him on the spot!"

"Yeah!!"

"We ain't going anywhere until we get the sheriff out of the jail cell. Somebody get the blacksmith! The rest of you who want to ride with us, get your horses and your guns! We'll be riding out as soon as Sheriff Dixon's ready!"

Mark was furious. He couldn't believe Marshall had broken out of jail! He told his father he was going to have one last drink before riding out with the posse, and he made his way back to the saloon, his mood black.

Sarah Jane had been upset by the ugliness of the mob, and she'd been nervous as she'd waited to see what was going to happen. When a few of the drunks began to straggle back in, aggravated because there had been no lynching, she was glad. She got herself a drink and was standing alone at the bar when Mark Larson returned and came up to her.

"I'll have another whiskey, Ed," he told the barkeep, "and the company of this pretty lady."

Sarah Jane managed a smile. "Evenin', Larson." The words almost gagged her, for she had no use for this bastard, and it wouldn't have taken much for her to tell him so.

"Evening, Sarah Jane. You're looking mighty lovely tonight."

Any of the other girls would have swooned to have his attentions, but she knew what he was capable of. She knew what he'd done to Jenny. "Why, thank you."

"Let's go sit at a table, shall we? There's something I want to ask you."

Sarah Jane wondered what he was after. He'd never wanted her before and she couldn't imagine what he wanted with her now. "All right. The girls tell me all the time that I'm the one with all the answers," she said with a laugh as she led the way to a table in the now almost-deserted bar. "What can I do for you?" she asked after they'd sat down.

"I need some information, and if anybody knows, it'll be you."

"Oh? About what?"

"Not what. *Who.* It's about Jenny. I want to know where Jenny is."

Anger flashed in her eyes for a moment and then was gone. It would be a cold day in hell before she'd tell him anything about the girl. "Ed threw her out and told her not to come back until she was looking good again. I don't know where she went."

"I'd like to believe you, Sarah Jane. I really would," he said in a low, threatening voice. "But you and Jenny were friends, and if anybody in town was going to know where she'd gone, it would be you."

"Like I said, Larson, I can't help you 'cause I don't know."

She started to stand up, but Mark caught her by the wrist in a painful grip and yanked her back down into her seat.

"I'm going to find her, Sarah Jane." His eyes bored into hers.

She could see the danger in his gaze and feel it in his painful hold, and she knew Jenny was in trouble, big trouble. "Good luck. Now, unless you want me to yell and let Ed know you're hurting me, I suggest you let me go."

"Hurt you? Why, I never meant to hurt you, Sarah Jane. I was just making my point," he said with a cool smile as he released her.

She cast him a contemptuous look as she got up and escaped his vile presence.

Larson finished his drink at his leisure and then left the saloon to join the posse. By the time he found his father, the sheriff had been freed from the jail cell and was getting ready to ride. More than twenty men had decided to go with him, and they'd gathered before the office to wait for him. When Dixon finally emerged, his expression was deadly serious.

"I appreciate your help, men," he told them.

"You shoulda let us kill him the day we first found him, Sheriff," Deputy Morgan prodded. He wasn't glad that Marshall had broken out, but he was certainly going to enjoy the chase of hunting him down again and, this time, killing him.

"A man's entitled to a trial," Dixon replied, his jaw set in fury as he reminded himself that he had to follow the law no matter how much he wanted to do otherwise.

"You ain't plannin' on bringing him back alive, are you, Sheriff?" one of the men demanded.

"Daniel Marshall's going to stand trial. There'll be no vigilante justice in my town," Dixon declared. He could see the hunger for violence in the faces of those gathered there, and though right now he felt the same, it was his job and sworn duty to uphold the law.

"But he kidnapped the McCord girl! No tellin' what he's done to her!"

"Any man who's riding in this posse because he wants to see a hanging might as well quit now and go home. I don't want you with me. I'm going to find Marshall and bring him in for trial. You got any different notions, get out now."

Morgan and Collins exchanged looks. They knew the sheriff wanted to do it all legally, but they were ready for revenge, and so was most of the town. Marshall had killed James McCord. Now, he'd broken out of jail and kidnapped a white girl. He deserved to die, and when the time came, they planned to see that he did just that. Neither man had any qualms at all about being the one to put an end to the half-breed's miserable life.

"All right. Let's ride."

"Where we goin'?"

"First, to Ben Douglas's office," he directed, and the posse headed there to begin their search for the fugitive killer.

Ben was working late in his office with the shades drawn, when he heard the sound of horses. When someone started pounding on the door, he hurried to answer it, fearing trouble. His fears were confirmed when he discovered the sheriff and his deputies, armed and ready, standing before him. There was also a heavily armed mob saddled up in the street.

"Sheriff Dixon, what is it? What's happened?"

"Your 'innocent' client pulled a knife on me and escaped from the jail!"

"He *what?*"

"You heard me! Now, step on out here while my men search your office."

Ben had barely moved when Morgan and Collins, their guns drawn, roughly pushed past him and began to search the office.

"How did this happen?" Ben demanded, thinking it a possibility that the deputies who were so intent on killing Daniel might have deliberately allowed him to escape so they could hunt him down as they were doing now.

"I wish I knew. He had a knife and he took the McCord girl hostage."

Ben was surprised by this news. She'd been devastated when they'd been together at the ranch, and he wondered why she'd come.

The sheriff nodded, "He threatened to kill me if she didn't go with him."

Ben swore under his breath, unable to understand his friend's reasoning. He believed unfailingly in Daniel's innocence, but he didn't understand why he had run. Running just made him look more guilty. "Have you sent anyone out to the Circle M to tell Mrs. McCord what's happened?"

"No, but I'll be doing that as soon as I'm sure they ain't hiding here with you."

Ben stiffened perceptibly at his insult. "Rest assured that I have no idea where my client is. But allow me to remind you, Sheriff Dixon, that he is to stand trial for James McCord's murder."

"Don't lecture me on the law, Douglas."

Morgan and Collins came charging out. "He ain't in there."

"Check upstairs!"

They rushed off again, leaving Ben, frustrated and maddened, with the sheriff and the rest of the posse. In minutes, they were back.

"Nothing," they reported.

"All right, then let's ride," Dixon ordered, and the two deputies quickly mounted back up. "If you find your client before we do, Douglas, you'd better make sure he turns himself in. Since he's taken a white girl hostage, I won't be responsible for what happens to him if the men find him when I'm not around."

Ben's expression was filled with contempt. "I'm riding with you, and I'm holding you personally responsible for Daniel's safety, Sheriff."

The two men stood, their hardened gazes dueling.

"Remember what I said, Douglas," the sheriff repeated as he turned and walked over to his deputies. "Morgan . . ." he directed. "You ride for the Circle M. The rest of you come with me!"

Fighting for control of his anger, Ben quickly prepared to ride out with the posse. He grabbed his rifle, locked the office, and went out to the stable to get his horse. He had no idea where Daniel had gotten the knife he'd used or what had possessed him to break out of jail, but he knew he had to be with the sheriff and his men when they found him.

Sheriff Dixon paused with the posse at the edge of town. "We'll split up here. Half you men come with me, the other half ride with Collins."

"Where you want me to search, Sheriff?" Collins asked.

"Go out to the fort to apprise Captain Greene of the situation. Then search south and west of town. We'll ride in the direction of the Cheyenne village. I don't think Marshall went there, but I want word spread that he's a wanted man and anyone giving him help will be in trouble. If you find him and the girl, bring them back to town. If not, we'll meet here in five days."

"We'll find them," Collins vowed fiercely, and they rode off in the direction of the fort.

Dixon turned in his saddle to speak to his men. "It'll be slow going until daylight, but I don't want to risk giving Marshall too big a lead. He knows this land like the back of his hand, and it's going to be hard to find him regardless. Anybody wants out, say so now. Otherwise, we're riding."

He paused, waiting to see if any of the men had had a change of heart. None did, so he motioned for them to follow him as he led the way from town.

The Larsons were glad they were riding with the posse, but they were less than pleased that Ben was going along. The half-breed had been set up perfectly, and they didn't want Ben stepping in to ruin things if the posse decided to take matters of justice into their own hands. They followed the sheriff, hoping it didn't take them too long to catch up with Marshall and the girl.

After Larson left, Sarah Jane was nervous and frightened. She waited until she was sure Larson had gotten out of town and then told Ed she was feeling sick and had to get outside for a while. Ed wasn't too happy, but let her go anyhow. Away from the bar at last, she hurried back to the small house and shook Jenny awake.

"What's the matter, Sarah Jane?"

"You gotta get out of here. Mark Larson's looking for you, and he means to find you."

"Oh, my God! Mark's after me again?" Jenny blanched at the news. "Where is he?"

"He rode out with the sheriff's posse to track down Daniel

Marshall, but he'll be back. Marshall broke out of jail tonight, and . . ."

"Daniel got away?" she said quickly.

Sarah Jane nodded and hurried to explain how Marshall had somehow gotten a knife and made his escape, taking Cari McCord hostage. "But none of that is important. What's important is that Larson's after you."

"I have to leave," she said in a panic. If Mark found out that she'd been the one to help Daniel escape, her life would be worthless. "I have to find someplace to hide. Someplace safe, where he'll never find me."

"Jenny, Mark's been with you many times. Why are you suddenly afraid of him?"

"I discovered the hard way that he can be a very violent man when he wants something."

"But what does he want from you?"

"I don't have time to answer your questions now. I've got to hide."

"Don't worry. I've been thinking about it all the way home, and I figured out the perfect place for you to go."

"Where?"

"To Mrs. Perkins's house," she answered, knowing what a safe haven the devout, little white-haired lady's home would provide.

Years before, when she'd first started working for Ed, Mrs. Perkins would often stop and talk to her on the streets. No other "good" woman in town would even acknowledge her, but Mrs. Perkins always did, and with a smile, too. Sarah Jane could still remember the last time the woman had tried to convince her to give up her work and begin another way of life. She'd been so endearing that Sarah Jane had almost agreed, almost believed it could happen, but then reality had returned. Not everyone was like Mrs. Perkins— loving and forgiving, and a girl did have to make a living when she didn't have a man to take care of her. Disappointed though Mrs. Perkins had been, the sweet lady had never given up on her. She continued to offer to take her to church services or help her in any way she could. Sarah Jane knew she herself was beyond "saving," but Jenny was another story.

"You mean that little lady we see who's always on her way to church?" Jenny stared at her in surprise.

"She's a kind old lady. She's always trying to help. I'll write you a note to give to her, but be careful getting to her house. Wear the dark cloak with the hood on it and stay out of sight. She'll take care of you once you're there."

Jenny stood and hugged her friend. "Thank you, Sarah Jane," she told her with heartfelt sincerity.

"Thank me later when this is all over and you can tell me the truth. Right now, get going. Ed's waiting for me, I gotta get back."

"Cari?" Elizabeth knocked softly at her daughter's bedroom door as she called her name.

She'd already been up for over an hour and had fixed breakfast, and still Cari had not come downstairs. Concerned, she'd decided to check on her. When no answer came to her knock, Elizabeth tried the door and found it unlocked.

"Cari? Are you feeling all right?"

She let herself into the room and was taken by surprise to find it empty. Frowning, she wondered where her daughter could have gone so early in the day. She moved to the bedside, and it was then that she noticed the piece of paper on the pillow.

Mother—
　　I've gone into town to get some answers.
　　I'll be back as soon as I can.

Love—
Cari

"How could she?" Elizabeth demanded aloud as she crushed the note in her hand. She felt betrayed and hurt as she stormed out of the room. In her blind fury she didn't see Elliot in the hallway and almost ran into him.

"Cari's gone," she told him, distraught.

"Gone?" Elliot repeated, confused. "Where?"

"According to her note, to town. She must have left late last night or very early this morning. Here, read this . . ." She handed him the note, and he quickly scanned it.

"Do you want me to go after her?"

"Oh, Elliot, thank you. I don't know what to think and I'm so worried about her . . ."

"I'll be ready to leave in a few minutes. Will you be all right alone?"

"The hands are here. I'll be fine."

Within minutes, he was ready to ride. Elizabeth accompanied him to where his horse was saddled and waiting.

"Bring Cari back to me."

"I will," he promised.

He gave her a warm hug and then mounted and prepared to leave. "I'll be back with her just as soon as I can."

Elliot reined his horse around and started from the ranch. He hadn't gone more than a mile when he saw a rider coming toward him, traveling fast.

"What's wrong?" he called out as he recognized him as one of the sheriff's men. "What happened?"

The deputy reined beside Elliot. "I'm Deputy Morgan, and I need to see Mrs. McCord right away!"

"Why? What is it?"

"The half-breed, Marshall, has escaped from jail, and he kidnapped Cari and took her with him! I gotta tell Mrs. McCord what happened!"

"Let's go!"

Elliot swore under his breath as they raced toward the ranch house. It infuriated him that Cari had gone into town alone, but for her to have been caught up in Silver Wolf's jailbreak outraged him even more. The man had claimed to care about her, yet he'd taken her hostage, and in doing so had put her in a situation where she could be hurt or even killed. He dreaded telling Elizabeth, but as much as he would have liked to have kept news of Cari's capture from her, there was no way he could avoid it.

"Elizabeth?" Elliot called as they reached the house.

She came out, a curious look on her face. "What is it? Why did you come back so soon, Elliot?"

"This is Deputy Morgan. Sheriff Dixon sent him."

"What's happened?" Elizabeth demanded, immediately sensing something was wrong.

"It's your daughter, ma'am," he began.

"Cari?" There was a note of hysteria in her voice.

"Yes, ma'am. Marshall broke out of jail last night, and he took her hostage."

"Dear God . . ." Elizabeth turned pale, grabbing the porch railing to support herself. "How could this have happened?"

"He had a knife. When your daughter went in to talk to him, he grabbed her. He was going to kill her unless the sheriff went along with him. So Sheriff Dixon did everything he said. The sheriff told him not to take Cari with him, but Marshall said he needed her for insurance." He quickly related everything he knew about the breakout.

"You have to find them! You have to get my daughter back!"

"Yes, ma'am. The posse's already out looking for them. I'll be joining up with them just as soon as I leave here."

"I'm going with you," Elliot insisted, stalking into the house to get what he needed.

When he returned, he not only had his bedroll, but he was wearing a sidearm and carrying a rifle. He laid them aside while he embraced Elizabeth.

"We'll find her. Don't worry. I'll bring her back to you," he promised solemnly.

She could only nod, for her throat was too tight with tears. Terror filled her. She had lost James, would she lose Cari, too?

"We'll be back as soon as we can, ma'am," Morgan assured her.

Elliot gathered his things and mounted up. His mood was grim as he rode off with the deputy.

"How long will it take us to catch up with the sheriff?"

"Not more than half a day if we're lucky."

Elliot nodded. He wanted to be there when they found Cari, for he could well imagine how devastated she was. Her note had said that she'd gone into town seeking answers. Elliot's expression turned harsh. Cari had gotten her answers all right, but he knew they weren't the ones she'd wanted. He hoped and prayed with all his heart that she was safe.

Elizabeth watched them ride away, and only when they'd gone did she allow herself to break down. Sobs choked her as she turned back into the house. She cried out mournfully for her daughter, aching to have her by her side. She'd known Cari had been upset about Silver Wolf, and she regretted that she hadn't taken the time to talk to her about it. But her own pain over losing James had been too great right then. Now, as she considered that she might have lost her daughter as well as her husband, she grew afraid.

For a moment, she wondered if Cari had anything to do with the half-breed's escape, but she quickly discarded the idea. Silver Wolf had killed James, and there was no way her daughter would have willingly helped her father's murderer escape.

Elizabeth searched desperately for a fragment of hope to cling to; the only hope she could find was that maybe, just maybe, Silver Wolf truly did care for Cari. As she prayed for her safe return, she agonized over her daughter's headstrong ways. Had Cari not gone into town to see him in the first place, she would have been safe. Elizabeth returned to her prayers, desperate to have her child back safe and unharmed.

Eighteen

For the posse, night had turned to day, and then the day had aged with no sign of the escaped prisoner and his hostage. They'd known it would be difficult to find them, but they were determined to catch him and see justice done.

"Are we riding into the village?" Sam Larson asked the sheriff at midmorning.

"We'll scout around the area, but there's no reason to confront Tall Shadow," Dixon said. He didn't want to start an Indian war, he just wanted to catch Daniel Marshall and free the McCord girl.

"I say we go in!" Sam argued, trying to rile up the posse to a fever pitch. "He's probably hiding there with the girl!"

Until that time Ben had said very little, but the thought of the posse riding into Tall Shadow's village, armed and angry, worried him. He thought of Star Blossom and all the other innocents there, and how fighting might erupt with the smallest provocation. Not wanting trouble, he knew he had to find a way to keep the posse from doing it.

"Daniel wouldn't have gone to the village. He'd never do anything that would put his people at risk."

"Ben's right, and, besides, there's no reason to stir up the

Cheyenne. We're only after Marshall and the girl," Dixon told him firmly.

"But what if the other Indians were involved with the rustling?" Sam demanded, frustrated by the sheriff's caution and eager to stir up trouble. "I say we go after them all!"

Ben glanced at the rancher. He remembered Daniel telling him that the Larsons might be the ones responsible for all the trouble, and he wondered at Sam's great desire to fight the Cheyenne. As small as the posse was, he wasn't sure that they would win any confrontation with Tall Shadow's warriors, and he wondered at the other man's bloodlust.

"Sam, we've got no proof they had a hand in it. We're tracking the half-breed."

Sam wanted to argue, but held his tongue for now. He hoped his time would come once they found Marshall and the girl.

The hours passed and the posse rode on, weary but vigilant. They were determined to find Marshall. At midafternoon, Morgan and Elliot met up with them and joined in the hunt. The hours dragged on as they searched futilely for some clue to the fugitive's whereabouts.

Late in the day, they came upon a stream and were about to take a moment to rest and water their horses when they heard the distant sound of a woman's voice. Anticipation filled the exhausted group, and they drew their guns as they rode in closer. Morgan was anxious to get his hands on the escaped prisoner again, and he barged ahead of the others, his horse crashing through the foliage in his rush to trap whoever was there. A feminine shriek of terror came to them from the direction he'd ridden.

"Well, well, well, what have we got here?" Morgan asked. "Sheriff Dixon! Look what I found!"

Ben had been riding toward the back of the posse, but when he heard the woman's cry, he pressed his mount forward and worked his way to the head of the group. As he did, Morgan came riding back, looking almost a drover on a cattle drive as he herded two frightened Cheyenne women before him.

"What the hell do you think you're doing?" Ben demanded,

seeing the women and their horrified expressions. He charged forward to defend them against the deputy's harshness.

"I'm going to find out where the damned half-breed is hiding!" the deputy declared, bearing down on the two helpless females. "And they're going to tell me!"

As Ben neared the women, he glanced down at them and immediately recognized Star Blossom.

He said her name without thinking and wheeled his horse in her direction.

Star Blossom had gone down to the creek with her friend, Calling Dove. The day had been so perfect that they'd decided to take a walk and just enjoy the sunshine and warm breezes for a while. They'd been shocked when a white man had appeared out of nowhere, startling them and chasing them in the direction away from their village and help. Unable to escape, they'd found themselves driven toward the menacing gang of white men. Memories of the tortured deaths of her mother and sister returned full force, and Star Blossom was quaking with terror as she and Calling Dove clung together.

They stood before the white men now, fearing the worst and knowing they had nowhere to run or hide. There would be no escaping them. Just as she was about to give in to her panic, Star Blossom recognized Ben's voice and heard him call her name. She looked up to see him charging toward her like an avenging warrior, his expression fiercely savage. Her breath caught in her throat as a tremendous sense of joy flooded through her. It was Ben! Ben was there! Ben would help them!

Ben saw the terror on her face, and, swearing violently under his breath, he commanded his mount between Morgan and the women. Reaching down, he snared the deputy's bridle and forced his horse away.

"Leave them alone, Morgan!" Ben ordered as he used his steed to shield the two women from his assault.

"Who are you to tell me what to do?" the deputy returned angrily. He'd been enjoying himself, treating the Indian women like the animals they were, and he had no intention of quitting so quickly. He figured if the sheriff wouldn't let them ride on the village, at least he could have a little fun with some of the women.

"I'm a friend to the Cheyenne, and they don't take kindly to their women being mistreated," Ben told him, looking the other man straight in the eye.

"I wasn't mistreating them. I just wanted to ask them a few questions."

"That's why you were riding them down like animals in a hunt!" he snarled.

Sheriff Dixon reached them then. "Enough, the both of you! Morgan, get out of here."

Ben hadn't been sure how the others in the posse would react to his defending the women. He was relieved to discover the sheriff was his ally, for he knew he wasn't strong enough or fast enough with a gun to take them all on should they turn on him.

The deputy relented grudgingly, and Ben let go of his horse. Ben waited until he'd moved away before dismounting to go to Star Blossom.

Star Blossom had watched Ben place himself in harm's way to protect her and Calling Dove. It was the second time he'd saved her from danger, and a strange, heart-rending emotion filled her as he came toward them. Her friend was still frightened and held tightly to Star Blossom's arm as she watched Ben approach, but Star Blossom gave her a quiet word of reassurance. "He is a friend."

The men of the posse watched from a short distance away as Ben talked to them.

"I'm sorry that happened. No one's going to hurt you." His words were softly spoken to the both of them, but his eyes were only on Star Blossom. "Are you all right?"

For just an instant, Star Blossom knew a crazy desire to throw herself into his arms and let him protect her forever, but she held herself back. She and Calling Dove nodded in response, and Star Blossom managed to say, "It is good to see you, Ben Douglas."

She spoke quietly, but he could see the shadow of fear still haunting her eyes and knew she meant what she'd said. He smiled gently at her. "It's good to see you, too."

"Why are you here? What do they want?"

"We're trying to find Silver Wolf. Have you seen him?" he asked her in low tones, not wanting the others to hear.

"No. He has not been to the village."

"If you see him, will you give him a message for me?"

"I will," she agreed.

"Inform him that there is much trouble in town and that he should turn himself in."

"I do not know that I will see him, but if I do, I will tell him your words."

"Thank you. Go on back now. I'll watch and make sure no one bothers you again."

Star Blossom cast Ben a lingering look, then drew the frightened and trembling Calling Dove along with her. They quickly disappeared from view, leaving Ben to face the posse.

"What did ya let them go for?" Morgan asked hotly. "They might have known something about Marshall!"

"They didn't know anything," Ben answered tersely. "Daniel hasn't been anywhere near the village."

"You believed what they said?" Sam demanded.

"I know Star Blossom. She has no reason to lie to me."

"All Indians are liars!" Morgan argued.

"I say we ride into the village!" Sam attempted to agitate the group.

Ben would have responded, but the sheriff cut them off. "Let's get back to our search. We've still got a lot of territory to cover."

They continued to comb the countryside, looking for some sign of Marshall or the girl, but found no clues to their whereabouts. At dusk, they could do nothing more and made camp. Elliot joined Ben as they ate the meager dinner.

"Do you think we'll find them soon?" Elliot asked, worried about Cari. He felt frustrated by their lack of success that day.

Ben cast a sidelong glance at him. He'd been surprised by his endurance so far, and his respect for the man was growing.

"I don't know," Ben answered. "Daniel was born and raised on this land. He knows every inch of it. If he doesn't want to be found, he won't be."

"If he's as innocent as you say, why did he break out of jail?"

"I wish I knew. Maybe he thought he'd be able to find the men responsible for James's death."

"But what about Cari? Why did he drag her along? Do you think she's all right?"

Ben's mouth tightened at his accusation. "Daniel would never harm Cari."

Elliot looked disgusted at his continued defense. "You say he had nothing to do with killing James, yet he took Cari hostage at knife point! If he cared for Cari, why would he put her in such danger?"

Ben shrugged. "I don't know and right now, it doesn't matter. What matters is finding him before something happens."

Elliot nodded and turned in for the night. As he lay there, he found himself regretting that he didn't know more about this land. He prayed, too, that luck was on their side, that they would soon find them, and Cari would be returned to them, unharmed.

Silver Wolf knew a posse would be after them as soon as the sheriff was found tied up in the jail, so he made certain that their trail was difficult to follow. Traveling over the roughest terrain, he backtracked as often as he could without losing too much time. He avoided all populated areas as he headed for the one place in the wilderness he knew they'd be safe— the place where his vision quest had come to him.

Exhaustion and pain filled Silver Wolf, but he didn't let it slow him down. Guiding the horse through the trees and up the hillside, they covered the last leg of their journey to the location where he'd camped that night. It was a private spot that offered a good view of the surrounding area and protection from the elements in the small cave nearby. The trek had been arduous but worth it, for he believed they would be safe there until he'd had the time he needed to find James's killer.

Silver Wolf had been torturously aware of the soft curve of Little Snow's body fitted perfectly against him as she rode before him. He wanted her desperately, loved her deeply, but his heart was heavy with the knowledge that though she had professed to love him, her love obviously hadn't been strong enough to withstand the attacks against him.

Reaching the clearing, Silver Wolf drew the horse to a halt and slipped from its back. He was glad to see that little had changed since he'd been there last, and he turned to Little Snow and lifted his arms to her to help her down.

Cari was bone-tired. The long hours in the saddle had taken their toll on her. She looked around, trying to figure out where they were, but Silver Wolf's efforts to lose those following them had also confused her and she wasn't sure.

When Silver Wolf came to her and offered to help her down, Cari wanted to refuse him, but every inch of her body ached and she doubted that she would be able to climb down on her own. Forced to accept his offer, she braced her hands on his shoulders as his hands went to her waist.

As Cari slid down, Silver Wolf accidentally brought her fully against him, and the contact jolted them both. Cari was stunned by the power of the feelings that swept through her, and for just an instant, frightened, too. It was that emotion that was reflected in her eyes when she looked up at Silver Wolf.

He had meant only to help Little Snow dismount,. but the moment he held her clasped against him, he knew he didn't want to let her go. He looked down at her, hoping to find that she was feeling the same way he was. But what he saw mirrored in her eyes was not burning desire, but what looked to be cold fear.

The thought that he frightened her touched Silver Wolf deeply, and he released her abruptly, unable to bear the exquisite torture of holding her so close and not being able to love her. He wanted to see her eyes shining with love for him. He wanted her to give herself to him freely as she had when they'd been together at the stream, not look at him with terror and loathing.

"We'll be staying here," he said in gruff tones as he moved away from her.

"For how long?" Cari didn't know why, but she felt almost bereft now that he'd let her go.

"For as long as it takes me to find the men who killed your father," he answered, turning his back on her. He took the reins and led the horse a short distance away.

Once again, his words struck at the heart of her confusion. If he was unjustly accused of the murder . . . then who had done it? Caught up in her roiling thoughts, she said nothing more, but only looked on as he tended to their tired mount.

Silver Wolf used the time bedding the horse down to work out some of his frustration. He didn't know how to prove his love to Little Snow. He wanted to grab her and shake her and tell her over and over that what they'd said about him were all lies, but he knew doing that would only make things worse. She had to come to believe in him on her own. He could only wait and pray that somehow, some way, some day, she would remember what they'd shared, and know.

Finishing with the horse, he picked up the saddle and blanket and headed into the cave. The fear he'd seen in her expression had hurt him, and he didn't even glance in her direction as he passed her. He knew he was leaving her there unguarded with the horse and that she could take her mount and run from him— and that was precisely what he wanted her to know. He wanted her to understand that he wouldn't use force to keep her with him, that she wasn't his hostage. He realized that she might very well flee, but it was a chance he was willing to take in his quest to convince her of his love.

Cari was stunned when he disappeared into the cave and left her alone with her horse. It would have been simple for her to escape, and she knew that he knew it. She stared at the horse, and then at the cave entrance, and in that moment a bud of truth swelled within her and she knew she had to talk to him. Following him into the darkened cavern, she found him just beyond the rim of daylight with his back to her, hunkered down building a fire.

"Silver Wolf?" She said his name softly, half in anticipation, half in dread.

At the sound of her voice behind him, he went still and a feeling of joy shot through him. He'd given her the chance to go and she'd stayed. . . . Forcing down the fierce emotion that welled up inside him, he glanced back over his shoulder at her.

Anguish gripped Cari as she saw once again the bruises on his face. She tried to read his expression, but found it inscrutable. Girding herself, she forced herself to go on, knowing she was the one who had to speak.

"Weren't you afraid that I'd take the horse and run away?" she finally managed.

"I was afraid you'd run from me," he admitted slowly as he forgot all about starting the fire and stood up to face her, "but I was more afraid of your fear. I don't want you to be afraid of me, Little Snow . . . ever."

"But I could have just ridden off. I could have gone for the sheriff . . ."

His gaze was stormy and his expression was serious as he met her wide, questioning gaze without reserve. "I trust you, Little Snow," he said with quiet intensity. "I trust you with my life."

His words were poignant, and her eyes filled with tears. "But why did you break out of jail? Why did you run?"

"The friend who brought me the knife told me that there was talk of vigilantes breaking into the jail to lynch me last night. I'm sorry if I frightened you, Little Snow, but you were my only chance to escape. I was hoping you believed in me enough not to run from me at the jail."

"I couldn't," she admitted, letting her gaze drop away from his.

He cupped her chin and lifted her face to him, forcing her to look as he spoke his next words. "I love you, Little Snow. You're the only woman I've ever loved. You alone hold my heart."

The bud of truth Cari had nurtured in her breast bloomed,

and the love she felt for him filled her with happiness. This was her Silver Wolf! He was the man she loved, not some terrible stranger. He always spoke the truth to her, and she'd been wrong, so very wrong, to forget that. He would never have harmed her father, no matter what evidence had been found!

"I'm sorry, Silver Wolf. I'm so sorry that I didn't believe you over the others," she whispered in an emotion-choked voice as she took a step toward him.

Her one step of surrender was all he needed to break the chains of restraint that had held him at bay. He took her in his arms and held her to his heart.

"Ah, Little Snow."

"I love you," she told him simply, glorying in the strength of his embrace.

At her words, he kissed her, and she welcomed him wholeheartedly. It was a deep kiss that told her of his desperate need for her, and she returned it full measure. They strained together as their lips met, then parted, then met again.

Silver Wolf had already spread the blanket on the ground, and he lowered Little Snow onto it now, then lay with her. His body was a searing brand upon hers.

The feeling of holding him so intimately was exquisite. She whispered his name in a tone of wonder. "Silver Wolf . . ."

"I know, my love . . ." he told her, barely in control.

He wanted to savor every moment of loving her, but his need for her was a driving hunger that could no longer be denied. His mouth claimed hers in a passionate exchange as his hands freed the buttons on her blouse. He parted the fabric and brushed it aside, baring her bosom to his kisses and caresses. Cari moaned in ecstasy as his lips sought the sensitive crests of her breasts. She began to move beneath him, urging him with her body to take her and fill the aching emptiness within her.

Unable to bear being separated from her any longer, Silver Wolf drew away only long enough to shed his clothing and to help Little Snow strip away hers. When at last she lay unclothed beneath him, he paused to gaze down at her, visually caressing her silken limbs, passion-swollen breasts, and the sweet curve of her hips. His eyes glowed with the love he felt, and he fitted himself to her, seeking the hot depths of her body with the proof of his desire. They came together in a heated rush of pleasure.

Cari opened to him like a blossom to the sun, and she followed his lead, matching his loving movements with a hunger of her own. They moved as one, giving and taking, sharing the beauty of their love in passion's oldest and most cherished way.

Caught up in the magic of their joining, there was only the two of them, caught up in their Elysian ecstasy.

In the quiet, blissful aftermath of their loving, they drifted. Neither spoke, for words were not necessary. Their bodies had expressed what mere words could never describe. They loved, and nothing would ever come between them again.

When at long last Silver Wolf felt strong enough to move, he rose above her, bracing himself on his elbows as he gazed down at her love-flushed features.

"You're beautiful," he told her in a husky voice. "I will never tire of looking at you."

Cari smiled up at him. "You're beautiful to me, too," she responded as she lifted her hands to tenderly caress the bruises that marred his face. Her heart ached, knowing what he'd suffered at the hands of his jailers. She vowed to herself to ease his pain and to never let him be hurt again.

Silver Wolf's lips sought hers in a cherishing, worshipful caress. "I love you."

"I'll never doubt you again," she promised, tears falling as she realized how close she'd come to losing him.

He kissed her once more, with infinite tenderness and care, then shifted away to the side so he could hold her, her head nestled on his shoulder as she curled against him. She rested her hand on his chest, and he covered it with his own as they lay together, celebrating the intimacy of their love.

Nineteen

Silver Wolf held Little Snow in his arms and treasured having her near. Gazing down at her as she lay quietly against him, he wondered how he'd existed all those days and weeks and years without her. When she was with him, he felt whole. Without her, his life seemed empty and pointless.

At the thought of being parted from her, Silver Wolf instinctively tightened his arms around her, as if believing that if he held her more closely, she would never slip away from him again. Little Snow stirred against him, and the movement of her satiny limbs was an unschooled caress that proved far more arousing than any learned loving. His passions soared, the heat hardening the manly center of him.

"Little Snow . . ." he murmured as he lifted her to him, needing to kiss her.

Cari opened her eyes as he brought her fully against him, and she gazed down at him with open, hungry desire.

"Somehow I always knew it would be this way between us . . ." she said in a husky voice.

She lay full-length against him, her breasts crushed against his chest and her hips fitted to his. The male heat of him seared her with the proof of his need.

"What way?" he asked, capturing her lips in a devouring kiss.

"Perfect," she sighed.

Emboldened by the knowledge that he loved her, she deepened the kiss, and when she felt a shudder wrack him, she knew a tremendous sense of feminine power. Suddenly, she wanted to know his body as well as he seemed to know hers. She became daring in her loving, caressing his hard-muscled frame with an eager, fiery touch.

When her lips followed the trail her hands had blazed, Silver Wolf could no longer control the blazing need that threatened to consume him. He clasped her to him and rolled with her, bringing her beneath him. In one sweet, powerful move, he buried himself within her. Little Snow gasped at the sensation. Silver Wolf tensed and started to pull away.

"Are you all right?" he asked worriedly, fearing he had hurt her in his frantic need to be one with her.

She held him tightly to her. "I'm fine," she told him with a throaty chuckle. "It just feels so good to have you inside me."

Her words turned the fire of his desire to a raging inferno, and he could no longer talk, he could only feel. He began to move, setting his passionate pace, as they sought the beauty of love's enchantment once again.

Tall Shadow saw the look of urgency on Strong Eagle's face as he listened to Star Blossom and Calling Dove tell of meeting the posse and speaking with Ben. When the women had gone, the chief looked at his grandson's best friend.

"You would go to him?"

"I believe I know where he is. Whenever he wants to be alone, he returns to the place where he received his vision quest."

"Then find him and tell him what we have heard."

"I will," he promised. "As soon as I have gathered what I need, I will ride to the cave."

The chief nodded. "I hope he is where you say. Tell him that my prayers are with him."

The warrior hurried to prepare for the trip to find his friend.

The night lark's song heralded the coming of dusk, and forced Silver Wolf back to reality from the Eden of Little Snow's embrace. His expression darkened as he realized they couldn't stay there alone in the cave forever. As much as he wanted to ignore the outside world, he couldn't. The law believed he was the murderer. He had to prove his own innocence.

Disquiet settled over him, stripping away the peace and contentment that had soothed him while he was with Little Snow. He'd warned himself that he'd been foolish to forget himself so completely, and he knew he would have to be more cautious from now on. He started to move away from Little Snow. It was important that he go outside and check the area to make certain that no one was near.

Little Snow felt him leaving her and roused herself from her drowsy splendor. "Where are you going?"

He could see concern in her eyes, and he wanted to reassure her. "Right now, to find us something to eat," he answered as he donned his clothes. He stared down at the loveliness of her body, and his heart beat a heavy rhythm. The look of love in her eyes renewed his deep conviction to do everything in his power to find her father's killer.

"Be careful," she whispered.

They regarded each other in silent understanding for a moment, and then he was gone. Without him, Cari felt chilled. She got up and dressed. Then she set about building the fire he'd attempted to start earlier.

Cari stayed inside the cave for as long as she could stand it, but finally, she grew restless and worried about him. When darkness settled over the land, and he still had not returned, she went outside to watch for him.

The moon had risen and hung low on the horizon. Stars twinkled in the clear, black velvet sky, and a cool night breeze swept away the heat of the day. As she stared off into the night, she could hear a wolf howling, its night song echoing hauntingly across the land.

"Little Snow . . ."

The sound of Silver Wolf's voice so close by startled Cari, and she turned to find him approaching from the other direction. "You're back . . ." She smiled in warm welcome, relieved.

"With dinner." He held up his bounty, a rabbit.

While he'd been out checking for signs of the posse, he'd come across the hapless rabbit. He'd already skinned and cleaned it, and now he headed for the fire so he could cook it on the sharpened stick he'd fashioned to use as a spit. Sitting down before the fire, he put the meat on the spit and held it out over the flames to roast.

Cari sat across the fire from him, studying him from beneath lowered lashes. The firelight bronzed him, his broad chest and wide shoulders glowing powerfully in the golden light. She remembered how hard and solid he'd felt beneath her questing hands, and a heat that had nothing to do with the fire warmed her. She forced herself to look away.

Silver Wolf patiently waited for the meat to cook. When it was done, he tore off a chunk and handed it to Little Snow.

She was hungry and gave no thought to her years of etiquette training as she ate it with her fingers.

Silver Wolf sat back and tore off a piece for himself. He devoured his portion with the same eagerness as Little Snow. His hunger for food satisfied, he realized for the first time just how tired he really was.

"I'm going to take a last look around before we bed down for the night. Do you want to come with me?" he invited.

There was no way she was going to stay behind alone again

and worry herself sick about him. She wanted to be by his side every minute she could.

He stood and held out his hand to her. They walked from the cave. He led her to the best vantage point, and they stood together, sharing a sense of peace.

"What are you looking for?" she asked, staring out across the darkened landscape.

"A campfire, or anything else that seems unusual," he told her, concentrating on the distance. He was tense until he was sure that there was no one near, then he allowed himself to relax, but only a little. He drew a deep breath as he glanced down at her and smiled reassuringly. "We'll be safe until morning."

She smiled up at him, loving him, trusting him.

His heartbeat quickened as he saw her expression. "Little Snow . . ." He lifted a hand to tenderly caress her cheek. "As soon as this is over, I want to make you my wife . . . by white law and by Cheyenne."

Pure ecstasy shone in her eyes, and she went into his arms and held him tight. "I love you, Silver Wolf. I want to be your wife in all ways."

He took her by the shoulders and held her away from him as his gaze met hers. It was time for them to face the truth, to talk about the future. "You know it won't be easy. Even after your father's murderer has been found, there will be those who hate me for my Indian blood and hate you for marrying me."

Her expression turned serious as she raised up on tiptoe and pressed her lips to his. "There's not another man alive who is as strong and brave as you are. I love you, Silver Wolf. That's all that matters."

"But is love enough?" he countered, worrying that some day she might regret loving him.

She answered him with her kiss, deepening it. "Your love is all I need . . . all I want. You are my life. Without you, I have nothing."

He groaned as she said all that he was feeling, and he kissed her wildly, his tongue delving into the honeyed sweetness of her mouth to meet and twine with hers.

"Tell me of the Cheyenne way of marriage," she encouraged as they stood beneath the silvery moon and stars.

"The brave sends one of his female relatives to take gifts to the girl's family. When she goes to talk to them, she tells them of the brave's love for the maiden. The woman's family then discusses the merits of the match, and the relative is told whether or not his proposal is favorably received or not."

Cari looked sad. "I wish it was that simple for us, but there is no gift that would convince my mother that our love is true and that we should marry."

"I know, but in my heart you are already my bride," he said with fierce devotion. "All my days, I will never want another woman."

She turned and lifted her face to look up at him. "If we can pledge ourselves to each other before God, then I am your bride, Silver Wolf, in my heart and in all ways."

Entranced, Silver Wolf gazed down at her. In the moonlight, her hair shone as spun silver. He touched the sleek beauty of it, then took her by the shoulders and gently pulled her to him. They stood locked in each other's arms in the moonlight, surrounded by the peace of the night and the power of their love. For now, at least, they were safe.

After a moment, Silver Wolf took her hand and led her back into the cave. They shed their clothing once again, and gilded by the firelight, they came together once more.

To Cari, this was her wedding night. She gave herself over to her husband's ardent lovemaking without reserve, and she returned his caresses with equal fervor. Her hands explored him with a hungry touch that left him breathless and panting for more. She grew daring and, straddling him, took him deep within her.

"Little Snow . . ." He was surprised, yet thrilled by her sensual move.

"Shh . . ." she whispered, a soft smile curving her mouth. "I only want to please you."

"You always please me, my love."

Leaning down to him, she kissed him as she began to move her hips in love's age-old motion. His hands caressed her breasts, then skimmed over her silken flesh to her hips. He held her as she rode him, each hungry thrust of her hips taking him higher and higher until finally the sensual torment was too much for him to bear. Bringing her beneath him, he took control, and together they reached pleasure's peak.

The exquisite glory of their joining sealed their lives as one. They lay together spent, their bodies still melded, their limbs still entwined.

Sleep claimed Cari first, and she drifted off in the arms of her dream warrior, her lover, her husband. Silver Wolf lay awake long into the night, worshiping the beauty of her and praying fervently for a lifetime with her and not just these few desperate hours.

When Cari awoke it was daylight, and she was surprised to find that she'd slept so well and so long. She smiled to herself as she thought of the night before, and she stretched sensually, remembering the excitement of loving Silver Wolf. She expected to find her warrior nearby, but there was no sign of him. Wanting to see him again, she quickly rose and went in search of him. She found him, sitting at the vantage point looking out over the valley below.

She greeted him as she went to him.

He returned her smile, thinking she looked even more beautiful this morning— if that was possible. He kissed her in welcome. "I've gathered some berries for breakfast, and there's a creek not far from here if you want to freshen up."

"I'd like that."

He escorted her to the stream, then discreetly disappeared while she tended to her feminine needs. Cari was grateful for the time alone. A short time later when he returned, she'd washed and felt refreshed. Silver Wolf enjoyed watching her as she finished up, and he remembered the first time they'd made love and he had bathed her in their stream.

When she was done, they returned to the cave, and she

feasted on the berries he'd found. They passed the hours together quietly, talking and growing closer.

"How did you find this place?" Cari asked, thinking it a
beautiful retreat.

"I came here when I was young. It's very special to me."

"It's so peaceful. You can almost pretend as if the rest of
the world doesn't exist." As she said it, she wished it were
true.

Silver Wolf knew exactly what she meant. They were safe
here in their haven. He wished it could stay that way.

"Let's walk outside for a while." He knew it was time to
keep watch again.

She went with him willingly, and as they reached the vantage
point and he glanced out across the valley, he froze. There in
the distance was a lone rider heading their way.

"Someone's coming . . ." He tensed.

"Who could it be?" Cari asked nervously. She grew pale at
the thought that they'd been discovered, for she knew the sheriff and his men would probably shoot first and ask questions
later.

"I don't know," he answered tightly. "Stay in the cave and
don't come out until I call you." He was already reaching for
the gun he was wearing in his waistband.

"What are you going to do?" Her expression clearly reflected her fear for his safety.

"Nothing, right now. I need to get a better look and see who
it is."

"And if it's the sheriff?"

He heard the terror in her voice and tried to reassure her.

Cari wanted to blurt out, "Be careful!", but she didn't get
the chance as he brusquely ordered her to go into the cave
again.

Silver Wolf watched until she'd disappeared out of sight,
and then, once he was sure she was safe, he left her and went
to keep watch over the intruder.

* * *

Because he had made such a late start, Strong Eagle was forced to camp for the night on his way to find his friend. As first light had stained the eastern sky, though, he was up and riding again. Silver Wolf was in trouble, and Strong Eagle was going to do everything he could to help him.

It was still morning when he neared the place of Silver Wolf's vision quest. As he rode in, he slowed his pace in case his friend was there and watching. He didn't want to alarm him. He had come to help. Strong Eagle kept his gaze riveted on the area where he knew the small cave was located. He was near the clearing when he heard Silver Wolf's voice ring out from nearby.

"Strong Eagle! My friend!" Silver Wolf stepped out of his hiding place and revealed himself to the other warrior for the first time.

Strong Eagle smiled in relief, glad that he'd found him. "Silver Wolf, it is good to see you! I was hoping you were here."

Silver Wolf strode forth to welcome him.

Strong Eagle swung down from his horse and went to greet him. "The news reached the village that the whites are searching for you."

"How did you hear this?"

He quickly explained how the women had run into Ben and the posse. He also told him what Ben had said about turning himself in. "Will you do it?"

"No. Not yet. I must find the man who killed McCord. Only then can I return."

Strong Eagle nodded. He did not trust the whites, and he understood why his friend didn't want to give himself up.

"I am glad that you came," Silver Wolf told him as they tied up Strong Eagle's horse and then made their way to the cave.

"You needed help," he answered simply.

"Have Tall Shadow's braves found McCord's bull?"

"We have searched in many places, but have not found it yet."

"I feared as much."

"Little Snow?" Silver Wolf called out to her so she wouldn't be frightened as they entered the cave carrying the supplies Strong Eagle had brought along.

"Little Snow?" Strong Eagle glanced at him sharply.

"She's with me."

Cari had been sitting by the fire, anxiously awaiting his return, and at the sound of his voice she jumped to her feet, ready to race to his aid. "Are you all right?"

"Strong Eagle has come to help."

Cari smiled in warm welcome as she went to them. "It has been many years since I saw you last, but it is always good to see a friend."

Strong Eagle stared at her in surprise. Not only was he shocked to find her there with Silver Wolf, but he thought she'd grown into the most beautiful white woman he had ever ㅤen. "I did not know that you were with Silver Wolf, but it is good to see you again and to know that you are both safe."

They sat down by the fire and opened one of his bags of food. As they ate, Strong Eagle told them everything he knew about the posse's location and the search for the Hereford.

"Has anyone searched on the Larsons' ranch?"

"The Larsons?" Cari was shocked. "Why the Larsons?"

"They're the ones who accused my people of stealing the cattle in the first place. They even tried to get the soldiers to ride against us."

"Papa always said the Larsons hated him for being friends with Tall Shadow. They even came out to the Circle M one time and tried to convince him that your grandfather was involved in the rustling."

Silver Wolf gave her a knowing look. "Their hatred for my people is an ugly thing, and their greed is strong."

"What Silver Wolf says is true," Strong Eagle agreed. "They and others like them want all the land, and they won't stop until they've taken it."

Cari remembered the scene on the front porch with the Larsons the day she'd returned from Philadelphia, and she knew the truth of their words.

"What do you want me to do?" Strong Eagle asked.

"Ride for the Larsons' ranch and search for the bull there, but be careful. If they see you, they'd just as soon shoot you as speak to you," Silver Wolf cautioned.

"Will you ride with me?"

There was nothing Silver Wolf wanted more than to find the clue that would clear his name, but he feared leaving Little Snow alone. "I must stay here with Little Snow."

"No," she spoke firmly. "Go with Strong Eagle. We'll know no peace until you find the ones responsible for my father's death!"

"I can't leave you . . ." His concern for Little Snow's safety warred with his desperate need to find the murderer.

"You must. I'll be safe. Thanks to Strong Eagle, I'll have plenty to eat, so there's no reason for you to worry about me. I was raised out here, remember?" Cari managed to smile at him as she tried to convince him that she would be fine. She never wanted to be separated from him again, but she knew this was something he had to do. He had to prove his innocence.

Silver Wolf turned his determined gaze to his friend. "I'll go with you."

Within minutes, the two warriors were ready to ride. Silver Wolf came to her and kissed her, then he handed her the handgun to keep for her protection.

"I'll be back, Little Snow. We'll find the man who murdered your father." He touched her cheek softly one last time before turning away to mount his waiting horse.

Silver Wolf looked the fierce, proud warrior as he wheeled the steed around and lifted his arm toward her in salute. He and Strong Eagle rode off, the sound of their horses' hoofbeats a fading thunder.

Cari kept watch until they'd gone from sight. As she did, she remembered that very first night in the snow when Silver Wolf and Strong Eagle had brought her home and then ridden away into the night. She had loved her warrior even then. She said a silent prayer that they would be safe and would return to her soon.

Twenty

Silver Wolf and Strong Eagle rode their mounts to their limits, covering seemingly endless miles of the Larson range in their desperate attempt to find the missing Hereford. As they made camp at dusk on their second day out, they faced the frustrating truth.

"We need help," Strong Eagle admitted, discouraged by their lack of success.

"It would take weeks for the two of us, and I don't have that much time," Silver Wolf told him. "At dawn, I'll ride to check on Little Snow while you ride for the village. Tell my grandfather that we need as many braves as he can give us, then meet me at noon the following day in the valley where the McCord ranch joins the Larsons'."

They bedded down for the night, but neither man slept well. As soon as dawn tinted the sky, they parted, agreeing to meet at the designated place and time.

Sheriff Dixon and the posse were tired. Five days of useless searching for the half-breed had left them frustrated and furious. Despite all the ground they'd covered, they'd turned up nothing. In defeat, they headed back to town, clinging to the hope that Collins and his men had fared better.

Elliot was silent, and his mood was anguished as he rode with the posse. During the time he'd been with them, he'd heard some of the men talk of the atrocities committed by the Indians, and he'd tried to reconcile what they were saying with what James had told him. The two sides were complete opposites, and with James now dead, supposedly killed by Silver Wolf, he could only wonder and worry.

With each passing day, his fears for Cari's safety had grown. He didn't know how he was going to return to the Circle M and tell Elizabeth that they couldn't find her daughter. Filled with despair, Elliot girded himself for the coming confrontation.

Ben rode along with the posse in silence, too, trying to ignore the angry rantings of the Larsons and some of the other men. Though Ben was glad that they hadn't found Daniel, he was concerned that Collins's posse might have. That possibility left him fearing for his friend's life. He hoped there would be word from Tall Shadow about the bull when he returned to town, but he knew it was unlikely. Whoever had stolen the bull had probably gotten rid of it as fast as they could, for the Hereford would be easy to identify.

"Do you want me to ride out to the ranch with you to talk to Elizabeth?" Ben asked Elliot when they reached town and reined in before the jail.

"No, I'll be all right. It'd be better if you stayed here to see what Collins came up with," he said as they realized the other posse had not yet returned.

"All right. If they've found anything, I'll send word to you right away."

"Thanks, Ben."

The two men shook hands, then went their separate ways, Ben returning to his office while Elliot started for the ranch. Elliot made only one stop on his way out of town, and that was at the telegraph office to send a message to his father telling him what had happened. Then he rode for the Circle M to face Elizabeth with the news that they had not found Cari.

The Larsons were angry with Dixon for not going into the Cheyenne village to hunt for the half-breed. When the posse disbanded, they went back to the Sundown Saloon with some of the other men to take up where they'd left off all those nights before. Tempers were hot as they gathered in the bar, and they grew even hotter as they drank and vented their hatred of the Indians. They managed to keep their fury in check, though, for there was still the chance that the other posse had found the breed and strung him up.

"Collins is back!" Howard shouted as he came running into the bar. He'd been watching for the other posse's return and had just seen them riding in.

"Let's go!" Sam stood up and led the way from the saloon.

The men headed for the jail, eager to hear the news that the breed was dead and the girl rescued. When they reached the jail, they found the men of Collins's posse milling around outside while the deputy met with the lawman in the office.

"What's going on? Did you get him?" Mark asked one of Collins's men.

"No. We didn't find anything," the man answered in disgust.

"You stopped at the fort, didn't you? Did Captain Greene send any help with you?"

"He sent a detachment of men along, but he ordered them to make sure we brought Marshall in alive if we found him!" the man snarled. "Not that it mattered. We never saw a trace of the red bastard anywhere!"

Sam was filled with rage, as was Mark. When Collins came out of the office looking angry, too, Sam told him, "Come with us back to the saloon. We've got some planning to do!"

Ben had come down to the jail when he'd seen the posse return, and he heard Sam. Knowing how vicious the man was, he went along to the bar.

For the next several hours, the men of the posse drank steadily, and with each round of liquor their need for bloodshed grew. Sam played upon their hatred of the Indians, and by midnight they were all ready to ride into Tall Shadow's village and destroy it as a message to Daniel. They believed he'd taken a white man's life, so they would avenge James by killing a hundred Cheyenne!

"We'll ride out first thing in the morning!" Sam directed the thirty bloodthirsty men who wanted to ride with him.

"Larson, you can't do this!" Ben argued as he faced down the rancher. "The Cheyenne are innocent in all of this!"

"Douglas, we don't need your Indian-loving kind here! Get outta here!" one of the men shouted at him.

"I believe in the truth, and what you're hearing here is not the truth!"

"Marshall killed McCord! He broke out of jail! That proves something, doesn't it? And he took the girl hostage! What more do you need to know before you join us?"

"Attacking Tall Shadow's village is not the answer!"

"It may not be the answer to you, but it is to us! If we can't catch the breed, at least we can make some of his relatives pay!"

"That's right!" Mark added. "Morgan, Collins, are you with us?"

The two deputies had been thwarted in their eagerness to make the half-breed pay, once by the sheriff and again by Captain Greene. They wanted to see the Cheyenne suffer for McCord's death and were glad to go along.

"We're with you!"

"We'll ride out in the morning!"

Ben stared at the rabid bunch and knew he was helpless against their numbers. Desperate, he raced to the sheriff's office.

"Douglas, what do you want?" Dixon asked, not at all pleased to see the lawyer. It had been a long five days, and he needed some rest.

"Sam Larson's got the men riled up again, and they plan to

ride on Tall Shadow's village in the morning! You've got to stop them. Innocent people are going to die!"

Dixon heaved a sigh as he stood up and grabbed his hat and rifle. "I'll talk to them, but it might be better to just let them sleep their rage off. Things can change by sunup."

The sheriff went to the saloon with Ben to find the men roaring with eagerness to kill Indians. As they walked in, Ben heard Morgan bragging about how he was going to take great pleasure in finding the two squaws they'd seen by the creek and maybe tasting of them before they killed them. When the deputy looked up and saw the sheriff and Ben, his expression hardened.

"What are you doing here with that Indian-lover?" Morgan sneered.

"You men aren't riding on the Cheyenne. I want you to let the law handle this."

"The law was handling this when the bastard escaped!" Howard yelled in drunken bravery.

"Justice is going to be done," the sheriff insisted.

"Where was the justice when our stock was rustled?" Sam shouted. "We're tired of waiting for the law to do something!"

"Yeah!" the other ranchers who'd lost cattle joined in the furor.

"You're either with us or against us, Sheriff. There ain't no in between!" Collins told him.

"You men listen to me! I don't want anymore talk about killing. I'll be the one who finds Marshall, and when I do, he's going to stand trial for McCord's murder."

"Not if we find him first!" someone shouted, and a roar of approval greeted his words.

Dixon stared about him at the faces filled with hate and knew he was helpless to stop them. He backed out of the bar, Ben following him.

"What are you going to do?" Ben demanded.

"You heard them. There's nothing I can do. I can't arrest them all. I'm just one man!"

"We're two men," Ben corrected.

"You have to do something!"

"Well, two men against thirty. We get ourselves killed, we're no better off."

"So you're just going to sit here and do nothing while they kill Tall Shadow's people?" Ben stared at him incredulously.

"Maybe it won't come to that. Maybe *your friend,*" the sheriff countered, "will turn himself in before any killing starts."

Ben's expression mirrored the loathing he felt for the spineless lawman as he turned away. There was only one thing he could do, and he didn't intend to let anyone know what it was. He would not, could not, stand by and let the whites attack an unsuspecting Cheyenne village.

Ben rode from the town. Larson had said they wouldn't leave for the village until dawn, so Ben knew he had time to warn Tall Shadow that they were coming.

Darkness slowed Ben's travel, and he didn't reach the village until early morning.

Ben practically threw himself from his horse's back as he reined in before Chief Tall Shadow's tipi. He expected the chief to come out of the tipi, and he was gravely disappointed when Little Cloud emerged.

Little Cloud started to greet him cordially, but he gave her no time to speak.

"Is Tall Shadow here, Little Cloud? I have to talk to him!"

"No, my husband has just ridden from the village a short time ago, and he will not return for several days."

"Damn!" Ben swore, his mind racing to find a solution. "Little Cloud, I must find Daniel right away. If you know where he is, you have to tell me now!"

"I do not know where my grandson is." Her answer was firm and her face betrayed no knowledge.

"This is a matter of life and death," Ben went on. "There was trouble in town last night. Some white men are planning to raid your village today unless Daniel turns himself in. I've got to find him!"

"The white men are coming here?" She looked horrified.

"Yes," he answered seriously, "and they're coming to kill. I have to find Daniel. There isn't much time!"

"I know where he is . . ."

Ben knew that voice as well as he knew his own. He whirled around to find Star Blossom standing behind them.

She'd watched Ben ride in and had seen how urgent his manner was as he spoke to Little Cloud. Sensing something was terribly wrong, she'd come immediately to see if she could help.

"Star Blossom," Ben said slowly as he took her by the arms in a gentle but frantic grip. "If you've ever trusted anyone in your life, you must trust me now. I have to find Daniel. There was more trouble in town. There are men riding for your village this morning. If Daniel doesn't turn himself in, they're going to attack."

"They wouldn't . . ." Her eyes widened with terror.

"Yes, they would. That's why I have to find Daniel before they get here! I have to convince him to turn himself in . . ."

Star Blossom stared up at him. Whites had caused nothing but pain in her life, and Ben was a white man . . . one of them. But as she gazed into his pleading eyes, she saw the truth. He was different. Instead of being filled with hatred, he was filled with love. Instead of seeing the differences in people, he saw the things they shared in common. He was gentle yet strong; proud yet fair. He had saved her life twice, and now he had put himself at risk to warn her and her people of danger again. There was no need to dwell on it further. She put her trust and her heart in Ben's hands.

"I will show you."

Ben's relief was tremendous. The time while he'd waited for her to speak had been the longest in his life. He couldn't stop himself from dragging her into his embrace, and he held her close as he murmured in a pained voice, "Thank you for trusting me."

She drew back to look up at him. "I do trust you, Ben."

They stared at each other for a moment as if really seeing each other for the first time.

"We will need to ride right away. I heard Strong Eagle telling the other braves that Silver Wolf had gone to the cave where he received his vision quest. It is a good distance from us, so we must hurry."

Ben turned back to Little Cloud. "Tell your people what I've told you. Are there many warriors in the village?"

The two women looked distressed. "Only a few. Most have ridden with Tall Shadow and Strong Eagle."

"Then we will ride like the wind to Daniel, and we will return as soon as we can."

Silver Wolf stood holding Little Snow to him, savoring the joy of having her close. Soon he would have to leave her to meet with Strong Eagle, and at the thought of being parted from her, his spirit grew heavy. He missed her already, and he hadn't even gone yet.

"I'll be back as soon as I can."

"I know," she murmured, her voice muffled as she buried her face against his chest, holding him tightly, for she never wanted to let him go.

The days they had been apart had passed in unending agony for her as she worried about his safety. Each minute had seemed an hour, each hour had seemed a day. When at last she'd caught sight of him in the distance returning to her, her heart had leapt in her breast. She'd run to him, meeting him at the bottom of the hill, and he had swept her up before him on the horse and kissed her. His kiss had told her everything she'd needed to know— he had missed her as desperately as she had missed him.

Cari clung to him now, wishing she could keep him with her safely there in the cave forever. It was a dream, though, and she knew it. He had to clear his name. Only then, when her father's killer had been brought to justice, could they be together as they wanted to be— as man and wife.

"How soon do you have to go?" she asked as calmly as she could in spite of the worry that consumed her.

"Soon." The regret he felt over leaving her was heavy in his voice. "Too soon."

He tilted her face up to him and kissed her softly. When the kiss ended, Cari gazed up at him. For just an instant, she could see all the torment of his uncertainty in his eyes. But he quickly hid his pain from her.

"I don't want you to go," she said.

"I don't *want* to go. Every minute I'm away from you, I think of you and worry that you'll need me, and I won't be here to help you . . ."

She managed a tremulous smile. "I feel the same. Our souls are bound together."

They embraced again, desperation fueling their need to share their love. Their lips met. In that frantic moment, they clung together, sharing the ecstasy and the pain of their love and their parting.

Finally, Silver Wolf ended the embrace. Even spending the last twelve hours in her arms making love to her hadn't been enough. Somehow, he knew he would never have enough of her.

"I have to go now."

"I know." She sighed.

"I'll come back to you as soon as I can."

He lifted a hand to touch her cheek, and she caught and held it against her, pressing a kiss into his palm.

"I'll be waiting for you."

They started outside to where the horse was tied. It was only then that he caught sight of the two riders coming their way. Fear seared him. He drew his gun and ran to the vantage point to get a better look at the intruders.

"It's Ben, and it looks like Star Blossom is the one riding with him!" he called to Little Snow as soon as he recognized them. "Wait here."

He started down the trail to meet them halfway, not revealing himself to them until they were nearly upon him.

"Ben! Star Blossom!" he hailed, moving out from where he'd been hiding, watching.

They reined in abruptly at the sight of him.

"Thank God, you're still here!" Ben said as he dismounted and rushed to his friend. They embraced and then Ben stepped away, the worry and the dread of the last days showing plainly on his handsome face.

Silver Wolf knew something was terribly wrong by the look on his face. "What is it, Ben? What's wrong?"

"It's the Larsons." He hurried to explain. "They rode with the posse trying to find you, and when they came up empty-handed, they decided any dead Indian was good enough revenge for James's death. They've got a gang of about thirty men, and they're riding on the village today."

Silver Wolf cursed. "They're probably the same ones who were planning to string me up the night I broke out."

Ben was shocked by this news.

"Someone came to the jail cell window in the alley that night and warned me that a lynch mob was forming down at the saloon."

"So that's why you ran . . ." Ben finally understood. "Who told you?"

"I'm not sure. It was dark, and they were talking in a whisper."

"Who would have known what was going on in the saloon?"

"Jenny . . ." Silver Wolf said her name in amazement, realizing she'd put herself at risk for him. "It must have been Jenny. If she hadn't brought me the knife, I'd be dead."

"You mean the girl who was with you at the Sundown the night of the dance?" At his confirming nod, Ben felt a little encouraged for the first time. The girl was still around somewhere, and she might know something that would help them. As soon as they got back to town, he'd start looking for her again.

Cari had followed Silver Wolf down to meet Ben and Star Blossom, and she'd remained quiet while they talked. When they spoke of Jenny, she felt a terrible pang of jealousy. Guilt

assailed her, too. While she'd questioned Silver Wolf's innocence, this Jenny had been there for him. Cari managed to
push the jealousy and guilt aside. She was at Silver Wolf's side
now, right where she belonged, and she would never doubt
him again. "I'll have to thank Jenny when this is all over," she
said.

"We all will," Ben agreed.

"You say the Larsons are riding for the village?"

"Yes, and . . ."

"And Chief Tall Shadow and many of the braves rode out
with Strong Eagle this morning," Star Blossom quickly put in.

The knowledge that his village was about to be attacked filled
Silver Wolf with a terrible resolve. His gaze hardened as he
looked at Ben. "Let's ride. I'll give them what they really
want."

"No!" Cari panicked. Running to him, she grabbed his arm
and stared up at him, her expression stricken.

Silver Wolf's features were stony and unrelenting as he
looked down at her. "I have no choice. My people need me."

Cari paled at his words. She tightened her hold on him, as
if trying to stop him from sacrificing himself.

"Don't you understand? They'll kill you without a thought,
and once they do, they may very well ride on the village anyway!"

"Little Snow . . ." Silver Wolf said her name patiently, with
great love. "I have to go."

Cari turned frantic eyes to Ben. "Ben! Tell him it's crazy!
Tell him you'll get the sheriff! Tell him the sheriff will stop
them! Tell him, Ben!"

"I've already talked to the sheriff, Cari . . ." Ben's pain
sounded in his voice.

Silver Wolf knew what his friend was saying. He knew the
fate of the village was in his hands. "Little Snow, there have
been no lies between us, ever, and there will be none now. I
must do this. My people are in danger."

Cari bit back a sob. As their eyes met, she saw honor and

commitment and love in them. He was her Silver Wolf. He could do nothing less than save his people.

"I'm going with you," she stated firmly.

"How much time do we have, Ben?" Silver Wolf turned to him.

"We have to hurry."

Silver Wolf nodded. "Let's get our things."

He and Little Snow rushed back to the cave without speaking. They gathered their few belongings and were ready to ride.

"I want you to ride with Star Blossom," Silver Wolf told Little Snow when she would have mounted with him. "Just in case there's trouble," he clarified, but he didn't explain further. He didn't tell her that he didn't want to put her in danger . . . that they might shoot him on sight.

He held her close one last time, then walked with her to where Star Blossom waited on her horse. As they shared a last passionate kiss, Star Blossom looked shyly away, and her gaze accidentally collided with Ben's. It startled her to find that he was watching her, and she gave him a small, almost sad smile.

Cari stared up at Silver Wolf, her heart shining in her eyes. "I love you."

"I love you, too." He echoed her heartfelt emotion, allowing himself one last moment of tenderness before facing the violence and hatred he knew was coming.

"I know you're innocent, and somehow, some way, we're going to prove it," she vowed.

Little Snow believed in him and loved him. At her words, an emotion more powerful than anything he'd ever known before strengthened him. He wanted desperately to believe she was right as he helped her mount behind Star Blossom. He swung up on his horse, then led the way from the cave. He rode slightly ahead of the others, a lone and solitary man, as he prepared to confront his fate.

Twenty-one

They reached the village and were relieved to find that everything was still quiet. After borrowing a horse so Cari wouldn't have to ride double, they prepared to head out again.

Ben stood with Star Blossom a short distance away from the others to tell her good-bye. There was so much he wanted to say to her, but there was no time. They had to leave now if they were going to intercept the Larsons and save the village from attack.

"You will never know how much your help meant to me," he told her. "Thank you for trusting me."

"You are a friend to Silver Wolf . . ." she replied simply.

"I am your friend, too," he insisted, his eyes darkening with the need to tell her everything that was in his heart.

"I know . . ." Star Blossom stared up at him, and the urge within her to kiss him was real and strong. She knew he was facing great danger, and she wanted to let him know how she felt before he left her. Unmindful that there were others around, she rose up on her tiptoes and pressed a kiss to his cheek. "Be careful. I will be waiting . . ."

Her kiss and words thrilled him, and before she could escape

him, he took her in his arms and held her to his heart. The
embrace was poignant, painfully so. He'd wanted to hold her
this way for so long, and yet now that she had come willingly
into his embrace, he had to let her go. He released her and
stepped away, looking to Daniel.

"We'd better ride," Ben said tightly, his control pressed to
the limit as he forced himself back on his horse.

Silver Wolf helped Little Snow up on her mount before
swinging up on the Indian pony. They bid farewell to those
gathered around them, and then rode out quickly to search
for the threatening whites.

They'd traveled less than an hour when they caught sight of
the Larsons coming their way. There were at least thirty men
following them. Ben reined in and glanced over at Daniel.

"Here," he said, tossing him his saddlebags. "You'd better
put the gun where they won't see it. I don't want them getting
any ideas and shooting you just because you're armed. I'll tell
them you turned yourself in to me and that I'm taking you to
the sheriff."

Silver Wolf knew he was right. The sight of him armed
would be all the excuse some of those white men needed to
shoot him.

"All right," he answered, slipping the gun reluctantly into
the saddlebag. If it came to violence, at least he'd be able to
get to the gun reasonably fast.

"Ben, what are we going to do?" Cari asked as she watched
the men riding ever closer.

"We're going to ride straight at them and face them down.
It's the only way."

"Let's go now," Silver Wolf ground out, wanting to stop them
before they got any closer to the village.

The two men exchanged knowing looks as they spurred their
horses forward.

* * *

"Morgan! Looks like riders comin' toward us!" Collins yelled to the other deputy.

"Hey, Sam! Look at that! Looks like Douglas found them!" Morgan called to Larson as he recognized Ben's horse.

Sam stared at the oncoming riders. Anger sliced through him as he realized that the deputies were right. "Damn!"

"Is it really them, Pa?" Mark asked.

"Yes. It's Douglas, and he's got both Marshall and the girl with him!" he snarled.

"What are we going to do? Are we still riding on the village?" Mark had been looking forward to some fighting today.

"I don't know. If we'd just found Marshall, it would have been all right, but now that the girl and the damned lawyer are with him, it changes everything. Douglas isn't a man to mess with."

Mark and some of the other men swore in frustration.

"Let's go get them!" Sam ground out as he put his heels to his mount. His horse sprung forward, and the others followed as they raced toward them.

Silver Wolf watched the intruders crossing his people's land heading toward them and knew they were the true predators. He reined in with Ben and Cari and waited.

Ben had already drawn his rifle and held it easily before him on the saddle as he watched and waited. Cari sidled her horse closer to Silver Wolf's as she prepared to face them by his side.

"Morgan . . . Collins . . ." Ben nodded toward the deputies when they stopped before them, then he turned to look straight at Larson. "Sam."

"So you knew where he was all the time," Morgan accused as he glared with open hatred at Silver Wolf.

"No, he's turning himself in. I'm just along for the ride into town to make sure there are no problems."

"There's no need for you to bother. Just hand him over to us. We'll make sure he gets to the sheriff," Collins said, moving forward in the gang of riders.

Ben gave them a knowing smile and chuckled almost evilly

as he shifted his rifle to bear on Sam. "I don't think so, boys. You're not the law."

"We're deputies!" Morgan and Collins countered.

"I know what kind of deputies you are. If I turn him over to you, he won't make it to town alive, let alone live long enough to see a trial."

"Listen, Douglas, I thought McCord was your friend. You got a lot of nerve siding with the filthy breed who killed him!" Sam charged, wanting to get the men angry about Marshall again.

Initially, Cari had been frightened, but at this first mention of her father, all her fears were replaced by fury. "He is not the man who killed my father."

A rustling of discomfort shifted through the gang as they faced the fact that McCord's only daughter was defending the man they thought had murdered him. If she thought he wasn't guilty, it occurred to them that there might be something to it . . .

"Now, Cari," Sam began in a patronizing tone, having heard the men mumbling behind him and wanting to discredit her in their eyes so he would have their full support again, "I'm sure losing your father was a terrible tragedy for you, and I know you've been through a lot being kidnapped and all. But we're on your side. You can trust us. We want to help you."

"You listen to me, Sam Larson!" Cari countered, turning her full fury on him. "I have been through a lot. But what I've been through is nothing compared to what you've done to Silver Wolf since he was accused of my father's murder and what you and these other men are planning to do in the name of revenge! Is there justice in the murder of innocent people, Mr. Larson?"

"Innocent people?" Sam spat the words.

"Only a coward would take pleasure in killing women and children," Silver Wolf told him.

At his statement, some of the followers muttered even more uncomfortably.

"They're Indians. They're not human! They're little better than animals!" he seethed.

"Perhaps sometimes it is better to be an animal . . ." Silver Wolf paused giving him a condemning look. When he spoke again it was in a steely voice that reflected the rigid control he had upon himself. "Animals never maim or kill for pleasure."

"Why, you . . ." Sam's temper exploded.

"I'm the one you're after, Larson," Silver Wolf said. "There's no reason for you to ride on the village. I'm turning myself in to Sheriff Dixon."

Sam didn't care about him turning himself in, he was furious and he wanted him dead. He started to go for his sidearm.

Cari gasped in horror as she saw him make his move, but Ben had been ready all along. He lifted the rifle in one smooth move and aimed it straight at the center of the rancher's chest.

"Don't do it, Sam," Ben warned in a deadly tone. "Marshall's going in of his own accord. There's no reason for any bloodshed unless you force me to it."

Mark, Morgan, and Collins started to go for their guns, too, but Ben knew what he had to do.

"Don't even think about it," he repeated in the same lethal tone. "I may only get one of you, but the one I'm going to shoot will be Sam."

Nervous mutterings went through the gang of whites.

"What do you think, Sam?" Ben challenged. "Has this gone on long enough? Are you ready to ride back to town and let the law handle it?"

Sam had gone red in the face and then turned ashen when he heard Ben's threat. By the look in the lawyer's eyes and the steadiness of his hands, Sam knew he wasn't bluffing.

"We're riding with you just to make sure the bastard doesn't escape again!" Sam snarled, trying to save some face before the others.

"That's fine with us. You just turn around and lead the way," Ben directed. "We'll be right behind you."

Temporarily thwarted, Sam, Mark, and the deputies took the lead and headed back.

Sheriff Dixon heard a commotion outside his office and someone calling his name. He rushed out to find Daniel, Ben, and Cari tying up their horses at the rail while Morgan, Collins, Sam, Mark, and the others looked on.

"Marshall!" He was shocked, and he drew his gun.

"I'm unarmed, Sheriff," he told him holding his hands up. "I've come to turn myself in."

"Miss McCord . . . are you all right?" the lawman demanded, ignoring Marshall's words and keeping his gun trained on him as he glanced in Cari's direction.

"I'm fine, Sheriff," Cari quickly reassured him.

Satisfied with her answer, he looked over at his deputies. He thought they were the ones who'd found Marshall, and he was pleased. "How did you do it, boys? Where did you find him?"

"They didn't find him," Ben corrected, coming to stand at his friend's side. He gestured at the handgun that was still aimed at Daniel. "And there's no need for the gun. Daniel decided to do this on his own. I rode with him to make sure he was treated fairly."

The sheriff eyed them both, then slowly holstered his gun. "Let's go inside," he ordered. He stood back to let them pass. "Marshall, you first."

Silver Wolf entered with Ben and Cari right behind him. The sheriff followed and directed Silver Wolf to go back to the cells. Cari almost cried out in protest at the thought of him being taken from her and locked up again, but she managed to remain strong and said nothing. Only when Silver Wolf cast a last glance her way did she allow him to see the pain she was feeling over being separated from him. He gave her a slight nod before doing as the lawman had directed.

Silver Wolf entered the same cell he'd been held in before, and he didn't turn around when the sheriff slammed the door shut and locked it behind him. The sound of the key turning in the lock had a certain finality to it that chilled his soul. He remained standing in the center of the cage that would be his home now until his fate was decided at trial. He thought of Cari, his love, and he wondered if he would ever get to hold her again. He thought of the look on her face when he'd glanced back at her, and he ached to hold her close and reassure her that everything would be all right. But he realized as he stood alone in the desolate cell, there was no guarantee that things *were* going to turn out all right.

Sheriff Dixon returned to the outer office to speak with Cari and Ben.

"Well, Miss McCord, you can go on and leave. I'll handle it from here. There's no need for you to worry or be afraid anymore. I'll keep Marshall locked up real tight. He won't be escaping again."

Cari met his regard squarely as she told him coldly, "I'm not worried about him escaping, Sheriff. I'm worried that some of the townfolks might decide to take the law into their own hands again and try to lynch him while he's in your custody. Will you guarantee his safety to me?"

"You're concerned about *Marshall's* safety?" He was dumb-founded. Wasn't she the girl he'd just kidnapped and held hostage? And now, here she was speaking out in his behalf. "He's the one who murdered your father!"

"He did not kill my father," she stated firmly. "I'm not sure who did yet, but I know Daniel Marshall is innocent."

Dixon snorted. "We have evidence . . ."

"Which could have been brought to the scene by somebody else and used to make him look guilty," she attacked. "Daniel Marshall is not my father's murderer, and somehow we're going to prove it." She looked over at Ben for reassurance.

Again, Dixon stared at her. He'd expected her to be a meek and mild miss, who'd be terrified at the thought of the breed ever getting loose again. Obviously, he'd misjudged her. She was more like her father than he'd thought.

"Well, you can figure you've got a week. We're going to trial just as quick as we can. The town's clamoring for justice, and I'm going to give it to them."

"The town's kind of justice or real justice?" Ben joined in, in support of Cari. "It came to my attention that the reason Daniel felt driven to escape that night was because he got word that vigilantes were going to raid the jail and hang him. Now, Sheriff, as Miss McCord has asked and I repeat, can you guarantee Mr. Marshall's safety or not?"

Sheriff Dixon felt the heat of anger rise in him. "I'll guarantee it."

"Good. That's what we wanted to know," Ben answered. "Now, can we see him before we go?"

The sheriff looked doubtful, then gave in. "This will be the last time I'll allow him any visitors, and you'll have to stay out of the cell. As his lawyer, you'll be able to talk to him, but I'm not letting any one else in until the trial's over."

Ben thanked the man and he escorted Cari back to see Daniel. "Daniel . . ."

Silver Wolf had not expected to see them again, and he came to stand at the door, his gaze feasting on Little Snow. "What did the sheriff have to say?"

"Not much. Just that he's going to go to trial within the week, so that doesn't leave us much time. I'll start checking on things again tonight."

"Perhaps my grandfather and Strong Eagle will find the bull."

"They will. I'm sure of it." Cari tried to sound optimistic.

She was gripping the bars that separated them so tightly that her knuckles were white, and Silver Wolf reached up to cover her hands with his. Their eyes met as their hands touched, and they both knew a terrible ache deep in their souls.

"It'll be all right," she whispered.

She leaned toward him, and as best they could through the bars, they kissed. It was a soft, fleeting exchange, but it was enough to give them the strength to do what needed to be done.

Silver Wolf glanced at Ben, whose face seemed to be set in

granite and realized from his expression just how serious the situation was.

"As soon as I have anything new to tell you, I will return," Ben told him, and with a hand at Cari's waist, he walked with her from the jail.

Cari and Ben stood on the deserted street outside the sheriff's office.

"I'm going to have to start at the beginning again," Ben explained, "but first we have to get you back to the Circle M so your mother knows you're safe."

"But I don't want to leave Silver Wolf . . ."

"You heard what Dixon said. He's not going to allow any visitors in to see him, so it won't do you any good to stay in town. Let's ride out and put your mother's mind at ease."

"You don't have to come with me. I'll be all right. I've made the ride alone before."

"I know, but there are a few questions I want to ask your mother, and since I'm over my investigation, I might as well start with her."

"Thanks, Ben," Cari said with great appreciation as she put a hand on his arm. "You're a good friend."

Ben was deeply moved by her words. "Right now, I just hope I'm a good enough lawyer."

Elizabeth heard the call go up that horses were coming, and she ran outside with Elliot to see Ben and Cari riding up to the house. Sobbing in happiness and relief, she raced to her daughter. Tears streamed down her face as she held her arms out to her.

"You're safe!! Thank God, you're safe!" she cried.

As soon as Cari dismounted, she was enfolded in her mother's loving embrace. Elizabeth hugged her tight, unwilling to let her go. She'd feared for her life. She'd thought the horrible half-breed had dragged her off, murdered her, and left her where she'd never be found again. There were no words to express the joy she was feeling over being reunited with her child.

"Oh, Mother . . ." Cari said in a love-choked voice. "I love you, and I'm so glad to be home."

"Cari . . ." Elliot had held himself back, allowing the women time to enjoy each other, but his happiness at finding Cari was safe wouldn't allow him to stay quiet any longer.

"Elliot . . ."

Elizabeth let her go, and Cari went to the man whom she knew loved her dearly. Cari lifted a hand to touch his cheek as she saw the depth of caring mirrored in his dark eyes.

"I'm glad you're safe," he told her, then embraced her. For just a moment, he closed his eyes and savored the ecstasy of holding her.

"Thank you. Thank you for everything," Cari told him, before kissing him.

In that kiss, a kiss of friendship, Elliot knew there would never be a future for them. He loved her, but she did not return the same passionate devotion. With a herculean effort, he managed to keep his heartbreak from showing.

"You know you can always count on me."

"Let's go inside," Elizabeth encouraged. "You have to tell us what happened. Did they catch Silver Wolf? Did they hang him already, or is he in jail? He didn't hurt you, did he?"

Ben and Cari exchanged quick, troubled glances, for they knew what they were about to face. It wasn't going to be easy, but somehow they had to convince her mother and Elliot of Silver Wolf's innocence.

It was an hour later that they sat together in silence in the parlor. Elizabeth's face was ashen as she twisted her hands nervously in her lap. Battling back scalding tears, she tried to understand everything they'd been saying to her. She found it next to impossible to believe that in spite of everything that had happened, Cari was still devoted to Silver Wolf and believed that he wasn't the one who'd killed James.

"You truly believe he didn't do it." She lifted her troubled gaze to her daughter, finding it difficult to accept her faith in the half-breed. She'd hated the man for so long that it was hard for her to think of him in kinder terms, especially with everything that had been said against him.

"I know in my heart that Silver Wolf would never have hurt Papa," Cari affirmed, kneeling before her mother and taking her hands in hers. "Mother . . . I love Silver Wolf. Remember how you loved Papa . . . wholly, completely, and without reserve? Well, that's the way I love him. He's innocent. In my heart, I know it."

"Elizabeth . . ." Ben spoke up as he began to gently question her. "James was a good friend to the Cheyenne. It just doesn't make sense that Silver Wolf or any other Indian would want him dead, rustling or no rustling. Did James ever say anything that might have indicated he was having trouble with anyone or that anyone hated him?"

"Just that first day when the Larsons came out to the house. You remember that, don't you, Cari?"

"Oh, yes. I remember."

"James told me before he went down to talk to them that they never paid social calls, that the Larsons didn't like his being friends with Tall Shadow and his tribe. He knew they meant trouble when he saw them riding up to the house."

Memories of those days came pouring back in a jumble— the memory of James's concern about the Larsons' hostility and of how he'd insisted on riding out that very next morning to warn Tall Shadow about their threats. Elizabeth realized reluctantly that it truly made no sense for the Cheyenne to have murdered him. He was their friend. She'd always known it, and she'd always hated it. Now, though, facing it clearly for the first time and realizing the implications it brought, she knew she finally had to accept it.

"If Silver Wolf didn't kill James, then who did, and how will you prove it?" she asked quietly.

"I don't know," Ben answered. "That's why I rode out here with Cari to talk to you. I'm starting all over again, hoping to find the one thing, the one missing clue that will bring it all together. There has to be something that will prove Daniel's not guilty. We've been trying to find the bull. No remains have ever been found, so we have to believe it's still alive . . ."

"And if you don't find it?" Elliot asked.

Cari, Elizabeth, and Elliot all saw the threatening edge of despair in Ben's eyes.

"The trial will be in a week. I've got that long to save him."

"We'll do it," Cari told Ben with all the confidence she could muster.

Ben looked at her and saw the unbending will of a woman of strength and courage. Inspired by her devotion, he shook himself free of the anguish that threatened to hold him immobile.

"I have to get back to town. I've got to keep looking . . ."

"I'm coming with you," Cari stated firmly.

Elizabeth looked at her daughter and saw the same look of resolve on her face that had often been on her father's face. She realized Cari was a woman full-grown now who knew her own mind. There was no denying she was James McCord's daughter.

"Be careful, darling," was all she said, not trying to stop her.

They hugged once more, and Cari hugged Elliot, too, before going upstairs to pack a few things. She didn't know when she'd be back, but she didn't intend to come home again until Silver Wolf could come with her. It was his home, too, now. Her father had seen to that.

Twenty-two

It was late when Ben and Cari reached town. They were both exhausted, and he took her straight to the hotel. After she'd checked in, he escorted her to her room.

"What are you going to do now?" Cari asked as they stopped at the door to her room to unlock it. Ben opened it for her, and they both stepped inside for a moment.

"I'm going to retrace Daniel's steps the night of the dance one more time and see if I can find out what happened to his medicine bag. It's the only thing that can help," Ben told her as he closed the door behind them to give them a moment of privacy.

"I know he went to a saloon that night . . ."

"Yeah, and by the time I found him, it was obvious he'd been there for quite a while. I went there once already to talk to Jenny, the girl he was drinking with but she wasn't there. Since I'm starting over again, I guess I'll go back there, especially since Daniel thought Jenny was the one who slipped him the knife and warned him about the lynch mob. Maybe she's returned and I'll be able to talk to her and find out if she remembers anything about his medicine bag."

Cari looked distraught. "Oh, Ben, I wish I could relive that night! If I could, I'd do everything differently, and then none of this would have happened . . ."

"What might have been doesn't really matter," he said gently. "What matters is proving the charges against him false. Now I'd better go. You get some rest, and I'll see you tomorrow."

"Thanks for everything, Ben."

Ben kissed her cheek. "Daniel's my friend, Cari. I love him, too."

When Ben had gone, she undressed, donned her nightgown and lay down. As tired as she was, she expected to fall asleep right away, but her worries about Silver Wolf kept her awake. All she could think of was him, lying alone in the jail cell.

Though Cari fought against them, mental images of what might happen if they went to trial assailed her as she stared into the darkness. The possibility that Silver Wolf might be convicted of a crime he hadn't committed and sentenced to death was just too devastating to her. Unable to still her troubled thoughts, she knew she couldn't just lie there and do nothing about Silver Wolf's situation. His very life was at stake!

Cari threw herself from the bed and began to pace the room. Tears threatened, but she held them at bay. This was no time to give in to her fears. She would be strong, and the only tears she would allow herself to cry would be tears of happiness when Silver Wolf was freed.

Cari went to stand at the window and gaze out across the dark town. In the distance, bathed in moonlight, she saw the steeple of a church, and though the hour was very late, Cari knew churches never locked their doors. Throwing on her clothes again, she left the hotel and made her way to the blessed haven. It seemed they'd exhausted just about every clue they'd had, and she knew a few prayers wouldn't hurt.

The church was small, but clean. Candles cast the place of worship in a golden glow. Save for one gray-haired lady sitting by herself up near the front, no one else was there.

Cari quietly settled in a pew and dropped to her knees. She bowed her head and folded her hands.

"God, please, if you've never listened to me before, listen to me now. I need your help. Silver Wolf needs your help . . ." she pleaded in a choked whisper. "Please, show me the way to help him. You can't let him die! You just can't! Show me how to save him. Show me what I must do. I'll do anything, God . . . anything . . ."

So fervent were her prayers, so fierce her concentration, that she didn't even realize she was crying. She remained in supplication, begging for God's help. After a while, she fell silent, waiting, hoping, listening. But all she heard in answer to her prayers was silence— a cold, unbroken silence that terrified her. She lifted her gaze to the altar, wondering why God wasn't answering her. A strangled sob escaped her, and she buried her face in her hands as she gave vent to the fear that threatened to overwhelm her.

"My child. . . . Let me help you."

Through her misery, Cari heard the soft, kindly voice. At first, she'd thought she'd imagined it, but then the woman spoke to her again.

"Please, let me help . . ."

She raised tear-filled eyes to find the elderly lady who'd been praying in the front of the church standing in the aisle beside her, holding out a clean, lacy handkerchief to her. The woman was petite, certainly no more than five feet tall, and her gray hair was done up in a prim and proper bun. She was dressed as well as any lady of quality from back East, and there was something in her manner, a quiet dignity, that inspired trust and put Cari at ease.

"Thank you," Cari managed, grateful for her thoughtfulness as she took the handkerchief.

"May I sit with you a while? You seem a little lost and lonely, and maybe I can help."

"Are you sure you want to?" Cari gave her a decidedly watery smile.

"Of course," she said with warm conviction, settling in beside her. She reached out and patted Cari's hand. "A good cry helps all of us at one time or another. I know I've had my share."

"I wish it were that simple . . ." She sighed as she dried her tears.

"Would you like to talk about it?"

"Talking about it won't help anything . . ."

"Troubles always seem a little easier to bear once you've shared them with a friend. I'm Lillian Perkins, by the way."

"I'm Cari McCord." Cari drew a deep breath. This gentle woman's smile was genuine, and her eyes sparkled with a special inner warmth and joy of living.

"It's nice to meet you, Cari," Lillian told her.

They sat in companionable silence in the flickering candlelight, experiencing the peace that surrounded them.

"I don't know what to do, Mrs. Perkins," Cari finally spoke.

"You've come to the right place. When you've tried your best and failed, this is where you need to be. God's always ready to listen."

"God may always be listening, but he doesn't necessarily always answer."

"What happened?" Lillian asked, her expression concerned.

"My father was murdered," Cari began, and she went on to explain all that had happened.

"I'm so sorry."

"Silver Wolf didn't do it, but there's no way we can prove it. I don't know what to do or where to turn. There are only two things that can save him now— finding the bull and the men who stole him, or finding out what happened to Silver Wolf's medicine bag the night my father was shot. Ben's gone to the Sundown Saloon now to try to find the girl named Jenny again, but I don't know if he ever will. When he tried to before, the bartender said she was gone and he didn't know if she was ever coming back."

Cari didn't notice the quick look Lillian gave her.

"I don't know if this Jenny can help us," Cari went on, "but if she knows anything about the medicine bag, anything at all, it would be more than what we know now."

"Perhaps he will find Jenny."

"I hope so, Mrs. Perkins. Silver Wolf's life depends on it."

Lillian didn't say anything more, but just sat with Cari. When at last Lillian stood, she took the young woman's hand and gave it a squeeze.

"I'll pray for justice for your young man and for your father, Cari."

"Thank you," she responded in a whisper. She turned her attention back to the altar. When she looked around again, the woman was gone. She was alone.

Cari stayed in the church a little while longer, then returned to her hotel room. She changed into her nightgown, but before lying down, she went to the window to gaze out toward the steeple one last time. She said another prayer for Silver Wolf's safety, then went to bed, but she didn't drift off until just before dawn. Her slumber then was not peaceful. It was restless, fractured by the fears that would not be forgotten, not even while asleep.

Lillian Perkins hurried back to her house, thoughts of her conversation with Cari McCord haunting her. As she started up the few steps to her front porch, she was almost positive that the Jenny Cari McCord was looking for was the same girl who was staying with her now. Sarah Jane had sent Jenny to her, Sarah Jane who worked at the Sundown Saloon.

Lillian liked Jenny very much, but she had found the girl very quiet. She'd been with her for quite a few days now, and during all the time they'd talked, Lillian had learned nothing about her past. She knew only that Jenny did not want to leave the house. Obviously, she was afraid of someone, but Lillian had no idea who, or why. Only the fading bruises on her face gave testimony to whatever terror she'd suffered and now refused to discuss.

Having learned of the man being held in jail and going to

trial for a crime he didn't commit, Lillian knew it was time to ask Jenny about her past. Usually, she believed someone's past was their own, but this situation was different. A man's life was at stake, and it seemed Jenny was the one who could save him. Determined to find out, Lillian entered her home and sought out the young girl who was reading in the parlor.

"Jenny? There's something important I must ask you," Lillian said as she came to sit in the parlor with her.

"Surely, Mrs. Perkins. What is it?" Jenny put the book she'd been reading aside and gave her her full attention. She was more than grateful that the old lady had taken her in, and she would help her if she could.

"While I was at church tonight, I met a young lady not much older than yourself. Her name was Cari McCord." Lillian watched her carefully for a reaction.

"McCord?"

"That's right. Do you know her?"

"No."

"She's very nice, but that's not why I mentioned her. Jenny . . ." Lillian's tone turned more serious. "Cari's father was shot and killed, and she believes an innocent man has been framed for his murder. Supposedly, there was a girl named Jenny at the Sundown Saloon who was with the man on the night he lost his medicine bag. His name is Daniel Marshall, although he is also known as Silver Wolf. He's a half-breed. Anyway, it seems his medicine bag was found right where the murder took place, and it's the main piece of evidence that will be used against him unless they can find out what happened to his pouch that night."

"So?" Jenny tried to sound disinterested.

"Are you that Jenny? Do you know anything about the missing medicine bag? If you do, you can help to save this man's life." She watched Jenny's face, hoping for some sign, some flicker, of acknowledgment in her eyes that she knew what she was talking about, but there was none. Disappointment filled Lillian as Jenny gave her a totally blank look.

"I'm sorry, Mrs. Perkins. It wasn't me. I don't know anything about it," Jenny denied, amazed at how coolly she could lie to the old lady. The memory of Mark Larson's threat as he'd taken the medicine bag from her room was very real, and the thought of him coming after her again was enough to cower her. She cared about Daniel and didn't want to see anything happen to him, but she knew Larson would come after her if she said anything, anything at all. So far, she'd been lucky, staying here with Mrs. Perkins, but she didn't know how long her luck would hold.

"You don't remember hearing anything about this while you were at the Sundown?"

"No. Nothing."

Lillian's spirits sank. She'd hoped Jenny would be forthcoming with her, but it looked as though it was not to be. "Well, I appreciate your listening to me. If you remember anything, anything at all. Please tell me. It's the right thing to do, you know."

"Yes, ma'am."

"I'm going on up to bed now. You have a good night."

"Good night."

When the old woman was gone, Jenny reached in her pocket and drew out the small stone heart she'd carried with her since the night Mark had beaten her. She stared down at the heart, thinking of Daniel in trouble, and, for a moment, she almost considered going to the sheriff with her story. But then she remembered how viciously Larson had beaten her and she knew she couldn't do it. It had been one thing to help Daniel anonymously that night at the jail when the lynch mob was coming, it was another to openly accuse Mark Larson of murder. What if no one believed her? She had no real proof, and she was just one girl, alone and unprotected. Fearing for her life, Jenny pushed away any thought of helping Daniel again. Even as she did, though, her hand closed tightly around the small heart.

At the sound of his voice behind her, a chill skittered down Sarah Jane's spine. Mark Larson. . . . He was back. . . . She picked up her glass of whiskey and took a drink, trying to ignore him, but when he moved to stand next to her at the bar and slipped a possessive arm about her waist, she knew there would be no easy escape.

"Evening, Sarah Jane," Mark said as he leered at her breasts where they swelled above the neckline of her gown.

"Hello, Mark," Sarah Jane said coolly. She'd worked at the Sundown for a long time and until now had always managed to avoid him whenever he came in. Knowing how he'd treated Jenny, she wanted to get away from him as quickly as she could.

"What do you say we go upstairs?" he suggested, his hand at her waist slipping lower to fondle her hip.

"I'm sorry, mister, but one of my regulars will be in any minute. He's expecting me to be waiting for him," she said easily. "I'm sure one of the other girls will be glad to take you up on your offer."

His hand tightened on her, and she flinched. "It's you I'm wanting."

"Tell it to Ed. He likes me to keep my customers satisfied, don't ya, Ed?" She deliberately brought the bartender into the conversation.

"You're the best at it, Sarah Jane," Ed agreed.

Mark was growing angry. He wasn't used to being told *no*, especially by any damned whore. "Well, since all I really wanted to do was talk to you, what d'ya say we step back in the back room for a minute?"

Sarah Jane swallowed nervously, but knew it was better than going upstairs. At least if they were in the back room, Ed would be able to hear her scream if Mark decided to get mean. "Sure. Ed, I'll be in back with Mark. Let me know if John comes in."

"I'll call you," he answered easily, busily tending to his other customers.

Mark took her arm and led her toward the back room, where he knew he could talk to her without anyone else hearing. He closed the door without releasing his hold on her.

"What do you want?" Sarah Jane asked.

"I want to know about Jenny." His voice was hard, and his grip on her arm hurt. He had to find out where the girl had gone. He didn't want her showing up during the trial and telling what she knew about the medicine bag.

"What's there to know? She's gone. She hasn't been back to the saloon since the night she left."

"Where'd she go?"

"I don't know where she is."

"Why don't I believe that?" he asked, an edge of menace in his tone. "You two were friends. If anyone knows where she is, you do."

Sarah Jane saw the cold, merciless look in his eyes. She knew if she displayed any weakness at all, he'd never give up. She looked him straight in the eye. "I don't know anything about Jenny, and I don't want to know. If you're so eager to find her, go look for her yourself!" She jerked free of him and rushed from the room.

Mark followed her and tried to grab her arm again and spin her around to face him, but she managed to elude him. She headed for the bar where she saw the lawyer, Ben Douglas, standing there.

"Good evening, Ben." Sarah Jane smiled up at him.

"Sarah Jane, I was asking for you. I'm glad you're here. I need to talk to you for a few minutes. If you've got the time."

"I always have time for you. I'm glad you asked for me."

"What I wanted to know is about the night of the dance, when Daniel Marshall was here with Jenny."

"What about it?" She didn't know why everyone was suddenly so interested in Jenny, and having seen Jenny's terror, she wondered what was going on.

"Well, I'm trying to find Jenny, and I was wondering if you could help me. The other girls seemed to think you knew her best, so I was hoping you could tell me where she is, so I could ask her a few questions about that night, too."

Sarah Jane's gaze slid to where Mark had come to stand at the bar near them. She could feel his presence like a living, breathing, evil thing. She didn't know what Jenny had done that night, and right now she was glad she didn't. "I don't know where she is. I haven't seen her," she denied quickly.

"It's important that I find her, Sarah Jane. She might have some information that will help prove Daniel Marshall didn't kill James McCord."

"Jenny?" This news surprised Sarah Jane.

"Yes, so if you see her, tell her I'm looking for her and need to talk to her right away."

"I really don't think I'll see her, but if I do, I'll tell her."

Ben saw something in her gaze that almost looked like a flicker of fear, but it faded too quickly for him to be sure. He couldn't imagine what she had to be afraid of. He thanked her and left.

Mark left the Sundown, too, but not before he gave Sarah Jane a dangerous look. Sarah Jane stayed at the bar until her regular customer came in and then went with him upstairs. As she thought about what Ben had said and about Mark's rough questioning, she realized that Jenny was involved in something very serious. Sarah Jane began to understand why the young girl felt the need to stay out of sight. She was glad she'd kept her mouth shut, and she vowed never to tell anyone what she knew about Jenny.

Silver Wolf lay on the cot in his cell, staring out the barred window. Through it, he could only see a tiny patch of black sky and a few sparkling stars, and he ached to be outside, sleeping in the open, a free man. He thought of Little Snow and of how much he loved her. He wondered if he'd ever get the chance to hold her again. He did not sleep that night.

Twenty-three

The courthouse was packed as the trial entered the third and final day. Today, the case would go to the jury.

Silver Wolf sat beside Ben at the table for the defense, his expression stony, revealing none of the dread he was feeling. He looked like a white man, dressed as he was in the tailored dark suit, but he knew most of those watching the trial thought of him only as an Indian. Most of those testifying so far had proven that. He knew Ben was doing his best, but he'd had little to work with. They'd found no trace of Jenny or the bull. Silver Wolf's fate would be decided today when the case went to the jury, and his mood grew darker with each passing hour.

Ben's mood was equally somber. He'd been worried when the trial had started, and now on the last day, his worries were turning to fears. The only bright spot in his whole defense was Elizabeth. She'd agreed to testify in Daniel's behalf. He hoped when the jury heard her explain her change of heart toward Daniel that she would, at the very least, create a reasonable doubt in their minds. Until now, though, the hard, condemning look in the jurors' eyes chilled him. He feared his efforts weren't going to be enough. He feared his friend was going to hang.

Ben glanced back to see how Cari was holding up. The strain of the trial was showing in her pale, tense features. Sitting directly behind Daniel, she had her gaze focused solely on him as if willing him all of her strength. Ben managed to get her attention, and he gave her a small smile, hoping to bolster her spirits. She returned his smile, but he could tell by the haunted look in her eyes that she realized just how badly things were going.

"Your witness," Boyd Williams, the prosecutor, was saying to Ben as he returned to his own seat. Williams had to push his chair back from the table to make room for his considerable girth as he sat back down to listen to Ben's cross-examination.

Ben gave Daniel a reassuring look as he stood up to question Hank, the ranch hand from the Circle M. Ben methodically reviewed with Hank how he'd found the body, how the prize bull had been stolen, and how the medicine bag had been found, held tightly in James's hand.

"And so, other than this one piece of evidence, this medicine bag, you have no real proof that Daniel Marshall was ever actually at the scene of the crime. Is that correct?" Ben challenged.

"We found *his* medicine bag in James's hand!" Hank declared, pointing at Daniel.

"Did you see Daniel Marshall at the scene of the crime?" Ben repeated, insisting on a reply.

"He did it. He must have!"

"Answer the question, please," Judge Englich instructed.

"Did you see Daniel Marshall at the scene of the crime?" Ben repeated.

"No, but . . ."

"Did you see Daniel Marshall shoot James McCord?"

"No," he answered sullenly.

"Thank you," Ben said quickly. "That is all for this witness." Turning his back on him, Ben walked back to the table where

Daniel sat stoically, his features schooled into an emotionless mask.

"For our next witness we call Nettie Jones," Williams announced.

Ben and Daniel sat side-by-side, listening to Williams question Nettie about the happenings at the dance.

"And you say there was a big fight?" Williams pressed her for more details.

"Oh, yes, Mr. Williams," the gossipy old woman told him with obvious delight. "Like I told you before when we talked, Elizabeth McCord was furious with Mr. Marshall. She slapped him right there in front of everybody at the dance. Many of us saw her do it. It was quite the talk the rest of the night."

"And why do you suppose she hit him?"

"Objection!" Ben came to his feet.

"Sustained," the judge ruled. "Go on with your questioning."

"Mrs. Jones, did you see James McCord talking to his wife a short time after the incident with Mr. Marshall?"

"Yes, I did, and he looked fit to be tied, I'll tell you!" she confided. "I'm sure he was upset with the half-breed taking such liberties with his daughter and . . ."

"*Objection!*" Ben rose again. "There is no way Mrs. Jones could know what James McCord's thoughts were."

"Sustained."

"Mrs. Jones, in your opinion, was James McCord angry when he left the dance that night?" Williams rephrased his question.

"Yes. He stormed out of there with fire in his eyes."

"Thank you." Williams looked to Ben. "Your witness."

"Mrs. Jones, did James McCord speak to you about the reason for his anger that night?"

"Well," she hedged nervously. "No, actually, we didn't speak."

"Then James McCord could have been angry about any number of things besides the one that you suggested, is that true?"

"Like what?" she returned.

"Like his wife insulting his good friend, the man who'd saved his daughter's life."

"Well, I . . ."

"Is that a possibility, Mrs. Jones?"

She glared at him. "I doubt it! Everybody knew Elizabeth was furious because Marshall had taken the girl outside unchaperoned. I'm sure James felt the same way."

"You're sure, Mrs. Jones?" he mocked, returning her glare before he stalked away. "No further questions."

Williams called the other ranch hand to the stand, and then several more witnesses from the dance, along with Sheriff Dixon, who testified about Daniel's escape from jail. Silver Wolf betrayed no emotion as he listened to the witnesses tell their stories to a jury that looked eager to convict him.

Ben was nervous. It was almost time for him to call his witnesses. He'd tried many important cases in Washington before he'd come to Cheyenne, but no case had been more important to him than this one, and no case had been worse to defend. Desperation alternated with despair within him.

"You may call your first witness, Mr. Douglas."

"I call Miss Carinne McCord to the stand," Ben announced.

Cari had never been so nervous in her whole life, and she spoke very quietly as she was sworn in.

"Miss McCord, did you love your father?" he asked.

"Oh, yes. I loved him very much," she answered quickly and surely.

"Did your father know about your relationship with my client?"

"Yes, he did."

"And did he offer you any resistance to it? Did he disapprove of your seeing Mr. Marshall?"

"No. My father loved me, and I know he cared deeply for Daniel." Cari looked over at Silver Wolf as she spoke, and he met her gaze. "They'd been close friends ever since Daniel rescued me from a snowstorm years ago, when I was eight."

Ben nodded, then turned to Williams. "Your witness."

The prosecutor stood, and after Ben had returned to his

seat, he walked slowly, calculatingly, toward the witness stand. "Miss McCord, is it true that your mother slapped the defendant at the dance that Saturday night?"

"Yes, she did."

"Is it fair to say that she was very angry that evening?"

"Yes."

"And is it true that she was upset because she believed Mr. Marshall had ruined your reputation?"

"Yes, but she was angry only because she didn't understand how deeply in love Daniel and I were. If she'd listened . . ."

"That'll be all, Miss McCord."

Cari was frustrated by Williams's tactic, but Ben quickly picked up the thread. "You were telling Mr. Williams that your mother might not have been so upset if she'd done something. What was that, Miss McCord?"

"If my mother had listened to us, she would have known from the very beginning that our love was too strong to be denied." Cari looked at her mother where she sat near the back of the courtroom with Elliot and his father. George had come to town to be with her as soon as he'd learned of James's death.

Elizabeth *was* listening this time, and her eyes were burning with unshed tears as she came to understand how much Cari loved Silver Wolf. She gave her daughter a tremulous smile across the width of the courtroom.

"Thank you, Miss McCord." Ben waited until she'd returned to her seat, then announced, "I now call Daniel Marshall to the stand."

Silver Wolf approached the bench and was sworn in. Ben began to question him as soon as he'd taken his seat.

"Mr. Marshall, how long have you known the McCord family?"

"I've known Cari for more than ten years, and her father longer than that."

"How would you describe your relationship with James McCord?"

"He was my friend."

"Did James McCord know about your relationship with his daughter?"

"Yes, he did."

"Did he object to it?"

"No."

"On the night of the dance, did you and Mrs. McCord have a fight?"

"Mrs. McCord disapproved of my escorting Cari outside unchaperoned. She slapped me, and I left the dance."

"What happened after that? Did you speak to James McCord later that evening?"

"Yes, I did. I was at the Sundown Saloon, and he came to see me there."

"What did James McCord want?"

"He came to apologize for what his wife had done at the dance."

"Is this your medicine bag?" Ben held up the evidence, then emptied the contents before Daniel.

"Yes, it is mine . . ." Daniel frowned as he looked up at his friend. "But there's something missing from it."

"There is? What?"

"I carried a small stone heart in it, too. The stone is gone."

The discovery puzzled both men, but Ben couldn't let it distract him. He had a point to make in his questioning.

"Did you have this medicine bag in your possession the night of the dance?"

"Yes. I was wearing it when I went to the dance."

"What about later that night? Did you still have the medicine bag in your possession?"

"I don't know. I went to the saloon and began drinking heavily. The next morning, I found it was missing, but I had no idea where I'd lost it. It might have been at the saloon or somewhere in town. I don't know."

"All right." He paused, changing to another subject. "Mr. Marshall, where were you on the day James McCord was shot?"

"I was alone, camped out."

"Did you see anyone during that time?"

"No. I didn't."

"Mr. Marshall . . ." Ben paused again for effect. "Did you kill James McCord?"

"No, I did not."

"Thank you."

It was Williams's turn now, and he approached Daniel, eyeing him warily. "Mr. Marshall, how close would you describe your relationship with James McCord?"

"I don't understand. I've already said that we were friends."

"What I mean is, what kind of friends? Were you close? Like father and son? Or more distant, like acquaintances?"

"We were close."

"That would explain then why James left half the ranch to you in his will, wouldn't it, Mr. Marshall?" Williams's smile was a sneer as a collective gasp erupted from the spectators. "No further questions."

Again noise tore through the courtroom, but it quickly settled down as the onlookers feared being ejected by the judge.

Ben had suspected that the subject of the will might come up, and he rose to question Daniel again. "Mr. Marshall, is it true that you were left half of the Circle M Ranch in James McCord's will?"

"Yes."

"And when did you learn about it for the first time? Remember, Mr. Marshall, you are under oath today."

"I didn't learn about the contents of the will until after James had been killed."

"Thank you."

"You may step down," the judge directed. "Call your next witness, Mr. Douglas."

"I call Elizabeth McCord to the stand."

Elizabeth made her way to the front of the court and was sworn in.

"Mrs. McCord, we've heard testimony here today that you had a fight with Daniel Marshall on the night of the dance. Is that true?"

"I'm afraid it is. You see, Daniel and my daughter had left

the dance unchaperoned, and they were gone for some time. I was worried about her reputation."

"Did you confront him and slap him as we've heard others say?"

"Yes, I did, but I admit now that I made a terrible mistake."

"What mistake was that?"

"I judged Daniel Marshall by his Cheyenne blood and not by the man he was. I was prejudiced, very prejudiced. Though my husband had been friends with the Cheyenne for years, I refused to believe that they were good people. I know now I was wrong. I understand why my daughter loves Daniel Marshall. He is a good and honorable man, and I'm convinced that he is innocent of the charges against him. Daniel did not murder my husband. He couldn't have. They cared too much for each other."

"Thank you, Mrs. McCord. Your witness."

Williams approached Elizabeth slowly. "Mrs. McCord, will you please tell the court why you've had this sudden change of heart about Daniel Marshall. Isn't this the man who took your daughter hostage when he broke out of jail? Doesn't the physical proof indicate that he's the man who shot and killed your husband? How can you sit there and tell the jury that you believe in his innocence, when his every action indicates his guilt?"

"All these years James told me how good a man Daniel was, but I refused to believe him. I've come to see how wrong I've been. Cari knew before I did. I changed my mind, because I finally understood what my husband stood for and what he wanted for the territory."

Williams stood before her, his expression smug. "You honestly believe this man is innocent?"

"Yes, Mr. Williams, I believe in Daniel's innocence."

Williams turned away abruptly. "No further questions."

The judge presided over the courtroom, looking at the crowd of people who had turned out for the trial. "We'll have the closing arguments now. Mr. Williams."

The prosecutor rose and approached the jury. He was sure

and confident as he began to talk. "We have here before us a man guilty of cold-blooded murder. We have witnesses who've testified that they saw the hostility and anger between him and Mrs. McCord. They have also testified that McCord was seen leaving the dance that night in a rage. I say James McCord saw what was happening between his daughter and Daniel Marshall and wanted to put a stop to it. I say they met out on the range and fought about it. I say Daniel Marshall won that fight by murdering James McCord! After all, with McCord dead, he could have his daughter and his ranch!" His voice was booming.

Williams fell suddenly silent as he walked up and down before the jury, looking them each in the eye. They watched him like a cobra watching its charmer.

As Cari watched the prosecutor, though, she thought he looked more like a snake than a charmer. High color stained her cheeks as she listened to his insinuations, and she had to clinch her fists in her lap to help control her temper. This was not the time to give in to her anger.

"I also say," Williams continued smoothly, "that the most damning thing of all, the one thing that cannot be denied, is the fact that Daniel Marshall's medicine bag was found in James McCord's hand. There must have been a struggle. They fought, and James must have grabbed the bag from Marshall's belt just as he was shot down." Williams paced more quickly before the jurors, dramatically using his voice to sway them. "There can be no verdict but guilty in this case! In no other way will justice be served and James McCord's death avenged! Thank you."

"Mr. Douglas." The judge nodded Ben's way.

Ben rose and walked slowly to confront the twelve men who would decide the fate of his best friend. Though he appeared calm and in control, in truth, his hands were shaking and his nerves were stretched taut. He was about to give the most important closing statement he'd ever made, and he prayed he was up to the task.

"Gentlemen of the jury . . ." he began, standing before

them to look them straight in the eyes. "For just one moment, I want you to put aside all your prejudice. For just one moment, I want you to stop looking at my client as an Indian and see him simply as a man . . . a man who's been accused of a terrible crime he did not commit. Daniel Marshall and James McCord were friends. With the help of men like James, Daniel was able to leave the reservation and go East to school so that he could get an education and better himself and his people. He did that. Against terrible prejudice and hatred, my client graduated from the university, and, after working in Washington, he came home to serve his people and his government."

Ben strode to the other end of the jury box. As he walked, his eyes never left those of the jurors. He knew it was important that they believe what he was saying, and he knew he couldn't do anything that might cause them to doubt his word.

"When he returned, he worked to make things better. He is a man dedicated to keeping the peace between the whites and the Indians."

Ben paused again for effect, giving them time to think about his words.

"Gentlemen, we have heard my client's testimony under oath that he did not have the medicine bag in his possession after the night of the dance. That it was lost some time that night. He did not know where it was until he was arrested for the murder of James McCord. As damning as it is, the evidence the prosecution has set before you is circumstantial. No witness has come forward to say that they saw Daniel at the scene of the crime. No witness has testified to seeing Daniel pull the trigger and kill James McCord. Mr. Williams would have you believe that this one piece of evidence proves my client's guilt."

Ben stopped and faced the jury. His emerald eyes were bright with the fervor he was feeling. "I say to you that someone either took the medicine bag or found it, and, realizing what it was, decided to use it to frame Daniel for murder."

He lowered his voice. "Daniel Marshall did not murder James McCord. Elizabeth McCord has testified that she believes in Daniel's innocence. It was her husband who was murdered, her husband whose life was ended in violence that fateful night. Yet, she is convinced that Daniel Marshall had no part in the murder. I say to you, gentlemen of the jury, if Elizabeth McCord can believe in Mr. Marshall's innocence, then you can do no less. Justice will be served only if you return a verdict of not guilty for my client. Thank you."

The courtroom was hushed as Ben returned to Daniel's side. Ben felt drained of all emotion. His plea had been given, but he'd had no hard evidence to present in Daniel's defense. He'd only had words. The bull was still missing, and he'd never been able to locate Jenny or find out what had happened to the medicine bag that night. It was going to seem like eternity waiting for the jury's verdict.

The judge gave the jury their instructions, then sent them out to deliberate. In the back of the courtroom, Lillian Perkins got up and rushed out of the building.

Cari had only a second to speak to Silver Wolf before he was taken away to be held under guard in a locked chamber.

"Silver Wolf . . ." She reached out to him as the guard led him away.

He had only enough time to touch her hand once before he was forced to go.

"What do you think our chances are?" Cari asked Ben as they stood together watching Daniel leave.

"I don't like it, Cari. I don't like it at all. But all we can do now is wait," Ben said, turning bleak eyes to her. "The longer the jury's out, the better it'll be for Daniel."

"Cari?"

She turned to find her mother there with George and Elliot by her side.

She was nearly distraught, but knew she could not break down now. She had to be strong.

"We're going over to the hotel dining room to get something to eat. Will you come with us?"

"I can't . . . I have to stay here, just in case the jury comes back."

Elizabeth didn't argue. She understood, and she gave her a warm hug. "We'll be back soon. If anything happens, please send someone to let us know."

Cari and Ben settled in on the hard courtroom seats to await the jury's return. The minutes passed slowly. They made feeble attempts at conversation, but couldn't concentrate enough to keep it up and finally just let the idea of talking die.

Lillian couldn't remember the last time she'd run anywhere. At her age, it wasn't quite the thing to do, but right now, she didn't care. It was too important that she hurry home. A man's life was at stake.

Since she'd met Cari in church and learned of her troubles, Lillian had made it a point to follow what was happening. She'd attended the trial every day and had seen Cari's desperation grow as the prosecution had presented its case. Each night when she'd gone home, she'd casually mentioned the day's happenings to Jenny, but now, with the jury out and things looking bad for Daniel Marshall and Cari, Lillian knew it was time to confront the young girl. She believed Jenny knew the truth, and she was bound and determined to convince her to come forth with what she knew before the jury came back and it was too late to save him.

She rushed into the house, calling Jenny's name.

"Is something wrong, Mrs. Perkins?" Jenny heard the frantic note in her voice.

"Something's very wrong, Jenny, and I've been quiet much too long about it." She confronted her in the hallway. As tiny as she was, when she was indignant, she was a giant.

"What happened?"

"What happened is, that poor man is going to be convicted of a killing he didn't commit! The jury has just gone to deliberate, and from the case presented, I would guess that it won't take them long to come back with a guilty verdict."

"Why are you telling me this?" she asked nervously.

"Jenny, I don't know what you're so afraid of, but I can tell

you this. If you think you'll be any safer once Daniel Marshall
has been hung for something he didn't do, you're wrong.
You'll be in danger until the day you die, because you know
something, something important . . . something that could
save Daniel's life. You won't get another chance to save him,
Jenny. The time has come to face up to your fears and tell the
truth. You can't hide for the rest of your life. The truth will
set you free, child."

"But . . ."

Lillian drew a sigh of relief as she saw the terror in the girl's
eyes. It was the first crack in her defenses. Jenny did know something. She'd been right all along. "We'll go to the judge together.
I'll be with you, and I won't let anyone harm you."

Ben drew a shaky breath as he glanced at the clock and
discovered one hour had passed. The spectators who'd gone
to eat started to return, lounging casually in the courtroom as
if this was merely a day of entertainment. He saw the Larsons
sitting near the back, along with some of the other ranchers
in the area. They seemed quite pleased. He thought they were
all ghouls who were eager to see an innocent man suffer. Ben's
temper frayed, but he controlled it.

Cari sat stiffly in the chair as she waited for the news that
would affect the rest of her days. Every fiber of her being was
aware that at any moment the jury could come back in and
announce that they had found Silver Wolf guilty of murder
and had decided to put an end to his life. The thought brought
a silent scream from her. It couldn't happen! She wouldn't let
it happen! Closing her eyes, she begged God— *Oh, please, don't
let Silver Wolf die!*

The courtroom door opened and Lillian walked in, bringing
Jenny with her. The girl's eyes were wide with fear as she
stared about the room. When her gaze collided with Mark

Larson's, she inhaled sharply and tried to pull free of the old woman's grip.

"Jenny? What is it?" Lillian asked.

Ben heard the name "Jenny" and looked around to see the girl he'd searched fruitlessly for standing in the courtroom. He was on his feet and beside the two women in an instant. Cari recognized her friend from church and ran after Ben.

"Cari, Mr. Douglas, this is Jenny," Lillian said with pride.

"Hello, Jenny. It's good to see you again. I've been looking for you." Ben couldn't believe that she was here. "Did you have something you wanted to tell us?"

"Yes . . ." Her voice quavered, but she felt safe from Mark when she was with this man.

Ben escorted her forward to see the judge who was still in the courtroom, while Cari hugged Lillian. The older woman sat with Cari as they watched Ben and Jenny.

"Your Honor, I know it's late in the trial, but a witness I'd been searching for has come forward with pertinent new testimony."

"Mr. Douglas," the judge said with exaggerated patience, "the jury is already deliberating."

"I know, Your Honor, but Jenny—"

Jenny interrupted him, blurting out, "I know what happened to the medicine bag!"

Judge Englich looked at her sharply and saw the terror within her. "Why did you wait so long to come forward, young lady?"

"I was afraid, sir. But I can't let Daniel hang . . ."

"All right. This is highly irregular, but under the circumstances, since a man's life is at stake. . . . Bring the jury back in. We'll hear one more witness."

"Judge Englich! The trial's over! You can't call another witness!" Mark shouted from the back of the room.

"Mr. Larson," the judge turned an icy regard on him, "until the verdict is in, the trial is not over. This is my courtroom and a life-or-death situation exists. The jury will hear the girl's testimony."

"Ben . . . what's going on?" Cari asked nervously when Ben returned to his seat. Jenny had remained at the witness stand and was being sworn in.

"The judge is going to let Jenny testify."

Cari and Lillian clasped hands, and their eyes shone with tears. Behind them the courtroom began to fill rapidly as word spread of the new witness. Elizabeth, Elliot, and George were quick to return and take their seats.

The guard brought Daniel back in to stand beside Ben. Daniel's expression was black. He thought he was coming back in to hear the jury pronounce him guilty. Pain had been tearing at him with razorlike claws as he'd tried to come to grips with the idea of losing Little Snow forever. Then he saw Jenny, and he looked over at Ben in amazement. Ben put a hand on his shoulder.

The judge called the court to order, then instructed his jury that they would hear one more witness. An eager quiet fell over the crowded room. Elizabeth, George, and Elliot sat nervously together, waiting . . . Sam, unaware of his son's sudden tenseness, sat confidently waiting . . . Ben sat beside Daniel waiting . . . Cari held tightly to the old woman's hand, waiting . . .

Ben approached Jenny easily, wanting to make her comfortable. "Jenny, how is it you know the defendant, Daniel Marshall?"

"I met him in the Sundown Saloon the night of the big dance."

"What were you doing in the Sundown, Jenny?"

"I worked there."

"I see. What happened that night?"

"Well, Daniel got pretty drunk. We went upstairs for a while, but when I started to unfasten his belt, he told me he didn't want to do anything but talk. He spent the evening with me—talking."

Cari's heart swelled to near bursting with love for Silver Wolf as she listened to Jenny's testimony. He could have made love to this girl that night when she'd hurt him so badly, and yet he'd declined.

"Did anyone come to see Daniel while he was with you?"

"Yes, sir. A man named James did, and then you did."

"What happened after Daniel and I left you in the bar?"

"I went up to my room and I found his medicine bag on my bed. I looked through it and found this heart." Jenny pulled Cari's stone heart out of her pocket and held it out for Ben and the judge and jury to see.

A murmur of surprise went through the court. It was just as Daniel had said earlier under oath.

"While I was looking at it, Mark Larson came in. He hit me when he found out I'd been with Daniel. He hit me hard, several times. He took the medicine bag when he left."

A rumble of shock reverberated through the crowd, and Mark, feeling trapped, lunged to his feet. Just as he reached the doors, they flew open, and Captain Greene strode in followed closely by Tall Shadow and Strong Eagle. A stunned silence gripped the court as everyone froze. Mark backed away, but the sheriff quickly grabbed him before he could run.

"Sheriff Dixon, bring that man before me!" Judge Englich ordered, then turned to stare at the intruders in his courtroom. "What is the meaning of this, Captain?"

"I have important new evidence, Your Honor. May I approach the bench?"

The judge waved him forward. "What is it?"

"Your Honor, Chief Tall Shadow and Strong Eagle rode to the fort to get me, for they feared that their word wouldn't be accepted here. I have come with them to tell you that the missing McCord bull has been found."

At his words, another explosion of shock erupted in the courtroom.

"Where?" the judge demanded.

Captain Greene turned to look at Mark, already in the sheriff's custody, and then at Sam who was trying to creep from the court. "The Cheyenne found the bull in a box canyon on the Larson ranch, Your Honor. Sheriff Dixon, please arrest Mark Larson for the murder of James McCord!"

Mark struggled frantically against the lawman's hold.

"Chief Tall Shadow, bring in our witnesses, please. Judge Englich, two of the Larsons' ranch hands were guarding the bull, and they are more than willing to testify to what happened that night. I think the court might find what they have to say quite informative."

Two more braves entered the courtroom dragging the terrified cowboys with them.

"Mark Larson did it!" one of them shouted as soon as he could see the judge. "He shot McCord!"

"Why you . . . !!!" Mark tried to break free and attack him, but Dixon held him.

"You're under arrest, Larson."

Judge Englich looked over at Ben and Silver Wolf. "Mr. Marshall, the case against you is dismissed. You are free to go, and you have the deepest apologies of this court."

A roar went through the room as Mark was dragged away, his father following.

Ben and Silver Wolf stood. They were numb, but happy. Finally, Ben turned toward him. Their eyes met in thankful understanding, and then they threw their arms around each other and embraced, slapping each other on the back.

"Thank God!"

"Indeed, thank God," Lillian echoed as she hugged Cari and then went to Jenny.

Williams crossed the room to speak to Ben, and Captain Greene came forward to shake hands with Daniel.

Silver Wolf turned away from the lawyers to see Cari making her way around the bar toward him. Tears of happiness were streaming down her face, but she had never looked more beautiful to him. He took a step toward her, then opened his arms to her.

Jenny watched from Lillian's side as Cari and Daniel embraced. She started crying, too. Her tears were joyful. Daniel was alive. "Thank you, Mrs. Perkins," she said in a soft, emotion-filled voice.

Her eyes sparkled with mischief and love. "If you really want to thank me, child, you'll forget all about working at the Sundown and stay with me. I like having you around."

The happy old woman and the redeemed young girl started to leave the room.

"Jenny!" Daniel called to her.

He broke apart from Cari for a moment. Still holding her hand, he brought her along with him as he went to speak to the young woman who'd just helped to save his life.

"Thank you." He lifted his free hand to touch her cheek. He could see the faint bruises and realized the horror that Mark must have put her through. "You really are beautiful without all that paint." He smiled at her.

Jenny went to him and looped her arms around his neck. She kissed him sweetly on the cheek. "Be happy, Daniel, my friend."

"You, too, Jenny."

"Jenny?" Cari knew she owed this woman Silver Wolf's life and more.

"Yes?"

"Thank you for helping Daniel."

The two women shared a secret smile, and then Jenny and Lillian started on their way.

Cari gazed up at her love, her heart filled with joy. Only moments before they had faced the possibility of his death, and now . . .

"I love you, Silver Wolf."

"I love you, too."

She went straight into his arms and was enfolded in his loving embrace.

Epilogue

Cari stood with Silver Wolf before the cave, gazing out across the land that stretched for miles in a moon-drenched vista before them. The night was warm and heavenly.

"I love coming here," Cari said in a soft voice as she relaxed back against his chest. They'd decided to make it a ritual to return to the cave at least once a year.

He slipped his arms around her thickening waist and held her close. The thought that she was bearing his child filled him with awe. "This place has always been very special to me."

Cari turned to face him, lifting her hands to frame his face. She gazed up at him, still thinking him the most handsome man in the world even after a year of marriage. "Any place is special to me as long as I'm with you, my husband."

Silver Wolf bent to her and kissed her tenderly. "You know I feel the same way."

They'd married with her mother's blessing shortly after the trial and had spent the last year working together to make James's dream come true. Their hard work was paying off, for the Circle M was gaining the reputation for having the finest stock in the territory. Elizabeth had gone back East to recover from her husband's death, but when she learned of Cari's pregnancy, she promised to return for the birth of her first grandchild.

Cari and Silver Wolf stood, locked in each other's arms, enjoying the intimacy of being alone, together.

"Do you suppose Ben and Star Blossom will marry, too, and be as happy as we are?"

"I think it's a distinct possibility. I heard him singing one day when I went into town and stopped at the office."

"Singing?" Cari didn't understand the significance.

Silver Wolf chuckled. "A warrior courts the woman he loves by sitting outside her tipi at night serenading her."

"Do you think he'll have any luck?"

"Not if that's the only thing she picks her husband by," he laughed.

"You're mean! First, you make fun of your best friend, and second . . ."

"Yes?"

"You never sang to me," she pouted prettily.

Silver Wolf was about to bravely offer her a rendition of an old love song he remembered from his time East, when the sound of a wolf's call came from afar, drifting to them on the night breeze. As they stood motionlessly, listening, an answering call was heard in the distance. The wolves' songs blended as one in the beauty of the night. Powerful feelings surged through Silver Wolf, filling him with more happiness than he'd ever known in his life.

"The wolf's song is my love song to you, Little Snow," he told her, lifting a hand to caress the silken glory of her hair as it shone like silver now in the moonlight.

Cari thrilled to his words, and when he lifted her up in his arms to carry her back inside the cave, she linked her arms about his neck. He lay her upon their blankets, and they came together in a blaze of passion. They reached the rapture together in breathless splendor. Silver Wolf knew no more perfect bliss than to love Little Snow . . . his wife.

Cari's eyes drifted shut as she surrendered to the paradise

she found in her husband's embrace. She listened to the thunder of his heartbeat, slowing now in the aftermath of their loving. The babe within her womb stirred, and Cari smiled into the night. They would raise their children to be loving and kind, generous and forgiving, brave and gentle. They would teach them to become a bridge between their two worlds. Then perhaps in the future, no one would have to suffer to be together as they had. Cari sighed and nestled closer to Silver Wolf. She knew this was where she belonged, at his side, with him forever.